The
NATURAL
SELECTION

Praise for *O'Brien's Desk*

"An intriguing and thoroughly researched story that gives us insight into the moral dilemmas of 20th century America. A well-told story that does not leave us with easy answers."

—Anne Perry,
bestselling author of the Thomas and Charlotte Pitt and William Monk mysteries

"Within the field of historical mystery, the time period of 1920s America chosen by Russell is a unique one that piques reader interest. Sarah Kaufman is an engaging protagonist, thrust into an authentic, sociologically driven mystery involving issues which still resonate today. The author handles the societal attitudes of the period with a sure and sympathetic hand, and with an eye for their parallels in the 21st century."

—Miriam Grace Monfredo, author of the Seneca Falls historical mysteries

"*O'Brien's Desk* is a terrific read because of its riveting story and because so much of the author's identity is invested in the events it so vividly portrays."

—Richard Lederer, author and host of NPR's "A Way With Words"

"The mystery of Ona Russell's first novel is deliciously seductive—you'll find yourself sleuthing out the clues right along with Sarah Kaufman, all the while hoping her bold spirit doesn't lure jeopardy. The rising stakes will keep you turning the pages to the end and leave you looking forward to more."

—Shaunda K. Wenger, author of *The Book Lover's Cookbook*

"Author Ona Russell has woven an intricate mystery around real people and events in Toledo during the first part of the 20th century. She has blended historical fact with fiction to create an intriguing story of the blackmailing of a prominent judge."

—*The Toledo Blade*

"A thrilling, suspense-filled, and vibrantly told novel."

—*Midwest Book Review*

"This is an engaging example of that popular cross-genre, the history/mystery. The daily details, smoothly integrated into narrative, give her tale a pleasing, authentic ring … Sarah [the protagonist] pushes the career edges of the possible, for in 1923 she is both a Jew and a Progressive. Her crusade to save her beloved bosses' sanity (and his job) in the middle of an election year draws her down some enjoyably puzzling paths."

—*The Historical Novels Review*

"An intense historical."

—*Library Journal*

The
NATURAL
SELECTION

AN HISTORICAL MYSTERY

ONA RUSSELL

SUNSTONE
PRESS

SANTA FE

Sunstone books may be purchased for educational, business, or sales promotional use.
For information please write: Special Markets Department, Sunstone Press,
P.O. Box 2321, Santa Fe, New Mexico 87504-2321.

Book designed by Vicki Ahl
Book Cover designed by Lauren Kahn

Library of Congress Cataloging-in-Publication Data

Russell, Ona, 1952-
  The natural selection / by Ona Russell.
    p. cm.
  ISBN 978-0-86534-628-4 (pbk. : alk. paper)
1. Courts–Officials and employees–Fiction. 2. College teachers–Crimes against–Fiction.
3. Scopes, John Thomas–Trials, litigation, etc–Fiction. 4. Tennessee–Fiction. I. Title.
  PS3618.U765N38 2008
  813'.6–dc22

                          2008004394

WWW.SUNSTONEPRESS.COM
SUNSTONE PRESS / POST OFFICE BOX 2321 / SANTA FE, NM 87504-2321 /USA
(505) 988-4418 / ORDERS ONLY (800) 243-5644 / FAX (505) 988-1025

For Kate,
And all the others

"For every complex problem,
there is a solution that is simple, neat, and wrong."
—H.L. Mencken

✢ Prologue

The gold sealing wax was a nice touch, the professor thought, a little extra to show his apology was sincere. He gave the envelope a final, satisfied glance and slipped it under the chipped wooden door. In one quiet push it vanished, and so too any last faint traces of remorse.

He listened. Still no signs of life. He stole down the empty hall and exited the building, greeting the muggy dawn with a line from Nietzche, Hegel—one of the Germans, it didn't really matter which—suddenly in his head: "What is right is what the individual asserts is right, but it is only right for him." Precisely, he thought. Precisely. Of course, some rules were necessary; the mass of men couldn't be trusted to think for themselves. Indeed, the professor had dedicated himself to reversing the damage the thinking of lesser minds had done. But the sentiment applied quite well to men compelled to live by a different code. Men like himself who were educated, admired and followed.

He smiled, imagining the objections of all those bleeding hearts. Wasn't such a view contradictory? Didn't it imply that the very deed he had just cleansed himself of could be worthy of punishment in someone else? Perhaps. But then the professor was, if nothing else, a man of contradictions. This morning it simply had been easier to explain them away. Everything seemed easier in the summer. Warmth might slacken the body, but it filled the spirit, leaving no barren space for doubt to creep in.

And so later that day, he strolled content and free in the college woods, only yards from campus, but worlds away. Believing he was alone, he inhaled deeply and loudly the honeysuckle bouquet, took in every hallowed branch of petal-like dogwood. Students would trample over this same path in only a few weeks, but for now, these were his woods. He loved this place. Of course, everyone else did too: his colleagues, students and neighbors, all staking their unearned claims to its quiet beauty. But his love came from deep within his veins—a love that stemmed from his family having once owned the very ground upon which he walked. Land for which his grandfather, a Confederate spy, gave his life.

The South. Another passion. Another contradiction. In the study of books, the professor was avant-garde, continuously pushing against the boundaries of convention, lecturing on the newest strains of literary criticism. "Literature should be judged on its own terms," he boomed to the hall of young, adoring eyes, "not according to some rigid sense of morality." But on the subject of his heritage, he was firm. Here, tradition was sacred, morality absolute. Right and wrong were literally divided into black and white.

As he forged deeper into the thicket, his thinning white hair beginning to mat with sweat, he thought, as he often did, of the need to restore order and erudition to the region. The South had been turned on its head since the Civil War, and he was committed to putting things—and people—back in their natural place. He was, he liked to tell himself, reclaiming the Golden Age.

In the pursuit of such a noble goal, there were bound to be casualties along the way, and today's was not the first. Survival of the fittest, his trusted Darwin proclaimed. And so it was with particular pleasure that he took in nature's best—the sheltering verdure, the familiar canopy of oaks, the gentle slope leading toward the creek whose clear water he would cup to his mouth.

But the professor was not, as he had thought, alone. Mirroring each turn, shadowing every step was someone following closely behind, silently, invisibly, until the moment was just right.

"Jesus Christ!"

"Hello Professor Manhoff," the familiar voice said evenly.

"Oh, oh, hello there. My God, you scared the life out of me. What are you doing here? I thought you were . . ." And then a fleeting realization. For a moment, the corners of his mouth formed a slight grin of understanding until . . . the quiet rage . . . the gleaming barrel. He opened his mouth to speak, to plead for mercy. "No. Please. God." But it was wasted breath. One shot rang out, clear and resonant, and he fell, heavy, into a bed of moss and branches. A bright pool of blood gathered in the full growth. It spread, feeding the soil and staining the land of his ancestors until, finally, the ceasing of his heart halted the flow. And then he was alone, truly alone in the college woods.

❧ 1

SARAH CLOSED HER BOOK, drew back the miniature, velvet curtain and peeked out the window. Finally the flat, grassy checkerboard had given way to rolling hills, which, from the vantage point of the speeding *Pan-American*, appeared to fold in upon themselves like emerald waves in a land-locked sea. As the conductor strolled the aisles, bumping every now and then against the slumped shoulder of a half-dozing passenger, he announced that they had just entered Kentucky, halfway through the all-day ride from Toledo to Knoxville. Right on schedule, Sarah thought.

She leaned back and exhaled. Now she could relax. As long as she was in Ohio, she wasn't free. Work could always track her down: dockets in need of review, people in need of counseling, each requiring her immediate attention. And memories. They seemed to find her, too, especially the ones she wished most to forget. But at last she'd managed to escape, each minute speeding farther away from it all. And up ahead lay the holiday she'd put off for years.

She glanced around and for the first time really noticed the car. How trains had changed. So modern! Not at all like the stuffy Victorian parlors they used to resemble. This was her first trip on the *Pan*, and now that they had crossed the state line she took in every detail. The black upholstered seats, the steel frame sheathed in glossy mahogany, the wide, carpeted aisles. Simple but elegant, with the exception of the portly man snoring across from her whom she was ready to clobber with her handbag.

One month. Four weeks. Thirty-one glorious days. Time to do with as she pleased. As her mind raced with the possibilities, she stretched her stockinged legs out as far as they could reach and closed her eyes. It would be hot, of course. Hot and muggy. But late breakfasts, hiking in the Smokies, a trip or two to the baths would balance out any ill effects. Besides, she'd just read that a little perspiration was good for the pores. And of course, there would be her cousin, Lena. Indeed, if Lena hadn't invited her down, pleaded with her to visit, Sarah still might be cooped up in her office, attempting to finish the work that never really would get quite done.

Little Lena. Though ten years younger, a kindred spirit. The person Sarah might have been had she been blessed with the same opportunities. Imagine. Graduating from Vassar, with honors. And then landing a teaching job at Edenville College. Quite a feat for a woman. Unheard of for a Jew. Which is precisely why, Lena told Sarah, she believed she was hired. To be observed and poked at like a newly discovered species. If anyone could handle herself, though, it was Lena: brilliant, feisty and deceptively clever. Sarah suspected that in no time her cousin would have her colleagues so charmed, they'd have no choice but to abandon their experiment and simply let her do as she pleased.

The train slowed as it passed one of the many nondescript towns along its route, and Sarah picked up her book again, tracing her fingers along the cover. An outline of a simple, ivy-covered cottage, under which gleamed the gold embossed lettering: *Uncle Tom's Cabin*. Despite its renown, Sarah had never read it. "Overly sentimental," Obee had warned. *"Moby Dick*, my dear. Now that is a novel." Uncharacteristic for Obee—Judge O'Donnell, that is—who usually touted his broad literary taste.

As the tip of her finger traced the line of the cottage, she let it trail down to the author's name etched below: Harriet Beecher Stowe. A Northerner whose portrait of slavery was so powerful that Lincoln was said to have credited her with starting the Civil War. Sentimental? Perhaps. But Sarah wasn't beyond judging for herself, especially now that she was traveling from one side of the former divide to the other. She turned to an earmarked page and read, silently mouthing the words:

> *I have tried—tried most faithfully, as a*
> *Christian woman should—to do my duty*

to these poor, simple, dependent creatures.
I have cared for them, instructed them,
watched over them, and known their little
cares and joys, for years; and how can I ever
hold up my head again among them, if, for
the sake of paltry gain, we sell such a faithful,
excellent, confiding creature as poor Tom.

"Excuse me, ma'am." Sarah slowly raised her eyes. "Ma'am?" A tap on the shoulder now accompanied the smooth, low voice.

"Yes?" she said, craning her neck toward the passenger in the seat behind her.

"Pardon me. I'm sorry to bother you, but I couldn't help notice your book." The young man leaned so far over her seat Sarah thought he might fall onto her lap, and she instinctively shifted positions to spare herself. "You've read it?" she asked.

"Oh, yes. Quite a coincidence, in fact. You aren't taking a class at the university, are you?"

"No," she said, with a restrained smile, knowing full well he knew she was a tad too old to be sitting in any lecture hall. "Why do you ask?"

"Well, Mrs. Stowe isn't often read for fun. Not these days, at any rate."

"Really? I'm finding her fascinating."

"I could only hope my students feel the same."

"My goodness, you look like a student yourself. Where do you teach?"

He studied her for a moment and without asking, maneuvered himself in one rather clumsy half pirouette into the seat directly across from her. She had wanted to be alone, but now, like it or not, he was here. She smiled to herself and watched as he settled in. Up close he actually appeared even younger than Sarah initially thought. Twenty-one, twenty-three tops. Framed by angular, straw-colored eyebrows, his gaunt, narrow face and high cheekbones gave him a startled look, which intensified when he spoke.

Handsome, in a struggling artist sort of way, especially with his rumpled white shirt, stained with a chunky remnant of what appeared to be mustard, and blond Byronic curls that crept haphazardly down his long neck.

"You know," he said, "their stance against slavery was often theoretical."

"Their?"

"Oh, I am sorry. There I go again. Starting *in medias res.*"

Sarah knew that meant "in the middle of things," but noted that he didn't seem to care if she did or not.

"Name's Paul Jarvis. I'm a graduate student in history at UT, the University of Tennessee." He took her hand and shook it vigorously. His palm was soft and moist, and Sarah quietly wiped his sweat off of her hand onto her dress. "I've been assigned my first lecture next week, and, to tell you the truth, I'm terribly nervous. An overview of Tennessee history." He pointed to her book. "When I get to slavery, I'm going to discuss Mrs. Stowe a bit."

Sarah nodded, observing his unlined face. No trace of nervousness there. She wished she could say the same of her own, which, she worried, manifested every harrowing moment of the last year.

Sarah cocked her head and twisted the long string of pearls that hung in a heavy loop around her delicate neck. "You know, Mr. Jarvis, my cousin, whom I'm actually on my way to visit, thinks Mrs. Stowe is terribly underrated. She's a new hire in the English Department at Edenville," Sarah said, puffing out her somewhat underdeveloped chest.

"Really? That *is* interesting!" he said, smiling broadly to reveal deep dimples and a slightly chipped front tooth. "What about you?"

"So far, so good. I need to read more to judge."

"No, I mean what do you do?"

"Oh." Sarah blushed and straightened in her seat. "I'm head of the Toledo Women's Probate and Juvenile Courts."

"My, that sounds impressive too. Seems like you've got something special runnin' through that family blood of yours."

He asked her to explain what her job entailed, which she did in the simplest of terms: "wills, property and marriage," she said, not caring to elaborate upon the actual unpredictable and varied scope of her duties under the Honorable O'Brien O'Donnell.

"So, what is it you plan to discuss in this class of yours, Mr. Jarvis?" she asked, wanting nothing more than to avoid the topic of her own work. And that was all it took. Before she knew it, he was opening a worn leather satchel overflowing with notes and papers, though it still had room to hold a short, wooden pipe, already filled. He bit down on the tooth-marked stem and held it in his mouth in perfect suspension. "Do you mind?" he asked. She shook her head, and without hesitation he lit the aromatic substance, puffing in and out rapidly until it burned on its own. He closed his eyes and exhaled.

"Since you asked, ma'am, would you be at all interested in hearing a condensed version of my lecture? I could use a fresh set of ears and considering what you were reading . . . well, I'd forever be in your debt."

Sarah raised one freshly plucked eyebrow and glanced down at her book. She hoped to have been further along, but for once there was no rush. "All right," she said, with just a hint of resignation. "Mind you, I'm a tough critic."

"You're a peach." He laid the smoldering pipe on the armrest and rearranged the papers until he was satisfied with the order, pulled himself up in his chair, and began.

"Now, I know most of y'all call Tennessee home. But it's surprising how much we sometimes don't know about the place where we live. So bear with me."

Sarah found his folksy opening endearing, and nodded her head in encouragement. Even if she hadn't, however, she probably would have reacted the same. She was, as everyone told her, a good listener. Really, she couldn't imagine being otherwise in her line of work. She hated to hurt anyone unnecessarily, and there was nothing more hurtful than being ignored.

"Tennessee, the sixteenth state to enter the Union, has a long history of oppression. In 1830, President Andrew Jackson, the Tennessean who allegedly gave the state its name, signed the Indian Removal Act. Can anyone tell me what that was?"

Sarah was tempted to raise her hand. Fortunately she caught herself, for an invisible student had apparently already answered the question.

"That's right," Mr. Jarvis said. "It was the forced relocation of the Cherokee and other tribes from their southeastern homes to territories west of the Mississippi. 'The Trail of Tears' as it has been termed, borne of white supremacy and greed for land." He relit his pipe and licked his lips. "It was also in Tennessee, in Pulaski, a small town in the middle of the state, that the Ku Klux Klan was later formed."

Sarah shuddered. The KKK? Six months had passed but the mere mention of the name still nearly undid her. She felt for her rings and began to twist. One, two, three.

"With white hooded robes, rapes, whippings and murders as their calling cards, the group, which rapidly spread to other states, succeeded in instilling fear among Negroes and Union representatives, those they considered enemies of the Southern way of life. Though the organization disbanded during Reconstruction, it reconstituted and is now an even more intolerant group, widening its net of undesirables to include Catholics, immigrants and Jews."

As if in perfect theatrical timing, the train jerked to the right, and Sarah's stomach, already on edge, turned inside out.

"The group has become more powerful and currently has candidates on political tickets nationwide. The most, I might add," his voice now bellowing, his eyes directly on Sarah, "in the North, in Indiana, just a skip and a jump from Ohio."

He needn't have gone to such dramatic measures. Sarah already knew about Senator Stevenson and his bunch of thugs. And she knew too, more intimately than he ever could have imagined, about the Klan's presence in Ohio. In the last election, the Toledo chapter had tried its best to remove Obee from office, something that nearly cost him his sanity . . . and Sarah her life.

❖ ❖ ❖

Steadying herself as the train turned another hard corner, Sarah grabbed hold of the cool handle to the restroom door and locked herself inside. It was hard to maneuver in the cramped space, but she needed a private place to recover after Mr. Jarvis' speech. Of course, she knew he was blissfully unaware of the turmoil he had stirred inside of her—how could he have known?—and she had made every attempt to happily congratulate him on a well-presented lecture. Now that she was alone, though, she let herself go. After a moment, her stomach eased a little and she ran the hot, mildly sulphuric water and lavender scented soap over her hands, splashing cupfuls onto her burning cheeks. By the time she dried off, steam had completely fogged up the small oval mirror hanging on the wall directly overhead and she wiped it with a towel until her image reappeared.

She let out a little self-deprecating laugh. Sarah knew that now that the past had resurfaced she couldn't prevent it from playing itself out; she only hoped it wouldn't carry her too far away. The stubborn past. Like a perpetually rewound film waiting for the next flip of the switch. She stared into the mirror, seeking her own reflection, but one by one the images came fast, stuck in time and place, blotting her out. Obee, weak and frail in his hospital bed, the blackmail note, horrible words and terrible threats, and always, the moment she thought she would die. Panic. Suffocating breath. Hands tightening around her throat. She felt them all now and had to pinch herself to stop from going any further.

Of course, Sarah was no stranger to murder. Counseling victim's families, visiting perpetrators in prison, listening to innumerable attorneys prosecute and defend in its name. But until six months ago, it had always felt . . . distant. Then, suddenly, unexpectedly, death and fear grew close, hovering around her friends and family, haunting her dreams, until finally, she saw it, felt it, tasted it for herself.

Holding firmly to the basin's rim, she breathed in deeply and exhaled. Whether fate, luck, or the grace of God had intervened Sarah wasn't sure, but she reminded herself now that she had managed to escape. And that she had helped Obee, her boss, her mentor, her friend to regain his health and return to the Bench. She had found the strength, risen to the occasion.

Thinking of these things always calmed her nerves, and soon her hands dropped to her side, her breathing slowed, and she once again saw her own reflection before her. Her involvement in the matter had come at a stiff price, but she was alive and now determined to move forward. And Sarah reminded herself there was a reason she had come so close to death's door. She was glad she had helped put things right, but she'd traveled too far afield. She wasn't a detective. She was an officer of the court, and a good one at that. When she returned from her holiday, she would be so again. The more routine the case, the better.

Feeling steadier and stronger by the moment, Sarah reached into her purse and pulled out a small, gold compact. Normally, she wouldn't have bothered—she could reapply the tiny amount of powder she used blindfolded—but since the events of last fall, she had become somewhat self-conscious about her appearance. Not about her so-called imperfections: the outward curve of her rather prominent nose, the slight gap in her front teeth, the tiny, half-moon scar on her left cheek. Those she had accepted long ago, had even grown to half-heartedly believe that they gave her the character everyone said they did. No, it was the loss of youth, or more precisely, no longer looking younger than her years, that had prompted vanity to rear its ugly head. Having been complimented on the trait so often, she had, even at forty, simply taken it for granted. Not any more. Not when nearly everyone she encountered offered instead their well-meaning advice: "You know, my dear, you could benefit from a trip to the baths." "Sarah, I have a wonderful doctor." "You're familiar with the Rest Cure, aren't you, Miss Kaufman?"

If she interpreted such remarks correctly, time not only had caught up with her, but was threatening to pass her by.

As she examined herself now, however, she observed a slight improvement. She never might be quite the same, but she had regained most of the weight she lost last year; at five foot six still thin, but healthy-looking at one hundred and twenty pounds. The angles of her heart-shaped face had softened, her olive skin had lost its sallowness, and the velvety quality of her deep-set dark eyes had returned. She held out her hands. Still perfectly average in length and width, still squarish in shape with a deep nail bed. The only change was on the underside of her right ring finger. The callous had grown from a small ridge to a thick bump, the result of metal continuously pressing against flesh. It drove her sister, Tillie, crazy, the way she incessantly twirled her rings, counting each turn just under her breath. But something about the motion comforted Sarah, a simple way to feel pacified and protected. Mismatched and awkwardly stacked, the rings glistened under the bathroom's soft white light. Her mother's thin cluster of marcasites, the gold encircled garnet Obee had given her for her birthday, and the plain silver band, a place holder for the one she used to think would someday permanently grace her other hand.

She moved closer to the mirror. Perhaps a few more lines were etched on her forehead. And there definitely was more grey scattered throughout her chestnut hair, especially at the base of her widow's peak, which became more obvious as she pinned it up into its usual French twist. But such minor alterations were a small price to pay. Not bad, she thought, as she straightened her pink silk chemise . . . all things considered. And with that, she swung open the door. Suddenly she was ravenous.

❧ ❧ ❧

Although it was noon, a few tables were still unoccupied. The dining car retained some of the luxury of the older trains: brass lamps, leaded glass windows, plush, thickly cushioned chairs. A uniformed Negro waiter escorted her to a white-clothed table midway down the isle. "Coffee or tea?" the man asked, as he placed a starched napkin on her lap.

"Tea, I think. Thank you."

"Chicken consommé or Roquefort salad?"

"Salad."

He smiled and wrote down her order, glancing at her book enigmatically before turning to a beckoning customer. She briefly tried to decipher his expression, but then decided that some things were best left unknown. Soothed by the gentle motion of the train, the tinkling of glass and silver, the gamy, citrus aroma of duck a l'orange, she marked her page and gazed out the window to the summer haze. At such a dreamy vision, the past retreated, wound itself back on the reel, and was held once more in suspended animation.

⇻ 2

WHEN SARAH ARRIVED IN KNOXVILLE, the air was warm, but still fresh from rain. Thunderstorms were the mainstay of summer afternoons in the South. As the day progressed, plump white clouds had gradually gathered into tall grey plumes, and the haze had thickened, turning the landscape into a shapeless mass. Only when a yellow-white flash of lightening periodically electrified the sky could she distinguish one hill from another.

Still, Sarah had mostly enjoyed the ride. Despite the fact that it was hot and steamy outside, she had the cozy feeling of being indoors on a winter's day. Not until the young Mr. Jarvis inadvertently sent her reeling did she begin to feel the heat of the storm. But for her cousin's sake, as well as her own, she had pushed the worries out of her mind and relished the remainder of her ride. Lunch had been satisfying, and with her appetite and nerves calmed, she had managed to make progress on her book. In between chapters, she had followed the storm's trajectory, from the first relieved droplets to the torrential downpour that signaled the beginning of its end.

By the time the conductor announced their arrival, the sun was out, streaming onto the landing where Lena was waiting. She waved at Sarah with both hands high above her head, plaid bloomers billowing out around her narrow hips, black bobbed hair swaying in the heavy breeze.

"Sarah! Sarah!"

Sarah dropped her suitcase on the wooden landing and ran toward her cousin. The two hugged and cooed for several moments, then drew back to examine one another. It had been five years. Much too long. Sarah held onto Lena's bare, narrow shoulders, eyeing her up and down. So small. Only five tiny feet. Five and a quarter as she knew Lena would be quick to correct her. At the most one hundred pounds. But what a package! And evidently, still possessing an acute eye for fashion. Those French pumps with their curved heels and cream-colored suede were up-to-the-minute, not like those worn by any academic type Sarah had ever seen. "Lena, you little smarty. I'll bet your male students have a hard time concentrating."

Lena's raven eyes gleamed. "Look who's talking," she said, or rather "tauwkink," her Philadelphia accent especially pronounced at the moment. "You look marvelous, Sarah. You always were the pretty one—if you'd just do something with that hair!"

They both giggled, Sarah in her soft pianissimo, Lena in her throaty pianoforte. Lena had wanted Sarah to bob her hair ever since the style became popular several years ago. Although Sarah repeatedly said she would sooner stroll nude through the center of town, her cousin had raised the topic so often that it had become something of a private joke.

Bob or not, Lena was not pretty in the conventional sense, even less so than Sarah. Though she too was blessed with a clear, olive complexion and was shapely in the right spots, her nose was curved like a hawk, her square teeth were undersized, and her lips, today painted candy-apple red, were wide and thin. "A real *meiskite*," as she said of herself. Regardless, Lena possessed that certain something, an ineffable quality that cannot be broken down into parts. Charisma, magnetism, whatever one called it, it drew people in—men, especially.

"C'mon," she said. "Let's go get your suitcase. You must be exhausted. I've got a driver ready to take us home."

The two locked arms and walked through the stately brick depot toward a waiting jalopy spewing mildly noxious fumes. Lena already had slid across the seat when Sarah heard her name being called. She turned around to find Mr. Jarvis running toward her, sweaty . . . again. "You left this," he wheezed.

Her book. She shook her head. "My mind was clearly somewhere else. Thank you so much, Mr. Jarvis."

"Paul."

"Paul. Paul," Sarah said, yanking Lena playfully out of the car, "this is my cousin, Lena Greenberg. Professor Greenberg."

Lena extended her small hand. "Hello, Paul. You'll have to forgive my cousin. She knows full well that as a mere woman I can't actually claim that title, but it's the thought that counts."

Blood rushed to his cheeks as he stared at her awkwardly. "Yes, I've heard a bit about your work on the trip here," he said. "It's nice to meet you." Sarah eased the tension by summarizing, as best she could, his ideas about Mrs. Stowe. But when Lena simply responded with a "hmm," and suggested, rather abruptly, that they discuss the work at some future date, Sarah was stunned. It wasn't like her to be so curt, let alone turn down an opportunity for debate.

Paul didn't seem to notice, however. He ripped out a piece of paper from his notebook, scribbled his telephone number and handed it to her. "I'll look forward immensely to talking with you. Safe trip," he called out, and dashed away.

As they drove off, Sarah grabbed her cousin's hand and asked if she was feeling well.

"Absolutely. I just wanted you all to myself."

"Well, that didn't stop you from taking Mr. Jarvis' number. He's a little young for you, isn't he?" Sarah joked.

She smiled mischievously. "That depends. I can think of a few things for which he might be just right."

And then they both laughed, laughed to the point of tears. Perhaps Lena was fine, after all. She certainly seemed okay now. And besides, Sarah was already having more fun than she'd had in months.

❖ ❖ ❖

By the time they reached the small town of Edenville, perspiration was clinging uncomfortably to her dress. Sarah fanned herself with her book, trying to remember the benefit to her pores. Their driver, an ambitious business student who got paid by the hour, suggested they take a brief ride through the school before heading to Lena's rooms. To sweeten the deal, he offered to roll back the car's flimsy top. Though heavy now, the air was fragrant with the sweet smell of honeysuckle and blew sufficiently to unstick Sarah's dress from the small of her back. Dusk, falling in varying shades of blue and orange, found the campus empty, save the fireflies, their bright tails flickering like miniature beacons in a darkening sky.

"The school was started by a group of Presbyterian ministers," Lena said, assuming the impromptu role of tour guide as they passed through the entrance. Engraved on a gold plaque next to the magisterial gate was the college's founding date: 1819. "One of the first fifty small colleges in the country."

Sarah counted ten four-story, red brick structures with arched, Gothic windows and white plantation-like columns bearing names of local heroes, former presidents and generous patrons. They drove past Preston, Simmons, and Jackson Halls. Thickly foliaged oak trees peppered the trim lawns on which each building stood equidistant, collectively framed by woods so dense that, at least from here, they were indistinguishable from the encroaching night. Forming a star-shape pattern, each hall led to the chapel, a high-domed, wooden edifice with colorful stained glass depicting the life of Christ. Like planets circling the sun, the chapel, with its towering oversized steeple was the fixed point around which mathematics, English, music and all the other disciplines turned.

"You can't imagine how many here still view the church as the life-giving force," Lena said. "The anchor. The final word. Without its watchful authority, they think we'll all go spinning out of control."

"I don't know how you do it, Lena," Sarah said. It's hard enough being a Jew. Even at court, where the separation of church and state is enforced, I have to watch my back."

"You know me. I just let them believe what they want and keep going my own way. Besides, my department is different. The zealots don't worry about us much. We only teach fiction, after all. It's science they keep their eye on."

As they exited the campus Sarah yawned deeply, covering her mouth in a failed attempt to hide the exhaustion that had suddenly overtaken her. On their way to Lena's, they passed through Main Street, an eight-block paved road with quaint stores on either side selling the staples of modern life. City Drug, Duke Dry Cleaning, Coleman Tires, Luke's Sandwiches, the names blurred together until Lena gave her ribs a little nudge. She shook herself just in time to see a soft, blue light rhythmically flashing: Cohen's. Cohen's. Cohen's.

"Don't want you to miss the Jew store, my dear," Lena said.

Sarah watched the light as it flickered and faded from view. She'd heard the moniker was common in the South, a reference to Jewish-run shops selling dry goods inexpensively to farmers, Negroes and anyone else short of cash. Still, it was disturbing.

"It's not as bad as it sounds, though," Lena said, no doubt seeing Sarah suddenly stiffen. Most people down here don't know enough about the Jews to know the term is offensive. Their ignorance isn't malicious."

"Oh come on, Lena. You're smarter than that. Inexpensive is a euphemism for cheap, and cheap for Jew."

"Well, of course, I know that's true in many places. But it's more complicated in these parts. The Cohens are well-liked, and their store does a good business. The euphemism isn't fully realized."

"Maybe so," Sarah said. "But I wonder if they would mind if we called, oh, I don't know, those little religious shops popping up everywhere the 'Goy' stores."

Lena laughed. "You're right, of course. But we're not going to solve that problem today. I know what you've been through, and you've cause to be wary. We all do. But remember what you told me. 'Lena, I want nothing more than to relax my body and rest my mind.'"

Sarah squeezed Lena's hand and smiled. "All right, all right. I suppose I'm overreacting. You certainly seem to be surviving. Thriving, even."

Lena turned away for a moment and was silent. "Yes," she replied, "I'm great." But the tone in her voice said something else. Sarah touched her shoulder and Lena turned back, smiling, perhaps just a little too much. Had the last year made Sarah so nervous that now she was misjudging her own cousin? She needed to watch herself, reading into things this way. "So, Lena, where is your place, anyway?"

On cue, the driver turned down a tree-lined street and stopped in front of a white clapboard house with a wide, inviting porch. Lena pointed to an upstairs window. "Right there."

❧ ❧ ❧

Lena occupied two spacious rooms in a Colonial-style house for faculty women. One was a bedroom, in which there were two comfortable-looking twin beds, a large walnut desk strewn with papers, and three windows, on which, thankfully, the lace curtains were lightly blowing. The other room served as living space. An overstuffed maroon couch, black leather chair, Art Deco lamp and ebony Victrola surrounded a worn Oriental rug. The remaining area, except for a small icebox in the corner, was filled with books. Packed in the built-in shelves, stacked in neat piles on the floor, tossed here and there. Lena ordered Sarah to sit down and then went to fetch a snack.

"I'm sorry things are a little untidy," she said, her head in the icebox. "I had meant to clean up more, but things have been a bit . . ." she paused, "busy here the past few days."

Sarah hadn't even noticed. She had already kicked off her shoes and unrolled her stockings, and was rubbing her sticky feet on the floor. The silk had been hot and the hardwood was wonderfully cool. "Your place is lovely. Don't give it a second thought. But what have you been so busy with?"

Lena walked over with a plate of sliced Georgia peaches, a wedge of Swiss cheese and a pitcher of iced tea, a drink that she claimed was a rite of passage in the South. She put the Brandenburg Concerto on the Victrola as Sarah took of a sip of the sugary drink. "Oh, um, nothing worth mentioning. You know, just work. What do you say we go to dinner in a few minutes? Meals are served downstairs."

"Forget dinner," Sarah said, leaning back like the worn-weary traveler she was. "This is all I want. Cheese and fruit. Bach and tea. Three-quarter time." She didn't feel even a need for the drop of "imported" whiskey she'd become accustomed to taking at night. Yes, she'd brought the flask with her, just in case. And yes, in doing so she was technically breaking the law, however destructive that law had proven to be. But her doctor, who ignored Volstead entirely, had given her orders.

"You sure you want nothing else to eat?"

"Positive. I think I'll even put off a bath until tomorrow."

And so she did. For the remainder of the evening, Sarah sat right where she was, talking, laughing and sipping tea to the strains of her favorite classical composer. With each note, another muscle relaxed. By the time the last chord was struck, she was ready for bed. "Good night, Lena," she said rising.

"Good night, Sarah. Sleep well."

→ 3

SARAH'S EYES FLICKERED OPEN. The room was still—it couldn't have been any later than one in the morning—and just a hint of moonlight washed the room in muted purple-grey. She pulled herself up on one elbow and felt a bead of sweat trickle down her arm and rest in the folds of her wrist. Her whole body was drenched. The sound that had jolted her out of her slumber came again, a soft knocking at the door, this time with a girl's voice calling out in a desperate whisper, "Miss Greenberg, Miss Greenberg!" She peered at Lena to see if she had heard and saw that she was already wrapping herself in her robe. "What's going on?" Sarah's voice cracked.

"It's nothing. Go back to sleep."

Lena motioned to Sarah to stay where she was and went to the front door just outside the bedroom. It creaked open.

"Kathryn?"

"Oh, Miss Greenberg. Did you hear?"

"Yes, yes, my dear. Shhh . . ."

The girl started crying.

"Kathryn . . . shhh. It'll be okay." Sarah couldn't make out any more. Just soft whispers now and the girl's weeping.

After a few moments, Lena returned to the bedroom.

"Lena, what on earth?"

"I'll be right back. Don't worry, Sarah." She slipped a dress over her head, grabbed her heels, and hurried out the door.

Unable to do anything else, Sarah sat on the bed and stared into the darkness. Maybe if she cooled off she would be able to go back to sleep. She got up, exchanged her moist, floor-length silk nightgown for a short, cotton slip and pulled all the windows wide open. It was hot, the curtains motionless. She sank back in bed, knowing she should have trusted her intuition. Something *was* wrong.

⇴ ⇴ ⇴

Sleep came in fits and starts, a restless conclusion to what she earlier thought, as she eased under the soft cotton sheets, would be a peaceful eight hours. Instead she dreamt, as she often did, of the past. Nightmarish visions of white ghostly figures, then hands squeezing her throat. In reality, she'd escaped. But not in her dreams.

No telling how long she might have continued to toss and turn had the landlady not awakened her with breakfast. Never did Sarah think she'd be glad to see a complete stranger hovering over her. She smiled gratefully and took the tray. A feast by her toast and coffee standards. Fresh squeezed juice, scrambled eggs and syrup-laden grits. The round, flat-faced matron introduced herself as Nan and told her that tomorrow Sarah would have to come downstairs like everyone else. "I ain't no slave," she said.

Sarah thanked her, took a few bites, and went to fill the tub with cold water. By the time she bathed and dressed, she was ready for a shower. Of course, Toledo summers were humid, too. But nothing like this. If the experts were right, soon her pores would disappear altogether.

To stop her mind from racing—wondering where Lena was, what had happened, why that girl was crying and what it had to do with her cousin—she perused some of the titles squeezed together on one of the shelves. *Hard Times, Madame Bovary, Daniel Deronda.* An abundance of Victorian novels, French philosophy, *Walden.* The complete works of Edith Wharton. A thick volume entitled *Literary Criticism.* Better finish her own book first. She picked up the red, leather-bound work she'd left on the nightstand and started to read:

> *You ought to be ashamed, John! Poor, homeless, houseless creatures! It's a shameful, wicked, abominable law, and I'll break it, for one, the first time I get a chance; and I hope I shall have a chance, I do!*

Sarah silently applauded Mary Bird for standing up to her senator husband, John. How could he, an Ohioan no less, have supported the Fugitive Slave Act? Both were fictional characters, of course, but Stowe based them on the actions of real people. Leave it to the women to put things straight.

An hour or so later, Sarah marked the page and watched as her cousin came in, shuffled to the edge of the bed and fell back. For several moments, she lay there, flat and still. Then, as if awakened by the mesmerist's snap of the fingers, she turned over and shaking her head, looked at Sarah. "I need to tell you something."

"So I gathered. Are you okay?"

"Yes, I'm all right, don't worry about me. But, well, it's unbelievable," she said. "The day before you arrived, a colleague of mine . . ." She stopped and swallowed. "He was found in the woods. Shot dead."

"My God! How did it happen?"

"The police think it was an accident, a hunting accident."

"That's horrible, Lena."

"Horrible, and a waste," she said, still shaking her head. "Such a brilliant man. And so beloved. He had just been appointed to chair my department, and we had even begun work on a paper together."

"I'm so sorry. I've been worried about you since you left with that girl this morning. Who was she?"

"One of his students. One of mine, too. The news is starting to spread, I guess. She'd just learned of it and was terribly upset."

Lena sat up and pulled off her shoes.

"Lena," Sarah said, "maybe . . . maybe I should go home."

"What?"

"I said, maybe . . ."

Lena widened her eyes. "I heard you."

"But . . ."

"No! I knew you would say that, which is precisely why I didn't want to tell you. I may be needed here for a couple of days to help sort things out, but after that everything will go as planned. Beginning with our hike in the Smokies."

"Maybe they'll ask you to take his place."

"Hardly."

"Still, you'll probably need to—"

"Not another word. I order you to stay! This is sad, very sad, but life will go on."

Sarah sighed and smiled uncomfortably. "Okay. But if you change your mind—"

"I won't."

In fact, there was a part of Sarah that desperately wanted to go. To flee as quickly as possible. It was selfish, but she had come here to enjoy herself, to escape the unpredictable facts of life. After all, it only had been six months. She deserved a respite. But of course that was unrealistic. Life was full of the unpredictable. A vacation offered no immunity. Thankfully, it didn't involve someone she knew. She sighed and relaxed her tight shoulders. Lena was right. Surely it wouldn't take that long to do whatever needed to be done. Lena wasn't a relative or even a close friend of the poor man. In the meantime, she could look around, explore the town. She glanced at her cousin, who had stretched out on the bed. Her eyes were closed.

"Sarah, I think I need a short nap."

"Of course."

"I can trust you not to hop on a train, can't I?" she said, peering out from one eye.

Sarah smirked. "I suppose. Maybe I'll take a walk into town."

"Good idea." She turned on her side. "That'll take you about an hour," she said groggily. "Timing wise, that should be just about right."

Sarah put on the coolest outfit she could find. She didn't go in much for hats, despite their popularity, but today she needed protection. From the two she brought, she grabbed the beige canvas one with the extra wide brim and left quietly. Lena was already fast asleep.

❖ ❖ ❖

Despite her light clothing, the humidity weighed Sarah down, forcing her to slow her usual rapid pace to an amble. It smelled different here. Rich, thick, fruity. Earthier than Toledo. Nevertheless, the fragrance was familiar. Not quite as sweet perhaps, but familiar just the same. It was in Nashville, 1918, the only other time she'd been in Tennessee. As chair of the Toledo branch of the League of Women Voters, she had attended the suffrage ratification conference there, held at the palatial Hermitage Hotel. She could still see vividly the walnut paneled conference room, inlaid marble walls and strangely intricate, stained glass ceiling: images of Madonnas and harpies, gods and devils. She remembered too, the roses everyone wore: yellow for suffrage, red against. "A fragrant sea of yellow and red," as one reporter put it. Having worked tirelessly on this issue—even speaking to President Wilson at one point—Sarah naturally was elated when yellow prevailed, and even now she couldn't help but smile a little in satisfaction.

She walked down two blocks, past a mix of Victorian and Colonial dwellings, all situated amidst foliage so lush there was no need for fences. When she reached the intersection, she turned left. On one side of the road was the college, on the other the courthouse, a smaller version of her own, granite and marble with Grecian columns. Up a long hill, and there was Main Street. In the daylight it looked smaller, less quaint, more provincial. She strolled past a shoe repair shop, a rustic, pre-industrial looking little place with a Gepettoish cobbler hammering away at a tall leather boot. Immediately next door was a dingy but crowded diner with a sign announcing the daily special: fried chicken, greens and "Joe's" peach cobbler, seventy-five cents. And then, up ahead, Cohen's. The Jew Store. She was curious, to say the least, and soon found herself peeking in its sparkling front window where thread, needles, shoes, work clothes and toys were all displayed in perfect order. Soon she realized that while she was looking in, someone was looking out at her, too. She raised her eyes and encountered a smiling face and a hand motioning her in.

"Well, hi there ma'am. What can I do ya for?"

The accent was strange. An unlikely coupling of West Brooklyn and East Tennessee.

"Oh, I'm just browsing."

The man eyed her and nodded. He was at least two inches shorter than Sarah, with a thick crop of graying hair, pale blue eyes and a warm, full-faced smile. A Jewish smile, Sarah thought to herself.

"Well, y'all take ya time."

The man kept looking at her, though, as if in recognition. "You're not from these parts, are ya?"

"No, I'm from Ohio."

"Well, I'm Charlie Cohen, and it's good to have you here, dahling," his accent suddenly favoring the Brooklyn half. "What is it that brings you to our fair town?"

"I'm visiting my cousin. She teaches at the college."

"Oh. That right? What's her name?"

"Lena. Lena Greenberg."

"Ah," he said nodding, smiling even more broadly. A second later, though, a shadow crossed over his face. "The college. Oh my. You must have heard about the death of that professor."

Sarah sighed deeply. "Yes, I just found out."

He shook his head. "Terrible. Did your cousin know him well?"

"Not well, but they did work together."

He sucked air through his teeth and kept shaking his head. "Such a shame."

"Shame my ass." A heavy-set man with worn overalls and a leathery face walked over holding a small shovel he had just picked out. "That there's a tragedy. Man was a true Southerner. Too few of 'em these days."

Sarah, feeling suddenly uncomfortable, gave a little smile and walked down the narrow isles. Toward the back of the store, she stopped to examine a paisley wool scarf, similar to one her mother had owned. The same swirling pattern and soft feel. It would be perfect with her grey winter suit. She couldn't find a price tag, so she started back to the counter, where Charlie was nodding, his smile tighter, more reserved.

Clearly, the disgruntled customer had not been satisfied to let the conversation end, and indeed seemed to be fueling his own fire the longer he talked. "That professor, he was the kind gonna bring back the Confederacy. That's what I heard. Gonna show 'em this ain't no lost cause. Those good for nothin'—" He picked up a plaid fleece blanket. "How much, Cohen?"

"How much can you afford, Mr. Sloan?"

The man didn't answer. Fingering the blanket, he eyed the upstairs of the store, where a sign read: Negro Dressing Room. "Hey, anyone up there," he shouted. Receiving no response, he yelled louder, undoubtedly aware that the room was occupied.

At that, a black teenage boy stuck his curly head out of the dressing room. "Yes, sir?" he said.

The man just glared, so the boy shut the curtain. Either he was drunk or just itching for a fight, mad at himself or the world. Whichever, he started for the stairs. But his wife, standing quietly until now, grabbed his arm, causing him to trip and knock over a neat row of fishing rods. Charlie walked over calmly and picked them up. "Now, now," he said. "Let's not start anything. He's just a boy."

The man shook him off. "I don't need no kike tellin' me what to do!"

"Bobby, c'mon. Let's go," his wife calmly pleaded. "The kids are in the wagon." He shook her off. "And I don't need no bitch bossin' me around neither!" He stuck the blanket under his arm, threw two dollars on the counter and stormed out. Giving a slight nod to Mr. Cohen, his wife followed.

Charlie shrugged his shoulders and looked at Sarah, who was standing in stunned silence. This wasn't quite the harmonious picture Lena had painted for her.

"Don't let it bother you, ma'am," he said. "No point."

→ 4

FOR ONCE, the guidebook had not exaggerated. The Great Smoky Mountains were indeed "nature at its most sublime." Sublime and gloriously indifferent. Away from the noise and crime, away from the lingering curious stares of her neighbors and friends—each waiting to see if she might yet break. Away from it all, and now, protected in a thicket of pines, she realized how grateful she was that Lena had encouraged her to stay . . . if hiding her suitcase could be considered a form of encouragement. Sarah couldn't blame her, though, for resorting to such extreme measures. Had the bag been at her disposal she probably would have left. The professor's death had already put her on edge, and the run-in at Cohen's had proved more than she felt she could handle. But now, trudging up the dusty trail, dressed in overalls that sagged in all the wrong places, she felt better. Looking at Lena in the same silly outfit, she felt almost giddy.

They had decided to start with a hike up to Hotel Le Conte for breakfast. Sarah, whose stomach had been talking to her for an hour, was just about to ask Lena how much longer it would be until they arrived, when she spotted a pointed tin roof. Rustic, isolated, with an unobstructed view of seven-thousand-foot Mount Le Conte, the place, Lena said, was a well-kept little secret. A two-story frame building situated near a clear, stony river, the remote outpost complemented the rugged land in both design and scale. Their other option was the Allegheny Springs, but with its velvet-upholstered furniture, crystal chandeliers and imported French coffee, they decided it was too opulent, not at all in keeping with the spirit of the wilderness. Besides, they couldn't have shown up there with sweat trickling down their foreheads and dirt clinging to their hems.

Once inside, Sarah, unwilling to let go of the view, peered back out again through the large, rectangular window in the entrance to the dining room. Had a blue jay not just splattered a white dropping as it flew by, she very well might have reached for the billowy cluster of pastel wild flowers dancing amidst the pines—it was that transparent. As they waited to be seated, she entertained herself by speculating on the quantity of vinegar required to attain such an effect—a quart, a gallon?—and made a mental note that she must get around to cleaning her own windows upon returning home, though the view outside of her little house on Fulton was not so grand.

She opened up her guidebook again and read a passage to Lena as they waited to be seated: "The Great Smokies are the western segment of the high Appalachian Mountains, majestically shaping the land from Asheville, North Carolina, to Knoxville, Tennessee, arguably some of the most spectacular scenery in the world. Wildlife that would stun the most jaded naturalist, slopes to both soothe the weak and challenge the hearty, flora of infinite variety. With each rise in elevation a dazzling explosion of color, shape and texture—purple-pink blossomed rhododendron, mountain laurel, red spruce, hemlock, silver bell, black cherry, buckeye, yellow birch. Towering pines. Chestnut trees reaching seventy to one hundred feet, softly blanketed in the region's characteristic haze."

"Right on the money," Lena said.

Yep. It was all here, Sarah thought. Right there, on the other side of the vinegar divide.

She read on. "To preserve the region for future generations, efforts are currently underway to turn the region into a national park. Logging is threatening to destroy the last remaining sizable area of southern primeval hardwood forest in the United States and leave world-weary city dwellers one less pristine habitat in which to rejuvenate." Sarah nodded in agreement at no one in particular. She was all for the park. Especially since it was a fellow Ohioan, Dr. Chase Ambler, who had started the organization that would bring it to fruition. But she was somewhat guiltily relieved that the area was not recognized yet as such, knowing that as soon as the official designation came, the crowds were sure to follow. Although in the last few years visitors to the region had increased dramatically, one could still travel for miles without encountering a soul.

❦ ❦ ❦

Only two of the eight tables in the dining area, a bright, surprisingly homey space with wood plank floors, red checkered tablecloths and bunches of wild geraniums, situated to take full advantage of the view, were occupied when they made their entrance. Seated at one of them was an overgrown Dutch family of five who had just received their food and were arguing in their guttural idiom about who had ordered what. Mr. J. W. Whaley, the owner and host, rearranged their plates until the brood was satisfied and then stretched out his arms and motioned for the cousins to come in.

"Mornin', ladies. Late risers, aren't cha?"

"Actually, we woke up earlier than usual. We've come up from Edenville."

Towering over Sarah in a red flannel shirt, rolled up sleeves, with veins bulging over thickly muscled arms, was a Paul Bunyan of a man. The advertisers of the Big Six would have loved him, although his high-pitched drawl counteracted the effect a bit. "Y'all must be hungry, then, from such a long walk," he said with enthusiasm, as if they were the first customers he had ever served.

"Yes, we're starved."

"Well, then, you've come to the right place."

Escorting them past the empty tables, Mr. Whaley seated them near another gleaming window, directly across from a young couple on their honeymoon. "Traveled all the way from Alabama to be married by Justice of the Peace Ephraim Ogle," he whispered, "down ta Ogle's general store in Gatlinburg. Ephraim's gettin' to be a popular fellow these days."

From the scavenged look of their table, the honeymooners had worked up a good appetite, too. Sarah smiled at them congenially before turning her attention to a bulky, dark mass moving in the distance outside.

"They's been a bunch of 'em this mornin'," the woman said in a syrupy sweet twang.

Sarah turned around and smiled again. "What's that?"

"Baars. A whole family, cubs and everthang."

"Really?"

"Yep. They's lovely, don't ya thank? But scary, too."

"Well I definitely wouldn't want to get too close. But from here they do look beautiful."

"Plannin' on goin' to the top?" the woman asked.

"We're not sure," Sarah said.

"We neither." She looked at her husband who was loosening the notch of his beaded belt and then back at them. "If ya don't mind me asking, where'd you'ns get them work clothes?" They look very comfortable, raht for hikin'."

"I ordered them from the Sears catalog," Lena said quickly.

Sarah raised one brow at her cousin. She knew Lena had purchased them at Cohen's.

"I was just admiring your husband's belt, too," Lena said, not meeting Sarah's gaze. "I sure could use something to help keep these things from sliding off me."

"Cost me two dollars for this heah belt," the man said. Them injuns ain't cheap but they sure do make some handsome things. The Cherokee— they're everwhar round heah."

"Well, I'll keep that in mind. Enjoy your hike."

She turned back to Sarah, and before Sarah could even form a word, simply said, "Leave it alone."

"But . . ." Sarah stopped herself and started to giggle. "Injuns?" she whispered. It's almost too funny to be offensive."

"Then don't let it be, Sarah. R and R, remember?"

Lena fixed her dark eyes on her. She obviously wasn't going to budge until Sarah relented. "Right," she said, returning to the comfortingly unaltered view.

Looking out into the miles of untainted forest, though, Sarah couldn't help but wonder about the professor's shooting in the college woods. She thought of what a lonely death that must have been with no one there to speak to or hold his hand as he slipped from this world to the next. Lena hadn't spoken of him for a few days now, and Sarah didn't want to remind her of something she was trying to forget. But she also wanted Lena to know she should feel free to talk about it without worrying Sarah was going to plan her escape again. "Lena," she started, "you've been fairly mum on your colleague's death. Would you rather not talk about it?"

"No, not at all. There's just not much to tell. The memorial service is next week. Apparently, it's not uncommon for hunters to shoot birds in those woods. They don't know who was responsible yet. The person who shot him probably doesn't even know himself."

"Have you heard anything about who will take the professor's place?"

"The former chair has agreed to take the job for another year. By then the good 'ole boys will find a replacement."

"What about his personal life. Was he married?"

"He was. His wife died a few years ago."

"Children?"

"No. And that apparently was a sensitive topic. When I asked him about it one time he abruptly changed the subject. I found out later that he was sterile." Sarah felt a familiar lump starting to form in her throat. "Well, at least he had a legitimate reason."

"Now, Sarah. You know that's been your choice."

"I suppose. Anyway, what about that paper you two were working on together? What's it about?"

"You really want to know?"

"Of course."

Just then Whaley came by with a steaming, speckled blue pot of coffee. "Breakfast will be ready in a jiffy," he said, filling their mugs.

"Better drink up lest you fall asleep right here at the table hearing about it," Lena said.

Sarah stirred in two teaspoons of sugar and took a giant swig of the nutty brew. "I'll try my best not to doze off. Go ahead."

"Okay. To begin, how does one teach literature? That is the question the professor and I were trying to address.

"I thought you already knew how. Isn't that why you were hired?"

Lena laughed. "I suppose you're right. But like everything else, education is always changing. You know, some think the imagination is the bane of society, that fiction is the devil's work. Others, like myself, believe it's a source of truth. But as an academic discipline, it's essentially been taught as another part of history, a way to teach a moral lesson, a reflection of the author's time and place."

"Uh huh," Sarah said. "That's pretty much what I was taught."

"Me too. But a growing group of scholars have begun to think that the literary work should stand by itself, you know, viewed as art, judged on its own merits. The question is, how? To be taken seriously in academia, you've got to have a serious method. Otherwise, the whole thing becomes too subjective, simply a matter of opinion. Are you with me, so far?"

Sarah nodded. "I think so, but, well, I don't mean to sound simplistic, but what about enjoyment? Isn't that an important part of reading?"

"Definitely. And actually that's part of the argument. Students of literature are too bogged down with the background. They aren't encouraged to see the beauty of the language, the soul of the story. Professor Manhoff . . . Nick . . . was helping develop a method to do so, a nearly scientific method."

"Beauty and science. Sounds somewhat contradictory."

"Well, yes. It is, sort of. That's why the work isn't complete. It's really just begun. Because the theory is only in the beginning stages, contradictions are inevitable. But Nick was on the forefront of change." Lena heaved a deep sigh and shook her head. "It's so sad. We were even planning to present my . . . his . . . our paper to the next MLA convention."

"MLA?"

"Modern Languages Association. That's where we scholars show each other how brilliant we are!"

"Ah! I see. Teaching literary types how to appreciate literature."

"In a manner of speaking. To rigorously appreciate it. Anyway, as I said, we had just started, but he was looking for a way to bridge the gap."

"Gap?"

"Between fact and value, investigation and appreciation, in a sense, to resolve the contradictions you spotted."

"How?"

"By moving from the particular to the general. By examining closely each word, each sentence, each image. First the parts, then the whole. He wanted students to see, as he said, 'beauty in the making.' After that's accomplished, and only after that, would he put the book back in history. He wanted the words to enlighten the context rather than the other way around."

"Interesting."

"And he used modern writers as his examples, too. Modern *American* writers."

"Why emphasize American?"

"Well, there's this idea that anything written after the Greeks isn't worthy. Old is good, new bad. And therefore literature by Americans is really bad. De Tocqueville said we were a bunch of boors a half a century ago, and we took it to heart. Perhaps he was right. But since the War, you know, with patriotism on the rise, there's been growing acceptance, an interest in homegrown writers. Nick planned to use Mark Twain for his paper, and he hoped I would do something by Edith Wharton. He even had a working title, 'The History of Aesthetics, the Aesthetics of History in Two Modern American Writers.' "

"Very clever. If I don't think about it too much, I even might understand it. And he asked you to help him?"

"Uh huh. Basically. Seemed to have no problem with my being a woman . . . or a Jew" Lena said, winking at Sarah.

"It really sounds like such a great loss, Lena."

"I know. And he was so loved by his students, became a real father figure to many of them. Even more than that. They hung on his every word. Worshipped him, I'd say."

"So what now?"

"Well, I'll try to finish the paper as best I can. Try to fulfill his goal of reading at the MLA. I, uh, thought that, um, maybe between our outings you could even help a little, if you don't mind. He was a prolific writer, and it's going to take me a long time to go through all of his notes."

"I'd be glad to do whatever I can. You know Lena, it doesn't sound as if his students were the only ones who were smitten with him. There wasn't anything . . . more going on between you two, was there?"

"What? No! No, Sarah. I admired him, but not in that way."

Just then Whaley appeared at the table, balancing two plates overflowing with griddlecakes browned to perfection, thick-cut ham, buttered toast and a fresh pot of coffee.

"Here you go. And there's plenty more where this came from," he said.

"Thank you, sir. We may take you up on that."

Lena started immediately, picking up a piece of each item on her fork and devouring them all together. After a prolonged glance at her plate, Sarah started with the ham, cutting off a small piece and slowly raising her fork. With a silent apology to her parents who sooner would have been tortured than let any pork pass through their lips, she bit into the piece of dark, honey-basted meat, enjoying the perfect blend of sweetness and salt. Then a bite of bread. And a slice of griddlecake. For several minutes she and Lena ate contentedly, each employing her own gustatory method. In the end, though, they were cousins, demonstrating their kinship by fulfilling the family mandate to "clean your plate."

⇛ 5

THE TIGHTNESS IN SARAH'S CALVES was pleasantly uncomfortable. It felt good to have used those muscles. Still, if she didn't move her legs soon she was liable to become petrified in her crouched position, so she grabbed a thick folder from the bottom drawer, stood up and limped over to the table.

For her taste, the college was a bit too much like the courthouse, designed to announce the importance of the activity for which it was built. Dark wood, marble floors, high domed ceilings framed with intricate molding. Imposing, sober, enlightened, the exact kind of environment she had taken a vacation to escape. Not to mention that the tiny file room to which she had been relegated was smaller and even narrower than her office. With no window, it felt both claustrophobic and stiflingly hot. But she was happy to help Lena. It was just for the afternoon, anyway. Tomorrow they were returning to the Smokies—she just hoped her legs would be ready to carry her.

"History teaches us what men are; literature teaches us what they should be." The name "Voltaire" was scrawled on the cover of the folder. Sarah agreed with the great French philosopher. She invariably felt more inspired by a good novel than a scrupulously footnoted account of some war. All she learned from history was that men were prone to violence. Nothing new there. But in, say, well *Uncle Tom's Cabin,* she was learning about redemption, forgiveness, about the importance of seeing beneath the surface of things. Of course, as Mr. Jarvis had said, Mrs. Stowe had her limitations, and she did spark a war. But in her novel, love and justice seemed to be the animating forces. For that matter, even in the stories of Sir Arthur Conan Doyle, to which Sarah was somewhat embarrassingly addicted, she found inspiration in the power of the human mind, in man's ability to overcome fear and unravel seemingly unsolvable mysteries.

She looked at the quote again, at the bold printing, so full of life, trailing across the folder in a diagonal line. She then opened the folder and started thumbing through the mass of papers. Some notes, typed documents, some full-length treatises written in a meticulous, slightly backward-leaning hand. The first was titled "Interpretive Criticism." Lena had asked her to look for anything that appeared to relate to the topic of her and the professor's MLA paper. Better pull that one out. The next was a mimeographed essay by Joel Spingarn. Was this the same person who founded Harcourt Brace? She and Obee had worked with the man at the NAACP. Probably. *Creative Criticism.* "Works of art are unique acts of self-expression whose excellence must be judged by their own standards, without reference to ethics." Yes, definitely include this one. A mimeographed quote by a Martin Wright Sampson from the *Dial* in 1895: "I condemn as an obsolete notion the habit of harping on the moral purposes of the poet or the novelist." This too, Lena would want to see.

"Excuse me?" A wheat-haired, lithe young woman knocked quietly and stood halfway through the doorway. "Excuse me, but have you seen Miss Greenberg?"

"She should be back shortly. Can I help you? I'm Sarah, Miss Greenberg's cousin."

"Oh, hello." Sarah recognized the voice. Calmer, lower-pitched now, but the same as the other night. "I'm Kathryn. Kathryn Prescott. Miss Greenberg asked me here to help."

"Yes, she told me you'd be coming. Nice to meet you. I guess my cousin feels I need some supervision!"

Kathryn smiled, her cupid-like lips curling around small, childish looking teeth. "No, it's not that. She said there's a lot of material to go through."

Kathryn's mouth didn't quite match the rest of her angular face, which, though attractive in a natural, farm girl sort of way, hinted at a maturity beyond her years. Sarah wasn't quite sure what it was. Something in the set of her pale blue eyes. "Well, that's true," Sarah said. I guess you know what to look for?"

"Uh huh. Um, where is Miss Greenberg?"

"At the police station. She and a few others were called in to hear the coroner's report. Just a formality, I imagine."

The girl motioned to someone in the hall, then eased in the rest of the way. Quickly assuming her place in the doorway was a tall, hovering male figure holding himself back cautiously. "I hope you don't mind," Kathryn said, taking the man's sinewy arm. "Jim's a friend. He was a student of Professor Manhoff's, too. I think it would be okay with Miss Greenberg."

A pleasant-looking fellow, Sarah thought. Straight, slicked back auburn hair, freckled up-turned nose, wide, open face. Average, in a good sense of the term.

"It'll be a bit tight," Sarah said, "but the more the merrier. We'll need another chair."

"Leave that to me, ma'am," Jim said, smiling, and returned quickly with the required seating. He put down the chair and rubbed his palm on his trousers before extending his hand. "Nice to meet you," he said.

"You, too."

"Sad occasion though," he added.

"Yes, I'm so sorry for you both, for the whole college."

"Jim's in the economics department, Miss Kaufman," Kathryn said, resting her hand on his shoulder maternally, "but he told me he's never enjoyed a class more than the one he took with Professor Manhoff. So many of us here felt the same way about him."

"Well," Sarah said, "at least you'll be helping to further his work. How about I divide this stuff into thirds?"

They each took their share and began poring over his notes. After almost an hour, Sarah needed a break. The heat was overwhelming, and sifting through the piles of papers was a bit too reminiscent of the newspaper clippings she had searched through not so long ago for clues, anything that might help Obee. She got up and offered to get everyone something to drink, which the two were apparently craving, as both responded with an emphatic nod; Jim, in particular, who put his hand up to his throat in an exaggerated pantomime of thirst. Sarah clicked her way down the hall to the faculty rest area where pitchers and cups were kept. She filled the pitcher with water from a rusty faucet, grabbed the cups and walked back.

"Thanks," Kathryn said. "Sit down, and I'll pour."

Sarah repositioned her wire-framed reading glasses and glanced at the students. Were they sweethearts? They were sitting very close. Whatever the relationship between these two, though, they were doing a great job. Their pile at least equaled hers. Lena would be excited to have so much to work with.

Sarah took a sip of water and thumbed through the remaining few papers. She was becoming accustomed to the terminology as well as to the professor's verbose style, which is why the last item gave her pause. Short. Terse. Fragmentary. Just the opposite. She pulled out the hand-written sheet and squinted, as if her glasses had suddenly lost their potency, and read the first line. "Meeting with Mencken, four-thirty p.m. July tenth, Morgan home—Dayton." She read it again. Mencken. *The* Mencken? Dayton—Dayton, Tennessee, she assumed. That's where the John Scopes trial was being held, and as everyone knew, the *Sun* was sending its famed reporter to cover it. Sarah had been made particularly aware of this fact. Mitchell Dobrinski, who had helped her so much with Obee, was covering the trial too, for the *Blade*. For weeks he could barely contain himself at the idea of meeting, as he repeatedly said, the "greatest journalist of all time." Mitchell, she thought, giving her rings a few spins. She had tried to keep her distance, but he was such a persistent fellow.

Anyway, Sarah knew Mencken was brilliant, but she didn't quite view him as the second, or, more accurately for her, the first coming, as Mitchell did. The man had enemies for a reason. She did know, however, that in addition to being a famed newspaperman, he was a noted literary critic, and thus assumed that the professor's meeting probably would have had something to do with books. That seemed to be confirmed by three names written directly underneath the reminder: *Smart Set* (the literary magazine that Mencken edited), Theodore Dreiser and Mark Twain. And then this quote: "A good critic is like an artist . . . So with criticism. Let us forget all the heavy effort to make a science of it; it is a fine art, or nothing." By H. L. Yes, Sarah thought. Henry Louis Mencken. But below this were words, a list of some sort, which caused Sarah's heart to skip a beat.

1. *The Origin of Species*—BY MEANS OF NATURAL SELECTION OR THE PRESERVATION OF FAVORED RACES IN THE STRUGGLE FOR LIFE.

2. George William Hunter—*Civic Biology*—Caucasian race—finally the highest type of all.

3. Nietzsche—A democracy of intelligence, of strength, of superior fitness . . . a new aristocracy of the laboratory, the study, and the shop.

4. Eugenics—the science of improving the human race by better heredity.

And scrawled across the bottom: Mencken = Natural Selection. All men are created UNequal. The strong will naturally prevail over their inferiors. Convince M. to publish and join the Brotherhood.

She removed her glasses, leaned back and massaged the bridge of her nose. How strange. Brotherhood. Usually a noble concept. But, *the* Brotherhood. That could be . . . that could mean . . . No, it didn't make sense. Not at all given what she'd heard of the professor. Maybe these were notes for a novel. A work of fiction he was planning to discuss with Mr. Mencken. Convince M. to publish. That must be it. There was no other reasonable explanation.

Feeling satisfied with her conclusion, Sarah picked up her folder again, just as Lena walked in. Everyone looked up eagerly, but as soon as they saw her, their expressions changed. She was pale. And trembling, so much so that she had to steady herself against the table. Sarah started to get up.

"The coroner's report is in," Lena said.

Sarah glanced at the others then back at Lena.

"Nick's death was not an accident."

6

*The lead bullet entered the head at too close
a range for it to be a hunter's—or anyone
else's—mistake. The slug came from a six
point thirty-five millimeter, a pocket pistol.
'Probably a Beretta.' So says County Coroner,
Foster McClean.*

Sarah put down her copy of the *Edenville Times*. This changed
everything, of course. Ever since she arrived, it seemed fate was sending her
a message. Go home, Sarah. You're not tough enough for Dixie. Go home.
But now, Lena didn't just want her to stay, she needed her to. Her cousin's
usual air of imperviousness had given way to vulnerability, even a bit of fear.
Murder? That was only in books, a literary device, an imaginative way to
make a theoretical point. The reality of it confused her. The proximity put her
normally calm nerves on edge.

Sarah had never had children, hoping to find a man to marry first.
But she suddenly experienced something like a mother's protective instinct.
An instinct lying dormant, waiting to be ignited, allowing her to keep her own
demons—which, at the very mention of murder, surely would have otherwise
risen to haunt her—at bay. Lena needed her support now. The kind of support
that comes only with the bonds of blood. And so she would stay, at least for a
while.

❖❖❖

Now that the professor's death had been deemed a homicide, the
town took on an entirely different aspect, as if suddenly electrified, as if an

especially powerful bolt of lightening had hit one of their shady old trees. Sparks flew everywhere, a high voltage mix of gossip, fear and excitement.

During the next week, all the available university staff was questioned and dismissed, as were the students, who frequently came away from their interviews in tears. Of course, many were gone for the summer, a source of aggravation for the authorities. Perhaps the murderer escaped, was already out of the country. If a clue didn't surface soon, they would have to broaden their search.

Lena's interview was conducted in the downstairs parlor. When she and Sarah entered the sweltering, fussy room, they were met by two uniformed officers gulping tall glasses of iced tea; a young, slender, redhead and a pot-bellied, crusty old codger with droplets of sweat threatening to drip from his deeply creviced forehead onto his vein-ridden, bulbous nose. The latter, clearly in charge, reluctantly allowed Sarah to remain in the room. "I'm Officer Perry," he said, "this heah's Officer Briggs. He'll be takin' some notes, if y'all don't mind."

Lena turned to Sarah, raising her eyebrows, as if to question whether this was appropriate. Sarah nodded, and the interview got underway.

"So, Miss . . . Miss Greenberg," Officer Perry said, glancing at a list of names, "when was the last time you saw the professor?"

The man's grey, filmy eyes were accentuated by a florid complexion. Probably due to having arrested so many bootleggers, Sarah thought. After all, one occasionally needed to test the evidence, just to make sure. Near his chair, a dull brass spittoon awaited the detritus of the weed-like substance he dug out of a burlap pouch.

"The day before his body was discovered."

"Under what circumstances?"

"We had been working on a project together."

"What sort of project?"

Lena took a deep breath and exhaled. "A paper."

"'Bout what?"

"About the direction the teaching of literature should take."

He rubbed his nearly non-existent chin. "How do y'all teach literature, anyway? Don't you just read it?"

Lena tried to smile. "That's an important first step, of course."

Having finished the tea, Officer Perry now placed a wad of tobacco deep in his cheek, and then pressed the cold glass against his forehead. That gave his partner an opportunity to break in. Mild-mannered and well spoken, he had no detectable accent. "Tell me, ma'am. Do you know any reason why the professor might have been killed? Anyone who'd want to do him harm?"

Lena shook her head. "No. Absolutely not."

Sarah took Lena's hand. It was cold and clammy. The notes, she thought. She hadn't stopped thinking about them, but for some reason hadn't told her cousin. Why? She had started to, and then . . .

"Do you, ma'am?" He was staring at Sarah. He had been watching her.

"Of course she doesn't," Lena said, shaking her hand free. "My cousin's just here for a visit. She arrived the day after Nick was found."

He kept his gazed fixed on Sarah. "Ma'am?"

"No, no I don't," Sarah said slowly. "Lena's right . . . except . . ."

Officer Perry leaned to the side, politely covered his mouth, and spit. A direct hit.

"Except?"

Lena turned toward her abruptly. "Except? Except what?" she asked, her face scrunched like an overly tight frock.

"Well, it's probably not important," Sarah said. "Obviously, my cousin doesn't know about this." Sarah shifted her gaze from Lena to the officers. "But the other day, when I was going through the professor's papers for her . . . for you, Lena . . . I came across something . . . some information. I don't know. It might be of some use."

Lena now just stared at her blankly.

"I don't know why I didn't mention it to you earlier," she said, taking Lena's hand again. "I really don't."

"What is the nature of this information, ma'am?" Officer Briggs asked, keeping his small, blue eyes on Sarah.

"Um, some notes."

"Notes? What kind of notes?"

"Oh, an appointment, a list. They're hard to explain, really."

"Where are they?"

"At the school, in the folder I set aside for you, Lena," Sarah said, as if her cousin had asked the question.

"Well, then," Officer Perry said. "What are y'all waiting for? Let's go."

All eyes were on Lena now.

"By all means. Let's all go," she said, suddenly standing up. "Let's go right now!" She then folded her arms, pressed them immovably on her chest, and marched toward the door.

⇻ ⇻ ⇻

Lena had every right to be annoyed with her. Sarah shouldn't have allowed her to be taken off guard like that. After all, her cousin was just beginning to establish herself here. Of course, she would have encountered those notes at some point anyway, probably quite soon. But why did Sarah wait to tell her, embarrassing her like that in front of the police? She couldn't form a clear answer. She had reacted to some instinct, but what? She was confused by her own action.

Fortunately, the officers didn't seem to notice. They were rather nice fellows actually, and treated both women with respect. At one point, Officer Perry even said he hoped his granddaughter would grow up as smart as "you two gals. Yep," he added, nodding, "the town would be a whole lot classier if there were more of you Hebrew folk around." Surprising to say the least, considering what she'd encountered thus far, not to mention the questionable reputation of law enforcement in the South. Was it a trick? She didn't think so. Was it their much-touted chivalry, that sugary patina of practiced courtesy? Perhaps. But if that were the case, then Sarah didn't mind, and she knew more than a few Ohioans who might benefit by a course in the subject themselves.

They continued in this manner, too, when it came time to question Lena about the contents of the note. According her the deference her position warranted, Officer Briggs handed her the paper, folded his feminine-looking hands and said: "You understand this stuff better than we ever could, ma'am. What do you think these references might mean? Mencken equals natural selection? All men are created unequal?"

Lena was non-committal. Her eyes panned back and forth, reading through the notes Sarah directed them to again and again, as if suddenly the next time it would all make sense. But as she read and no explanation came, the color slowly drained from her cheeks and her usually animated, slightly mischievous expression settled into fixed confusion. She struck Sarah as an alabaster figure carved by an exceptionally ambivalent sculptor. "Well, I don't know," Lena said. "It could mean nothing, of course. It could mean . . . well, like my cousin, here, said, it could be notes for a story. I don't know."

"Uh huh. Well, now, what else might it be, ma'am?"

Lena shrugged.

"You know," Officer Perry said, "I'm no scholar, but at face value these views seem a bit extreme for an educated type."

Lena nodded in agreement. "At face value, yes."

"And you, Miss Kaufman, is that perhaps what you thought when you saw them?"

"Yes, I suppose it is."

"Well then, we'll do some investigatin' and let you know." He turned to Lena. "Ma'am, in the meantime, if you think of anything, you know where to reach us." He tipped his dark blue cap, motioned to his partner, and the two walked off, leaving Sarah the awkward task of apologizing for something for which she didn't have an explanation.

➤ 7

THAT WAS ON JULY FIRST. By the fourth, they had not heard again from the officers. Just as well. Though still as perplexed by Sarah's behavior as Sarah was herself, Lena had forgiven her. Certainly the matter of clearing up the professor's notes, and his death, wasn't over. Perhaps the worst was yet to come. But they made a pact. Today, they wouldn't speak of it. Today, they would act as if nothing had happened and join in the celebration of the country's independence.

Most of the town seemed to have the same idea. Yesterday, murder was the only thing on people's minds, the only thing that could make them forget that it was the hottest summer in years. Today, the focus had shifted. The calendar dictated that it should, that the cares of the world temporarily should be suspended. Already Sarah could hear the happy shrieks of children playing outside. Chicken was being seasoned, corn shucked, watermelon sliced. And Nan herself was busy making pies, the holiday smell of baked apples and cinnamon drawing all of the boarders out of their rooms earlier than usual. A different kind of excitement had taken over, just as palpable as when the coroner's news was announced, but gentler, far more benevolent. Even nature cooperated, dropping the temperature a precious few degrees.

After a light breakfast, Lena and Sarah, arms looped around the back of each other's waists, headed for Main Street where the annual parade was about to begin. A light breeze had picked up, and in their thin, cotton frocks, they were almost cool. The rambunctious children playing in front yards, rich, meaty aromas mingling in the air, and red, white and blue streamers hanging from several trees along the way all did their part to excite the two.

"Mornin', ladies." An aging man, barely able to stand straight over his wooden cane, greeted them as they passed. "Happy Fourth," he said, raising one shaking hand. "Happy Fourth!" they both echoed, waving back. In the front yard of the next house, a robust young woman looked up from her gardening and smiled. "Goin' to the parade, are you'uns?"

"Yes we are," they again answered in unison. Feeling as energetic as two young schoolgirls, though they knew better, they almost began to skip down the street. In part they sensed that they had better enjoy themselves while they could. And in part they knew that unlike Christmas, this was a celebration in which they could partake without any guilt. And so they would.

When they finally spotted the center of town, they could see a conglomeration of chairs and benches lined up along the parade's path. Many were already occupied, but Lena found two vacancies right in front of Cohen's. Sarah chose not to speculate about why they were empty. A chair was a chair, and she hurried with Lena to make sure hers didn't get away. Mr. Cohen was there, setting up a makeshift stand next to a sign that read "Hats and Fans." He beamed when he saw them, stretching out his arms as if they were long lost relatives. "Hello! Hello! So good to see you."

"Good to see you, too, sir. These chairs aren't taken, are they?" Lena asked.

"No, of course not! Right here, my dahlings," he said, pulling them out with a gentlemanly flourish. "I saved them for you."

"You did?" Sarah said.

"No, but I couldn't be happier that you two ended up here. Uh, by the way," he said, fixing his narrowing blue gaze on Lena, "that's terrible about the professor." Lena silently nodded. He then gazed at both of them, rubbing his chin. "I think I've got the perfect remedy. I'll be right back. Don't move."

"I hope he doesn't mean that literally," Sarah said. "This seat is hard!"

Lena smirked. "You've got enough padding."

"Hey, I worked my tush off to get some meat back on my bones."

"I know. Just kidding. You know I envy your tush."

Just then Charlie returned with a package wrapped in brown paper and handed it to Lena. He leaned down and whispered: "Enjoy."

"Thanks," Lena said, "for whatever it is."

"You're welcome. Now, I've got to finish setting up. I'll see you girls later."

Lena examined the package, moist from something inside. "Should I open it?"

"Why not?"

She peeled off the masking tape and gingerly ripped open the bag. Ha! Not exactly the remedy she imagined, but a decent one nevertheless. The familiar briny aroma drifted in Sarah's direction. Pickles. Lena picked one up and took a generous bite. "Just as it should be," she said, crunching loudly. "Not overdone."

Sarah was a bit too full of toast, but she agreed that it looked perfect. "Thick, firm and juicy." Lena gave her a sideways glance and pinched her on the leg. "I love it when you're naughty," she said, and they both laughed out loud, not caring who heard them.

✤ ✤ ✤

Edenville's parade reminded Sarah of Toledo's, and for a moment she wondered whether Obee was sitting in their usual spot watching it right now. Stars and Stripes flew in abundance. A high school band played a drum-heavy version of "America the Beautiful." War veterans, precariously perched on an old fire truck, blasted a horn and waved proudly. A few Model Ts carrying some of the town's notables sputtered down the street followed by several horse-drawn wagons advertising local businesses, while people of all ages sat or stood on the sidelines, clapping, singing and drinking lemonade . . . some no doubt sweetened with more than sugar.

There were, however, a few discernable differences. This celebration was smaller. Toledo was a large city, and thus there was simply more of everything. But that was just a matter of scale. The Rebel flags were something else again. Not that many really. Just here and there, punctuating the crowd like some long out-of-use exclamation point. But they made Sarah uneasy, reminded her that she was a foreigner. And another thing. Though the town was nearly one-third black, not even one Negro had come out to watch the parade. The only faces that weren't white, in fact, were the Indians'. Several Cherokee dressed in short-sleeved buckskin costumes and colorful beads had set up shop, selling their wares close to where Mr. Cohen seemed to be making a killing. One certainly wouldn't see that in Toledo either. What, she wondered, did this holiday mean to them?

She turned back to the parade in time to see an ice truck plastered with an oversized picture of President Coolidge drive by. Hard to believe. Coolidge's inauguration was only a few months ago. Four long years still lay ahead. She heaved a deep sigh. Already the brute had signed that despicable bit of legislation, the National Origins Act. "America must be kept American," he'd argued. What he meant was, restrict Eastern European immigration and exclude the Orientals altogether. And she thought Ohio's native son, Harding, was bad. Thank God she was born here, she thought, or she'd surely be turned away, too. She glanced back at the Indians. Of course, they were born here, and look where it got them. She remembered Coolidge's campaign slogan: "Keep Cool with Coolidge." Cold is more like it. No wonder they put him on an ice truck. His image alone was probably keeping the blocks from melting.

As the parade neared its end, the crowd had swelled to several hundred. Many students even had made an appearance, including Jim and Kathryn. When they spotted Lena, they ran over, their hair sopping wet.

Lena smiled. "You two just take a shower together?"

"Miss Greenberg! Of course not! We were swimming in the river," Kathryn said. "It felt so wonderful, but then too many people started coming, so we decided to come over here and watch the rest of the parade."

"I was just kidding."

"Any word, Miss Greenberg?" Jim asked, somewhat out of breath.

"No, not yet. I'll let you know. You're both taking summer classes, aren't you?"

They nodded.

Sarah observed their smooth, unmarked bodies, their sensuality brimming over. How long it had been. Despite all the supposed free love, opportunities had rapidly dwindled in recent years. Of course, there was

Mitchell, had she just given him the sign. But why start anything? She was an old maid, yes, an old maid! Love, especially sex, was for the young. She worked all her life for women's rights, but like any good Victorian, was repelled by her own desires.

"Good. I may need your help again," Lena said.

Kathryn leaned over and squeezed the excess water out of her hair. "Anytime."

"Okay, now run along, and have fun."

"You're terrible," Sarah said, when they were out of earshot. "Embarrassing those kids like that."

"I know. I'm just jealous."

Sarah nodded. Me too, she thought.

※ ※ ※

The sun was more than halfway through its descent when, bringing up the rear of the parade in a shiny new Studebaker, the mayor stopped to deliver a concluding message. The loudspeaker helped with the volume but muffled his words. Sarah could discern only "freedom," "God," and "America." That was probably enough. She could guess the rest.

After he was through and the parade had come to a close, most of the town lingered and talked on the sidewalk. Without a doubt, everything had gone well. It had been a lovely day, absolutely delightful, and just what the local folks needed. As they stood there, debating who would make the best barbecue later that evening, a sound approached from the distance that stopped the chatter and turned their heads. The parade wasn't over after all and a renewed excitement spread through the crowd, necks craning in unison. Who was coming? A surprise celebrity? As the sound of heavy, rhythmic footsteps grew closer, louder with each pace, they could begin to see it wasn't anyone famous.

Infamous was more like it. Down the street they strode, one, two, one two. Sarah stood up abruptly, twisting her rings to the beat, pressing firmly on the garnet with each complete turn. Bold, aggressive, determined, a self-appointed army shrouded in flowing white robes and topped in cone-shaped hoods. As they came closer, Sarah spotted a few holding similarly garbed babies. Brainwashing the innocent before they even could speak. Realizing it was the Klan, some in the crowd waved, a few clapped and hooted but most just went back to talking. They had seen it before. Sarah had seen them before too, but her gaze remained fixed, unblinking. The scene was strangely fascinating to her, like a horrible accident from which she could not turn away. Perhaps they would march by and be done with it. After all, this was America. It was their right to assemble. And to speak freely, she thought, when they started their thundering "white power" chant. But at that moment, a few Negro boys who apparently had been watching the parade from a distance, had ventured closer when it started to wind down. No one had seemed to mind, until now. "Stay off the white man's streets, boy!" a Klan member yelled. "Go to your nigger parade!"

Lena grabbed Sarah's hand. "Relax," she whispered in her ear.

"I'm tired of relaxing."

"There's nothing you can do."

Sarah watched the entire group slow down as the boys backed away, but didn't leave.

"Hey boy, I said git!" The speaker now broke step with his troop, running toward the boys, who, fortunately, were quicker on their feet. "Git out," he yelled, breathing hard. "Git out and stay out!" He waited until they were out of sight, filed back in line and continued to march. Sarah looked around in amazement. Nobody tried to stop him. A few shook their heads. "Don't pay 'em no mind," one woman said. "Leave 'em alone," said another, as the ghostly figures turned the corner and disappeared from view. What could they do anyway? After all, it was the Fourth of July. They had hot dogs to cook, fireworks to ignite.

Sarah, though, could think of nothing else. The KKK. Again, the loathsome group had entered her sphere. The ignorance, the hate, even more menacing as a collective force. Lena certainly hadn't seemed so affected, though. If only a look had the power to transform, her cousin's bemused smile would have turned their venomous performance into the lowest form of parody. Sometimes Sarah longed to be more like her. A couple of days ago,

Lena seemed ready for the Cure. Now, even with the loss of a colleague and the murder investigation looming, she could take this ominous display with a grain of salt. Sarah knew better, however. These people might look like clowns, but they were more than adept with a gun and a rope.

Sarah sat back in her seat and tried to relax as Lena talked with one of her students. But her mind wouldn't stop. Her pledge to enjoy the day ended at the sight of those white robes. So did her promise not to think about the professor's murder. The KKK. His notes—"Convince M to publish" . . . and to join the Brotherhood. The KKK. Also known as the Brotherhood. Was there a connection?

Perhaps, Sarah thought. Perhaps, also, she was beginning to discern her own inexplicable behavior. Yes. Wasn't it because she knew precisely what the Klan and its kind were capable of that she hadn't said anything to Lena about the nature of the professor's list? At first it seemed a stretch in logic, a forced attempt to make herself feel better about her decision. But the more she considered the idea, the truer it felt. Whatever his reasons, this Manhoff fellow clearly had held some disturbing views. Caucasian—finally the highest type of all. All men are created unequal. She and Lena both knew deep down they weren't notes for a novel or any other kind of story. Even the officer understood that. What they could suggest, however, is a motive for murder. Few obviously knew this side of the man. Lena certainly didn't. But say someone did, someone not a member of his "favored" race. That is surely how the police would see it. Even now they probably were rounding up suspects. And if they'd read even slightly between the lines, that would mean only one thing.

At the time, she hadn't consciously reasoned it out, but now she was certain. Her reaction had been one of instinct, of the emotions rather than intellect. The race was so often wrongly accused, so often scapegoated. Even back home, for no good reason, that poor colored woman sent to prison. And then, the lynching in Columbus of all places. Wasn't that why she worked for the NAACP? How could she knowingly then throw them to the wolves? How could she admit that these notes could be critical evidence, suggesting that the professor's killer was quite probably black? So she had said nothing. Let someone else figure it out.

When Sarah later explained this to Lena, her cousin nodded, but still wasn't convinced that the professor held the opinions Sarah accused him of. "I wouldn't want someone to judge me based on one measly piece of paper. I make lists that out of context could be construed as grounds for commitment. There must be something we don't know," she said. "I worked with the man. If he were that extreme, wouldn't I have sensed it? Why would he be so good to me? A Jew, a woman?"

"Some bigotry is narrowly focused," Sarah said. "Certainly he wouldn't volunteer the information. Maybe he was even using you as a front. "

"Oh come on, Sarah. As an English teacher I can tell you that's not a very credible plot."

"Of course, you know your stuff. But books are one thing. Believe me, the courts are filled with stories that would make even that volume of Edgar Allen Poe you sent me seem like the dullest history."

"Well, let the police take care of it, then. If they find something, so be it. Be sensible, Sarah. According to what you just said, there's nothing you can add now anyway."

Be sensible. Sarah thought that a bit self-deceptive. Of course, it was best not to worry about something over which one has no control. But Lena tended to avoid problems altogether, a strategy that worked as long as one's unconscious had enough room. When over-burdened, all hell could break loose. If Sarah's experience with Obee had taught her anything, it had taught her that much about human psychology. But as usual, Lena did have a point. What could Sarah tell the police that they hadn't figured out? She already imagined that every Negro in town would be questioned in a matter of days. To take her belief to the police now would make Sarah seem like a racist herself. Better to wait at least to see if her assessment was correct. And why involve herself at all? Wouldn't that be doing precisely what she had come here to escape? A man had been murdered. With luck, his killer would be found.

❧·❧·❧

The fireworks lent a lambent glow to the night sky, each new burst of light bringing the holiday one step closer to its end. Sarah stood at the window, watching a sparkling diamond-like cluster trickle softly to the ground. Stiff competition for the fireflies. Silly as it was, she loved these brilliant, celestial explosions. A magical union of man and nature.

Thankfully, the morning papers recorded no serious accidents. Reformers were apparently successful in making the devices safer down here, too. Yet fire is a tricky thing, Sarah thought. Its purposes are varied, its effects dependent on the intent of the user. When shaped for good, it can be, as it was last night, a light in the heavens. But in the hands of evil, it can instill fear and dread, can read like a message from the underworld.

Sarah clenched her jaw to the point of pain as she read the headline recorded on the next page. "Six-foot wooden cross set ablaze in Negro's front yard." A burning cross, the Klan's latest calling card. The first ever in Edenville. Why did they choose this symbol anyway? She couldn't figure it out. From what she knew of Jesus, she didn't think he'd have endorsed it either. As she read of the incident to Lena, she felt herself grow warm, her eyes burning as if feeling the heat of the flame. A vicious act. Vicious, but as cowardly as their ridiculous disguise. They really were a bunch of cowards, and yet, as she well knew, quite capable of inspiring fear. In her case, paralyzing fear. When she finished reading the article to Lena, her cousin shook her head. "Horrible," she said, "still, there's nothing we can do." Sarah didn't agree. There was something they could do, more specifically, something she could do.

8

NEARLY TWO WEEKS HAD PASSED, but finally the day had come. Lena stood waving on the hot, empty landing. "Good luck." Sarah read her lips and watched until the petite, polka-dotted figure became a tiny unrecognizable speck. She then turned around, facing in the direction of the lumbering train.

The tracks led south. Southwest to be exact, toward Dayton. When she first told Lena of her plan, her cousin thought she was joking. "Yeah," she said, "and I'm going to teach at Harvard." Only when she observed Sarah studying the train schedule did she start to believe her. Then she just thought she was nuts. After everything Sarah had been through. All her talk about simplifying her life. Besides, she said, it would be a waste of time.

Maybe, but once the idea of going to Dayton had occurred to Sarah, the reasoning easily followed. Mencken was a much sought after figure. His time, as he let the world know, was valuable. Therefore, if in fact he had scheduled a meeting with Professor Manhoff, especially during what was already being called the "Trial of the Century," he must have considered whatever they were going to discuss important. Probably he knew the man. Perhaps he knew him well. If so, he might be of some assistance, might, at the very least, decipher the notes and confirm or deny their troubling implications.

When Sarah suggested this to Officer Perry, he stuck another thick wad of tobacco in his cheek, leaned back in his swivel chair and closed his eyes. Except for a few nonchalant, sideways spits, he was silent. Then finally he said, "Uh huh. Might work."

As Sarah had guessed, Officer Perry was considering the possibility of a racial motive for the murder. But she had underestimated him. He was by no means planning to "round up" the Negroes. He shook his head resignedly, as if he'd expected more from her. "That wouldn't be fair to them now would it, ma'am? Understandably, they'd resent such an action. And can you imagine what effect it might have on the town's bigots? Why, the whole place could go up like dry leaves under a lit match." What he needed, he said, was a concrete lead. So if there were even a remote chance that Sarah could find it in Dayton, he would send her off with his blessing. In fact, to make it easier, he would deputize her. Since she worked for the courts and all, it wouldn't be hard to explain. And if anyone had a problem with it, he'd just remind them who was in charge.

The buttons on his tight, overly starched shirt had looked ready to pop, and tobacco had stained what were left of his teeth. But after listening to him, Sarah was impressed . . . and humbled, for even with a twang that sounded like a painfully out-of-tune guitar, he had single-handedly reminded her that all Southerners were not alike. She, who shouldn't have needed such a reminder.

The truth was, however, she would have gone to Dayton anyway. She was glad to help in the investigation of the professor's murder; the sooner this matter was solved, the sooner justice would be served. Yet her decision to make the trip was also a test. A personal test. To be sure, she had come here to enjoy nature, to visit with Lena. But she also had come to escape. As if her demons would somehow stay put in the North. As if an imaginary boundary could contain them. Instead, like hoboes, they had hopped a car and followed her wherever she went. At Cohen's, the Smokies, the parade. When she left Toledo, she was certain she needed a rest. Now she felt differently. Perhaps it was seeing Lena, who dealt with her fears by avoiding them. Perhaps it was remembering Obee, who nearly died trying to do the same. Perhaps it was the burning cross. Whichever, she was starting to believe that the key to overcoming her own fear was work; the very kind of work she swore she would never do again.

She wished she could have gone immediately, but the appointed date had still been days off. So she had waited, as unsuccessful in her efforts to relax as Officer Perry had been in finding a lead. He, too, had been eager for her departure. Ignoring the fact that she was an Ohioan, a Jew and a woman, he placed her hand on the Bible and asked her to uphold the law. Was she worthy of his trust? Was she up to the task? She was about to find out. Dayton was just up ahead.

✢ ✢ ✢

Sarah turned and apologized to the scowling man behind her. He looked like a bulldog ready to bite. She didn't blame him. Startled by the commotion in the depot, she had abruptly stopped while disembarking, causing him to trip. He caught himself, but not before initiating a disagreeable chain reaction. What was wrong with her? She was so concerned about how Mencken would receive her, she'd forgotten the event that brought him here in the first place. Of course, there would be a crowd. The papers had said it for weeks: the eyes of the world focused on this tiny backwater town. The press, cameras, even radio, the first broadcast ever of a trial. She grabbed her suitcase and exited the train, scolding herself for being so oblivious.

"Sarah, Sarah, there you are!"

A shot of adrenalin raced through her body, making her momentarily weak in the knees. The tall, lanky figure was loping towards her. His thick salt-and-pepper curls and heavy brows were coming into view. As usual, he needed a shave.

"Mitchell," she said, stiffly extending her hand, "thanks for coming."

He ignored the gesture and gave her an affectionate hug. "Of course."

She pulled back and repositioned the red felt hat Lena had labored over to get at just the right angle. She wished he didn't smell so good. That same slightly woodsy scent.

"Sarah, Sarah, you look wonderful," he said, his large, downward sloping hazel eyes moving over her as familiarly as they would a child's bedtime story.

"You've got to be kidding. I'm hot, tired and just about caused a wreck to rival the B. & O."

He laughed and took her arm. "That's my Sarah," he said. "Come on, let's get out of here. The Southern's got extra trains from Chattanooga about to arrive. I've got this timed to a science."

My Sarah. She thought she had made the purpose of this trip clear. Perhaps in his excitement over the possibility of an interview with his hero, he had misinterpreted her call. She'd have to straighten him out immediately. Their friendship in Toledo was one thing. People don't share an experience like that and not develop some kind of bond. After all, without Mitchell she very well might not have lived to tell the tale. It was natural to feel some warmth, to confuse gratitude with attraction. But when things had settled down, he had persisted. He wanted her, but she wanted to be alone. She hadn't been ready, perhaps never would be, for anything more.

As they strolled toward the center of town, she freed her arm, about to kindly remind him of just that. But her attention was diverted. On July tenth, the first day of the trial, the *Edenville Times* described the atmosphere in Dayton as "carnival-like." It was now five o'clock on the evening of the twenty-first, and the term still seemed apt. Several blocks of the main street were blocked off to traffic. Vendors were everywhere, some selling souvenirs—stuffed animals, banners, commemorative coins—some food, especially snacks such as ice cream, or "eye scraim," as they called it down here. With the help of its master, or maybe the other way around, a live monkey in a three-piece red and white checked suit was taking a picture of a banana. Across the street, another was playing a toy piano, undoubtedly much more comfortable in its undershirt and knickers. If this didn't prove Darwin's theory, she didn't know what. Only a descendant of these sweet little creatures would participate in such a ridiculous display.

The entire town indeed was adorned for the occasion. Shop windows were decorated with pictures of apes and monkeys. To her right, a music store displayed a poster of a hot new tune, "Darwin's Monkey Trot." To her left, a billboard showed an orangutan drinking a bottle of milk. And amidst it all were signs admonishing people to "READ YOUR BIBLE."

Mitchell slowed his pace. "Bizarre, huh?"

"Utterly. It must be hard to remain objective writing about this stuff."

"Nobody's even trying to be. You should read what the French are saying."

"I can imagine. Something about De Tocqueville having it right?"

"Worse. Much worse."

Continuing on, the blur of faces slowly came into focus. Sarah observed primarily two distinctive types. Farmers and reporters. Overalls and white suits. Duck-billed caps and fedoras. The contrast was striking. Conspicuously absent were the hordes of tourists that were predicted, or as Mitchell had told her, consciously planned for by the city leaders.

Mitchell stopped and pointed to a small building. "That's it."

"It?"

"Where it all started. The drugstore. Robinson's."

"Oh." Sarah eyed the small, red brick building. "F. E. Robinson and Company." Through the window she observed the usual hodgepodge. Several glass-cased cabinets. A fully stocked bookshelf. A beverage counter, ceiling fan and a cash register. Medicines, cosmetics, spectacles. Quite a selection of spectacles, in fact. She needed a new pair; maybe she'd come back later.

Near the window was a small, round wooden table; according to Mitchell's sources, the very spot where the deal was made. A calculated deal, at that, not the chance encounter the city claimed it to be. Drummed up by a guy who worked for Cumberland Coal and Iron. Supposedly, the man read an article he thought might help turn around the local, failing economy. The ACLU was offering to pay the expenses of a teacher willing to break the recently passed Tennessee Butler law, which forbade the teaching of any theory that contradicted the Bible. No telling what the publicity of a case like that could do for a town. He took his idea to Robinson, brought in lawyers and town officials, and convinced John Scopes to be the victim. Unbelievable. The whole thing was a scheme, nothing to do with either science or religion. Nevertheless, it had gotten people thinking, a major accomplishment, intentional or not. Perhaps history selected this place ahead of time. Sarah touched the window to see if any mysterious energy emanated from it. It did feel strange.

Mitchell came up from behind and tapped her lightly on the shoulder, his woodsy scent preceding him. "Want one?" he asked.

Sarah turned around, brushing up against his chest. He looked down and smiled. She suppressed a desire to smile back.

"Want one what?"

He motioned to a sign near the store's front door: "Simian sodas, twenty cents."

Now she couldn't help but smile. "No, thanks."

They continued walking, she thought to her lodgings. But several minutes passed and still they walked. She was afraid of the answer, but she would have to ask. "Mitchell, did you manage to find me a room?"

"Well, as I said, Sarah, there were very few options. Most of the reporters are staying at the homes of locals. Many residents left town and rented out rooms."

"So you told me on the phone."

"Yeah, well it was a bit more difficult than I thought."

"So you couldn't find one?"

"No, I mean yes, I did."

"Great. Is that where we're heading?"

"Yes, but I have to get a cab. It's a couple of miles out of town."

She didn't like the sound of this. "Oh? Well, that's all right. Tell me the name of the place, and I'll get a cab myself."

"I'll accompany you."

"No, you don't have to. I'm tired, anyway. Why don't you call me in the morning."

"Sarah, I'm afraid I must go with you."

"What? Why?"

"Because I'm staying there, too."

❖ ❖ ❖

They were heading for the Morgan Springs Hotel, perched atop the Cumberland Pass, six miles to the south of Dayton. In the taxi Mitchell laughed and said it was literally the last resort. Sarah gazed straight ahead and remained silent. She was not amused, and the winding road was upsetting her stomach. "Seriously," he said, "every other room was taken. Even the extra cots in the lobby of The Aqua, the best hotel in town, Sarah, have a waiting list." She doubted him, but didn't have the energy to argue. If he was up to something that was his business. She could take care of herself. She had experience telling him no.

The sign said it was a quarter mile to the summit. It was about time. One more curve and she would have lost her lunch. When they reached the hotel, Mitchell hurried around to open the door, but she was already out, taking in some deep breaths.

"Pretty nice, huh Sarah?"

She looked around. It was lovely. Cooler too. "It'll do."

"And they've got a special rate during the trial, only seven dollars."

Sarah nodded slowly and walked over to a marked lookout spot. A vast green expanse framed by a reddening, smudgy sky. She stood for several moments and watched the color subtly change, as if consciously searching for the perfect shade. Apple, rose, ruby, then fading out over the horizon. She felt the muscles in her jaw relax. Even if one had been available, certainly this was better than a cot, in a lobby no less! Perhaps Mitchell was telling the truth. And if he were lying, she ought to be flattered. She turned to where he was patiently waiting and told him she was ready to check in.

Her room was on the second floor, tiny and a bit musty, but charmingly decorated with a polished brass bed neatly covered in a multi-colored patch quilt. On a small, unvarnished nightstand rested a carved, wooden duck and a cobalt blue ceramic vase overflowing with dried mountain laurel. Not a style Sarah would choose for her home, but just right in this country setting. Above the bed was a painting of a grove of pines, a fairly good rendition of the view out the room's four-paned cottage window.

Before Mitchell left for his own room several doors down the hall, he asked Sarah to dinner, and she accepted. Why not? They were here, the restaurant was open, and now that her stomach had settled, she was hungry. Fortunately, she had brought her one and only evening dress, a black velvet, sleeveless chemise. She slipped it over her head, glanced in the mirror and smiled. It fit. At least better than a few months ago when it had hung on her like a limp noodle. Over it she draped the long string of white pearls her mother gave her shortly before she died. She always wore them when she went out. Now then, just a bit of kohl around the eyes, a touch of rouge and lipstick. Contrary to popular opinion about women over forty, the older she got, the less makeup she used. Age was better left alone. Caked with powder, even the smallest line widened into a deep crevasse. She twisted her hair and fixed it into place with a square rhinestone clip. Enough. Already Mitchell might think she was sending him mixed messages.

⇥ 9

SARAH HAD CONSIDERED ORDERING the fried chicken. After all, she was in the South. But the special was lamb stew, one of her favorites, and it turned out to be the right choice. Meaty, succulent, with just a touch of salt. Served with buttery mashed potatoes and a bottle of mineral water from the nearby springs from which the hotel got its name. Healing waters, the waiter said. She gulped down a glass and poured another.

After dinner, they took the advice of a couple at the next table and went to the hotel's lounge, the only such place for miles. Not the Cotton Club, they said, but hot music and "larapin" strawberry shortcake made from the local crop. "With all that's goin' on, you might even see someone famous."

Even though he was on the wagon, Mitchell thought jazz without booze was like a Christmas tree without lights. A sturdy backdrop, but bare, lacking the spark that brought it to life. In most places, speakeasies solved the problem, but not here. "If Dayton has any bootleggers, no visitor has heard of them," he said, quoting a statement Mencken made yesterday in the *Sun*. But even he had to admit, the music sounded pretty good. Not like any hillbillies he'd ever heard. A band of seven filled the intimate room with a surprisingly robust sound. Two clarinets, two trumpets, a sax, a flute and drums. Mitchell said the trumpet soloist sounded like Louis Armstrong himself, someone whose music career he had ardently followed after seeing him perform in Chicago.

Small round tables with flickering candles surrounded the raised wooden stage. They were seated near a tall, narrow window just as the group finished a set. The small crowd clapped and whistled when they promised to return shortly.

"This is some business you've gotten yourself into Sarah," Mitchell said. "Not that I'm complaining, but I thought you had sworn off detective work."

He lit a cigarette and took several long drags. No doubt he would try to quit smoking again when he returned to Toledo. "A woman is allowed to change her mind."

He frowned and made a hissing sound. "That, I know. But do you feel well enough?"

"Yes, I'm fine."

"I'm glad. You certainly look fine."

Sarah smiled and looked away.

"The meeting is at four-thirty, you said?"

"Uh huh."

"And he doesn't know about the professor's death?"

"I'm not sure, but he certainly doesn't know about me."

Mitchell rubbed his cleanly shaved, dimpled chin. So clean, he looked ten years younger. She'd never noticed that small mole over his lip before. "Reporters like to be in control," he said. "He's a master, but I wonder how he'll react."

"Afraid the myth will turn out to be a man?"

"Ha!" What impertinence! You really have recovered."

The waiter delivered their order. Portions big enough for an elephant, but the cake was stale. The strawberries, however, were delicious, soft, pulpy and incredibly sweet.

"Rhea County is known for these," Mitchell said, holding a perfect specimen between his long, tapered fingers. "They're served with every meal. I've seen people even pass them around in court. By the way, that reminds me, I can get you a press pass tomorrow, if you're interested."

Sarah almost hugged him. "Interested? Absolutely! I was hoping to get in. That would make it so much easier."

"Glad to help. The place is jammed, but maybe you even can sneak a peek at Mencken. Size him up before he does you."

"I don't know that I want to. I might lose my courage."

"I won't let you. At any rate, I think you'll find the trial fascinating, unlike anything you've seen back home."

"You know, with all that's been going on, I haven't been able to keep up with the proceedings. What's happened so far, anyway?"

"The long or short version?"

"Before the band returns."

"Oh, alright. Let's see." Mitchell lit another cigarette and sat back in his chair. "First of all, the jury was selected. Or rather tolerated. What a fiasco. Darrow had a hell of a time. A choice amongst brethren. All anti-evolutionists, just some less so than the others. The man was a joy to watch, though. He disposed of one fellow in particularly short order, a minister who claimed he could be impartial, despite the fact that he was, as he put it, "'strictly for the Bible.'" Darrow pushed him to answer if he had ever preached for or against evolution. "'Well, I preached against it, of course'!" he said. "'Why, 'of course'?" Darrow asked. And that was it. He zeroed in on those two little words and convinced the judge—no small feat, let me tell you—that the minister's conviction against evolution was too firm."

"I've met him, you know," Sarah said, twisting her pearls.

"Darrow?"

"Uh huh. At Obee's. They were in law school together. Pretty good friends, too. Of course, as a dedicated agnostic, he found Obee's Catholicism hard to take. They had some pretty heated debates on the matter. When Obee said his religion gave him a measure of peace, Darrow reminded him of the wars fought in its name. When Obee said he believed in a strict division between church and state, Darrow asked him why he kept a Bible in his chambers. When Obee said he believed in religious freedom, even the right not to believe, Darrow clapped, but said he still couldn't understand how such a smart man could believe in all that hocus-pocus."

"No one ever said he wasn't opinionated."

"True. But for someone who preaches tolerance, he can be fairly intolerant himself. And uncompromising. During dinner, he lambasted Obee for the few times he took the side of business. To him, the unions were right, even when they were wrong."

"Did you tell him that?"

"I might have, had he asked." She smiled. "Does he still wear pastel shirts?"

Mitchell rubbed his chin again, this time targeting his perfectly centered dimple. "Hmm, come to think of it, yes. Yellow, I believe, on Monday, blue yesterday, and today . . . pink, yeah, pink. And suspenders. The guy looks like a bumpkin, but his eyes gleam like a wizard's."

"I remember them," Sarah said. "Exceptionally blue. And I remember his brows too, a very devilish shape. Especially when he spoke. I doubt whether he'd remember me, though."

"And I doubt that."

"Mitchell, you're the limit. If I didn't know you better, I'd think you've been reading Jane Austen, or one of those romance novels you claim to hate."

"Well, I mean it," he said, blowing a loose strand of hair out of her face.

She felt herself flush. "Go on, the jury was selected and then what?"

He grinned mischievously and cleared his throat. "Each side stated its case to Judge Raulston, who, by all accounts, is firmly in Bryan's court . . . no pun intended. Darrow argued that the Butler Act was illegal because it promoted a certain religious viewpoint. Bryan countered that the issue was about State's rights. Darrow pleaded for tolerance and enlightenment, Bryan for the Bible-believing majority. The literal interpretation of the Bible, that is. Tomorrow Raulston decides whether the case goes forward. No doubt he'll rule in the prosecution's favor. Bryan certainly had the crowd's support. Every time he spoke, they applauded, so much so that Darrow finally had to ask the judge to shut them up."

"I don't get it," Sarah said. "True, I'm Jewish, and skeptical at that, but why isn't it possible for a god, Christian or otherwise, to have set evolution into motion? Even Obee believes that. Why does it have to be either or?"

"I don't know." He smirked. "But then I'm agnostic."

"You know that Darrow supported Bryan for president."

"So did I. Didn't you?"

She nodded. "Most Progressives did. But the Great Commoner has gone a little mad, I think. Either that, or he's playing to the audience for political purposes. What else would explain this backward move?"

Mitchell shrugged. "Life is full of contradictions. Take you, for example. You aren't progressive on everything."

She ignored the suggestion. "So what else?"

"The big question will be whether Judge Raulston will allow Darrow's witnesses."

"Why wouldn't he?"

"They're experts. Science experts."

"So?"

"Well, today a local minister opened the session with a prayer asserting that God is, how'd he put it, the 'creator of the heaven and the earth and the sea and all that is in them.'"

Sarah shook her head. "In Toledo that would count as judicial bias."

"If you hadn't noticed, this isn't Toledo. Ah. Just in time," Mitchell said. "There's the band."

⇥ 10

EIGHT IN THE MORNING and perspiration had already left its indelible mark under the arms of Mitchell's blue pin-stripped shirt. He loosened his tie and rolled up his sleeves. If she had any, Sarah would have done the same. The taxi felt like an oven on wheels. Sarah slid off the sticky leather seat and smoothed out her dress, a white, sleeveless chemise with lemon-yellow polka dots. Actually, it was Lena's. A little too short, but her cousin assured her that it traveled well. She glanced down at the wrinkles. Well, it was stylish, anyway.

Mitchell locked her arm familiarly. She started to pull away, but then relented. After all, he didn't have to take her along. He was in Dayton for a story, and would unquestionably write a better one without her. Besides, last night he had behaved himself. After the music and another cup of coffee, they went straight to bed . . . Mitchell in his room, Sarah in hers. She had raised her defenses, prepared to do battle, but all he did was wish her goodnight. Whatever his desires, whatever his motives, he played the gentleman. She was almost disappointed.

"Sarah." Mitchell pointed to an energetic knot of women chanting Bryan's name and waving hand-painted signs: SWEETHEARTS COME TO JESUS. READ YOUR BIBLE. DARROW GO HOME. "Not your suffragette type, I'd wager."

"Probably not," she said. "Still, it's good to see them exercising their rights. The Women's Movement takes many forms."

"You know, you really should have been a lawyer. Or better yet, a judge!"

"Tell that to the good old boys running the Bar."

"Ha! No question about it. Your health is restored."

Yes, Sarah was better. But had she been on her deathbed, she would have reacted the same. She had in fact thought about law school. But that was ten years ago, before women even had the vote. With a brother and sister to support, she didn't have the luxury to wait. Not that it would have made much difference. Men still ran the show, still thought the female mind wasn't logical enough for the job. As with everything else, acceptance would probably come when she was too old to do anything about it.

"You're cute when you pout," Mitchell said.

"Now that's just the kind of statement that keeps us down."

"Okay. You're ugly when you pout."

"Thank you. Now shall we continue?"

He took her arm again, and they continued walking northeast on Market, toward the sizzling center of town. Tillie would have said that she could cook an egg on that street. And she would have said so with pride, thinking she invented the phrase.

Forty miles behind them was Chattanooga—a sooty, industrial center they refer to around here as the Pittsburgh of the South—and in the opposite direction, Knoxville. A short distance to the east, the lazy Tennessee River, to the west, the Trail of Tears, the rugged dirt path that so many years ago took the Cherokee from their home. A diaspora prompted by a belief of racial superiority and intolerance. Still, the tribe had endured, not vanished as predicted. They were still here, in the names of mountains and valleys and the little shops in which they sold their wares to the descendants of those who had sought to destroy them.

The railroad followed the curved, grassy valley floor, and Market Street loosely paralleled them both. Georgia, Delaware, California, Alabama; each of these roads intersected with Market. After that, the streets were numbered. As they crossed First, the crowds thickened considerably. A few trained monkeys were already performing their tricks.

Sarah glanced to her left and spotted a red brick building flanked by two white pillars. A flight of concrete stairs led to a set of massive wooden double doors. In front of the structure, people were vying for space on a wide, manicured lawn. "Something tells me that's the courthouse."

Mitchell nodded. "Yep."

"It's lovely, what I can see of it. Romanesque Revival. Italian Villa style."

"If you say so."

"I do. I know my courthouses. Hard to believe what's happening here. Looks more like a church picnic." Sarah squinted. "What does that sign say?"

"Prayer meeting tonight. Eight p.m."

Mitchell pulled out his camera, fiddled with the lens and clicked. He was a very good photographer, despite his claims to the contrary. In addition to a few requisite shots for the *Blade*, he had already taken a book's worth of pictures here for his own pleasure.

It was Wednesday, July twenty-second, the hottest day so far. The trial wasn't due to start for an hour, but newsmen already were lined up four deep along the rectangular rail surrounding the sanctum of the sweltering court. With every minute that passed, another hard wooden seat was taken, until by nine-thirty none was left. The general public, which, according to Mitchell—Sarah's source now on all things trial related—was comprised mostly of locals from Dayton and the surrounding countryside, began to spill out into the hallway.

During the next half hour, everyone, seated or not, was preoccupied with the fruitless task of trying to cool down. Even the installation of the radio microphone set to broadcast via Chicago, the first such event of its kind, was treated with relative indifference—except by Sarah who immediately recognized the announcer as the one and only Quin Ryan. His sunken chin and prominent forehead were legendary. But she remembered him for announcing the Cubs game in April. That, too, was a first, the first time a regular season game had ever been broadcast. Exciting, even though the Cubs won. The Tigers were her favorite team, after the Mud Hens, of course. But even Ty Cobb going six-for-six couldn't compare with the thrill of listening to that game as it happened.

Sleeves were rolled up, straw hats removed, and palm leaf fans waved rhythmically, an oddly sensual sight in this parochial setting. When frosty pitchers of water were placed on the attorneys' tables, Sarah observed several people lick their lips, and could almost feel a collective, concerted restraint. Had the mercury risen one more degree, she felt certain decorum would quickly have given way, and they would have jumped over their seats to see who could get to the water first. A basic human need providing living proof of survival of the fittest.

Judge Raulston entered the room, waving and broadly smiling to the crowd. "They don't wear robes here," Mitchell said in response to Sarah's perplexed look. The tall, balding, meticulously groomed man wore an off-white linen suit, something she never had seen in all her years in court. As he approached the bench, he ran his hand reverentially over the oversized, leather-bound Bible resting near his gavel. Mitchell had warned her, but she still couldn't believe it. "I thought justice was blind," she whispered.

"You did?"

She nodded. Well, it's supposed to be, at any rate. She knew that judges could be biased, even in Toledo. But in a case in which religion was so central, this gesture was more blatantly prejudicial than any she had witnessed. Or so she thought. A moment later, she noticed another one of those "Read Your Bible" signs next to the jury. And then, without a trace of irony, Raulston asked a local minister—someone Sarah later learned was radically fundamentalist—to lead the crowd in prayer.

What would Obee say? No doubt he was glued to the radio like everyone else, listening to the Trial of the Century. Of course, Obee wasn't exactly perfect. Certainly he had his own problems, his own detractors. But no one ever could accuse him of not striving to be fair. Indeed, if anything, he often went overboard in this regard. Nevertheless, Obee, the Honorable O'Brien O'Donnell, would probably pass into history unnoticed, whereas this judge, she sensed, would be known to the world.

Despite his relatively lowly status here, Mitchell had managed to get seats fairly close to the bench. No surprise, really. He was known for being resourceful—mischievous, but resourceful. That's why she still doubted his hotel story. Had he really wanted a room in town, he would have found one.

"Recognize him?" Mitchell said, nudging her. It was only then that she noticed Darrow: his spiky hair, rutted face, strong but somewhat sagging jaw. She agreed with a description she had once read, that his "skeptical, twisted mouth was softened by the quizzical twinkle of his deep-set eyes." These competing qualities, rather than canceling each other, ebbed and flowed, each threatening but never succeeding in overtaking the other. It was a fine balancing act. His Honor, however, seemed unimpressed. When Darrow objected to the prayer, Judge Raulston turned to the heckling crowd with a twinkle of his own. "Overruled," he said.

Next to Darrow sat John Scopes. The scene was a study in contrasts. Darrow, the celebrated defender of hardened criminals, a crusty, larger-than-life public figure, with lavender suspenders supporting his well-fed, middle-aged stomach. And Scopes, the tall, fair, smooth-faced defendant. Plucked out of obscurity, his plain cotton shirt was already clinging to his bony frame.

Undoubtedly, both were relieved that Judge Raulston had loosened the dress code for the proceedings. Even though Raulston himself wore a coat and tie, he hadn't required anyone else to do so. Perhaps he assumed that in this heat, even God would have understood. Women were not affected by this ruling, of course. They still had to dress up, although admittedly, they had more choices where temperature was concerned—one of the few things in which they did.

The morning started with the long-awaited ruling on Darrow's motion to throw out the indictment. Sarah felt her stomach tighten. She hadn't even come here to see the trial, shouldn't let herself get drawn in. But she couldn't help it. Such an auspicious occasion. The jury, the spectators, the reporters; everyone looked on anxiously. If the judge ruled in Darrow's favor, the trial would be over before it began. Only Mitchell seemed relaxed, leaning on his elbow, notebook and pen in his lap. The crowd grew quiet as Judge Raulston cleared his throat: "I cannot conceive how the teachers' rights under this provision of the constitution would be violated by the act in issue. The relations between the teacher and his employer are purely contractual, and if his conscience constrains him to teach the evolution theory, he can find opportunities elsewhere."

Appreciative noises erupted while reporters wrote furiously. Mitchell just grinned. "As I said, the trial will go forward."

✥ ✥ ✥

Judge Raulston let court out early for lunch, but Sarah wasn't hungry. It was too hot to eat, even though they managed to find a spot to sit under a shady, full-leafed dogwood. Only after Mitchell repeatedly insisted that she take a bite of his roast beef sandwich did she relent. It would be hours, he said, before they would eat again. She would need her strength for Mencken. As she started to chew the tough meat, she felt a tap on her shoulder and turned around. It took her a moment to focus. When she realized who was squatting beside her, she let out a little gasp. "At O'Brien's," Darrow said, "at Judge O'Donnell's, right?"

Sarah coughed, nearly choking on a piece of wilted lettuce. "Why, yes. That's right."

"What are you doing here?" he asked, as if his approaching her were no big deal.

"Well," she said, still clearing her throat, "it's a rather long story."

"No matter, as long as you're with us."

"Yes, of course."

"Good girl. And you?" he said, eyeing Mitchell's notebook suspiciously.

"Journalistic objectivity. I'm neutral."

Darrow squinted and rose stiffly. "I see."

"But Mr. Darrow," Mitchell said hopping up, appearing to suddenly realize the unique opportunity, "if you wouldn't mind, I would like to ask you a few questions."

"It's lunch, my man." He turned back to Sarah. "Be here tomorrow?" he said.

"No, just today."

"Too bad. Well, give O'Brien my best. And remind him that variety is the spice of life. Fish every Friday will do him in."

Sarah laughed. "Will do."

Darrow adjusted his suspenders and headed toward a group of reporters.

"I wonder what they have that I don't," Mitchell said.

Sarah almost jokingly told him to look at the size of their feet, but caught herself. Lena's dirty mind was rubbing off. Instead, she simply shrugged her shoulders and declined another bite.

✦·✦·✦

Thankfully, Judge Raulston had banned smoking from the courtroom. After lunch everyone would have lit up, and in this heat, the stench of stale smoke would have turned her green. The already pungent combination of perfumed sweat and leftover lunch was bad enough.

A few puffs from a cigarette might have helped the young Scopes, however, who now appeared somewhat confused, as if awakening from a long sleep. Perhaps reality was beginning to sink in. According to Mitchell, he was not particularly committed to this cause. It wasn't even clear if he really had ever taught Darwin's theory. He was more a chosen victim than a principled defendant, appointed by city officials to help a failing economy. Maybe he was wondering what impact the trial would have on his future, on his career, on his students. Or maybe he was just thinking he'd rather be fishing.

As if on cue, Darrow leaned in close and whispered something in Scopes' ear. Glancing to the side, he caught Sarah's gaze. The blue eyes froze for a moment, and then turned back to Scopes. He looked at her again, and this time saluted her familiarly.

"I told you so," Mitchell said, witnessing the exchange.

"Told me what?" Sarah suddenly felt even warmer, if that were possible.

"That he couldn't forget you."

"Don't be ridiculous. We just spoke outside."

"Right, but he still remembered you."

Sarah didn't respond, but secretly she was pleased. Even if he couldn't identify her by name—which indeed he hadn't—it was still gratifying to know that she hadn't gone entirely unnoticed that night at Obee's. Could she feel his eyes on her again? She looked up, but immediately turned away. No need to press her luck.

On the other side of the aisle, furiously waving what was surely the biggest fan in the room, sat Bryan, the Great Commoner. Also larger than life. Not lined like Darrow, but pasty, plethoric, and sweating profusely. Sparse grey hair at the base of his skull stopped abruptly at the top of his ears, a demarcation as sharp as the tree line. Clearly, the man was uncomfortable, even without a jacket, even with his bow tie drooping and shirt half open at the collar. Yet he was smiling. A stretched, confident smile that said he was among friends. Directly behind him in a wheelchair sat his wife, a dignified looking woman who purportedly opposed his participation in the case. Waving a slightly smaller fan with a visibly arthritic hand, she kept her eyes fixed adoringly on her husband's massive, shiny crown.

Bryan's mix of Christian zealotry and left-wing politics was something Sarah had difficulty understanding. She agreed with Mitchell that human behavior was often contradictory. But this particular combination seemed impossible to reconcile. How could one vehemently uphold an absolute notion of truth, of good and evil, right and wrong, and truly empathize with the sufferings of those who did not believe the same? Then again, Christ himself had a rather radical bent, feeding the hungry, helping the poor. The meek shall inherit the earth. She smiled. Of course, Christ was a Jew, not a Christian.

Like his rival, however, Bryan was a skilled rhetorician, and Sarah would have liked to see him in action. Would he be as persuasive as he'd been at that Chautauqua, where, against Sarah's better judgment, he convinced her to join the temperance movement? But apparently it was not to be. Technically, Bryan was Special Counsel, only an assistant to the lead prosecutor, Attorney General Stewart. Though she doubted whether the Commoner would be content to take a back seat for long, for now he leaned back in his chair, silently waving his fan.

It was Stewart—younger, taller, with a full head of black hair— conducting the questioning today. The crowd settled down as he tonelessly made his opening statement: "Scopes violated the anti-evolution law by teaching that mankind is descended from a lower order of animals. Therefore, he has taught a theory which denies the story of divine creation of man as taught in the Bible." He sat back down and turned to his opponent.

Sarah leaned toward Mitchell. "That's it?"

"Apparently. Malone is already on his feet."

"Malone? What about Darrow? I'm not going to miss him too, am I?"

"Now, now. Don't get greedy."

"I know, I know. I'm lucky to be here at all. Who is Malone anyway?"

"Dudley Field Malone. He's on Darrow's team."

"Obviously."

"Oh, you mean his background. He's a divorce attorney from New York."

She knit her brows. "I see."

"You do?"

"No, but Darrow must have his reasons."

"You're really smitten with this guy, aren't you?"

"Jealous?"

"You know I am," he said, wrapping his arm around her bare shoulder.

The blood rose to her face. She should know better than to joke about such things with this man. Fortunately, Malone was about to speak. She twisted out of Mitchell's embrace and turned toward the well-dressed figure.

Malone's open, grandfatherly face didn't match her image of a divorce attorney. An image based on experience, for she knew many of that particular breed personally. It wasn't that she was against divorce per se. How could she be? She'd never been married, didn't know how she, herself, would hold up. But at court, she had counseled many couples ready to call it quits, and found, more often than not, that all they needed was a good listener. She was proud to say that in being such a person, she had helped save far more marriages than she'd lost. No thanks to the attorneys, however, who, in general, hoped for the worst. Naturally, they had to make a living, but doing so through the destruction of relationships seemed to cost them a bit of their humanity.

In this case, of course, Malone was hoping for the best: that his client would be exonerated. In an even, sincere tone, he read from a prepared statement: "We will prove that whether this statute be constitutional or unconstitutional the defendant Scopes did not and could not violate it. We will show by the testimony of men learned in science and theology that there are millions of people who believe in evolution and in the story of creation as set forth in the Bible and who find no conflict between the two."

Then Malone went on to argue, rather brilliantly, Sarah thought, that Christianity takes many forms, that just because Bryan's particular brand of fundamentalism finds science incompatible doesn't mean that other branches of the faith feel the same. And that, therefore, since our country is predicated on religious freedom, to forbid the teaching of evolution is to deny the rights of other Christians.

Sarah agreed, despite the fact that her own religion apparently didn't figure into the issue at all. However ruthless Malone might be in a divorce court, he was compassionate enough here. Compassionate and succinct. His logic was inescapable. Did others feel the same? She glanced around the silent room. Evidently not.

"There's your man," Mitchell whispered excitedly, as Stewart stood to call his first witness.

"Man?"

"Over there." Sarah turned around. All she could make out was a stocky figure in a rumpled striped shirt and dark pants marching into the courtroom, chewing on a fat cigar. She couldn't catch his features, but felt his energy. Confident, determined, annoyed. The other reporters must have sensed his presence too, for as soon as he approached, they opened a path, letting him pass like Moses through the Red Sea.

"Oh, the man." Sarah pulled back, not wanting him to catch her looking. Mitchell was right. Good to size him up before the meeting. Lessen the tension. She jutted her head out slowly, but it was too late. Henry Louis Mencken, journalist extraordinaire, the man who might hold the key to the professor's murder, already had been swallowed up.

Stewart first questioned the school superintendent, Walter White, a slight, old geezer who yawned as he testified that Scopes had admitted teaching about the theory of human evolution from Hunter's *Civic Biology*. Mitchell leaned toward her. "Don't let him fool you. He was in on the original deal at Robinson's."

"Could you repeat the name of the textbook, please?" Stewart asked.

The man lowered his head. "Hunter's *Civic Biology*."

Sarah smiled to herself. She would have to get a copy of this shameful work.

Next to take the stand were two of Scopes' students. The overly muscled captain of the football team began, seeming to relish the task. Yes, he testified with a self-satisfied toothy grin, Mr. Scopes had used the book in his class. The second, a curly-haired freshman named Howard Morgan, appeared more reticent, stating in a halting, cracked voice that he remembered the defendant only once discussing the topic of human evolution. He smiled sweetly, but his heavy brows were continuously lowered.

"I ask you further, Howard," Stewart said, "how did he classify man with reference to other animals; what did he say about them?"

"Well," he said, swallowing, "he classified man along with cats and dogs, cows, horses, monkeys, lions, horses and all that."

"What did he say they were?"

"Mammals."

"Classified them along with dogs, cats, horses, monkeys and cows?"

"Yes, sir."

At that, the crowd made noise. Some gasped, others just laughed. "Thank you," Stewart said, and sat down. "Your witness."

Darrow pushed back his chair.

"Looks like you'll get to hear him after all," Mitchell said.

"So it does."

Darrow placed his thumbs in his suspenders and gently rocked on his squat legs. Then, in slow motion, he approached the defendant. With each step, the room seemed to gradually shift, from one to three dimensions. "Now, Howard," he said with a half grin, "what do you mean by classify?"

"Well, it means classify these animals we mentioned, that men were just the same as them, in other words—"

"He didn't say a cat was the same as a man?"

"No, sir: he said man had a reasoning power; that these animals did not."

"There is some doubt about that, but that is what he said, is it?"

Sarah laughed. She looked around, pleased to see that a few others did as well.

"Order," the judge said obligatorily.

Darrow then asked him to relay how Scopes had defined a mammal, which the poor boy couldn't remember. "Well, did he tell you anything else that was wicked?" he asked so gently that had Sarah not known his views, even she might not have been able to discern the sarcasm.

"No, not that I remember . . ."

"Now, he said the earth was once a molten mass of liquid, didn't he?"

"Yes."

"By molten, you understand melted?"

"Yes, sir."

"After that, it got cooled enough and the soil came, that plants grew; is that right?"

"Yes, sir, yes, sir."

"And that the first life was in the sea?"

"Yes."

"And that it developed into life on the land?"

"Yes, sir."

"And finally into the highest organism which is known to man?"

"Yes, sir."

"Now, that is about what he taught you? It has not hurt you any, has it?"

"No, sir."

"That's all."

❧ ❧ ❧

The final witness was F.E. Robinson, but Sarah couldn't focus on his testimony. Her thoughts had shifted to Mencken, who had skulked out of the courtroom before the man was called.

"You are Robinson, the owner of Robinson's Drug Store?" Stewart asked.

"Yes, sir."

She glanced at the courtroom clock.

"Where all this thing started?"

"Yes, sir."

Had he heard of the professor's death and already made other plans? If Mitchell hadn't needed to stay, she would have gotten up and followed him. She might do it anyway.

"Did you have any conversation with Scopes along about the time that this trial started with reference to his teaching the theory of evolution?"

"Yes, sir."

No. Where would he go? Besides, she wanted Mitchell with her. Just in case Mencken lived up to his reputation.

"Get the date of it."

"I don't remember what date; all I know is that Scopes said that science teachers could not teach Hunter's biology without violating the law."

"Okay," the judge said, "the witness is excused. Court dismissed."

⇥ 11

THE AIR OUTSIDE WAS NO COOLER than in the courthouse, but at least there was more of it. Sarah took in a few deep breaths and turned to Mitchell, who was already halfway through a cigarette. They had an hour to spare, but she didn't want to take any chances. Was Mencken in his room? If so, she'd wait nearby until the appointed time. If not, she'd keep watch until he returned.

Mitchell blew a masterful smoke ring, flicked the butt onto the ground, and then tossed a stick of Wrigley's spearmint into his mouth. "Have a piece?" he asked.

"Yes, thanks, but remind me to spit it out before we get there. I doubt if he'll take me seriously if I go in popping my gum. Speaking of that, where did you say Dr. Morgan's place is?"

"On Seventh Avenue. Just four blocks south."

In minutes they were standing in front of a two-story wood-planked house with a wide porch. A simple engraved sign out front read, "Dr. Thomas Morgan."

"Stay here," he said. "I'll check. You know how they are down here."

They? Actually, in this regard, they weren't that different up in Toledo. A woman entering a man's quarters unescorted would raise an eyebrow up there, too. Although admittedly, at her age only slightly.

In seconds, Mitchell returned. Yes, he was in his room. "The landlady asked if I was the visitor Mr. Mencken was expecting. I said I was, and that I'd be back soon . . . with my wife."

Sarah opened her mouth to protest, but stopped herself. Let him have his fun. Besides, it wasn't a bad idea. No need to identify herself. It would speed things along. She smiled and nodded. The only problem was that now that she knew Mencken was in there, she had no excuse. She would have to follow through. Investigate—was she actually doing this again?—a murder. A murder of man she didn't even know, a murder of which Mencken was apparently unaware. Henry Louis Mencken. The most celebrated journalist of her time. Who did she think she was? Still, she was here. Lena, and indeed perhaps all of Edenville were counting on her. Anyway, he was just a person. She straightened her back. The trial had been a fascinating digression, but it was time to return to the topic at hand. She glanced at a nearby clock, gave her rings a few concentrated twists, and tried to ignore the man dressed like a monkey coming her way.

⇢ ⇢ ⇢

Mencken's room was up a short flight of worn carpeted stairs. Mitchell raised his fist to knock on the door, but Sarah motioned him away. "Let me do it," she whispered.

"Okay, you're the boss."

She smoothed her hair, swallowed and knocked.

No answer.

She knocked again, louder.

"C'mon in, Nick." The voice was deep and raspy, the tone at once commanding and familiar. Sarah and Mitchell stood motionless.

"Nick, door's unlocked." Now he sounded irritated. Sarah glanced at Mitchell and slowly turned the cut glass knob. The door creaked open. Still she didn't move, so Mitchell gently pushed her forward. The first thing she noticed was a pleasant mingling of scents—spicy cologne, ripe strawberries and fresh cigar smoke. Since a child, she had possessed a heightened sense of smell, an almost uncanny ability to detect even the tiniest hint of a substance. A drop of fragrance behind the ear, a lone strawberry at breakfast would have been enough. Sometimes this trait was rewarding, sometimes a curse.

Next her eyes fell on what appeared to be a two-fingered typing machine and several sheets of paper that lay on a small writing table. Squinting, she could just make out the title: "The Hills of Zion." Bessie Smith was belting out (or was it Ma Rainey?) a throaty tune on a small gramophone. Finally, she saw Mencken himself, gazing out the window, stripped to the waist, his bare rounded back facing them. She glanced at the open door. They could still get out before he saw them. It was okay for a man to go shirtless, of course, but this was an embarrassing invasion of privacy.

"Nick, my man." Too late. He turned around, grinning. Instantly, his face dropped. He craned his thick neck forward. "I'm afraid you've got the wrong room," he said, tapping cigar ashes into his cupped hand.

Sarah tried to keep her eyes focused on his slickly parted hair rather than his fleshy chest.

"Mr. Mencken?"

"Yes, you've got that right," he said, not self-conscious in the least. He faced them squarely, shoulders back.

"Actually sir," Sarah ventured, "we're here to see you."

He narrowed his eyes. "Oh, yes, yes, now I know," he said, ignoring her and pointing at Mitchell. "You're one of my breed. I've seen you in court. Well, nice try. But I'm not available to give interviews just now. Perhaps later. If you'll be so kind as to . . ."

"Mr. Mencken," Sarah said. "Nicholas . . . Professor Manhoff . . ."

He stopped. "Nick, yes, what about him?"

Sarah swallowed hard again. "I'm afraid . . ."

"Yes?"

"He's dead, sir."

At first the man didn't seem to hear her. He stood still, legs apart, puffing silently on his cigar.

"Is this some sort of joke?" he finally asked.

Sarah exhaled. "I'm afraid not."

Now he scrutinized them, shifting his cynical, metallic eyes from one to the other. What the hell happened? How do you know Nick?"

"Well," Sarah said, "I was visiting my cousin . . ."

"Just a minute. I need a drink." He opened a drawer and pulled out a half-full bottle of whiskey. "I'm a wet. You're not temperance folks, are you? Prohibition nut cases?"

"No," they said in unison.

"Join me?"

Mitchell licked his lips. "No, thanks."

Sarah glanced at Mitchell. Surely he wouldn't want her to decline just because he had a problem with the stuff. After all, she hadn't touched the flask since she'd been here. And this might earn her some leverage with Mencken. "Don't mind if I do," she said.

"Good for you," he said. He turned off the music, handed Sarah a cloudy water glass, and poured her a shot. "I'm ambibulous, you know. "Drink every known drink and enjoy all of it. Never drink alone, though. Way to become a drunkard." Mitchell averted his eyes. "Never drink when the sun is shining, either." He glanced outside. "Well, almost never. But I'm fond of drinking a reasonable amount. Benefits the heart muscle. Please . . ." he said, gesturing to a dusty, velveteen love seat.

Mitchell looked stunned but said nothing as Sarah guzzled the burning liquid, then relayed the details—as much as she knew, anyway—of the professor's death. Mencken listened with his heavy brows knit together, sipping his drink, puffing on his cigar and occasionally shaking his head. He too was silent until she told him about the coroner's report.

"Murder?" His face contorted. "Jesus Christ."

"Yes," Sarah said, "it's terrible . . . shocking for you I suppose. Were you close to him, Mr. Mencken?"

"Murder," he said again, shaking his head.

Sarah repeated her question.

"Close? No, not really. But then we Americans bat that word around too easily. I can count on one hand the people I'm close to. Still, I knew him fairly well. Or his type, anyway."

"Type?"

"College professor. English, no less. Despicable profession. He didn't deserve this, though. Poor fella."

Sarah winced a little, remembering how hard Lena had fought just to get her foot in the door of that "despicable profession."

"Any idea who did it?" he asked.

"No, but, as I said, that's why I'm here, to see if you might know something . . . anything."

He squinted again, and then stared blankly into space, his face empty of expression. "Doubt it."

"Doubt what?"

"Doubt whether I can help."

"Well, you never know. Please, if I could just ask you a few questions."

"You say the police sent you?"

She nodded.

"That's surprising. But then the South is its own planet."

"Surprising because I'm a woman?"

Mitchell stared at her, the downward slope of his eyes reversing course.

Mencken chuckled. "Well, yes. Mercifully, the women's movement hasn't really found its way down here yet. Oh now, don't go lookin' at me like that—I'm not a misogynist, you know."

"No?" Sarah said, maintaining her expression, whatever it was.

"Hell, no. A misogynist is a man who hates women as much as women hate one another. I don't even approach that. Besides, I'm married to a wonderful woman . . . her name is Sarah, in fact. Love is the triumph of imagination over intelligence, you know. I love her deeply, so I must not be that smart." He snickered, but Sarah was silent.

"I guess you're right," he said. "This isn't a laughing matter." Suddenly he looked thoughtful, serious. "I'll tell you what. Let me finish my article, here, and then I'll meet you for dinner. You said you're staying at the Morgan Springs? Yeah," he said, answering his own question. "They've got pretty good food, I hear. And music. Say, at seven?"

"Thank you. Thank you, sir."

"Yes, thank you." Mitchell said. It was the first word he had spoken since their inauspicious entrance.

"What d'ya say your last name was?"

"Dobrinski."

"No, I mean you," he said, motioning to Sarah.

"Kaufman."

He stared at her intently. "Ohhh, yes. I see. Well, seven o'clock then," and abruptly showed them the door.

❖ ❖ ❖

Mencken was already seated, again chewing on a cigar when they arrived five minutes late. "Hope you don't mind, he said. "I already ordered."

"No problem."

"For all of us," he added. "Salisbury Steak."

Mitchell smiled obsequiously. "That's my favorite."

"Really? I thought it was chicken," Sarah said.

Mencken looked from one to the other and smirked. "Sound like a married couple to me."

"Hardly," Sarah said.

Mencken smirked again as they settled in. "Now then," he said, "what would you like to know?"

He certainly gets right to the point, Sarah thought. No wonder he's so prolific. "Well, I guess to begin with, why was the professor meeting with you?"

"Why? Mainly to convince me to publish one of his articles in the *Mercury*. I met him at a convention, and he's been after me ever since. You may have heard that my magazine has had some impact on authors, brought some vitality into the literary world."

"Theodore Dreiser. Isn't that right?" Sarah said. She had loved *An American Tragedy*.

"Yeah, he's one. Although I've cooled a bit on his work. Too ideological. Same reason I wouldn't publish Nick's work . . . that, and it was miserably written. Amateurish. Nick would have never made an author. He was a teacher. A professor, mind you. But from my experience, teaching literature is a subjective enterprise by people who can't do anything else."

"But Mr. Mencken," Sarah said, thinking again of Lena, "surely you believe it can be a noble profession. Discussing ideas, explaining complex topics, helping people understand what they're reading."

"If someone can't figure this stuff out on their own, they should do something else."

Sarah took a long sip of medicinal tasting water, wondering if his attitude was in part a case of sour grapes. She had heard he'd not finished college. She kept those thoughts to herself, but they must have been written on her face.

"Ha! I admire your spunk, young lady."

She felt herself blush. "I'm not so young."

"No, but you are Jewish."

Her stomach turned. "Yes, so?"

"So, you're assertive, aggressive even."

There it was again. One could never tell where it would surface. "Excuse me, sir, but isn't that generalizing a bit?"

He smiled thinly. "You mean, am I anti-Semitic? I've been accused of it. But you know my partner, George Nathan, is Jewish. Been my partner for over ten years."

"That's like saying some of my best friends . . ."

"I call 'em like I see 'em, Miss Kaufman, but I judge people individually. Take Hayes, for instance, one of the attorneys on Darrow's team. He's a Jew. Good man, too. If Raulston will ever let him speak. Ha! Raulston. Now there's a man with some strong feelings about your people."

"The judge?"

"Uh huh. You're right, though. The general does not always apply to the particular. But I will admit that some groups do have rather predictable traits. That's what Nick believes . . . believed, too." His face darkened. "Christ."

Just then the waiter came with hearty plates of gravy-soaked meat, buttery mashed potatoes and fried okra, the house specialty.

"This needs a nice glass of Cabernet. Wouldn't happen to have any, would ya?" Mencken asked. The waiter blushed, shook his head and walked away. "No, no, I suppose not." He cut into the soupy substance and took a bite. "Pretty fair," he said.

Mencken spoke in a manner that made rebuttal difficult. It was not only what he said, but also how he said it. Accenting the last word in each sentence—pretty *fair* is how his comment actually sounded. He added weight, a heavy certainty to it. His tone was hard to pin down, too: at once folksy and erudite, quizzical and condescending. In a word, it was maddening.

"Can you elaborate on the professor's views?" Sarah asked.

"He believed in survival of the fittest, as do I."

"In what sense exactly?"

"In the sense that the stronger races will rise to the top, beat out the others. If that means certain groups die off, become extinct, well that's the natural way of things. If the damn do-gooders don't get in the way, that is. Nature abhors the weak . . . and morons." He twisted his napkin into a weapon and squashed a buzzing mosquito unaware. A streak of blood marred the otherwise stark white tablecloth.

Sarah pushed down the piece of meat that had caught in her throat and said: "You can't mean that, someone of your intelligence? I've heard this attributed to Darwin, but do you really think that's what he had in mind?"

"The term actually belongs to Herbert Spencer. But read *The Origin of Species*. Darwin may not say it explicitly, but it's the logical conclusion of his theory . . . and it is what Nick believed. Sink or swim. For that matter, it's what the Commoner believes too. He's got it backwards, of course, the old fool, but that's one of the reasons he's against Darwin . . . and Hunter, the author of the textbook that started all the hubbub. I imagine you might be too, if you knew what was in it."

"I see no reason to doubt the theory of evolution," Sarah said.

"Yes, but do you believe that epileptics, the mentally ill and other unwanted types are lower animals, that we would be best to kill them off to prevent them from spreading?"

"Of course not."

"Do you believe we should prevent intermarriage and the possibility of perpetuating such a low and degenerate race?"

"No!"

"Well, that's a direct quote from *Civic Biology*. Now, Bryan thinks this means Darwin himself operated on the law of hate. Never mind that he was merely recording scientific fact. Government handouts and prayer is what he'd prefer. I don't know about you, but I'd take hate any day."

Sarah glared at him and then looked down at her plate unseeingly. To say this so matter-of-factly. Sickening. Frightening. She didn't care who he was; she had to speak her mind. "Mr. Mencken, with all due respect, in a vacuum the theory of evolution might be construed this way, but in practice don't you think it has actually taken us down a different path? Toward a more enlightened attitude, a more compassionate view of existence? After all, conscience is a product of the evolutionary process too, isn't it? And at its best, isn't the government an extension of the conscience?"

"Nature doesn't have a conscience; it is neither kind nor cruel. It just is."

"But humans do, that's my point. We have a choice, we think. Remember Descartes! 'I think therefore . . .'"

"Yes, yes, 'I am.' But what about religion?" he asked. "Do you find that part of the evolutionary process? I may have my preconceptions, but remember what has been done to your people in the name of Christianity. Is that enlightened?"

This was true. Sarah agreed with him about religion. At least the fundamentalist sort. One could certainly be ethical, moral and agnostic. In fact, in her experience, this was at least as often the case as it was with the devout. And that quote from Hunter—using Darwin to justify intolerance. She knew this kind of argument, but didn't imagine it would surface in a high school textbook. That did muddy the situation a bit. She didn't say any of this, though. They were getting off the point. For a few moments they sat in silence, then she said: "But how can you believe in this, this . . . social use of Darwin and also treat people as individuals, as you say?"

"Nature takes care of itself. I would never attempt to mandate my views. I am a libertarian in the truest sense of the word. Live and let live. Humans have a right to at least the pursuit of happiness."

"So I assume you are a States rights advocate?"

"Absolutely."

"Well then, how can you support John Scopes? Disobeying the Butler Law—Tennessee state law—is what this is all about."

"Very good, ma'am. But then I never claimed to be consistent."

They ate, rather the men ate and Sarah played with her food. They ordered coffee that even doused with cream and sugar tasted like dirty water.

"Did Professor Manhoff treat people individually, as you say you do?"

He sat silently and puffed. He seemed hesitant. "Not quite."

"What do you mean?"

"Let's go hear the music, shall we?"

They sat in the back of the lounge, where they could hear each other talk. Fewer tables were occupied than the previous evening, but the same talented band was on stage.

"Well, Mr. Mencken?" Now it was Sarah who wanted to get to the point.

He lit a new cigar. "You know, there are two main strains of thought on this topic."

"What topic?"

"Social Darwinism. I'm more in the Spencerian vein. Laissez-faire. As I said, let the forces of natural selection take care of society. Nick, well, he believed in intervention. To assist nature in decreasing the, uh, unfit elements of the population. More a follower of Francis Galton, you know, Darwin's cousin."

Sarah thought of the professor's notes. "You mean he believed in eugenics."

"In a word, yes. He was, I must say, quite knowledgeable on the topic."

"And who did he feel were the unfit?"

"Well, certainly Coloreds topped his list." He picked up a plate with peppermint candies sitting on the table. "Have one?"

Sarah recoiled. Eugenics. She and Obee had fought against the idea for years, most memorably when there was a call to sterilize a group of women in Toledo, simply because they were poor and black. Fortunately, they succeeded in squashing the effort. If the procedure had been allowed in their city, others in Ohio would have jumped on the bandwagon.

"Don't judge poor Nick too harshly, Miss Kaufman. I would imagine that if you scratched beneath the self-righteous surface of many modern reformers, you'd find some place where they draw the line. "Italians, Hungarians, Russians . . . Jews."

Sarah was silent.

"Don't judge me too harshly either," he said. "As I said, I believe in leaving things alone. Whoever can rise up on his own accord should be applauded. Fact is, Nick was coming to try and convince me to publish a new piece on the folly of that view. A piece of fiction." Mencken shuddered, as if trying to rid himself of the memory. "How America devolves, becomes a primitive, backward society when a Negro becomes president. Horrible stuff. Told him I'd never do it, and not just because the prose was abysmal. But he wouldn't give up."

Sarah thought as she watched Mencken smoke. Hard to believe. Knowledge was supposed to enlighten. Tolerance, compassion, empathy. These were the characteristics she admired most in the teachers she knew. Perhaps it was as she had originally feared. Perhaps the motive for the professor's murder was revenge. Someone, some Negro on the receiving end of his hateful views. Certainly people had been killed for far less cause.

"Mr. Mencken. Did Professor Manhoff ever mention anyone in particular, someone who might have held a grudge, or even threatened him?"

Mencken looked at the band and tapped his foot irregularly to the syncopated rhythm. There were only two other parties left in the room. Mitchell, so quiet she had nearly forgotten he was there, shifted in his seat. "I see where you're going," Mencken said, biting hard on his wet cigar. "Yes, of course, I see. But no, no we didn't talk about particulars. Our discussions were purely theoretical."

Sarah exhaled. She was almost relieved.

"Except . . ."

She stiffened.

"Except . . . for that one young Colored. A few years back. Let me see. He rubbed his forehead, dislodging a thick strand of hair from the right side of his symmetrical part. Lee, Lee something. Something Lee. I don't know."

"What about him?" Sarah said.

"Yeah, what about him?" Mitchell finally echoed.

Nick had worked to, shall we say, enact the policy of intervention. The fellow had applied for entrance into his college. Nick simply saw to it that he didn't get in. Not too hard a task, I would imagine. I don't think many Negroes had been admitted yet anyway. Doubt whether there are many there yet."

"How did he do it?"

"Don't know exactly. Didn't want to know."

"Why did he tell you about it?"

"Because he thought I'd sympathize, even thought I'd consider writing something about the dangers of miscegenation. He didn't really know me."

Sarah glanced at Mitchell, who, by his far-off expression, was undoubtedly composing a story about this incredible matter in his head. Between this and the trial, he'd hit a goldmine. He would have to be reined in. She thought for a few moments. "Do you think there's any possibility this man could have discovered something?"

"Unlikely. Highly unlikely. I think Nick would have covered his traces. Besides, it'd be pretty hard for a Colored to get access to something like that. Especially here, in what I like to call the Bible Belt. Despite all their praying, blacks have little access to anything."

Sarah agreed. But this was her only lead. A place to start. "Do you remember the fellow's first name, sir?"

"No, I don't. Shouldn't be too difficult to find out, though, considering he's black. I imagine there are records."

"Yes."

The waiter marched impatiently by their table several times, casting them a side-glance. Sarah looked around. Although the band was still playing, everyone else had gone. Apparently he wished them to follow suit. "Well, it's getting late," she said.

They all stood up, but Mitchell seemed reluctant. Reaching in his pocket for a pencil and paper, he was not about to let the moment pass. "Mr. Mencken," he said as they headed toward the door, "please, what is your real opinion of the trial?"

"Come now, you've read my columns, haven't you?"

"Yes, but . . . "

"But you'd like to quote me in your newspaper, the *Blade*, isn't it? Tell me, don't you think a newspaper is a device for making the ignorant more ignorant?"

"Do you, sir?" Mitchell asked.

"Of course."

"With all due respect, Mr. Mencken. I have always admired you, but you do seem to hate everything."

"Not true. I am strongly in favor of common sense, common honesty, and common decency." Sarah and Mitchell waited for the punch line.

"Of course, this makes me forever ineligible for public office."

They both lightly chuckled.

"You know, I'm really with the Modernists on this one. Ever heard of the Higher Criticism?"

"Not exactly."

"Well, it uses historical and literary tools to uncover the Bible's historical context. If there is a god, evolution is part of his continuing revelation. That's as far as I go. But the Christian church, in its attitude toward science, shows the mind of a more or less enlightened man of the thirteenth century. It no longer believes that the earth is flat, but it is still convinced that prayer can cure after medicine fails. No different than believing that a horse-hair in a bottle of water can turn into a snake."

Mitchell smiled as he scribbled. "But for someone who questions a belief in absolutes, you seem to believe absolutely in this."

"As I stated before, contradictions don't bother me. I'm with the Modernists. For instance, I myself am incredibly superstitious, never do anything risky on Friday the thirteenth." He slowed his pace, then stopped. "What would bother me immensely, however, Mitch, is if you printed anything about my relationship to Nick . . . about our conversation tonight. No scoops. At least until after this case has been solved."

"Don't worry about that," Sarah said, darting a look at Mitchell she knew he would understand. "He wouldn't think of it."

Mencken faced Mitchell with raised eyebrows.

"No sir, I wouldn't think of it."

"Good. Most scoops are bad stories, anyway, played up in an idiot manner. I can tell you're no idiot."

"No, sir, I am not."

⇒ 12

THE AIR HUNG LIKE A HEAVY SACK as they bid the man goodnight. "Please," he said in parting, "keep me informed, Miss Kaufman. "May I?" he asked, motioning to Mitchell's paper and pencil. "Here is my telephone number. I trust that you'll keep it to yourself."

"Of course."

"I wish you luck. See you in court, Dobrinksi."

"Yes, see you there."

Mencken got in the hotel's one and only car. They watched the dust rise as the rickety machine started its slow descent down the hill.

Sarah shook her head. "Whew! I don't know what to feel about that man."

Mitchell drifted to the lookout spot and gazed into the hazy darkness. Very few stars were visible in the thick sky. The band could still be heard in the distance, belting out a jazzy tune.

"Everything you hoped he'd be?" Sarah asked, coming up beside him.

Silence.

"Mitchell?"

No response.

"Something wrong?"

Mitchell turned around. Even in the dark, she could see his clenched jaw. "I don't like being made a fool of, Sarah."

"Fool?"

"You shouldn't have spoken for me. I'm a grown man. I can answer for myself."

"Oh, you mean about the article. I'm sorry. I shouldn't have . . ."

"No, you shouldn't."

"I know I overreacted. I thought you might be considering printing something about the interview."

"Of course I was. But do you really think I would if, for good reason, I were asked not to? After all we've been through, Sarah?"

Sarah thought back to the time she had been the one to make such a request of Mitchell. He had agreed to it then, even though the story would have made his competitors play darts on his image.

"You're right," she said. "I was out of line." Although she didn't say it, she knew her remark was particularly offensive because she was a woman. He had a long way to go in the area of female equality, but even the most enlightened man might have bristled.

He turned back around, lowered his eyes and shut his mouth so tightly his full lips all but disappeared. A childish expression. She half expected him to cry. Why she did what she did next, she wasn't sure. That same maternal instinct? To make amends? Perhaps to avoid laughing. He did look rather silly. Whatever the cause, she softened her expression, took his hands and with an ease that surprised her, placed them gently around her waist.

At first he responded skeptically, raising an eyebrow, squinting as if to penetrate the meaning of the gesture. He had misinterpreted her before. "What is this, Sarah?" he whispered.

She sighed. "I don't know. I really don't." Maybe the altitude had clouded her judgment. Since arriving, she had resisted. Begrudged every smile, protested even the slightest touch. She liked Mitchell, enjoyed his company, but didn't want to lead him on. No more mixed messages. Yet, was that the whole truth? Wasn't she still torn between her longing and her embarrassment over the very thought of it? And wasn't she also afraid? After all, it had been a long time. So long, she wondered whether that summer— how many years ago?—in the Catskills was a figment of her imagination. How she adored that fellow, thought for certain they would marry. But he never asked, and Sarah couldn't help but feel used. Her sister's "I told you sos" didn't help either.

The rejection made her wary, too much so perhaps. For years afterward she'd put all her hopes in Obee, a great friend but someone she on some level knew would never return her affection. And now she was no longer young. An old maid. Though she'd never had children, her body wasn't what it used to be. Her skin was still supple, especially considering she had lost all that weight. But the pounds had redistributed themselves . . . less in her breasts, more in her stomach and thighs. Mitchell might very well be disappointed, she thought, spinning her rings until it hurt.

Still, she could reconsider. No doubt he was expecting as much. But that music! Searing the leaden air with its sharp, exotic notes. Why was the band still playing, anyway? The lounge had closed. Perhaps they were practicing. Or maybe jazz was just hard to stop, no predictable pattern, no final measure. Unsettling with that rambling melody, that dark, irregular beat. Reaching inside her, traveling from her mind to her body, to places she far too infrequently allowed herself to be stirred. Taking her, after all this time, to the point of no return.

Without speaking, they entered the stuffy, brightly lit lobby and silently walked to her door. Her heart was racing. Disquieting, but impossible to deny. Spontaneity at this stage in life was difficult, with all those years of fairy-tale love scenes carved into her brain. Still, with more confidence than she felt, she found herself touching his hot cheek and smiling. "As you said, Mitchell, life is full of inconsistencies. I'm allowed to change my mind . . . again."

He pressed his body against her and kissed her softly. "Okay."

And with his promise not to expect too much, that this was just for tonight, Sarah guided him inside and shut the door.

⇻ 13

WHETHER MITCHELL WOULD HOLD TO HIS PROMISE when they returned to Toledo remained to be seen. Whether Sarah would want him to would as well. Her mother didn't live long enough to teach her sexual pleasure was wrong, but the world she grew up in—and Tillie—did a good enough job. The present culture was different. Men *and* women were encouraged to explore. But old ideas die hard. Then again, so do old maids.

She pushed all of these thoughts temporarily out of her head. It had been awkward, shaky, embarrassing, even funny. And yet nice. Quite nice. Better than she expected. She thought of his long legs wrapped around her own, half the size, and experienced a wave of desire so intense she was tempted to rush to his room and demand entrance. Forty years old, and she could still experience the thrill of it. Fortunately, he hadn't balked at her request to keep the lights off. It allowed her to be less inhibited than she surely would have been otherwise, to indulge in the pleasure without worrying about this or that wrinkle. Nor did he protest very much her request for him to return to his room afterwards. Sleep was something she told him she could not do without. Dreading him seeing her in the harsh morning light was something she kept to herself.

She tightened her garters and pulled down her dress. White silk with black polka dots, this time. Another of Lena's loan-me-downs. Yes, it had been nice. Mitchell had been a tender, sensitive lover. She grabbed her suitcase and opened the door, nearly missing a small note lying on the floor. No envelope, no name. "All is forgiven," it read, "except for the booze." She smiled and headed toward the taxi, concerned about what awaited her, but lighter in her step than when she arrived.

✢ ✢ ✢

Sediment compressed into immense, wafer-like layers. Mountains and seas, rising and falling, marching to the slow, steady beat of geological time. The evidence was there, spectacularly on view through the train's half-opened window. Sarah gazed at the slanted earth, jagged sculptural formations of rock, mineral and sand. Seeing is believing. But not always. Faith doesn't care about evidence. Evidence, however, must be handled with great care. Had Darwin known to what dangerous purposes his evidence might be used, perhaps he would have thought twice before sharing it with the world.

Sarah planned to go directly to police headquarters, but reconsidered as soon as she disembarked. Her evidence, such as it was, could be dangerous too. Better do some checking first. Talk to Lena. See what had transpired in her absence.

Lena was downstairs when she arrived, engaged in what appeared to be a spirited tête-à-tête with a man whose hunched-over back was all Sarah could make out. He turned around upon her entrance.

"Miss Kaufman!"

Sarah should have known. It was Paul Jarvis, the graduate student from Knoxville. "Well, Mr. Jarvis."

"Yes, it is I, Paul," he said, bowing theatrically. I bet you're surprised to see me so soon."

"Oh, I wouldn't say that," she said, darting a knowing look at Lena.

"I tracked your cousin down to talk about Mrs. Stowe."

"I see. You tracked *her* down."

He explained. "Yes, I called, we started to talk, but, well, Lena suggested that since it was such a short train ride here, why not meet in person. I only just arrived myself."

Lena leaped over a small leather footstool and embraced Sarah heartily. "Sarah!"

"'Lena' is it? Quick work, cousin," Sarah whispered. Something had transpired, all right. Something quite different than she had imagined. She turned to Paul and smiled. "Would you excuse us for a moment?"

"Certainly."

"Just a minute," Lena said, taking his arm. "Sarah, he knows about Nick."

"Fine. Still, I'd like to talk to you in private."

"Not a problem," Paul said, pushing open the front door. "I'd like to take a look around anyway."

Sarah waited until she heard his footsteps trail off, and then turned to Lena shaking her head. "You slay me. Here I was worried about leaving you. You seemed to have managed quite well, although I am a bit surprised you're in the mood for an academic debate."

"Nick's death was consuming my thoughts. I needed a diversion, that's all." Lena eyed her curiously. "You know, you look like you've had a bit of a diversion, yourself. You're positively glowing."

"I don't know what you're talking about. I'm just not used to this heat."

"You forget, dahlink, I know my cousin pretty well. But I'll let it go . . . for now. Tell me what happened with Mencken. Did you talk with him? Did you discover anything?"

"If you don't mind, first tell me what's happened here."

"Not much," Lena said, sitting. "After all, it's only been three days."

"Does 'not much' mean anything?"

"Only that Officer Perry came around to see if I'd heard from you."

"That's all?"

Lena nodded.

"Well, then," Sarah said, and relayed the events in Dayton (leaving for a more appropriate time her night with Mitchell), during which Lena's expression shifted from amusement to disbelief and back again. "I'm proud of your chutzpah with Mencken," she said, patting her on the head. "Runs in the family."

Regarding this Lee fellow, Lena agreed that Sarah should of course go to the police, but only after they went to the admissions office. Why stir up trouble until they had something more concrete to go on? Mencken might be a genius, but his information was still second-hand. Better verify it in the school's files. Find out the student's first name. See if there's any record of Professor Manhoff's influence in determining his status. Though Lena admitted that wishing didn't make it so, she still clung to the hope that all these discoveries about her dead colleague were a terrible mistake.

Sarah, too, clung to a hope: that in providing the police with as much information as possible, she would help thwart a witch-hunt. God knows, she hadn't come here for an altruistic purpose, but now that she was confronted with this situation, she couldn't betray her principles altogether. She knew from experience that an entire group could be blamed for the purported sins of one of its members.

"Done yet?" Paul asked, peeking through an open window. "I'd like to take both of you ladies to lunch!"

"Just one more minute," Lena said, and then turned to Sarah. "You know, I don't think we really have to worry about Paul. If anything, he could be of some help. There's apt to be quite a few files. Besides, he's a staunch advocate of the Negro. He even thinks Harriet Stowe was a bigot, for God's sake. I never imagined I'd be defending her against that charge."

"It's not his progressiveness I doubt, Lena. It's his age. The young have difficulty keeping things to themselves."

Lena winked and lightly licked her lips. "I'll see to it that he does."

"You're incorrigible," Sarah said smiling. "All right. But let's take him up on his offer for lunch first. I'm hungry."

→ 14

A PETITE CLAUDETTE COLBERT LOOK-ALIKE escorted Lena, Sarah and an exuberant Paul to a relatively cool brick room. "The applications are in here," she said, pointing to several rows of splintered, wooden drawers. "Now, y'all let me know if you need anything, Miss Greenberg . . . oh, and do mind them ghosts!"

Sarah tossed Lena a sideways glance. "Does she mean the people in the files?"

"No. She means ghosts. Several buildings here are said to be haunted." Lena waved to the woman. "Don't worry, we've got a man with us."

Paul half-grinned, not quite sure if Lena was joking or not.

After a greasy, but filling grilled cheese sandwich, they had settled down to their task. Sifting through files. Again. Searching for a name. Wondering if a dry, lifeless document would have anything to say.

"Are there many Negroes at Edenville?" Sarah asked.

"No, Mencken was right on that score. Not many at all."

Paul chimed in. "This college has one of the worst records in Tennessee."

"That's unfortunately true," Lena said, "but at least that should make our work a little easier." She pointed to one of the applications. "As you can see, students are asked to list their race."

The Edenville College application was clean and elegant, gold-embossed script against a crisp, white background. On each was the required information: name, address, education, desired occupation and so forth. They went back quite a ways. Indeed. The wilted and yellowed one Sarah picked up was dated 1830! "Samuel P. Bushnell. Caucasian. Knoxville, Tennessee,

Andrew Jackson High School. Teacher." She blinked several times before asking the others. Was it possible? The applications from this drawer were nearly a century old. Thousands of men had died, but these little bits of paper had somehow remained intact, eluded the cannons and mortars, survived the hatred and division. Fascinating, but not relevant. Or so she thought. Lena grabbed her arm as she started to close the drawer.

"Luke Thomas Jameson." She pronounced his name slowly as her eyes ran across the page. "Colored. But this can't be. It says he was admitted."

In short order, Paul found two further black applicants, and Sarah several more. Each had been admitted, and they hadn't even reached 1885. "What the devil?" Lena said. "How could I not know this?"

"It was a little before your time," Sarah said.

"Before Nick's time too," Lena said. "He wasn't hired until 1910. But this is such a curious finding. Not in any of the university literature I was given."

During the next hour or so, they counted at least sixty Negroes admitted by 1885. Five before 1860. Sarah shook her head. This was curious. Was it possible that a Southern college admitted Negroes even before the Civil War? Before the North? She had always believed that Oberlin was the first in the nation. Everyone in Ohio did. Paul tapped his fingers impatiently and then jumped up. "You two keep going. I'm going to do a little research on my own."

After he left, Lena pursed her lips. "Research my eye. He's gone off to make time with that doll."

"She can't hold a candle to you, cousin."

"Perhaps, but she might offer to hold something else."

"Lena!"

Her cousin chuckled in that husky Philadelphia tone. "Come on. This is more important, anyway. Men are a dime a dozen."

1890, 1900, 1905. They were getting more adept at their search. Wade Johnson. Caucasian. Adam Templeton. Caucasian. Thomas Black. Caucasian as well. Something had changed. As they approached their own decade, the number of black applicants dropped precipitously. One Negro admitted in 1912. A couple more in 1914. After that, a few applied but were denied entrance. Sarah did notice with some satisfaction that female admissions rose considerably after 1902, but they, too, were all white, Southern belles with reassuringly Christian names.

Paul walked in and stood before them waving a thin, blue notebook.

"Have fun?" Lena asked.

"Fun?"

Sarah smirked.

"Never mind. What's that?"

"Lena," he said, "you know that Edenville was sponsored by the Presbyterian Church, right?"

"Yes?"

"And you know that the Presbyterians valued education. Their frontier log cabin schools and all."

"Yes, why?"

"Well, that included the education of Negroes."

"I know. So?"

"So, according to this little document, their financial support of this college was dependent on its willingness to admit freed slaves."

"Now, that I didn't know."

"Right. Well, there's more." Paul was wearing the same white shirt he had on the day Sarah met him; though faded from apparent washing, the mustard was still there.

"Edenville," he continued, "essentially broke the law in the antebellum period," he said excitedly, "because Tennessee, like other Southern states, had outlawed the education of Negroes."

"Of course. After Nat Turner's Revolt. But I wasn't aware that the law applied to private institutions," Lena said, stretching.

"It didn't, but most acted as if it did. However, Edenville continued to admit Negroes. And Cherokee Indians. The Presbyterians saw to it."

"What is that document?"

"A draft of the school's history. Lent to yours truly by that nice, young woman who showed us in."

Lena rolled her eyes. "Ahhh. Who wrote it?"

"She didn't know. Someone started working on it years ago, but it was never published. It's been in the archives gathering dust."

"Well, that's very interesting. But since you've been gone, Sarah and I found only one Negro admission. Something happened after the turn of the century."

"I can explain that too," he said running his hand through his damp hair. Matted with perspiration, the curls had congealed and darkened. "After the Civil War, the Presbyterian Synod of Tennessee met and voted to reopen the college. Here was their resolution: ' . . . we have in the midst of nearly four million freed men . . . [the] obstacles to their improvement and elevation . . . having been swept away, a door is now opened . . . there can be but one mind and one voice among Christians . . . we deem it our solemn duty to encourage . . . every exertion made for their intellectual, moral, and religious improvement. No person shall be excluded by reason of race or color.'"

"That explains nothing," Lena said.

Paul touched her cheek, which instantly reddened. "Be patient, my dear professor. This policy was embraced by a number of northern philanthropists who made substantial contributions to the college, with the caveat that blacks continue to be educated there. And apparently they were. But not without protest. Consider this. In 1872, three Negroes applied for admission into the Animus Cultus."

"That was the old name for Alpha Sigma, wasn't it? The literary society?"

"Right."

"So what happened?" Sarah asked.

"Well, they were rejected . . . on account of their race. And the society made no excuses for its position."

"But according to what you've said, that would have violated the school's policy. Did anything happen to them?"

"Eventually they were reprimanded, but a year later when a black freshman applied for membership, he was rejected too . . . because of a mistake in punctuation. And a few years later, they were at it again, in much grander form. This time the society presented a petition with fifty signatures to the college president demanding that he dismiss all Negro students at once."

"And?"

"He obeyed!"

"Just like that?"

"Until the northern contributors threatened to withhold funding and he was forced to reinstate them. But this caused an outright rebellion by Animus Cultus members and other students claiming States rights and protection under the Constitution."

"Animus Cultus, States rights." Sounds a bit like what's going on in Dayton," Sarah said. "All those dressed-up monkeys. Does that mean the students won? Is that why black enrollment dried up?"

Paul flipped through a couple of pages in the notebook. "Not exactly. The college needed that northern money, so it threatened the students with dismissal if they didn't back down. Negroes were permitted to attend the school, and in fact, at the commencement of 1895, the cash prize for an oratory contest was awarded to a Negro. The man won fair and square, but so many parents protested that they never again had such a competition."

Lena glanced at the clock and sighed. "So what caused the decline?"

"1896, separate but equal."

"Plessy versus Ferguson? Northerners wouldn't let that stop them."

"Maybe not, but in 1901 the Tennessee State Legislature passed a bill extending segregation of the races to private schools."

"You're telling me the funding stopped after that?"

"I don't know. That's where this document leaves off. Don't you know who your current donors are?" Paul asked somewhat haughtily.

"Show your elders some respect, young fella!"

Now it was Paul who blushed. "Sorry."

Lena tousled his hair. "Never mind. The school is privately funded . . . by various individuals. In truth, it wasn't one of my priorities when I interviewed for the job."

They smiled at each other apologetically.

"You know, this really is fascinating," Sarah said, "but why don't we finish examining these applications. Law or no law, a few Negroes have apparently managed to overcome the system, haven't they Lena?"

"Yes, that's true," she said, turning her gaze slowly from Paul.

It wasn't long before they seemed to have found exactly what they were looking for. An application dated 1918. Sarah read: "Jacob Stephen Lee. Nashville, Tennessee. Jackson High School. Negro. Minister." Boldly stamped across the top: "Admission Denied." And in a space for interview comments, a notation by none other than Professor Nicholas Manhoff: "Strongly advise against admission. Deceptive. Dangerous. Godless." Deceptive? Dangerous? Godless—that alone would probably bring down the axe. The professor didn't leave anything to chance. Sarah thought back to her talk with Mencken. He hadn't known, or chose not to relay, any details about the student. Only that he was black. But if Manhoff's motive was race alone, then why had he not prevented other Negroes from being admitted? Indeed, as they continued their search, they located ten additional black applicants: two had been denied, two had graduated, six were still matriculating. And Manhoff had not commented on any of their applications. Why had he singled out this man in particular? Deceptive, dangerous, godless. Were those characteristics chosen at random? Or was there something more to them?

One by one they scrutinized each of the applications. All eleven were from Tennessee. All high school graduates. All men who possessed the same goal, to become a minister. No distinguishing feature.

Paul shrugged his shoulders. "Strange," he said.

"Incredible," Lena said.

Sarah nodded. The school obviously had a checkered history where race was concerned. Donors on one side, traditionalists on the other. The donors demanded Negro admission, but the school officials admitted only those who would literally preach the gospel. Pulling for, tugging against social progress. But did Professor Manhoff's targeting of this Lee fellow lead to murder? Highly improbable, as Mencken had said. A young, Negro student; what would he have to gain? How could he know? But she was doing it again. Letting her own wishes get in the way. She would have to take this to the police, and that was that. It was not up to her to figure out anything, not up to her to judge.

❧ ❧ ❧

Grateful for her efforts, Officer Perry shook her hand and politely relieved her of her duties. "Good job," he said. He had relatively few leads himself and therefore would act on the information immediately. Would he keep her apprised? As long as it didn't compromise the investigation, he said. He would call if he required her services again. In the meantime, he suggested she have some fun. No doubt it would do Miss Greenberg some good, too.

"Evah been to the caves?" he asked, his right cheek swollen with tobacco.

"Caves?"

He grinned, pushing on the wad with his tongue. "Guess not. How 'bout your cousin?"

"She's never mentioned them."

"Well, then. That there's a trip you'll neva fergit. To the centa of the earth . . . or at least of the Smokies. Closest ones are in Townsend, not fifteen miles from here. Take your mind off evrathin'. You said you hiked Mount Le Conte?"

"Yes, it was wonderful."

"It's somethin', all right. But I'll bet those caves are like nothin' you've evah seen. Course you'll have to be careful. Slippery in spots. And dark. You gotta watch out for them moonshinas, too. They set up shop there. Caught up with 'em a couple a times. But it's a maze down there. Impossible to keep on top of 'em. Still, if you like the works of Mutha Naycha, you'll love the caves."

Sarah left the police station and decided to walk the mile or so back to Lena's. The temperature was tolerable, and she needed the exercise. Besides, there was no need to hurry. She had done her part, more than she ever could have imagined. Upon her return, Nan gave her a note written in her cousin's familiar scribbled hand: "We're walking in the woods. Be back soon." "We're?" Paul was supposed to have gone, said he had to study. Hmm. Perhaps he was doing just that . . . he hadn't said what subject.

Sarah thanked the woman and dragged herself upstairs. She had either underestimated the distance or the humidity. She was dripping, and her legs felt like lead. She grabbed her glasses, sprawled across the bed and opened her guidebook.

Caves were abundant in Tennessee. They weren't officially open to the public, but obviously it wasn't against the law to visit them. Sarah knew about these hidden structures, but wasn't planning on any direct encounter. She had, figuratively speaking, just been to the depths. She longed for open space, heights, for mountain air. But now she reconsidered. Officer Perry's enthusiasm was contagious. A new natural wonder to explore. She read:

> *According to legend, the Cherokee Indians knew of the Caverns and hid in them before the white man discovered them about 1850. Written reports tell of the discovery of the Caverns by the white man about the middle of the last century when sawmill workers watched water from a heavy rain pour into a sink hole in the area. The hole was filled with debris but one of the men found an opening in the rock and made his way into the Caverns.*

Fifteen miles he said. Not too far. "A crystal clear, cool stream flows through the length of the Caverns, draining much of the surface water from a small Alpine cove." Huh. No wonder moonshiners like it there. Cool water. Perfect for distillation. She was no scientist, but from her experience in the temperance movement, which she deeply regretted, this much she knew. "As old as the mountains themselves. Calcium carbonate—cave onyx—formed by surface water which combines with carbon dioxide given off by plants." She scanned through the remainder of the scientific explanation: "pressure . . . low temperature . . . rate of drip . . . " Her eyelids felt heavy. "The only value of cave onyx is the beauty it adds to the cave." Only? She blinked and read on:

"A stunning, natural display of color and shape" . . . Hmm. "A constant fifty-eight degrees." And a refuge from the heat! That clinched it. As soon as Lena returned, she would convince her to make the trip.

❧ 15

The 'Paris Soir' this evening, describing the case as one which will decide whether "a monkey or Adam was the grandfather of Uncle Sam writes: 'On this side of the ocean it is difficult to understand the susceptibility of American citizens on the subject and precisely why they should so stubbornly cling to the biblical version. It is said in Genesis the first man came from mud and mud is not anything very clean. In any case, if the Darwinian hypothesis should irritate anyone it should only be the monkey. The monkey is an innocent animal—a vegetarian by birth. He has never placed God on a cross, knows nothing of the art of war, does not practice the lynch law and never dreams of assassinating his fellow beings. That day when science definitely recognizes him as the father of the human race, the monkey will have no occasion to be proud of his descendants. That is why it must be concluded that the American Association which is prosecuting the teacher of evolution can be no other than the Society for Prevention of Cruelty to Animals.'

Mitchell folded his copy of the *Chattanooga Post* and laughed out loud. The French. If only he possessed half their wit. Of course, he was particularly receptive to humor just now. Indeed, he felt almost giddy. It was a good thing court was over; his stupid smile might have begun to attract attention. All day he'd had trouble focusing on the trial, preoccupied instead with the previous night, lingering on every delicious detail. Sarah turned out to be, well, quite a woman. Definitely worth the wait. He had long wondered what it would be like to make love to her. More cerebral than physical, he had imagined, a polite, intellectual meeting of the flesh. He grinned and bit his full lower lip. He was wrong.

"Afternoon, Dobrinksi."

Mitchell rose from the courthouse steps just in time to see H. L. Mencken purposefully coming his way, his half-smoked cigar accompanying him again. The thing was glued to his mouth, like a baby's pacifier. Hmm. Perhaps he was ready to give him that interview. Mitchell smoothed down his hair and extended his hand. "Mr. Mencken."

"As they say, how y'all doin'?"

"Fine, fine, sir."

He reached in his pocket, pulling out another cigar. "Care to join me?"

Mitchell had just pledged to himself once again to stop smoking, but he wasn't about to decline this offer. "Thanks, don't mind if I do."

"Why don't we walk a little."

"Sure." Mitchell felt a surge of adrenalin, imagining the bonus he might get if the interview went well.

Mencken lit a match and puffed several times. "What would be your headline today?"

"Headline?"

"Yeah, headline. You're a newsman aren't ya?"

Mitchell took a deep drag and coughed.

"You'll kill yourself if you inhale that thing like a cigarette."

Mitchell felt the blood rush to his head as he suppressed another cough. "Expert Testimony Debated."

"What's that?"

"My headline. Expert Testimony Debated."

"Ah. Well, true enough. But it doesn't grab."

Mitchell knit his brows. "Perhaps not in Baltimore, but it'll do for Toledo."

"I mean no offense, man. Just one reporter to another. What'd you think of the arguments?"

Mitchell wondered what he was up to. This guy didn't really care what he thought. Still, he wasn't about to make a fool of himself, even if he'd only lent half an ear to the proceedings. "Well, it was fascinating of course to hear Bryan at last. He's quite the showman. But I think his partner, Hicks, made the most compelling point, you know, when he quoted Darrow as saying that evolution was a mystery. If the theory is a mystery, then even the most informed experts couldn't be of much use. Quite clever."

"Do you agree with that, Mitch?"

"Agree? Hell, no. I have faith in science, imperfect as it is. To refuse to hear testimony from some of the greatest minds in the field is outrageous. But the point is nevertheless well taken. And it'll probably convince the Court."

"Yeah, yeah. Hicks did Bryan pretty proud. But Malone, now he was pure genius, don't you think? Remember what he said?" Mencken opened a small pad of paper, thumbing through several note-filled pages.

"We feel we stand with science. We feel we stand with intelligence. There is never a duel with the truth. The truth always wins and we are not afraid of it. The truth is no coward. The truth is imperishable." Mencken bit down hard on his cigar and fixed his steely gaze on Mitchell.

Mitchell felt himself squirm.

"I've been thinking about Miss Kaufman," Mencken finally said.

"Oh?"

"There is something I neglected to tell her. It's been bothering me ever since you left yesterday."

Mitchell raised one eyebrow but was silent.

"This is not for the papers, you understand?"

"Of course."

"I mean it. I don't make hollow threats. You'll never work again if you let this out."

Mitchell nodded.

"Come down here, Mitch." They had just reached a relatively uncrowded area, a few blocks past Robinson's. Mencken led him down a cobbled side street and held his arm tightly as he spoke. "The truth always wins and we are not afraid of it. The truth is imperishable." He repeated this until Mitchell nodded in agreement.

"That kid, that Lee fellow. He may not have been just any old student. Any old colored student."

"No?"

Mencken opened the top button of his collarless, blue pinstriped shirt and grimaced, like a child preparing for an injection. "He claimed to be a descendent of *the* Lee. Robert E."

"What's that?"

"You heard me right."

"The general?"

He nodded. "What's more, Nick believed him. Of course, the believing mind is externally impervious to evidence. The most that can be accomplished with it is to induce it to substitute one delusion for another. He may have believed it because he wanted to."

Mitchell blinked and rubbed his chin, uncertain what to think. "Why would he want to?"

Mencken shrugged his shoulders. "Don't know."

"But you must have some . . ."

"No, I don't. Nor do I have any idea what bearing this might have on the investigation into his murder," Mencken said, anticipating Mitchell's next question. "But your lady friend came all this way. I admire that kind of moxy, even in a woman. I thought I owed her . . . and Nick . . . the truth. As much of it as I know, at any rate." He tossed his cigar on the ground. "So there it is. And now I've gotta go. I'm leaving early in the morning."

"You're not staying to the end of the trial?"

"Nope. I've had enough. You said it yourself. It's pretty clear where this is headed. I don't need to stay here to write the rest of the story. For all its wit, 'The Hills of Zion' has a predictable plot. Now, if you'll excuse me."

Mitchell watched the man as he started to walk away. Having relieved his conscience—if that's what he'd done—he obviously no longer had any use for him. Just then, however, Mencken stopped, walked back, and put his hand on his shoulder. "You know Mitch, you seem like a decent fellow. But let me give you a bit of advice. Don't ever take yourself too seriously as a reporter. Freedom of the press is really limited to those who own one." He smiled, winked, and with that was off for good.

❧ ❧ ❧

Mitchell's assessment of the judge's ruling on expert testimony proved correct. Geologists, psychologists, anthropologists and even religious scholars from the top institutions in the nation were rejected as defense witnesses. Zoologist Dr. Maynard Metcalf of Johns Hopkins University was the only exception, and that was because he attempted to reconcile evolution with biblical accounts of creation.

Back in his room, Mitchell ripped off his sweaty clothes, lay on his bed and wrote: "Friday, July seventeenth. Years of study, commitment to intellectual progress and IQs undoubtedly rivaling Newton's and Galileo's held no sway. Judge Raulston brushed these men off as irrelevant: 'The state says that it is both proven and admitted that this defendant did teach in Rhea County, within the limits of the statute that man descended from a lower order of animals . . . and that no amount of expert testimony can aid and enlighten the court and jury upon the real issues, or affect the final results.'"

Sad, Mitchell thought, stretching his thumb, which had begun to cramp. No expert testimony. God help us if that idea ever took hold in the courts. He continued to write: "The excitement today came when Darrow's frustration boiled over. 'I do not understand,' Darrow said, 'why every request of the state and every suggestion of the prosecution should meet with an endless waste of time, and a bare suggestion of anything that is perfectly competent on our part should be overruled immediately. 'I hope you do not mean to reflect upon the Court,' the judge answered. 'Well, Your Honor has the right to hope,' Darrow said. 'I have the right to do something else, perhaps,' Judge Raulston answered, getting the last word."

"We may see," Mitchell concluded, "what the judge meant by that remark on Monday."

He put down his pen and stared unseeingly at the ceiling. Mencken was right about the so-called freedom of the press. As a reporter you could say what you pleased as long as it agreed with the publisher's views. He had learned that the hard way. Thankfully, on the Scopes matter, he and the *Blade* were in accord.

It was particularly in his reporting of O'Brien O'Donnell that Mitchell had come to understand his place in the overall journalistic scheme of things. The mere suggestion of anything untoward about the judge, and he was abruptly ordered to stop. Of course, had he not been assigned to cover the campaign, he might never have gotten to know Sarah, for whom he voluntarily shelved the juiciest story ever on the man. Sarah. Thanks to Mencken, he now had an excuse to call her. He would have eventually done so anyway, but would have at least tried to wait a few days. He knew how that woman could be. He closed his eyes. She liked him. Of that much he was finally certain. But she was stubborn and often too analytical, picking things apart until there was nothing left. He nodded to himself, remembering her reaction months ago to that unexpected embrace. So brief, it was nearly undetectable, a vulnerable moment, gone before it had even begun. Yet she'd regretted it, politely telling him she was not ready. Lord knows what was she feeling now.

She was worth fighting for, though. He believed that more than ever today, but he did back then, too. After the O'Donnell ordeal was behind them, he had cautiously pursued her, letting her dictate the excruciatingly slow terms under which she wanted their relationship to proceed. Any other man would have given up. Of course, he did have to admit, a few times her snail's pace got the better of him. "What are you waiting for, Sarah?" he asked impatiently, we're not children." When his own words didn't work, he attempted to persuade her with those of the sly Andrew Marvel: "Had we but world enough, and time, This coyness, lady, were no crime . . ." The gesture was intended as a respectful and light-hearted plea, but it only made her dig in more firmly.

He had wanted her, wanted her badly. But he was also worried about her. In spite of the judge's overdose, the blackmail attempt, in spite of all of those unbelievable events, O'Brien himself had come out just fine. Sarah, however, hadn't fared as well. The attempt on her life had affected her profoundly, causing her to turn inward. Having had her trust betrayed by someone she considered her friend, she grew wary of just about everyone. Her usual vitality fled, leaving her gaunt and pale. It was only recently that she agreed to see him—but then only in short intervals—continuing to leave nothing to chance. Until last night, that is. He felt a flash of heat and smiled. No planning whatsoever. Utterly spontaneous, and she never seemed better. Whether that could be attributed to him, or, ironically enough, to finding herself back in the sleuthing business, he wouldn't care to speculate. Either way, he was happy.

Still, he'd have to tread gently. He put on the only clean pair of trousers he had left and skipped downstairs to make the call. The phone rang. It seemed hardly possible that this young Negro was related to Robert E. Lee. But then there were so many stories, he wouldn't bet money against it. True or not, however, Sarah should know.

The phone rang again, a third time and then a fourth. An annoyed female voice finally picked up and told him that Sarah was not there. She and her cousin had gone to visit some nearby caves.

"By themselves?"

"No, a young man accompanied them."

Mitchell didn't know whether to feel relieved or upset. He asked the woman to please have Sarah return his call. Yes, she had his number.

Back upstairs, he picked up his camera and paced around the room. The floor creaked. He hadn't noticed that before. Probably some interesting shots in those caves. It was Friday. The trial didn't resume for two days. Trains left on the hour. He could . . . oh for Christ's sake! No. Tread gently, remember? He put the camera down and undressed. Show some restraint, man! He closed the blinds, lay back down and fell instantly asleep.

⇾ 16

"I THINK YOUR MR. MENCKEN IS ONTO SOMETHING about our society, Sarah," Lena said. "Our Puritan roots are coming back to haunt us. Conservative politics, conservative culture. I've read some of his stuff on Harding and Coolidge, too. What did he call Harding, a "hallucination?" Are these fellas really the best we can do? What the devil happened to the Progressives anyway?"

Sarah turned around from the front seat of the dilapidated car wheeling them precariously to the caves. Kathryn's friend Jim, who had helped go through Professor Manhoff's papers, was driving. He had been to the caves many times before. Kathryn herself was subject to motion sickness so declined to come along, but promised Jim would make a good guide and keep them safe. Lena sat with Paul in the back seat. Paul promised to keep them safe too, and to return to Knoxville in the evening. That, she thought, remained to be seen.

"He's not my Mr. Mencken, but I have to admit," Sarah said, "national politics have been terribly discouraging. Progressive suddenly seems to be a dirty word. But then we did gain some ground in the mid-term elections." She looked forward, stretched her neck, and then turned back around. "For now, I think we have to keep our eyes out for some charismatic figure to emerge that can take us out of, out of, what did you say the poet Eliot called it, the wasteland?"

"Yes, *The Wasteland*. Marvelous piece of writing that could never be appreciated by the *Reader's Digest* crowd."

Sarah winced at her cousin's uncharacteristic snobbery, although there was some truth to her point. She thought of President Harding. A

Reader's Digest figure if she ever saw one. Condensed, reductive, easy to read. God rest his soul, it was terrible to have died in that hotel room. But she was ashamed to say he was from Ohio. His vacuous oratory had been bad enough. But Teapot Dome, all those corporate scandals. Interior Secretary Fall secretly leasing those government oil reserves in California. Anyone with a brain would have thought that would have spelled the end for the Republicans. But no. People didn't care. As long as they were getting a tax break and could shop at the A&P, they didn't care. Didn't care that Congress lowered income taxes for the well-to-do. Didn't care that the forest service said our very air was filthy from all the oil consumption. Didn't care that influential businesses reversed all those reform measures, including the two laws she and Obee had worked so hard to pass: imposing punitive tax on the products of child labor and that minimum-wage act for women workers. And now Coolidge. Already found napping on the job. Literally.

"The Democrats need to regroup," Paul said. "They're too indecisive, too wishy-washy. That's what hurt Cox. He couldn't stand firm. And they're too divided. The rural and urban wings are different as night and day. We need our party to stand for the welfare of all the people."

Sarah observed Jim tighten his grip on the steering wheel. "Don't worry young man. We're not Socialists, although that's what the Republicans would have you believe."

The affable economics major smiled, but said nothing.

"You've got to be careful what you say these days," Lena said. "If you speak in favor of labor, they think you're a Red. If you believe in science, next thing you know Billy Sunday will be trying to save your soul."

Sarah nodded. "He should have stuck with baseball."

"It's all you flappers that have done it. Women should have stayed in their place," Paul said, tickling Lena in some unmentionable spot. "You, and all those foreigners; your wicked ways are tearing apart the country's moral fabric. God-fearing, like-minded, culturally identical people. More churches. More Stop and Shops. That's what we need."

They all laughed, except for Jim, who made a hard right onto an unpaved road. The jalopy rocked to and fro, spraying fine dust everywhere.

Sarah pulled down tightly on her straw hat, yet another of Lena's loaners. "You know, I agree with all of this," she said. "But there's another side. Mencken is brilliant. There's no disputing that. But he's got some pretty disturbing beliefs, too. His anti-Semitism, for example. He downplays it, but hardly denies it. And he twists Darwin into an evil knot. How do you reconcile this?"

"I don't know," Lena said. "That's true of Eliot too. He, Hemingway, Fitzgerald. There's an anti-Semitic strain throughout their writings. They lament the decline of our culture, and somehow the Jews get blamed." She sighed and shrugged her shoulders. "But Sarah, we still listen to Chopin, even though he was no lover of our people either."

"Maybe we shouldn't."

"And miss all that beauty? It's his beliefs, not his music, that should be ignored."

"Art is the expression of beliefs, Lena. You know that better than I."

"Perhaps. But Christianity is the glue that binds. As long as they think we nailed their god to a cross, we're fighting an uphill battle. We might as well sit back and enjoy ourselves."

"You're putting your head in the sand. You'll sing a different tune when they cut it off."

"Ladies, ladies! Calm down. Remember, I'm one of the 'they,' and I don't want to do anything of the sort," Paul said. "Nor does Jim here, do you Jim?" Jim shook his head. "People just need someone to blame . . . anyone except themselves."

"You're a pal," Lena said, pointing to a small wooden sign. "Caves one mile ahead."

❊ ❊ ❊

Jim agreed to lead the way, respectfully joking that they needed a Republican for balance. Cave onyx was apparently very fragile, and would break like glass under such left-leaning weight. Obviously pleased when they all laughed, he straightened his back and directed them down a winding path toward a cluster of massive granite boulders, behind which lay the entrance to the caves. "Here we are," he said, pointing to a narrow, tunnel-like opening.

"Duck down." Single-file, they followed in a crouched position for several hundred feet. Only Jim had thought to bring a flashlight, a practicality he also attributed to his politics.

"We never said you didn't serve an important function," Paul said, good-humoredly. Actually, they were all grateful. Without a light source, the trip would have been a waste. The cave was dark, dark and dank. Sarah was not usually claustrophobic, but she was beginning to feel a little panicky, and her back was starting to ache from being hunched over. "How much farther?"

"Just a few more feet."

Finally they reached a wide, cathedral-like area where they could stand up. "Whew!" Paul said, vocalizing what they all felt. Sarah was gradually becoming accustomed to the dark, but glancing around, still couldn't believe her eyes. "Incredible," she whispered, as if in some sacred place where talking were forbidden. Science had a name for it. Calcium carbonate. But mixed with carbon dioxide, time, and just the right amount of water, a work of art. Graceful curves, twisted lines, deeply etched grooves.

For several minutes they stood silently. Jim added drama by directing his flashlight quickly from one formation to the other. "You know, the Cherokee knew of these caves before we did," he said, just as Sarah observed a structure resembling an intricately carved totem pole. The one next to it, standing about twelve feet high and barely a foot across, looked like a giant toothpick. "Stalactites and stalagmites," Paul said, not wanting to be edged out by the precocious undergraduate. "The stalactites hang down, the stalagmites go up."

"Yes, and the ones that touch, like that one, are called columns," Jim said.

A rushing noise indicated water nearby, and indeed, around a small bend flowed a delicate waterfall. Moonshiner's gold, Sarah thought, looking around for signs of their activities.

"Another world," Lena said.

Paul nodded. "Alice in Wonderland."

They all searched in vain for an expression that would capture the vision before them.

"Amazing, isn't it," Paul said, "carrying on all this time without our input."

"That was kind of Professor Manhoff's view," Jim said.

They all spontaneously jumped, as if the boy had just uttered some terrible profanity. Collectively, they had put the murder on hold, laughed and frolicked as if nothing were wrong. Humans could do that, Sarah knew. Something in their psyche seemed to require a purposeful respite from tragedy. A diversion, as Lena said. But the event was just beneath the surface. It took only the mention of the professor's name to bring it back to the forefront of their minds. Not appearing to notice, Jim continued: "He talked of the caves in class, encouraged all of us to visit them. He called it a perfect alchemy. The epitome of nature doing its job, indifferent to Man, quietly evolving, changing a vast darkness into a thing of beauty. He could put things so poetically. Even a God-fearing economics student such as I could appreciate it."

They were all silent.

"We didn't mean to offend you earlier," Sarah said.

"I wasn't really offended. I do believe in God, but I'm not one of these new breeds of fundamentalists. What's going on in Dayton is a travesty. By the way, we've all been so curious. How, I mean, do you mind me asking how the investigation is going?"

"The police prefer we don't talk of it, Jim," Sarah said, suddenly recalling with a bit of a thrill her night with Mitchell.

"Oh, oh, I understand. I, all of the students, just hope they find his killer. Maybe he had some unusual ideas, but he made English tolerable. He was one of those special teachers. Everyone wanted to take a class with him, even we financial types, even the divinity students!"

They explored the caves for the next hour or so, during which their talk returned to the sorry state of the nation. Feeling more at ease, Jim stood up for his party: "What about Harding's appointments?" he asked. "Look at Andrew Mellon, he's balanced the budget!"

"Yes," Sarah said. And we have corporate and financial interests all over the world. But we've neither joined the League of Nations nor the World

Court. We're isolationists, greedy and self-centered. Pardon me. But business isn't everything."

"Have you heard of Bruce Barton?" Paul asked, looking at Jim.

Jim cowered, as if expecting a right hook. "Yes, yes I have."

"I haven't," Lena admitted.

"He's the son of a Protestant minister, who described Jesus Christ as a managerial genius who, 'picked up twelve men from the bottom ranks of business and forged them into an organization that conquered the world.'"

Lena sniggered. "Business and religion. What a strange coupling. What blasphemy!"

"It's the hypocrisy that gets me," Sarah said. "The country is supposedly prosperous, but look at all of those who've lost jobs. Remember that article I sent you from the *Independent* a few years ago, Lena? 'American stands for one idea: Business. Through business, properly conceived, managed, and conducted, the human race is finally to be redeemed.' What it should have said, is part of the human race is redeemed . . . the rich part!"

"Not all financial types are so single-minded, ma'am," Jim said earnestly.

"I know." Poor fellow. He feels attacked, Sarah thought. "I'm sorry, Jim. I don't know why I'm getting so revved up. Maybe it's the change in oxygen."

Paul nudged him. "You're a good sport, Jim. We better be nice to this chap, or we'll have to walk home."

They explored the cave a bit more, seeing in each encrusted hollow and fissure a unique, intricate design. Unique, but continuously in the process of becoming something new. In one little crevice, from which water was steadily dripping, it was almost possible to see the colorful minerals thinning out, changing shape.

Jim reclaimed the front spot as they prepared to leave. Lena and Paul followed, with Sarah holding up the rear. As she crouched down, she glimpsed a small, shimmering object. Cave onyx? She moved closer. No, the shape was too regular, crafted by man. She reached for it and saw that it was a bottle with some sort of label. "Wait a minute," she said to the others. They all stopped. She asked Jim to come and shine the flashlight on it. She squinted, but it was no use without her glasses. "What does it say, Jim?"

"Authentic Chattahoochee River Water."

"What's that?"

Paul read the name again and then said: "the Chattahoochee River is in Georgia. Sorta near Atlanta."

"That's odd. Do you suppose it's used for moonshine?"

"I don't know why it would. There's plenty of water here."

"Probably some snake oil," Paul said. "One of those miracle cures."

"It does look like that." Sarah shook the bottle. Empty.

"Why don't you take it for a souvenir?" Lena said.

"No, that's all right. I like to leave things as I find them. Let's go."

A blast of hot air greeted them at the exit, but the sky had darkened. Thick clouds were gathering, signaling an inevitable downpour.

"How long do you think we've got?" Lena asked, stretching.

Paul studied the sky. "An hour."

"Less than that," Jim said.

They exchanged knowing glances and hurried to the car. Paul may have been a fine interpreter of books, but on statistical matters, they'd put their bets on the numbers man. Including Paul himself, who, as soon as they were all seated, ordered Jim to step on it.

⇥ 17

MONDAY MORNING, JULY . . . WHAT WAS IT? Ah, yes. The twenty-fourth. Mitchell coughed several times and rolled over. He'd been sick all weekend. Some kind of virus, he assumed. Sore throat, achy muscles and, though he'd had no thermometer to verify, undoubtedly a fever. Hot and chilled simultaneously, and then sweating until his sheets were drenched. He knew the human body was composed mostly of water, but the humidity in this blasted place had surely already left him with precious little. How could a person lose that much fluid without some permanent effect? He drained the glass of water by his bedside, lifted the pitcher that had magically been replenished, and poured another.

He glanced at the neatly folded stack of linens on the wicker chair, vaguely recalling the housekeeper placing them there. She must have filled the pitcher, too. He'd have to leave her a nice tip. Another dim memory flashed before him. He'd called Sarah again. Or had he? He wasn't sure. It might have been a dream. She'd popped in and out of his thoughts frequently over the past couple of days, occasionally in poses even he, with an eye for the photogenic, didn't know he knew. If that's how his unconscious worked, he wouldn't mind getting sick more often. Dream or no, however, he hadn't spoken with Sarah. Of that he was certain. Someone, whether real or imaginary, had told him she was still out.

He sat up slowly to assess his condition. Congested, and a bit weak, but over the worst. And hungry, a sure sign of improvement. He glanced at the clock. Seven a.m. Too early to call her, but time for some breakfast before the trial. His stomach growled. Even the restaurant's sticky grits sounded good today.

***

Mitchell scoured the packed courtroom for Mencken. He couldn't believe the man had really gone, but, indeed, he was nowhere in sight. Too bad. His searing prose would have best captured the spectacle. Only a few minutes into the trial and Darrow, as Mitchell had hinted at in his Friday article, was held in contempt. Raulston may have been a small town judge, but he wielded his authority with the best of them: "The criticism of individual conduct of a man who happens to be judge may be of small consequence, but to criticize him while on the bench is unwarranted and shows disrespect for the official, and also shows disrespect for the state." Clad today in lavender suspenders, Darrow sat quietly with an inscrutable expression as the even more informally dressed Raulston continued: "It is my policy to show the same courtesy to the lawyers of sister states that I show the lawyers of my own state, but I think this courtesy should be reciprocated; those to whom it is extended should at least be respectful to the court over which I preside. He who would hurl contempt into the records of my court insults and outrages the good people of one of the greatest states of the union—a state which, on account of its loyalty, has justly won for itself the title of the Volunteer State." He then ordered Darrow to pay a bond of five thousand dollars and answer to the citation the next morning.

The room buzzed, most audibly from the swarm of impatient reporters. Despite the fact that the trial was being broadcast on radio, newspapers were still the world's primary source of information, and each one sought to top the other in timing and wit. Or for lesser rags like Toledo's *Bee*, in sensation. At the morning break, Mitchell observed several of his overly anxious kind engaged in this contest by attempting to beat each other to the phones. Mitchell himself, however, just sat on the court steps and jotted some notes. Darrow's face had been hard to read, but not impossible. Immediately before Judge Raulston announced the recess, Mitchell saw something—compressed lips, a slight nod of his head—to indicate they would not have to wait until tomorrow to hear from the man. And indeed, as soon as court resumed, he somberly asked to speak to the court.

Initially, Mitchell thought the man was going to get himself in further trouble. "I tried to treat the court fairly," he said, his entire left hand locked in his suspender, "even more fairly than usual because I recognized the odds were against me . . ." He stuck his other hand in his pocket. "I don't know as I was ever in a community in my life where my religious ideas differed as widely from the great mass as I have found them since I have been in Tennessee." Mitchell perked up his ears, waiting for the catcalls. But then, a stroke of genius: "Yet, I came here a perfect stranger and I can say what I have said before that I have not found upon anybody's part—any citizen here in this town or outside, the slightest discourtesy. I have been treated better, kindlier and more hospitably than I fancied would have been the case in the North, and that is due largely to the ideas that southern people have and they are, perhaps, more hospitable than we are up north . . ." Flattery. Works every time. Immediately afterwards, Darrow apologized for his earlier remarks, prompting hearty applause and His Honor's complete, if hesitant, forgiveness.

❧ ❧ ❧

Yes, Raulston forgave him, and Darrow watched himself after that. But later that evening, Mitchell would write of the irony of the judge's reasoning in the matter, predicated as it was on the example of Christ pleading with God to forgive the men who crucified him. In the same article, he would also describe how Darrow visibly winced when Raulston admonished him: "Learn in your heart the words of the Man who said; 'If you thirst come unto Me and I will give thee life.'" And finally, he would relay how in the afternoon, the judge moved the court outside for fear that the floor would give out. Mitchell smirked. God may be omnipotent, he thought, but it was apparently not His job to protect His flock from the room's dangerously overloaded capacity. Whether Mitchell would actually include that last bit of editorial flourish remained to be seen. It was best not to act too impulsively when it came to such subjective remarks. "The spontaneous overflow of emotion recollected in tranquility." William Wordsworth said that of poetry, but it was an idea worth emulating, even in a two-column article. So, he'd wait a bit to decide.

Now was now, however, and for this he'd waited long enough. He picked up the receiver, dialed and held his breath. He exhaled. This time, she was there.

≫ 18

SARAH HUNG UP THE PHONE with a mixture of pleasure and dread. The outing to the caves had helped put things in perspective. The trip had been fun, just as Officer Perry predicted. Including the ride home. Twenty minutes into it, drops appeared on the cracked windshield. Thirty, and the roads were slick. By the time they reached the rooming house, rain was falling in sheets, and the car had offered little protection. But they'd all remained in good humor. Troubling as Professor Manhoff's death was, it had made them appreciate being alive. One of those rare moments of brotherhood, Sarah thought. Differing sensibilities, common humanity. Contrasting notes playing to the same beat. She had been toweling her wet hair, nearly nauseating herself with happy clichés when Mitchell called. Initially, she felt annoyed. It was too soon. She'd enjoyed letting their encounter slowly seep in, at times even willing the memory of it away so as to experience it anew. But as he spoke, she felt herself soften. Would she really prefer aloofness? He wasn't asking her to marry him, for God's sake. In fact, at first, he didn't mention anything about their night together at all. Instead, he questioned her about the caves and talked of the trial, the trial and Henry Louis Mencken.

"It'll go to the jury in the next couple of days, Sarah, and I suspect we'll have a verdict in less than an hour."

"You sound as if it's a *fait accompli*," Sarah said.

"Well, H. L. certainly feels that way."

"H. L.?"

I thought that would get your attention.

"You've been talking to Mencken?"

"Actually, yes. That's the main reason I called."

"Oh?" She felt slightly disappointed.

Mitchell's voice sounded hoarse, deeper than usual, as he relayed the gist of his conversation with the man. "It's bizarre, I grant you, Sarah. But for whatever it's worth, Mencken wanted you to know, and to pass it on to the police."

Robert E. Lee? Of course, racial mixing was more common than some people liked to believe. She'd been reminded of that in *Uncle Tom's Cabin*. The hypocrisy of the slave owners was beyond belief. But the South's top general? Imagine if it were true! More immediately troubling, however, was that Mitchell had reminded her of the murder, which for a short time had receded to the background of her thoughts. Lena had gone to see Paul off at the station, and even though alone, her mind had been quiet. Now it was racing. She hadn't a clue what this strange detail might mean for the investigation. And the idea of contemplating the possibilities made her head ache. Nevertheless, H. L., as Mitchell said, thought it important enough to go out of his way.

"Sarah?"

"All right, I'll call the station tomorrow."

"Good."

"Anything else?" She cringed at her own short tone.

"Sarah, Sarah, I enjoyed the other night . . . very much."

She tried to say something, but the words caught in her throat. "I, uh . . ."

"It's okay. No need," he said.

Silence.

"Are the monkeys still performing?" she finally asked.

He coughed. "Ha! Sure are. Animal and human." He coughed again.

"You know, you don't sound so good."

"You mean the hacking? I've had a touch of the flu or something."

"Oh, I'm sorry," she said, feeling a sudden wave of tenderness.

"It's nothing. I'm much better."

"Still . . . Mitchell, I, I, uh . . . alright, dammit, I had a good time, too!"

He was quiet for a few moments. "There, that wasn't so hard, was it?"

"Yes, yes it was."

He laughed. "Fair enough."

She did as well.

"Call me with any news, Sarah?"

"Of course. You do the same. And Mitchell, take care of yourself."

She stared at the phone for several moments, her expression locked between a smile and a frown. She checked the clock. Fortunately, no time to think. She needed to dress quickly. Lena had asked her to a dinner to discuss Professor Manhoff's memorial service. Tomorrow he would be buried in the old cemetery near the woods, a place for which he apparently had a deep affinity. It would be a quiet affair. He had no known living relatives, and many people were gone for the summer. Still, everyone felt the man deserved a special tribute.

Sarah at first refused. She didn't belong. She'd prefer to stay home and finish her book. But Lena pleaded. Despite their somber task, she promised an agreeable evening. Sarah would get to meet some of the other faculty. Conversation and tolerable food. Besides, she added, Sarah belonged as much as anyone else, considering all the help she'd been.

Yes, she'd been of some help. And it had been good for her. But now she was being squeezed, drawn in tighter to the murder investigation, and to Mitchell. Thus far, she was still in one piece. But how much longer? If she left today, right now, she could escape them both. She could go to the Yellowstone or even Yosemite. Mud baths. Mineral water. Dry air! She started for her suitcase. Yes, she'd go. Write Lena a note. Leave the back way. For a moment, she actually took the idea seriously. But then she sighed. What was she doing? She should have learned by now. If it had been another person, she'd have diagnosed the problem instantly. Fear. Fear of, well, of the very things that might give her life more meaning. She sighed again and checked herself in the mirror. At least it didn't show. In fact, she looked rather well. Even without her glasses, she could see the brightness in her eyes, the color in her cheeks. She grabbed her handbag and headed downstairs, wondering if these were signs of a new beginning or simply the early stages of the flu.

➤ 19

SHE AND LENA LOCKED ARMS as they walked down the narrow, brick path that led to the faculty dining room. It was lucky they had decided to meet there. Having given Paul a longer than anticipated farewell—waving kisses, as she theatrically demonstrated, until the train was out of view—Lena had made it just in time. It was no use asking her cousin where this little dalliance was going. She would say she didn't know and didn't care. In matters of the heart, she lived in the moment, a modern woman through and through. Work came first. Until, perhaps, the right man came along.

The storm had cooled things down considerably. Tomorrow promised to be another scorcher, but right now it certainly didn't feel like one of the hottest summers on record. Sarah drew her velvet wrap tighter around her bare shoulders as they picked up their pace. In no time, they reached their destination and were soon warming their hands before an unseasonable but nevertheless welcome crackling fire. Standing before its stone hearth, Sarah instantly felt at ease.

With its dark paneling, lacy curtains and richly colored tapestries, the cozy room belied its institutional purpose. This was a place to unwind, a place where strangers could become friends, she thought. Contributing to its homey feel were the glowing flames, doubling in size as they reflected off the polished, planked wood floors. Sarah turned her back to the fire. Spanning nearly the entire length of the room was a narrow, rectangular table covered in a beige satiny cloth. She counted fourteen place settings, each comprised of plain white china, silver utensils and matching napkins triangularly folded. Two pewter candelabras flanked a cut-glass vase filled with lilac so fragrant she could detect its scent over the burning pine. A series of gold-framed landscapes adorned the ruby-painted walls within which the illustrious crowd had already gathered.

Lena took Sarah's hand. "C'mon dahlink, it's time to meet everyone."

Sarah loosened her wrap and followed obligingly. "This is my cousin, Sarah Kaufman. Sarah, this is so and so from such and such department." Sarah shook their hands one by one. Professor David Michelson: History. A meticulously groomed, middle-aged man, with a poetic demeanor but a slightly lascivious gaze. Professor Winston Hallwood: Biology. Tall, black hair, large, pointy teeth that seemed made for the jugular. Professor Shelby Byeerst: Theology. A fair redhead with a dimpled chin whose cherubic cheeks could not soften his icy blue eyes. Chester Aurosa: Economics. Swarthy, somewhat disheveled, a communist, Sarah mused, quietly reaping the benefits of capitalism. And Nathan Lovell: English. Thinning, sandy hair. The one who would probably take Manhoff's place, Lena said, known as much for his shoe fetish as his expertise in eighteenth-century British literature. Though possessing an open face, there was something in the arch of the man's brow that made Sarah not want to turn her back to him.

Such thoughts! Hopefully no one could read them. She wasn't usually so quick to judge, so cynical. Perhaps it was because she knew what they had put Lena through. Her cousin was tough, but the hiring process had been brutal. Or perhaps it was the power of suggestion, Mencken's jaundiced views penetrating her unconscious. When Lena next introduced her to a bland, young man from the geography department, she forced herself to think something nice.

Fortunately, that was easier to do with the remaining guests: two no-nonsense women from the department of home economics who shared a room at Lena's boarding house but whom Sarah had not yet formally met, as well as five students who had been particularly close to the professor: Kathryn and Jim, Emily and Eric—a Nordic-looking couple who Sarah later learned were fraternal twins—and Penny, a tall, striking young woman with lightly tanned, glowing skin, a wavy, blond bob and violet, cat-like eyes. With the exception of her full bust, which she didn't attempt to flatten, Penny could have walked out of the pages of Vogue. Off the rack, her simple white jersey would have looked like a Butterick pattern. On her, it was pure Coco Chanel.

During dinner, Sarah wondered if she'd not been on to something about the faculty after all. The meal began honorably enough, with a solemn tribute to Professor Manhoff. "A man of courage." "An original intellect." "A dear friend." "The best teacher we've ever had." As a deferential Negro waiter silently delivered the first course of lettuce and tomato salad, they continued to sing the man's praises. By the time the roast beef arrived, they had set the date of the service for next Tuesday at noon in the chapel. They knew the professor had not been a particularly religious man, but they all agreed that his high moral character entitled him to the privileges of one. True, he did hold some rather radical views, which only now were coming to full light. But no one seemed particularly concerned. Theory is not the same as practice, they said. A genius was entitled to hypothesize.

Naturally, they were somewhat curious about Sarah's participation in the investigation. "Mind you," Professor Lovell said with an affected-sounding drawl, "we're enormously grateful, but it's rather odd, don't you think? I mean, granted, you work in the courts, but you're not a detective. And you're from Ohio."

Sarah agreed that it must have seemed odd. Odd and certainly not part of her holiday plans. But she explained that she did actually have some experience in this area. When they pressed her for details on the status of the case, however, she politely refused. "I've been sworn to secrecy," she said. "Officially." Not that it really mattered. They already knew who killed their colleague. A mad man. A black mad man that is, which Professor Hallwood quietly clarified after the waiter left the room.

With that put to rest, however, the conversation quickly shifted to themselves, a topic that clearly interested them as much if not more than the murder. What they were reading, what they had taught and especially what they had published. The importance of what they had published, in minute and excruciating detail. I argued this. I argued that, I argued the other. The philosophy of symbolic forms. Pure and impure poetry. The anatomy of criticism—Lena was right, Sarah thought; they really were trying to turn literature into a science. This theory, that theory. The words blurred together.

Peach pie came and went. Seconds and thirds on coffee. Cigarettes, cigars and pipes were lit as they droned on. Lena sat quietly with folded arms. What was she thinking? She might have been truly interested, but her pursed lips suggested that she was more likely feigning the respect demanded of a junior faculty member. The students tried to appear engaged, but even in the dim light, Sarah could see that their eyes had glazed over. Earlier in the evening, Kathryn had scolded Jim for reaching for the rolls. Now, apparently too bored to care, she unabashedly defied dining etiquette herself by resting her smooth, bony elbows on the table.

Sarah never tired of truly intelligent speech, but she quickly grew weary of people who merely liked to hear themselves talk. And yet behind their bravado, there was something else. A slight tremble, a shrillness of tone that said perhaps they protested too much. During the initial introductions, she thought she had sensed a unique treachery in each man; lust, greed, duplicity, whatever it was that had prompted such a strong reaction in her. The longer she listened, however, the more she wondered if those weren't just the superficial signs of a common insecurity, a self-doubt that made them dread any new thought that wasn't their own. She glanced at Lena and the other women. As of yet, they appeared relatively uncorrupted. But then they were still struggling to get a word in edgewise. It might very well be only be a matter of time.

As the evening wore on, Sarah became convinced. Their colleague lay dead, murdered, hadn't even been put to rest and they were more worried about whose article would get published first. This wasn't just diversionary; it was mercenary. "When did you say yours was coming out, Win? " "Next month." "Ahh," Professor Byreest said, smiling while gritting his teeth. "But then, the sciences do review more often than religion." "And yours, Shelby?" "In the fall," he answered quickly, and then, appearing to think better of the answer, said: "winter at the latest."

Lena had promised an agreeable time. Well, it had been educational, at any rate. Don't judge the general by the particular, Sarah told herself. Really, she should give these fellows the benefit of the doubt. Perhaps this was their way of dealing with the tragedy. Most probably, they were fine teachers. Still, if they hadn't already been questioned and found to have rock-solid alibis, she'd have suspected any one of them of committing the crime himself. Then again, under a microscope, rock revealed itself as sand. Clearly, they respected Professor Manhoff, no matter how perverse the man's thinking had been. But they also must have envied him, and that was a motive as old as the oldest books on their shelves.

The last business of the night was to divide the tasks for the ceremony. This was obviously what the students had been waiting for. Instantly, they brightened. Apparently suddenly aware of her impropriety, Kathryn darted an embarrassed glance around the table and slowly brought her arms down beside her. Then, the volunteering began. The twins would send out notices and order the flowers. Kathryn, Jim and Penny would prepare the room.

"It's the least we can do," Penny said tentatively, "for someone who has given us so much."

Kathyrn nodded and smiled at Penny maternally, like a mother whose normally introverted daughter had finally found her voice. Penny smiled back and blushed.

Sarah turned from one girl to the other. Very different types, she thought. Kathryn might be a stickler for etiquette, but she was self-possessed, someone who made things happen. Her fresh, unmade-up face fit her outgoing personality. Penny was objectively prettier, probably more appealing to men. But her cultivated look suggested an underlying lack of confidence. Then again, first impressions could be misleading. The two seemed to be friends, no doubt had much in common.

The home economics teachers, Phyllis and Samantha, offered to make finger sandwiches, cookies and iced tea. Lena agreed to play hostess, welcoming mourners, watching the time and introducing the speakers, who, of course, would be the men. Women were too subject to tears, they said. Eulogies needed the calm, masculine touch.

On that somber note, the shifting of chairs and rustling of coats signaled the evening's close. All that remained were the goodbyes. Sarah and

Lena offered theirs and were near the door when the twins stopped them. "Please, Miss Greenberg, wait." Emily turned to the others. "Everyone, please wait. We'll be right back." Sarah looked at Lena questioningly, but her cousin just shrugged. An air of anticipation filled the room, but for what no one evidently knew. It wasn't long before they found out. When the pair returned a moment later, it was with what appeared to be a large canvass draped in a white sheet.

"Would you all please move to the other side of the room?" Eric asked.

The request was heeded.

"Now," they said in unison, dropping the sheet. Collective gasps, then silence. For several seconds, no one moved. "I painted this last year, Eric finally said in a soft voice, after Emily and I did some research with Professor Manhoff." The lanky towhead stared at his shoes. "I'm sorry if I've upset you."

"No, no, no, Eric," Professor Aurosa said," it's just so . . . so very realistic."

"Yes," Professor Byeerst added, "especially against the firelight, it comes quite alive."

"It's exceptional," Professor Michelson said. "I didn't know you were such a talented young man. How long have you been painting?"

"All my life, really."

"That's true," Emily confirmed, in a voice only slightly higher in pitch than her brother's. "Our mother swore he was born with a paintbrush in his hand."

"I'm surprised you aren't attending some prestigious art academy, the Sorbonne or even Carleton."

Eric stammered for a moment. "Thank you for the compliment, sir, but art is my avocation. Teaching English will allow me ample time to paint."

Professor Michelson nodded. "I see. Very mature of you." He turned to the others. "We should display it at the service."

They all nodded.

"I admit, that was my hope," Eric said, brightening.

"Why don't you put it over there?" said Professor Aurosa, motioning to the buffet table in the far corner of the room.

The twins lifted the painting—a large, unframed rectangular oil—and rested it against the table. For several moments, everyone again was still. Then, as if suddenly magnetized, they huddled together, joined in what felt more like apprehension than communion. No one spoke of it, but she knew the reason. The professor's image had cast an invisible shadow in the room. A good portrait could do that; blur the boundary between one world and the other, capture the subject's essence, transcend time and space. It could bring comfort to the living. But it could also remind one of death; in this case, of a violent death, of murder. Sarah raised her right hand to her head and pressed the dark red garnet against her skull. She pushed harder, imagining the bullet, the hot piercing pain. Then, nothing. Murder. Perhaps it was the college's reputation for ghosts. Or, perhaps her own experience doomed her forevermore to be sensitive to the word, to empathize with the victim whether or not he deserved it.

Eventually, the departures resumed, but now with gentler steps. On their way out, the men collectively tiptoed past the painting, glancing out of the corners of their eyes. Jim and Kathryn gazed at the apparent uncanny resemblance too, holding hands with their fingers tightly laced. Penny stood quietly before it and wept. Turning to leave, Kathryn wiped her own eyes and gave Eric a full, long embrace. Such physical gestures could reflect a spectrum of emotions, but even out of context, Sarah would have recognized this as one offered in appreciation.

She and Lena were last. Lena kept her distance from the portrait, looking pale, even in the room's soft, yellow glow. Sarah alone moved up close and studied the features. Wide face, a mildly pockmarked, ruddy complexion. Closely cropped, silver hair. Eric's heavy brush stroke and funereal, grey background seemed appropriate. Maybe he had sensed what was to come. Small, brown, medium-set eyes and a blank expression. The bold, Cezanne-like style didn't match the surprisingly ordinary appearance. She stood back a bit and looked again. Professor Nicholas Manhoff. Now she had a face to go with the name. Nothing to inspire greatness. But not particularly sinister either.

On the way back, Sarah confessed to Lena her impressions of her colleagues. Lena nodded, laughed a little, but seemed distracted, still shaken by the portrait.

"It's just a painting," Sarah said, reassuring herself as much as her cousin.

"I know, but Nick really is dead. I think it has finally sunk in."

❧ ❧ ❧

Nothing more was said. They both knew that until the culprit was caught, the reality of the professor's death would dominate their thoughts. Sarah folded her wrap over her arm. The humidity was back with a vengeance, and she had the feeling that it, too, was here to stay. They were nearly home when she remembered Mitchell. "God," she mumbled. Robert E. Lee. As soon as they arrived, she would call the police and schedule a meeting for tomorrow. Down the path, turn right. Up the stairs onto the porch. Lena pushed opened the door, allowing Sarah to enter first.

"Thanks, cousin." She walked in and abruptly stopped, leaving Lena to straddle the doorway. The call wouldn't be necessary. Officer Perry was pacing in the parlor.

"Miss Kaufman," he said, with a note of exasperation. "Sorry to botha you so late." His uniform was wrinkled, and sweat had formed a curved pattern under each arm. He must have caught her looking, for he said: "Excuse my appearance, ma'am. It's been a long day."

Before Sarah could respond, Nan marched into the room and frowned. "I'm not used to having trouble 'round here, you know. This is a respectable establishment."

"Now, now . . . don't worry, Nan," Officer Perry said. "There's no trouble. How about you git me some more of this heah tea." He swigged down what was left in the glass he'd been gripping in his meaty hand. "You make the best in town, you know." She gave him a hard look, but set about fulfilling his request. The woman reminded Sarah of her sister, Tillie. A gruff exterior that a little kindness could turn to mush.

Officer Perry motioned for Sarah to sit down. Lena remained standing, and asked if she was needed. When Officer Perry said no, she excused herself and went upstairs.

"You know, Officer, I'm glad you're here."

"Oh?"

"Yes, I was going to call you in the morning."

"Oh?" His eyes widened.

"With some information."

"Oh. Thought maybe ya just wanted to see me, ma'am."

Sarah felt herself redden.

"Sorry. Just joking. I'm punchy. What d'ya have?"

"It's nothing really. You must have come for something more important."

"No please, go ahead."

Sarah leaned back on the crocheted doily decorating her chair. "Well, Mr. Mencken said that, uh, well, it sounds so silly. Even if it were true, I don't know what use it might be. But at any rate, he said that Professor Manhoff told him, well, that this Lee fellow might be related to . . . to Robert E. Lee. General Robert E. Lee."

Officer Perry looked at Sarah blankly. "And?" he said.

"And? And nothing. You don't seem surprised."

"Those sorts of claims are common round heah. I'll keep it in mind."

"Do you think it's possible?"

"Course it's possible. Many of us white folk hate to admit it, but Negras are human too. And when humans get together, you know."

Sarah forced an image of Mitchell's arched back out of her mind.

"But like you said," he added, "I don't know what it might mean. We'll see. Is that it?"

"Yes," Sarah said, pleasantly confused.

"All right then, my turn."

The landlady came in with more tea and a glass for Sarah. "If y'all be wanting anymore, you'll have to get it yourself. I'm going to get my beauty rest."

"All right," Officer Perry said, "not that ya need it, mind ya."

The woman actually smiled before turning to leave. He followed her with his eyes and waited until he heard her door creak shut.

"I'm not gonna beat around the bush, ma'am. I need your help again." He held up his hand, silencing her protest. "Please, let me explain. I don't rightly know if this Lee fella has any white blood, but it's lookin' more like he could be our man. We've done some investigatin' and found he's been in some trouble. Minor offenses mostly, petty theft and such. I know," he said, reading her mind. "That in itself doesn't mean much. But there's more."

Sarah kneaded her neck as he continued. A knot the size of a walnut was making her entire left side ache.

"Everyone we've spoken to about him said he has a hot temper. Even his pals. Gotten into fights because of it. He belongs to some underground group demandin' rights too. Wants to do away with the law . . . ya know, segregation law."

"Plessy . . . Plessy versus Ferguson."

"Yeah, yeah."

"Well, there's nothing wrong with that. To me anyway."

"No. But it depends on how a feller goes about it. Especially down here. He's apparently had a few scrapes with white men. Put one in the hospital. Downright fortunate that the man didn't press charges. At any rate, he's the kind that could hold a grudge, ma'am . . . if you know what I mean."

Sarah didn't respond, but she knew exactly what he meant. If he found out about Professor Manhoff's efforts to squash his admission . . .

"What about the crime scene? Any evidence?"

"Does this mean you're interested?"

Sarah thought for a moment.

"That depends on what you want me to do."

"Well, as you can imagine, we've been to his home already. Lives two towns over. His mama said she hadn't seen him in months. Doesn't know where he is. Now, that was just a little too convenient. There was something in her expression that told me she knows more than she's sayin'."

"How about his father?" Sarah asked.

"Father's dead. He's an only child too, so the woman said. Frail little thing. All alone, 'cept for a mangy mutt."

Sarah already knew where this was heading.

"Now, as we both know, you've had a lot of experience in this area. Considerin' your job and all. You're an expert, aren't ya, in talkin' to women, drawin' 'em out."

Yes, in this she was an expert. She thought of the poor soul, alone, afraid. Sarah would know how to comfort her. But dammit, she didn't have to come here to do that. Women were waiting in line back home for her services. Besides, it would be deceitful. Then again, if the boy were guilty . . . "So you'd like me to visit her, see if she'll open up."

"Precisely."

Sarah sighed. "All right. I'll do it. But that's it. And I do have a few questions."

"Shoot."

"No pun intended, I assume."

"Ha! Y'all are quick."

"Are you looking at other suspects?"

"Of course. There's a burgeonin' list." He puffed out. "Like that word?"

Sarah smiled.

"But motive. That's the thing. This is the only person so far with a motive . . . and, by the way, the skill. I failed to mention that the boy is supposedly an excellent marksman."

Sarah shook her head. Naturally. "Isn't everyone down here good with a gun?"

"Now, Miss, that's the last kind of remark I thought I'd hear from you."

"You're right." she said. "I'm generalizing." She had to stop feeling sorry for a fellow she didn't even know. It did look bad for him.

"Oh, and you asked about the crime scene?" Officer Perry said.

"Yes."

"Nothin'. Nothin' so far."

Sarah sighed deeply. "All right then, I suppose you'd like me to go tomorrow?"

He nodded and handed her a piece of paper with the woman's name and address. "You should probably go alone. I'll arrange for a cab. Better than arriving in a police car."

"Shouldn't we call her first?" Sarah asked.

"Doesn't have a phone. Say nine a.m.?"

Sarah glanced at the ticking grandfather clock, walnut with gold inlay, indifferently marking time. It was about to chime midnight. "Ten. I'll be ready by ten."

"Okay. Sleep well. And thanks, ma'am. You know, if this boy's innocent, you may be able to help prove it. If he's not, the sooner he's caught the better."

He put down his glass and tipped his cap.

Sarah started for the stairs when she heard him call out. "Oh, Miss Kaufman, you know the burial's tomorrow afternoon. Might be good if you could be there too, you know, see if you spot anything unusual. Catch," he said.

Sarah caught the silver badge in her palm and looked at him questioningly. Didn't she just tell him that this was it, that after tomorrow morning she was through? She opened her mouth, but nothing came out. Instead she just nodded and dragged herself to bed.

⇀ 20

MITCHELL AROSE EARLIER THAN USUAL, even by his insomniac standards. A sliver of sunlight crowned the purple peaks, which only minutes before had blended invisibly into the darkness. It was dawn, and he was there to witness it in all its glory, looking out from the same spot on which he and Sarah had stood only days before. This detective business could be nasty, and he worried about her involvement in it yet again. But talking to her last night had nevertheless put him in a very good mood. She was fighting it, but there was something between them. Something more than sex, but confirmed, made sweeter by it. He turned and ambled toward the dining room, thrilled at the prospect of the next, inevitable encounter.

The "morning room" was clean and cheerful but insufficiently ventilated. Heavy, gold curtains had been drawn back, and the yellow warmth streaming in through the bay window was rapidly wilting the Queen's Anne Lace—the delicate white wildflower, or weed, depending on one's perspective—that adorned each of the tables.

Mitchell ordered the breakfast special, rolled up his linen sleeves and opened the *Dayton Herald*, a small daily about one-eighth the size of the *Blade*. The front page bore two headlines: "Mine Explosion Entombs Ten Men at Rockwood," and "Jury Should Get Scopes Case Today." "One of the worst disasters known in the History of the Roane Iron Company," the first article began. He read it in its entirety, lighting his first cigarette since his illness. The last line particularly struck him. "When those who are acquainted with the mines were asked their opinion of the safety of the men, they shook their heads in grave fear." Over the years, Mitchell had covered similar events.

Such tragedies didn't always lead to reform, but when they did, a revealing news article was frequently the catalyst. That was one of the main reasons he had become a journalist. To expose the truth: in industry, politics, anywhere it was intentionally concealed. He was certainly less idealistic now, but not yet quite as cynical as H. L. Despite everything he'd been through, Mitchell still believed in the power of the press.

He inhaled and coughed sharply. Perhaps his lungs weren't quite ready. He smashed the cigarette out, and perused the Scopes article. In essence, just a recapitulation of what he'd already written himself, without the editorial flourish, of course, which he did ultimately include. "Darrow was held in contempt and apologized. The case for the defense is expected to wind up today."

He browsed the ads. A Chrysler Model B for two hundred and sixty bucks; not bad. Black-Draught Liver Medicine: "Your liver is the largest organ in your body. When out of order, it causes many complaints. Put your liver in shape by taking Black-Draught . . ." "We use Black-Draught in our family of six children and find it a good bowel regulator." Ha! I wonder how many commodes they have, he asked himself. Quinlan Violet Astringent: "Refreshed, refined and young again! This delightful preparation reduces enlarged pores, refines the skin texture, prevents wrinkles and makes the complexion radiant."

Mitchell sucked in air through his teeth. He hated going to the doctor, nearly fainted every time. But he'd sooner bend over for one than buy any of this crap. Health mongers, that's what they were, profiting off the fears and ignorance of well-meaning folk. They were everywhere these days. He would have to write a story about them sometime.

His ham and eggs arrived along with a day-old copy of the *Baltimore Sun* he'd requested. The paper had been available in Dayton since, in his first report on the trial, Mencken characterized the town as "full of beauty and charm." Whether he meant it or not didn't matter. It had the effect of endearing the man to the city, especially, Mitchell guessed, to those who had concocted this circus to draw in more business. Despite Mencken's overt disagreement with the majority of the citizens, despite even his overt satirizing of them, the paper had become a must read. Perhaps that was the real mark of a great journalist:

> *All that remains of the great cause of the State of Tennessee against the infidel Scopes is the formal business of bumping off the defendant. There may be some legal jousting on Monday and some gaudy oratory on Tuesday, but the main battle is over, with Genesis completely triumphant.*

"What do you think, Mr. Mr...?"

"Dobrinski," Mitchell said turning around. All he could see from this angle were pale yellow suspenders. That could only mean one thing. He swallowed and looked up. Clarence Darrow was reading over his shoulder. "Sir?" he said.

"Do ya think he's right?"

"You mean Mencken?"

"Uh huh."

"I don't know."

"Oh come now, you look like a smart fella. Up with the birds, just like me."

"I'm just a poor sleeper."

He glanced at the table, which was set for two. "You expecting company?"

Mitchell shook his head. "Care to join me, sir? I'd be honored."

"No, no . . . I'm meeting someone here. Just thought I'd say hello." He scratched his head. Little lady not here?"

"Little lady?"

"Sarah, Sarah Kaufman."

He is smitten, Mitchell thought. "No, she's already left."

"Ah. That's right. Back to Toledo?"

"No, to Edenville. She's visiting her cousin."

"Oh. Well, give her my best, will you?" he said, quickly losing interest.

"Of course. Uh, Mr. Darrow," Mitchell said, hoping to engage him a bit longer, "can I say that no matter what happens—and yes, I'm afraid you will lose, sir—that you've performed a great public service by fighting to the finish . . . and so eloquently, I might add."

"Attaboy! Tell it like it is."

Mitchell smiled, emboldened by the man's enthusiasm. "Sir, are you sure you won't join me," he said, his journalistic juices suddenly in high gear. He'd already blown one opportunity to interview the man. He likely wouldn't get another.

"Sorry, old man. I really do have a meeting. Maybe after the trial's over, eh? An exclusive, isn't that what you call it?"

"Why, yes sir. That'd be Jake."

"All right, then," he said, his eyes twinkling mischievously. He bowed, turned, and headed for a table on the other side of the room, leaving Mitchell with cold eggs and the distinct impression that he never would actually speak to the man again.

⇛ 21

THE DISSONANT HORN HONKED FOR THE THIRD TIME. Nine o'clock. Sarah stared at her watch and listened for the downstairs chime to confirm the hour. Yes. She guessed the cab would arrive early, that Officer Perry would forget or perhaps even consciously disregard her request. She stuck her head out the window. "I'll be there in a minute," she called out to the impatient driver. She was nearly ready, but wasn't about to hurry. It had been quite a while since she'd given her hair a good brushing. Slowly, methodically, a hundred strokes, just like the beauty experts said. She lifted, twisted and pinned the thick bundle into place. The style was sedate but approachable. She examined herself in the full-length mirror to see if her muted grey frock carried the same message. No, a bit too austere. She reached for her pearls on the nightstand and arranged them in her usual fashion; one strand hugging her neck, the other dangling to her waist. "Lena, I'll meet you there at noon then?"

Lena grunted, but otherwise lay motionless on her bed. Neither of them had slept very well, what with talk of Lena's colleagues, the portrait and, most of all, the mission on which Sarah was about to embark. A mission once again made official by the rusty badge she reluctantly dropped in her handbag.

She stood at the bedroom door for a moment, envying Lena. They must have had four hours tops. The last thing she remembered was discussing the burial, and then a half-dream of deteriorating headstones in a wind-swept cemetery.

The horn bellowed out again. "All right, all right!"

"'No breakfast today?" Nan asked hopefully as Sarah headed toward the door.

"No, not today."

The driver, a doughy figure with monstrous hands opened the door for her but said nothing.

"Thank you," Sarah said.

He nodded, closed her door and lumbered over to the driver's seat. The car looked new, a black, Ford Runabout with full balloon tires. Just the style her brother Harry was saving for. She had a coupon at home that would help with payments. They were all uneasy about buying anything from Henry Ford who, unlike Mencken, was an unambivalent anti-Semite. But his cars were well-made and affordable. There were times one had to hold one's nose and sacrifice principles for practicality.

The driver was silent for the duration of the twenty-mile trip, except when Sarah asked him the age of the aluminum plant they passed on their way. "Fifteen years," he grunted, as if the act of speaking were painful. Annoyed at first, she decided it was probably for the best. Better than that overly friendly fellow in Toledo who said whatever came into his mind. The quiet would allow her to focus on her task. She shouldn't judge, anyway. One never knew what a person might be going through. Maybe he'd just had a fight with his wife. Perhaps his child was sick. Even if he was just ill tempered, it was best to leave him alone.

Sarah stuck her head part way out the window and breathed in what was becoming the familiar, thick, sweet scent. As they left the Alcoa town limits, other smells intervened, became dominant and then faded: drying hay, honeysuckle, manure. The scenery, however, remained constant: rolling green hills, red barns with peeling paint and a few ramshackle houses. An occasional grazing horse or cow.

In the distance, she saw a cluster of buildings she assumed was Brody, their destination. As they got closer, the structures appeared to shrink, forming a town about half the size of Edenville. Before they reached the main street, the driver turned down a paved road which led into a small, modest neighborhood of generally well-kept, single-story brick houses. He stopped before number five twenty-three, distinguished from the rest by the wild, viney kudzu threatening to overtake the front porch.

"This is it. I was told by the boss to wait," he grunted again, opening her door.

"I may be a while."

He nodded and returned to the car. Sarah shrugged and started up the walk, smiling at a group of black children who giggled as she tripped over one of the steps. She smoothed her hair and knocked. A woman of approximately her own size and dressed in a loose, pink flowered jersey opened the door. A thin gold chain with a shimmering cross hung around her bare neck. She didn't appear frail at all, and the dog vigorously wagging its tail beside her was hardly mangy. "Yes?"

"Hello," Sarah said. "My name is Sarah Kaufman. I was wondering if I might have a word with you."

"About what?"

"About Jacob, your son."

Ignoring Sarah's outstretched hand, she looked her up and down and then glanced at the car. "You a cop?"

"No. I'm not."

"Well, then . . ." and she slammed the door.

Sarah adjusted herself and knocked again several times. The woman finally opened the door again and glared at Sarah silently.

"I'm not a officer," Sarah said, "but the Edenville police did send me." Reluctantly, she showed the woman the badge.

"I've already told them. I don't know where my son is."

"I know. I just want to talk to you a little about him. I understand he is a very bright young man."

"No need to soften me up. I know what you want."

"You do? That's strange. I don't even know what I want. I thought I was coming down here for a holiday."

"What kind of line are you feeding me?"

"Can't you tell by my funny accent that I'm not from these parts?"

The woman started to smile, but caught herself.

"Please," Sarah said. "If you don't want to talk, could I just come inside a moment? That cab driver may be a little fried. I'd like to give him time to . . ." She stopped and turned her ear toward the door. "Ma'am, is that a radio?"

"What do you think," she sneered, "Niggers don't have such things?"

Sarah cringed. She should tell the woman that she was a proud member of the NAACP. But anything she'd say would sound defensive and patronizing. "No, it's just since you don't have a telephone . . ."

"I don't, huh? I wonder what that thing is on the wall, then."

Sarah glanced over the woman's bare shoulder. She could just make out part of the receiver. "Oh, I see," she said out loud.

"What do you see?"

"The ways of men, Mrs. Lee. You are Mrs. Lee, aren't you?"

She nodded.

"I'm afraid I've been duped, ma'am, foreigner that I am."

The woman smiled this time, perhaps out of confusion. Sarah really wasn't making herself clear. Nevertheless, she needed to take advantage of the opening. "Please," she said. "That's the trial, isn't it? I recognize the announcer."

"Trial of the Century. Sure is." She cast another glance at the cab and then bore her sable eyes into Sarah, as if trying to read her mind. "All right, ma'am," she said cryptically, "let's see if you can prove me wrong." She ordered her dog out of the room and motioned for Sarah to come in.

⇥·⇥·⇥

Sarah was surprised by the radio, but it had nothing to do with the woman's race, and only slightly more with Officer Perry's—what should she call it?—little white lie about the phone. Radios simply weren't all that common. She herself had only purchased one a few months ago, in time to hear Quin Ryan call the game. And WGN was a Chicago station; its range was limited to the Midwest. But then, she knew very little of these matters. Signals were frequently crossed. Perhaps there were special accommodations made for this event. After all, the people of Tennessee were entitled.

Mrs. Lee offered Sarah a cane-back chair in the sitting room. "Thank you," Sarah said, inhaling deeply. "Mmm. Is that coffee I smell?"

The woman narrowed her eyes. "You've got nerve, I'll say that for you. Cream, sugar?"

"Both, thanks. Two lumps."

The coffee did smell good, but Sarah really just wanted to be alone for a moment to look around unobserved. She gave the room a sweeping glance. The space was tidy and clean, modest but cared for. Two open windows let in light and air, filtered and cooled by a full-leafed magnolia tree directly outside. Centered between the windows was a tan velveteen couch decorated with three embroidered pillows whose country scenes Sarah could vaguely make out by squinting. She shifted in the chair. To her immediate left, a round wooden table held an etched-glass Victorian lamp with knotted tassels, a few of which were missing. A few feet away, a rocking chair with knitting materials on the seat swayed nearly imperceptibly. The rust-colored ball of yarn appeared to be in the process of becoming a slipper. She shifted again. Against the wall stood an antique white upright piano, on top of which rested a vase of fresh geraniums and a gold-framed photograph. The radio was not in sight, but over the heavy static, Sarah could hear Quin Ryan's clipped baritone state that the lawyers were still convening with the judge.

Sarah reached for her glasses and walked over to the photograph. A tall, broad shouldered young man dressed in dark winter clothes leaned wistfully against a white picket fence. It had to be her son. Jacob. Jacob Lee. The lapels of his heavy coat pulled up around his neck, he gazed out at the cloudy sky, appearing to see something the camera couldn't quite capture.

Mrs. Lee came in with the coffee, her "specialty," she said begrudgingly, but with obvious pride, "made with chicory and cinnamon." She seated herself in the rocking chair and picked up the knitting. Her expert fingers were long and youthful; if white, the type one might see in a newspaper ad for hand lotion. From this distance, her face, too, appeared young. All things considered, she had to be at least thirty-five, but her chocolaty skin was as taut as that of a girl of sixteen. An attractive woman by anyone's standards.

But was there anything in the features that hinted at a white lineage? No, of course it had to be on the Lee side. Sarah lowered her eyes. This was nasty business. Against her principles. Still, she took note of the full lips and broad nose, the high cheekbones and black, tightly coiled hair, cut in a close-to-the-head style few women could carry off as well.

Mrs. Lee gazed directly at Sarah, while her hands moved with precision and speed. "You were trying to flatter me, but it's true about my son, you know. Jacob is smart. Like Frederick Douglass, he is." She continued to knit, her needles clicking methodically, as if keeping time with a metronome. "He built the radio."

Sarah had to consciously prevent her eyes from widening. "Built?"

"Go take a look . . . around that wall."

Sarah willingly obeyed. No doubt the small, square space was once a dining room. The chair rail, silky curtains and faint stains on the carpet reminded her of her own. But it clearly had not been used as such for quite a while. Instead, it appeared to serve as a kind of workshop, filled, as near as she could tell, with at least three different radios, a variety of wireless paraphernalia and other miscellaneous, electrical materials. One of the radios Sarah recognized as a Cats Whisker, only because Obee had once pointed out the tiny, thin wire for which it was named. Had she not known, she would have described it as a box with a knob. There was another larger instrument; curved, encased wood with thicker wires. Then, a long piece of metal with two black dials. This was the one currently broadcasting. A pair of headsets lay nearby, ready for use. On the wall hung a yellowed photograph of a distinguished, familiar face. She moved in close, put her glasses back on and read the words directly underneath. Ah, yes. Marconi, inventor of the telegraph.

"Amazing," Sarah said, returning to her chair. "Your son did all that?"

She nodded and rocked.

"He can do it all," she said. "Preaching was . . . is . . . his vocation. Mechanics is his passion. He picks things up quickly. From the time he was a young boy."

She concentrated on her knitting for a few moments. With each twist of the yarn, the muscles in her jaw visibly relaxed. Just like Tillie, Sarah thought; even when she was in one of her moods, the repetitive activity had a calming influence on her sister. Poor Tillie. She was skilled at all of the traditional female arts and couldn't understand why Sarah was so disinterested. Yes, she knew Sarah worked and that they couldn't survive without her income. But that didn't mean she should abandon her femininity altogether. To humor her, Sarah had tried, in fact somewhat mastered the basic stitch, creating a looping yard of shapeless, blue wool. She had even purled a few rows. But when it came to finishing, she lost patience. And so did Tillie. "You're hopeless," she had said to Sarah in her exasperated tone. Sarah smiled. Tillie tried to be tough, but she could never sustain it. Just a few weeks later, she presented Sarah with a pullover sweater made from that very same yarn, an exact replica of the one Sarah had coveted but couldn't afford at Laman's.

"You might not have noticed the big antenna outside." Mrs. Lee let herself smile this time, revealing crowded white teeth.

"No. I didn't. But then, I tend to overlook things I don't comprehend. She motioned toward the piano. I assume that's your son in the picture?"

"Yes."

"Handsome boy."

"Come on, Miss, what'd you say your name is?"

"Sarah. Sarah Kaufman."

"Sarah Kaufman. Let's get to the point."

Sarah took a swig of coffee. It was delicious, but she dare not give any more compliments. "All right," she said. "You say you know what I want."

Still knitting, the woman nodded. "Cops think my son had something to do with that professor's murder."

"I think they just want to ask him some questions."

"The cops never just want to ask a black man some questions."

"I understand why you would feel that way."

"Do you?"

"Yes, I do." Sarah spoke the truth, and perhaps Mrs. Lee believed her, for she said nothing, just stared at her unblinking. "I think in this case the officer is pretty fair," Sarah said, glancing at the telephone. A bit of manipulation not withstanding.

"My Jacob could no more kill anyone than fly."

"All the more reason to clear his name quickly."

"All right. Go on," she said.

"Well, for the moment, let's forget about his whereabouts. I've heard that he has a temper, that he's prone to, well, violence."

"Heard from who, that fair police officer?"

"Well, is he?"

"Violence? I'd hardly call it that. He's been in a few fights . . . but only when extremely provoked."

"What do you consider extreme?"

Mrs. Lee was silent. This was the first time she averted her eyes. "Look, Miss."

"Sarah."

"Okay, Sarah. You're from the North, don't really know nothin' about our way of life. Down here, our race is provoked daily. It's just a question of degree. When it's extreme, you know it."

"The North unfortunately has its intolerance too, ma'am. But let me ask you straight. To your knowledge, was there anything Professor Manhoff did that might have upset or angered your son, provoked him to a high degree?"

"Damn," she said, staring at her knitting. "Dropped a stitch." She slowly raised her eyes. "No."

"Are you sure?"

"Yes."

"Your son wasn't admitted to Edenville College. Did you find that strange, considering how bright he is?"

"I thought you said you understood such things. He's black, remember?"

"But others of your race were admitted."

"Many more were not."

Over the static, Quin Ryan's now quiet tone sounded otherworldly, neither here nor there, a disembodied voice caught between heaven and earth. "Mr. Darrow has just stood up," he whispered, "thumbs in his trademark suspenders."

"The defense desires to call Mr. Bryan to the stand as a witness," Darrow said.

"Bryan? Holy Christ!"

Both Sarah and Mrs. Lee jumped out of their seats. That exclamation had not come from the radio. Mrs. Lee froze, halting her knitting mid-stitch. Their eyes met briefly, then turned toward the sound of heavy footsteps squeaking on the planked, wooden floor.

"It's all right, Mama," he said, walking over to Mrs. Lee, "I'll talk to the lady." Now in light summer clothes, the handsome, wistful young man in the photograph wrapped his arms around the stunned woman and gazed at Sarah. "After the questioning of Bryan. If that's okay with you, ma'am."

Stunned herself, Sarah just nodded.

"Good," he said. "I'll turn up the volume."

⇀ 22

MITCHELL'S PENCIL NEEDED SHARPENING, but he wasn't about to lose his seat. He could have borrowed another, of course. However, once, when using a colleague's pen, he wrote a terrible article, full of clichés and grammatical errors. Admittedly, he was drinking then too, and the bulk of the piece was actually composed on a typewriter. But the experience had prompted him to develop a habit. One writing tool per story, always his own. Over the years, the habit had become an obsession.

With dull lead smudging his words, he wrote: "Because Judge Raulston had disallowed his scientific experts to testify, Darrow shocked the Court by calling the foremost expert on the Bible to the witness stand: William Jennings Bryan, the prosecutor, the Great Commoner himself. With reading glasses hanging from his pocket, the one-time presidential candidate waved to the crowd and took the stand." Mitchell looked over what would be the opening to his article. He would polish it later. He skipped a few lines and continued to write as the testimony began.

The Court: "Mr. Bryan, you are not objecting to going on the stand?"

Bryan: "Not at all."

The Court: "Do you want Mr. Bryan sworn?"

Darrow: "No."

Bryan: "I can make affirmation; I can say, 'So help me God, I will tell the truth.'"

Darrow: "No, I take it you will tell the truth, Mr. Bryan."

A championship match, Mitchell thought. Bryan sat unflinchingly in the witness booth as Darrow paced menacingly before him. Two heavyweights, throwing punches, battling for a knockout. He gazed at the scene for a moment, then turned back to his notes where he was startled to see Sarah's name scribbled in the right margin. When did he write that? Good God. Was he that far gone? He started to erase his lovesick doodling, but stopped himself and turned to a fresh piece of paper instead.

"You claim everything in the Bible should be literally interpreted?" Darrow asked, his playful tone betraying the delight he obviously took in having his opponent in a vulnerable position.

"I believe accepted as it is given there: some of the Bible is given illustratively. For instance: 'Ye are the salt of the earth.' I would not insist that man was actually salt, or that he had flesh of salt, but it is used in the sense of salt as saving God's people."

"But when you read that Jonah swallowed the whale—or that the whale swallowed Jonah—excuse me please—how do you literally interpret that?"

"When I read that a big fish swallowed Jonah—it does not say whale—that is my recollection of it. A big fish, and I believe it, and I believe in a God who can make a whale and can make a man and make both do what He pleases."

Darrow was attempting to apply logic to faith. A doomed approach, Mitchell thought, imagining how he himself would respond if someone tried to reason him out of his pencil. Nevertheless, Darrow continued in this manner and picked up speed to boot, forcing Mitchell to abbreviate and condense.

D.: "What if the earth suddenly stood still?"

B.: "Don't know, and don't care. God will provide."

D.: "Believe the Flood was true?"

B.: "Yes."

D.: "When did it occur?"

B.: "About four thousand B.C."

D.: "How was the calculation made?"

B.: "Don't know."

D.: "What do you think?"

D.: "I do not think about things I don't think about."

D.: "Do you know anything about how many people there were in Egypt three thousand, five hundred years ago, or how many people there were in China five thousand years ago?"

B.: "No."

D.: "Mr. Bryan, am I the first man you ever heard of who has been interested in the age of human societies and primitive man?"

B.: "Yes."

D.: "Where have you lived all your life?"

B.: "Not near you."

Mitchell laughed along with everyone else. Bryan had a sense of humor, all right, something Mitchell remembered from his presidential campaign. Still, in just about any other hearing, the cumulative effect of Darrow's questioning would have been devastating. He'd made an admired national figure sound like an idiot. But this was not any other hearing. The crowd was on the side of the Commoner, whether he made sense or not.

Darrow: "Do you think the earth was made in six days?"

Bryan: "Not six days of twenty-four hours."

D.: "I will read from the Bible: 'And the Lord God said unto the serpent, because thou hast done this, thou art cursed above all cattle, and above every beast of the field; upon thy belly shalt thou go and dust shalt thou eat all the days of thy life.' Do you think that is why the serpent is compelled to crawl upon its belly?"

B.: "I believe that."

D:. "Have you any idea how the snake went before that time?"

B.: "No, sir."

D.: "Do you know whether he walked on his tail or not?"

B.: "No, sir. I have no way to know."

Mitchell was a bit surprised to hear laughter this time, for it was clearly at Bryan's expense. And the man knew it. His wide mouth twitched as he glared at Darrow. "Your Honor," he said, "I think I can shorten this testimony. The only purpose Mr. Darrow has is to slur at the Bible, but I will answer his question. I will answer it all at once, and I have no objection in the world, I want the world to know that this man," he said pointing accusingly at Darrow," who does not believe in a God, is trying to use a court in Tennessee—"

Darrow objected but Bryan kept on going.

— "to slur at it, and while it will require time, I am willing to take it."

"I object to your statement," said Darrow. "I am exempting you on your fool ideas that no intelligent Christian on earth believes."

Before the crowd could react, Judge Raulston slammed his gavel. "Court is adjourned until nine o'clock tomorrow morning."

Mitchell scouted for a quick exit and hurried toward a cab. So that's it, he said to himself. Tomorrow closing arguments, and then the case will go to the jury. He thought of the *Blade* newsroom, waiting impatiently for his call.

"Back to the hotel already?" the driver said, recognizing him from earlier in the morning.

"Yep, short session today." Mitchell thumbed through his pad of paper. Fortunately, he was not subject to motion sickness. As the vehicle snaked up the hill, he reviewed his notes and began mentally crafting an article for the evening paper. In this age of the automobile, his equilibrium was a blessing.

⇨ 23

"REMARKABLE," JACOB SAID.

"Yes," Sarah said. "Remarkable." Remarkable that she just had been in Dayton, spoken to Darrow, met with Mencken, done, well, done *that* with Mitchell. Remarkable, too, that she was where she was right now. With everything she'd been through, such things should have ceased to amaze her.

"Ma, you've just heard history in the making." He gently stroked his mother's head. "Now, why don't you go check on Bea. She looked so forlorn, banished to the bedroom like that."

"No, no, I'm staying put."

He cupped her youthful face in his hands. "Eldora. Please."

She sighed. "All right. But if you need me . . ." She stuck her needles in the dwindling ball of yarn, rose from the chair and cast Sarah a fierce, hard look, one that said: "I will protect him at all costs." Sarah had seen it often in juvenile court, no matter what a child had done. The maternal instinct. One felt powerless in its presence. At times, envious too.

Jacob waited until he heard the dog howl gratefully, and then turned to Sarah. "Most mothers would be offended by their child calling them by their Christian name," he said in a smooth bass. "Mine's just the opposite. It's my ace in the hole."

Sarah smiled, meeting his direct gaze. He bore a striking resemblance to his mother. Handsome for the same reasons she was pretty. Wide-set sable eyes, high cheekbones, the same crowded teeth; a quality that added a touch of boyishness to his unequivocal masculinity. And then, his skin; the same color but darker in hue. If chocolate was the analogy, hers was of the milk variety, his bittersweet.

"So." He laced his shapely fingers together and leaned forward. "Ask away."

"I obviously was not expecting to have this opportunity," Sarah said. "I guess I should first explain why I've been selected for this task." Which she did, omitting the most important fact of all: that she was the one who had informed the police about him. Then she said: "I guess I'll just get to the point. Did you kill Professor Manhoff?"

He maintained his gaze. "No."

"Then why hide from the police?"

"The public is outraged over the murder. The authorities need a villain, and they somehow learned that I knew the professor. That's all they need to know."

Sarah briefly averted her eyes, and then turned back. "As I told your mother, I really believe the police chief, Officer Perry, is a fair man. I don't think he'd arrest you without cause."

He looked at her as if she were a naive child. "I heard you talking to my mother. I thought you understood something about Southern justice. Even if you're right about the chief, he's only one man."

"But you must see that running makes you look guilty."

"Well, that's why I decided to talk to you." He reached in his pocket and took out a plain, carved wooden cross and fingered it gently. "I'm a spiritual man," he said. "I believe in doing what's right. But sometimes the law of the land is unjust. Sometimes one must follow a higher law."

Sarah thought of Mrs. Stowe and all those in the Underground Railroad who indeed broke the law to help the slaves. Certainly, that was the right thing to do. But as a regular practice, such behavior was dangerous. Anarchy does not make for a civil society. And so-called higher law, God's law, is subject to interpretation itself. But these sorts of questions had no easy answers. Best to ask one that might.

"How well did you know the professor?"

Jacob knit his thick, wiry brows. "Not well, but better than any other faculty member at Edenville, including those in the department of religion. When I first thought of applying to the university, I talked to many of the professors, just to get a sense of the school. Professor Manhoff was the most willing to accommodate me. And I initially thought I made an impression."

"Why is that?"

"He just seemed engaged. He asked me numerous questions, for instance, about my interest in the ministry."

"Such as?"

"Well, first he wanted to know why I wanted to be a preacher. What were my goals? I guess he had certain expectations of what I would say. Because when I explained my reasons, he looked puzzled."

Sarah took a swig of her coffee. It was cold, but still flavorful. "What did you say? What were your reasons?"

"I told him what I tell everyone. That I wanted to help my people rise out of ignorance and poverty, and that entering the ministry was the best way I could think of to do that. To me, religion's chief goal should be to become a force for social good, for tolerance. You see, I don't think of Christianity, or for that matter any other religion, as centrally about sin."

He fingered his cross again and swallowed. Sarah watched his prominent Adam's apple protrude and retreat. "Is that all?" she asked.

"Oh, no. I also told him that a literal reading of the Bible is what keeps my people down, as surely as if they were in chains. Faith is salve for the soul, but the mind needs to be free. To focus on the reality of the Immaculate Conception, the Resurrection, and other biblical events fails to take into account their function as powerful metaphors. About human potential, love and redemption. If I were a preacher, that's what I would emphasize."

Guilty or not, Sarah thought, he would make a wonderful preacher. Even she might attend his service. "That is quite unconventional thinking for a Christian, isn't it?"

"I suppose so."

"What did Professor Manhoff say?"

"He immediately asked my opinion of science. Of course, you can imagine what I told him, what with all my tinkering. How could I not believe in science and be crazy for wireless, radio and such?" Jacob shifted in his chair and gazed off at some spot on the wall with an expression similar to the one in the photograph. "You know, Miss Kaufman, I was almost published in *Science and Invention*. They liked my article about the importance of keeping the airways free. Before they found out I was a Negro, that is. Ironic isn't it?"

Sarah nodded.

"Probably wouldn't have mattered anyway. Soon, the National Broadcast System will own even the clouds. Amateurs like myself will be shut down."

Sarah was impressed. Had she been asked to hand down a verdict at this moment, she would have let him walk. But she had to remind herself that intelligence and charm, both of which he possessed, did not equal innocence. Smooth talking crooks had hoodwinked her before.

"So what did Professor Manhoff say next?"

Jacob motioned to the room where the radio still hummed. "As a matter of fact, he asked me about Darwin, what I thought about his theory of evolution."

Darwin. Of course, Sarah thought. All roads seem to have led there for the professor. "And what did you tell him?"

"From what I knew of it, I told him I thought it made sense, that to me, this was science describing the bond that exists between all God's creatures. We come from apes. So what? It's only a threat if one views events in the Bible as entirely literal. And as I said, I don't."

"I assume you're on Scopes' side, then."

"Absolutely. God created Darwin as well as Adam. One doesn't have to be an atheist to believe in scientific fact. If some members of the church had their way, we'd still believe the sun revolves around the earth."

"You sound more like a Universalist than a Christian, Jacob, even if I myself agree with you. But just to play devil's advocate, couldn't restricting the teaching of creation be viewed similarly?"

"Nonsense. I never would say that this magnificent story shouldn't be taught. Only it should stay in church where it belongs. This country was founded on the separation of church and state. Darwin in the pulpit would be equally inappropriate."

"From what I've learned of Professor Manhoff, I assume he was pleased with your views."

"Oh yes, quite. After I explained them to him, he actually applauded. I must tell you, ma'am, at that point, I thought my admission to Edenville was guaranteed."

"But it wasn't."

"No."

"Did you ever think the professor played a part in your rejection?"

Jacob was silent and then laughed a little. "Did I think he played a part? I know he did. That's why the police want me, isn't it? They see a motive."

Sarah nodded, unsuccessfully trying not to show her surprise. "How did you find out?"

"From the man himself."

"Professor Manhoff told you?"

"In so many words. After he learned where I stood on evolution, he began talking more freely about the concepts central to Darwin's theory, you know, natural selection, survival of the fittest."

She nodded again, slowly.

"He started off rather generally, simply describing what he claimed was the logic of those ideas, how he himself had come to similar conclusions just by observing nature. He said that one didn't need to go to the Galapagos to see that certain species fail while others thrive."

Jacob suddenly stood up, walked to the piano and sat down sideways on the bench. He ran his fingers lightly over the keys. "Then the professor's speech turned. From description to interpretation. He grew more animated too, agitated even. He said that these processes were nature's way of weeding out the weak, the feeble: 'Everything's evolving, don't you know, human beings included. Evolving with the ultimate goal of reaching an ideal state, of being one with God!' He shook his head and smiled. 'Those silly religious folk against Darwin don't understand this,' he said. 'But you, my boy, you do.' When he asked if I was following him, I said yes. What I didn't say was that I was also feeling increasingly sickened about where he was heading."

"I can imagine," Sarah said, feeling rather queasy herself.

"I only became more so as he continued. 'Unfortunately,' he said, 'even the best theories are not foolproof. Sometimes, every once in a while, nature makes a mistake. That's when human beings must intervene. We help nature by weeding our gardens, for instance. In so doing, we restore their beauty and balance. A mother bear loves all her cubs, but she will not hesitate to leave the one that is impaired to die in the wilderness.' And then he said, 'And now, I'm going to tell you a little secret. I've never told anyone else. This should show how much I respect you.'"

Jacob stared at Sarah silently. She held her breath while he prepared to betray the dead man's confidence.

"He said that long ago he discovered that his lineage was not entirely pure, that one of his ancestors had committed a grave sin by impregnating a black woman." Jacob closed his eyes and exhaled deeply. "Professor Manhoff visibly shuddered when he admitted this, taking several seconds to compose himself. Then he put his hand on my shoulder, like a doctor about to give his patient bad news. No one knew about his past, he said, except for himself. No one knew he was tainted. Not even his wife. At the most, his blood was a sixteenth black. Just a sixteenth, Miss Kaufman! A drop of black paint into a bucket of white. No one would ever guess, he said, rolling up his sleeve to show me his pale flesh. But it was enough to make him realize his duty. With his blue eyes filling with tears, he said he swore he never would have children. Never. Why? 'Because I am like that mother bear,' he said, answering his own question. 'Better off though, because I prevented the birth of another defective being. Don't you see? I have helped along the process of natural selection. This mutation will stop with me.'"

My God, Sarah thought, had Manhoff taken his ideas that far? Was he not sterile after all? Or for some reason, had he concocted this lie to conceal his sterility? Which was it? Which to him would have been the greater humiliation? Then again, was Jacob telling the truth?

Jacob shook his head and continued. "Of course, I was shocked beyond words. He was either unaware or didn't care that he had offended me, cut me to the core. But believe it or not, the worse was yet to come. He was building to a crescendo."

Sarah drained her cup. "Go on."

"He told me I was a fine young man. But that I must know I was unusual for my race. An anomaly. The exception to the rule. 'If you believe in evolution,' he said, 'then you must know your race is inferior. Just consider all the white race has accomplished, in art, architecture, medicine, science.' Then he looked me straight in the eye: 'Now, really, what has the Negro done?'

"I, of course, could have named names, Booker T. Washington, Langston Hughes. I could have reminded him of all the Africans who fought in the Civil War, who endured despite being forbidden to read, to grow, but I was stunned into silence, which I'm afraid he interpreted as agreement. Then came the final blow. Most of the Negroes being admitted to Edenville, he said, were typical of the race: kind, soulful, but with limited intelligence and ambition."

Keep the Negroes in check and still satisfy the donors, Sarah thought.

"'Ah. But you!'" Jacob continued, quoting the professor. "'It's a hard lot, but you do see that, like myself, you need to help nature along. Intervene on its behalf. Act for the greater good. You must do the honorable thing.' Professor Manhoff then drew closer and whispered: 'Withdraw your application, my boy. Prevent your mind from becoming something it wasn't intended to be. Your people don't need metaphors; they need rules and boundaries. And you can help them. You can lead them. I tell you, if you plant this seed, it will grow into a monstrous plant, one that could devour all of mankind.'

"I see by your expression, Miss Kaufman, that you feel the same as I did. But I tell you, the man was dead serious."

"You misread me, Jacob. I'm appalled, really. But based on what I've learned of the man, I think him quite capable of harboring such views."

Jacob must have been telling the truth, Sarah thought. No one could invent something so outrageous. "I'm surprised, though, that he discussed them with you so openly," she said. "I can only imagine that the thought would have crossed his mind that you might expose him."

"Expose him? To whom? Do you really think anyone would take my word over his? Oh, no. He knew he had nothing to fear. Still, I told him I refused to do as he requested, that I had no intention of withdrawing my name."

"How did he respond?"

"With a kind of strange, dejected calm. He'd made what he must have thought was an irrefutable case, and lost. For a moment he appeared small and shriveled, as if his very life force had been sucked out. But he quickly recovered. He stared at me blankly, put on his glasses and picked up a book. 'Well, good day then,' he said. Just like that. Pff. Good day."

"And that was it?"

"Not quite. Before leaving, I asked him if he would try to prevent my admission. He didn't even look up. He just kept his eyes on his book and said nothing. That was when I knew it was over."

"For Edenville or for college in general?"

"In general, for a while. I could have applied elsewhere, but that would've meant moving away from home. My mother had scraped together every penny she earned teaching at the black grammar school to pay for college, but she'd counted on me living at home and helping out. Besides, I'd have hated to leave her alone." Jacob stared into space again, his expression both soft and hard, like a cloud made of steel. "So I went to work for a machine shop," he continued, "volunteered at the church and waited for a chance to make something of myself."

Anger crossed over his face. Sarah waited for his features to relax before asking the next question. "Jacob, would you say you have a temper? I've heard you've been in a few fights, that you put someone in the hospital."

"I detest injustice, that's what I'll say."

"Professor Manhoff committed a terrible injustice against you. You must have felt resentment, perhaps even longed for revenge."

"I wouldn't be human if I didn't."

Sarah examined him. He was still on simmer. "You own a gun, don't you, Jacob? And you're a pretty fair marksman."

"I shoot clay pigeons and occasionally real ones. That's all."

"Well, just humor me then. Do you own a pocket pistol? A Beretta, twenty-five caliber. Six point thirty-five millimeter to be exact?" Sarah adopted a serious expression, but knew she sounded like a parody of a tough cop.

He stared at his cross. "Yes, yes, I do. But I'll tell you one thing. If I seriously wanted to dispose of someone, it wouldn't be my first or even second choice."

"Why not? It obviously worked."

"Whoever used the piece got lucky. It's simply too small, too inefficient. Good for scaring away a burglar. Good for a lady like yourself to keep in your purse. I'll show you," he said, getting up. He returned a moment later and handed her the weapon. "Beretta, six thirty-five. Here. Almost delicate, isn't it? You take it. Give it to the police. Of course it's got my fingerprints on it, but they'll see it hasn't been fired."

He very well might own ten of these things, she thought, taking the metal object and dropping it in her purse. It did fit nicely. "You know, Jacob, you really do seem to be quite knowledgeable about guns."

"Yes. So are most men around here. Ma'am, did it ever occur to you that there could be others . . . a whole host of others, a whole university's worth of feathers the professor might have ruffled who also own such a gun?"

"Of course. They're investigating everyone possible. Do you have any ideas?"

"No, I don't." He leaned toward her. "But I'll tell you this. I did not kill Professor Manhoff. And unless the authorities come up with some hard evidence, which given what I just said, is impossible, I'll not turn myself in. If I do, I'll never come home."

"But . . ."

"Please. I think I've said everything I need to say. Now, if you'll excuse me. Ma?" he shouted.

Mrs. Lee appeared with the dog following closely behind.

"Please," Sarah said, "one last question."

Jacob nodded.

"Are you related to Lee, Robert E. Lee?"

The mother and son gave each other a knowing glance and laughed.

"No," Jacob said. "But that is the running joke around here. We tell everyone that."

"Including Professor Manhoff?"

"Professor Manhoff. Are you kidding? Hell, no. Not him. Why would you think so?"

"I don't know, perhaps when he confided in you about his heritage."

"No, ma'am. I wasn't in a joking mood. Besides, I'm black through and through. I think you can see that. What made you ask?"

"Never mind. It's not important." Or at least she didn't yet know the significance.

There was an uncomfortable silence. Mrs. Lee took that as Sarah's cue to leave for she stood up and motioned toward the door. "Well," Sarah said. "Jacob, if you change your mind . . ."

"I won't."

"I'm afraid the authorities will find you if they set their mind to it. You're only compounding the problem," she said half-heartedly.

"Thanks for the warning. Really, you've been very kind."

"Well, goodbye then." Sarah turned to open the door. It stuck a bit, so she twisted the knob and yanked. She gasped. "Officer Perry!"

"Thank you, Miss Kaufman," the uniformed man said. "I'll take over from here. You run along, now. The driver's waiting."

Jacob cast Sarah a pained look. "I guess they did find me, with your help. I thought you were different," he said with disgust. "I should have known."

"But I knew nothing about this," Sarah said. "Honestly, I didn't know!"

"She's telling you the truth, young man."

Jacob looked at her again, his expression softening slightly. "So, this is your fair officer?"

Sarah glared at the man as he unlocked a pair of handcuffs. "I was obviously mistaken."

"I'm sorry ma'am, but I have a job to do." He turned to Jacob. "Jacob Lee, you are under arrest for the murder of Professor Nicholas Manhoff."

Mrs. Lee grabbed hold of her son and began crying. "No! No!" The dog darted her pebbly eyes from one human to the other and whimpered.

"What evidence do you have?" Jacob demanded. "You can't have any evidence!"

"I'm afraid we do."

"What is it? What trumped up piece of garbage is it?"

"An eyewitness, sir. We have an eyewitness."

⇻ 24

SARAH SAT ON LENA'S FRONT-PORCH SWING scraping caked mud off her shoes. Accompanied by a light continuous rain, the burial had been an uncomfortable and somber affair, the earth wet and heavy as it received the dark mahogany casket. She had not been thinking straight when she'd put on her suede pumps.

The minister, a stooped, tubercular-looking fellow, offered words which made Sarah wince but which Professor Manhoff himself certainly would have approved. "An intellectual, a dedicated teacher, a native son who gave his all. A great man whom God, for reasons of His own, had unfortunately not blessed with progeny. It is up to the university to keep his memory alive. This proud son of the Confederacy who was taken violently and too soon."

Sarah felt a lump in her throat as he then picked up a clump of dirt and tossed it onto the closed lid. The sound reverberated in the heavy air. The final, symbolic act before all light is obliterated. She thought—as she always did at such times—of her parents. Her mother's loosely braided black hair, her father's ticklish red mustache. Their mingling smell of sandalwood and rosewater. Both died when she was old enough to remember, but young enough to still occasionally feel like an orphan. Another handful. The moment when it was really over, when all the knowledge in the world was useless, when differences of faith fell away. Dust to dust. Neither science nor religion could prevent it. Neither doctor nor priest nor even rabbi could explain it. Was there an afterlife, a heaven, a place where people were reunited with those they loved? If only it were true. Whoever claimed to know, didn't really. Whether we crawled out of the sea or were formed in God's image, all we could do was hope.

Sarah banged her shoes together, shaking off the remaining traces of mud. The here and now was all one had. The only thing over which one could claim a modicum of control. Except for yesterday, that is, when she had allowed herself to be manipulated like a puppet. One man was dead, and her actions in the matter unintentionally had helped put another in jail. Undeservedly, she still couldn't help but believe. Her eyes drifted to the nearby woods. Lush, green, and impenetrable from this vantage point, the sweet, earthy fragrance that had intensified with the rain gave no hint of the tragedy that had occurred there. The faculty—the same who attended the dinner—was equally devoid of clues. Flat surfaces. Inscrutable expressions. Huddled under their umbrellas, each appeared respectfully downcast, if a bit impatient with the minister's excruciatingly slow pace.

After the service, Lena stayed to console the girls; Kathryn, Penny and Emily, whose eyes had not stopped welling up since the casket was lowered. All clearly had loved the man. It must have been doubly difficult for Kathryn and Penny, who, like Sarah, had previously experienced deep, personal loss. According to Lena, Kathryn's parents both died when she was thirteen in a train accident. After that, she lived with her grandparents, kind, well-meaning people, but somewhat infirm. As an only child, the girl pretty much had to fend for herself. And Penny's father passed away a few years ago from a heart attack, tragically, the day before her high school graduation. Sarah recalled her initial impression of the two girls together at the faculty dinner, how different they appeared despite their closeness. They had seemed so just now at the service too, what with their contrasting high and low heels, short and long frocks, dark and pale lips. They even cried like opposites: Kathryn, audibly but controlled, Penny, in silent, heaving spurts. But now Sarah thought she perhaps understood what bound them, why in particular Kathryn exhibited that touch of maternal pride when her more voluptuous friend spoke up. Loss. Loss of a parent. Having lived with it longer, Kathryn knew Penny's pain and took her under her wing.

Jim offered Sarah a ride back, but despite the rain, she decided to walk, thinking it might help the throbbing in her head. The pills Nan had forced upon her, which she promised would provide instant relief, certainly had not. A swig from her flask, that's what she needed. Because, as Freud might explain it, the pain was more in her mind than her head, a physical result of her inner turmoil. A diagnosis in Toledo she both had given and received. Officer Perry had used her, and justified or not, she hated being used. But when he dropped by last night to explain, she reluctantly accepted his apology. He confessed that he'd thought all along Jacob was hiding out at home. He just needed someone who could draw him out. Sarah, he sensed, was just that person. But why, she asked, hadn't he told her of his plan? Surely he knew she could be trusted. Trust had nothing to do with it, he said. Despite her experience with criminal types, she inadvertently might have let something slip. It had happened before, even to some of his best officers. She would be more believable if she herself thought she had come alone.

Sarah knew he had a point, but she still loathed the tactic, especially since she had been the pawn. She was also confused. Her intuition told her Jacob could not commit such a cold-blooded crime. When Officer Perry relayed the details of the arrest, however, she wasn't so sure. The witness, a respected, male engineering student, was a prosecutor's dream. His name was Christopher Wilde, and until a few days ago, after returning from a trip with his parents, he hadn't even heard of the professor's death.

Officer Perry held up his hand at Sarah's raised brow, anticipating her question. Yes, the boy himself was in the clear. They'd eliminated him as suspect. First, he never had taken a class with Professor Manhoff, in fact knew him in name only. Nothing suspicious in his school file, nothing in the slightest to suggest a motive. That was substantiated by a number of other students. According to everyone he interviewed, Christopher was an intelligent, responsible and all-around decent chap. A somewhat disfiguring port-wine stain on his cheek had made him shy with girls, but he was generally well-liked.

Officer Perry admitted that when the boy first arrived at the station, he seemed uncomfortable. His mouth twitched and he nervously opened and closed a pocket watch dangling from his pants. But when he started to relay his account, he seemed perfectly at ease. He had been waiting for his parents by the chapel when he saw someone running toward him from the direction of the woods. As he approached, he could see that it was a young colored man whom he assumed was just passing through the school. As he got closer, he saw his features clearly and noticed a strange, wild-eyed expression. He was momentarily puzzled, even felt briefly uneasy. But then his parents came and he forgot all about it. Until he heard of the murder. When he realized the timing, he knew he had to do his duty.

Officer Perry turned to Sarah with a grim expression. "Miss Kaufman, I know how ya feel about bigotry, blamin' Coloreds and such, but accordin' to the information my investigators gathered about Jacob, this here youngster described him to a tee. We can't go lettin' our sympathy for the race get in the way of justice, ya know."

He was right about that, and really Sarah should have been glad. She very well might have helped capture a criminal and could resume her holiday to boot. Instead she was troubled, hardly caring that she had stepped into that muddy puddle. Earlier this morning, she'd heard that this Christopher fellow had easily picked Jacob out of a line-up. The evidence was mounting. Still, she wasn't convinced. Sympathy shouldn't get in the way of justice, but neither should the mere appearance of guilt. It all seemed a bit too theatrical. Mencken, H. L. Mencken, for God's sake, providing the suspect. The file providing a motive. And now, an eyewitness. Jacob was such an intelligent, inquisitive young man. And caring. His love for his mother, even his concern for his dog. But dammit, there was nothing she could do. He'd been identified. A jury would have to decide.

She sat up, her head still throbbing. No need to keep scraping; her shoes were ruined. She kicked them off and went inside. A jury would decide. A jury. Scopes. The trial! She checked the clock. Too early to call. Perhaps later. She thought of Mitchell, his full weight upon her, softly kissing her mouth, telling her to open her eyes. Yes, later. She headed upstairs in her wet stockinged feet and smiled for the first time that day.

⇻ 25

"NO CLOSING ARGUMENTS." Mitchell jotted down the Court's unconventional decision, but he sympathized completely with Darrow's request. What was the point of summing up to a jury when one has no witnesses? It was bad enough that Judge Raulston had disallowed the expert testimony. But ordering that Bryan's, too, be expunged from the record! Why not have him step down as soon as he saw the thrust of Darrow's examination? "The issue," Raulston said laconically, "is simply whether the defendant, Scopes, taught that man descended from a lower order of animals, and I feel that the testimony of Bryan can shed no light on any issue that will be pending before the higher courts."

Well, Mitchell thought, technically he may be right, but the broader issues raised in this trial would not go away. Certainly, this was only the beginning. He wondered too whether Raulston would have made his decision had the testimony not taken that nasty turn yesterday. Mitchell opened his notebook to July twenty-second, and read the exchange he'd recorded between the two men: "Your purpose," Bryan proclaimed, "is to cast ridicule on everybody who believes in the Bible, and I am perfectly willing that the world shall know that you and your cohorts have no other purpose than ridiculing every person who believes in the Bible." Darrow fired back: "We have the purpose of preventing bigots and ignoramuses from controlling education of the United States; and you know it, that is all." Mitchell smirked. At least Darrow would leave with dignity, protesting the way the case was handled by acknowledging the verdict was a forgone conclusion: "We have no witnesses to offer any proof that would be admitted as the issue is laid down here. There is nothing to do but bring in the jury and instruct them to find the defendant guilty."

At eleven a.m., Raulston heeded Darrow's first wish by calling in the jury, but he went through the motions of charging them with the case. "Take your time. Consider all the evidence." Mitchell wasn't ready for lunch, but he wanted a cigarette. He went outside, lit up and stood smoking on the courthouse steps. He wondered what the consequences of the inevitable decision would be. For other states. For the country. For the future of the separation of church and state. And what about Dayton? Would this event have the desired economic effect? What would they do with all those monkeys once the visitors left?

Mitchell watched some of his fellow reporters circle the attorneys as they exited the building. He, himself, had wanted to ask Bryan a few questions. Perhaps this was the time. He rehearsed them so he wouldn't fumble. What would have been his stand on teaching evolution had he been elected president? Would he have left it to the states, or would he have used the White House to impose his views? What role would science have assumed in his administration? Mitchell thought he knew the answers, but he wanted to get them directly from the Commoner. A novel angle, he thought, one that might alert the public to the dangers of electing a zealot. True, like Sarah, Mitchell had voted for the man. But that was before Dayton. Before the man's overt fundamentalism put his progressiveness into serious question.

What was that passage Mitchell had read? Ah, yes. Mencken. Naturally. It was by Mencken: "As democracy is perfected, the office of President represents, more and more closely, the inner soul of the people. On some great and glorious day, the plain folks of the land will reach their heart's desires at last, and the White House will be adorned by a downright moron." It didn't exactly fit, of course. Bryan was smart. Very smart. Indeed, beneath that garish coating of literalism lurked a great critical mind. But imagine a president with his same religious beliefs but without his intelligence!

Mitchell took a long drag on his cigarette, coughed and stamped it out. He really needed to quit. Inching toward Bryan, he looked up and surprisingly found Darrow's blue eyes on him, or so he thought. He smiled and extended his hand, but Darrow gave no response. Then someone behind Mitchell, one of the law clerks, walked up to Darrow and whispered something in his ear.

Darrow chuckled and turned back toward the reporters vying for his attention. Mitchell felt himself redden. Idiot, he said to himself. He started back toward Bryan, but now it was too late. The bailiff came out and requested everyone's attention. A verdict had been reached. Mitchell checked his watch. Less than ten minutes. The shortest deliberation he'd ever seen.

The crowd marched back into the courtroom rather nonchalantly, like satiated cattle heading toward another feeding. The trial's earlier tension and excitement were gone. Certainty permeated the air. Mitchell himself was so sure, that when the words were actually read, it felt like déjà vu. "On the charge of violating the Butler Act, we the jury find the defendant, John Scopes, guilty." The case would be appealed of course, but it was still a strikingly anti-climactic ending to one of the bitterest legal battles ever waged in the country. Gradually, people rose, chatting and laughing, and Quin Ryan, bereft of animation, made his final announcement: "The Trial of the Century is over."

Mitchell remained in his seat, and uncharacteristically began there and then to compose an article. He knew better than to fight the creative process when it was this demanding. Occasionally the immediacy of the moment could not be denied. After all, he was a newsman, not a poet.

Twelve men of the hills today found John T. Scopes guilty of teaching evolution and the young Tennessee high school teacher is on his way to a place beside Dred Scott on the shelf of lasting fame. Like the humble Negro slave, who was the instrument through which the chains of human slavery finally were broken, this pleasant young man whose blood comes down from the early Anglo-Saxon lovers of liberty, is the medium through which the Supreme Court of the United States finally will decide whether a state legislature may chain the mind.

He was editorializing again, he knew, but didn't care. He'd leave it to his paper to decide. So far, they'd printed everything he'd written on the case. Mitchell focused the rest of his piece on what he thought was the most interesting moment of the day, when John Scopes himself made a statement. "It was odd to hear from the soft-spoken young man," he wrote, "who had been silent throughout the hearing. His words were brief: 'I feel that I have been convicted of violating an unjust statute and I shall continue to oppose in every way I can a law which I feel violates the ideals of freedom, the teaching of the truth and my constitutional and personal freedom.' Whether Scopes was still performing for the city or had truly been convinced of this position over the course of the trial, I couldn't say. It will definitely be worth keeping tabs on the fellow."

Scopes' remarks were followed by a friendly exchange between the attorneys. Bryan showed a glimmer of his earlier days: "This case has stirred the world because it reached into the future beyond the power of man to see." Darrow thanked the counsel on the other side for their courtesy, Judge Ralston spoke of the importance of truth—which, he naturally associated with the word of God—and then ordered Scopes to pay a fine of one hundred dollars. After that, the crowd started thinning out. Mitchell closed his notebook and thought about giving Bryan another try. According to his colleague from the *Tribune*, however, Bryan's wife had just escorted him into a taxi. Apparently, he was not feeling well and she wanted to make sure he got some rest before dealing with the press. Mrs. Bryan's love for her husband had been evident throughout the trial, but now, brushing off reporters like flies, she also had demonstrated a strong will.

Mitchell waited until everyone had packed up their belongings and gone. Then he took out his new thirty-five millimeter Leica and began taking shots of the empty sanctum. He'd been waiting to do this since the trial began. The scene after the action. Motionless to the human eye, the officious space reverberated from the drama that had unfolded there. Hold. Click. Pop. Now, a section of the wooden seats, the half-filled water glasses. Shards of dust-filled light. The ever-present Bible on Judge Raulston's desk. These would catch the time, hold the place. Visible proof when he was too old to remember.

He approached the defense attorneys' table. That rumpled, white handkerchief might some day become valuable. Depending on whose it was, of course. Settling for a picture instead, he changed the lens, adjusted the flash and shot. Then off to the prosecution's side. What was that? He moved closer. A half-eaten radish! It must be true. Bryan did eat the bitter little things. Whether as frequently as rumor had it he didn't know, but here was surely a convincing piece of evidence. He shot. Perhaps he would submit this one to a journal. Then again, he was stinging from the last rejection. He took a few more—the three-starred state flag, the silent witness box, some left behind papers—then returned the camera to his bag and exited the building.

Out on the lawn, people mingled, and the souvenir stands had long lines. The trial was over, but apparently no one was quite ready to return to their mundane lives. Surprisingly, Darrow was out there too, still talking to the press. Mitchell thought he would have been one of the first to get out of town. Not because he'd lost, but to get back to civilization. Mitchell watched him for a while and thought: I've already made a fool of myself. What the hell. He waited until Darrow was alone, then approached. The man looked worn out. Half of his shirttail hung over his pants. His normally bright eyes were rimmed with dark circles. Perhaps the loss had affected him more than Mitchell thought. Perhaps somewhere deep inside, he'd held out hope.

Mitchell cleared his throat. "Mr. Darrow?"

He didn't answer.

"Mr. Darrow, sir?"

"Yeees?"

He sounded annoyed, appeared not to recognize him. "You said something about an exclusive, sir," Mitchell said, "you know, earlier today."

Darrow squinted. "Ah, Mr. . . Mr. . . . ."

"Dobrinksi," Mitchell said. "Mitchell Dobrinski."

"Right." He ran his thumbs up and down his suspenders. "Well, I've got three minutes. What do you want to know?"

"I guess whatever you'd like to tell me."

Darrow sighed, scratched his cheek, and then looked directly at Mitchell with a bit of the light back in his eyes. "Fair enough." He pulled out a pipe and tobacco from his jacket pocket, packed the bowl, lit and puffed. A few strands of greased hair fell over his forehead. "The anti-evolution movement has reached Washington," he said. "That's what makes it dangerous. There are several new proposals at the next meeting of congress. Specifically, it is their purpose to bar the Smithsonian Institution from investigating matters concerning the origin of man. Bar the Smithsonian! You tell your readers that, Mister Do . . . whatever your name is. You tell them to write their congressmen. You tell 'em Clarence Darrow, a native son, a fellow Ohioan said so. Hell, the last budget only allowed a few thousand dollars for the Bureau of American Ethnology as it is. From here on out, all such appropriations will be challenged. It is . . ."

Mitchell interrupted. "Could you please slow down a bit, sir."

"I'm in a hurry. Take it or leave it."

Mitchell nodded, resorting to a messy shorthand even he himself often couldn't read.

"It is in such proposals that the menace of the anti-evolution agitation is manifest. Their position is this: 'Don't ask these questions—don't investigate—don't accept the findings of those who do investigate.' We are told that we should not dig into the ruins of ancient cities where we may find records written before that eventful Friday, October twenty-third, 4004 B. C., when, at nine o'clock in the morning we are assured creation occurred. We should not invent microscopes, telescopes, spectroscopes and the like, should refuse to use them once invented. 'Don't question, don't look, don't investigate.' That leads to the closed mind, stops progress. You tell 'em that!"

"I will," Mitchell said, mesmerized by the man's off-the-cuff eloquence. Had he suddenly felt inspired or just regurgitated familiar lines? Either way, it was impressive.

"Now, I really must go," he said. "Quote me correctly, ya hear?"

Mitchell nodded. "Thank you, sir."

Darrow turned to leave, then stopped. "And give my regards to Sarah," he said, biting down on the pipe's oversized stem.

Mitchell smiled, conjuring up Sarah's delectable image. "Will do," he said, as the man walked away.

➜ 26

SARAH WOKE WITH A PAINFUL SORE THROAT. She swallowed a few times to make sure. No doubt about it. This was not in her mind. Had she been home, Tillie would have asked her for definition. Sticky or scratchy? Her sister needed to know in order to prepare the right remedy. Honeyed tea for the former, chicken soup for the latter, a distinction only someone with Tillie's meticulous attention to detail could have discovered. Sarah swallowed again. Scratchy, this one scratched like sandpaper. Lena said she shouldn't have walked home in the rain but Sarah thought it more likely she'd gotten it from Mitchell. The incubation period was probably about right. Either way, she doubted whether soup was in the offing.

Actually, she felt the nasty little thing coming on last night. Just a tickle, but that's the way of sore throats. They tease before they attack. Perhaps if she'd gone to bed earlier, she would have slept it off. But the phone lines had been tied up. She'd tried for hours to get hold of Mitchell, with no success. It must have been past midnight when she finally gave up. Of course, she learned of the guilty verdict anyway. Lena told her about it as soon as she returned from campus, and it even had made the evening paper. But she still wanted to hear Mitchell's impressions. And now, she also wanted to blame him for making her sick.

Sarah held her clammy hand to her forehead. No fever. She wasn't about to lie in bed, anyway. This bug would take its course, but she'd be damned if she would let it interfere with the time she had remaining. She got up, dressed and tried not to swallow.

Coming down the stairs, she smelled coffee and heard voices over the clanging of dishes. Breakfast was still underway. When she entered the dining area, Nan was serving scrambled eggs to Phyllis and Samantha, who she finally formally met last night. Lena was seated on the other side of the table. All were still in their robes.

"Come join us," Samantha said, wielding a fatty slice of bacon.

Lena narrowed her eyes. "Do you feel well enough?"

"I'm fine," she said, her throat on fire.

"You sick?" Nan asked, keeping her distance, a hair net covering tightly pinned up curls.

"Just a little. I won't breathe on anyone."

"Hungry?" she asked curtly.

"Yes, I am." Feed a cold, starve a fever.

"Well, help yourself, then. I'm going to Atlanta in a couple of weeks. Can't take any chances."

Sarah obliged and helped herself to eggs, toast and tea. Underdone, burnt and weak, but soothing.

"We've been talking about Scopes," Samantha said. The chubby blond woman had an audible lisp, which must have made the articulation of that name somewhat difficult. But she managed to get it out cleanly. Sarah admired little victories like that. A small hurdle overcome often affected her far more than a grand act of heroism. She breathed in the steam from her cup. "You have?"

"Yes, and it's been quite a stimulating conversation."

They looked at each other and nodded.

"Sarah, what do you think of the verdict?"

"Me? I guess I think it was predictable."

They all nodded again.

"We all did too. But," Samantha said, reaching for the salt, "Scopes did violate the Butler law. That we know."

"Well, technically perhaps. But from what I've heard, the whole business was a setup anyway. Dayton needed money. The ACLU believed the law was unconstitutional and sought out someone willing to break it. Dayton saw an opportunity, and Scopes was the patsy." Thank you, Mitchell, Sarah thought.

"That's right. You were there. Of course, either way, I personally feel that without the Bible, we're lost. Even Jewish people believe that, don't they? I mean, the Old Testament and all."

Lena wagged her index finger. "Like I said earlier, it's just a question of where the Bible belongs, in church and synagogue or the schools."

"Why not in both?"

"Oh, come on, Sam," Phyllis said. In appearance Phyllis was Samantha's near opposite. Brunette where Samantha was blond, short where she was tall, angular were she was round. But they were obviously friends. Phyllis nudged her affectionately and said: "We've talked about this before. Don't let Sarah think you don't know about our government. She'll wonder how you ever got a university job."

Sarah laughed, but couldn't help think of Mencken. "Those who can't . . ."

"Yes," Samantha said, "I know about church and state. But it doesn't mean I agree with it all the time. People need moral guidance."

"Some of the most moral people I know are atheists," Phyllis confessed.

Samantha shook her head disapprovingly.

Phyllis smiled and turned back to Sarah. "Tell me, Sarah, the Butler law aside, do you think Scopes got a fair trial? Did he have a jury of his peers?"

"I don't know. I wasn't there for jury selection. I think the odds were stacked against him, though, with the judge not allowing any testimony from the defense."

The woman was quiet for a moment, and then looked at Sarah conspiratorially. "Sounds as if we'll be having a trial of our own pretty soon."

Sarah sipped her tea and felt herself blink rapidly. Obee did that when he was troubled. Perhaps she was acquiring his habit. Better than permanently ruining her finger. "Do you think this defendant will have a jury of his peers?" she asked. "If he gets indicted, that is."

No one spoke. Then Samantha said: "You mean a Negro jury?"

"Well, I know that's unlikely. I just mean, well, do you think it's possible for this boy to have a fair trial?"

"I think so. I hope so. Let's just pray the truth comes out, whatever it is . . . Samantha," Phyllis said, "that reminds me, we've got to get to work on the bread." She turned to Sarah. "We're making sandwiches, you know, for the memorial."

Sarah nodded as they scooted out from their chairs.

Samantha smiled again. "Nice chatting with you, Sarah. Hope you get to feeling better."

They gathered their dishes and took them to the kitchen where Nan had sequestered herself since Sarah's appearance.

Sarah turned to Lena, trying to pretend her throat wasn't worsening. "So what do you think? Is there a chance in hell Jacob will have a fair trial?"

"Sarah, whatever Nick's views, he didn't deserve to die. If this fellow killed my colleague . . ."

"If. That's the point. You don't know for sure."

"You don't know that he didn't."

Sarah swallowed. Sticky. The thing was changing, adapting, evolving! "You're right, Lena. But I also know that when it comes to Negroes, justice has one eye open down here."

"And sometimes up there."

"I know, but that doesn't make it less true."

For a few moments, they sipped and thought. Then Lena said: "You sure you're feeling okay?"

"I'll live."

"C'mon, then. Let's get dressed. I want to show you something. Something that may help you see Nick from a different perspective."

"Now?" She had planned to try Mitchell again.

"C'mon. It won't take long."

Maybe it was better to wait, after all, she thought. The worse she sounded, the guiltier he'd feel. "Okay."

Nan came out from the kitchen and stood with her hands on her hips. Obviously she'd been listening.

Lena smirked. "After we clear off our dishes, I mean."

Numerous paths led from the college to the woods, but Lena took the one that some believed was already haunted, the one Professor Manhoff had walked that fateful day just weeks ago. Three weeks. It seemed like a year since she'd boarded the train in Toledo, a mere twenty-four hours after his body was discovered.

"Well, it's not the Smokies, but it's lovely," Sarah said.

Lena smiled. "I'm surprised your friend Officer Perry didn't ask you to come here before now. You know, to give your expert opinion."

"I'm not an expert. And he's not my friend."

Lena laughed, but Sarah wondered. No, Officer Perry hadn't asked her to view the crime scene, but why hadn't she herself taken a look anyway? Technically, the police were still investigating, but they hadn't barred anyone from the surrounding area. Was it again the reminder of death? Of murder? Of the brutality that seems to cling to a place long after a deed is done? Like the battlefield she'd once visited, so peaceful from a distance, a picture perfect postcard. But as soon as her feet touched the ground, a wave of nausea rippled through her, leaving her queasy for hours.

Lena turned to Sarah. "The air feels fresher today, doesn't it?"

Bouncing along in a billowy white dress, Lena reminded Sarah of a little sprite, an ethereal spirit out of *The Tempest*. With a Jewish nose, that is. "Yes, it does," she said. So fresh that Sarah was starting to feel chilled. It was lovely, though. Dense with foliage, white-streaked pine, trunks that were thin, stout, smooth and grooved. "They seem animated, don't they? Bowing, stalwart, that one over there even looks bawdy."

"The pathetic fallacy," Lena said.

"What?"

"The pathetic fallacy. Imbuing natural objects with human characteristics. The painter John Ruskin coined the term. He hated the trait."

"Oh, I am sorry, professor."

"Ha! Don't be so sensitive. She put her arm around Sarah. "I said Ruskin hated it. I myself use it all the time."

"And don't be patronizing."

"Your throat is affecting your head."

Maybe, Sarah thought, pushing her cousin away. At least it hadn't yet affected her acute olfactory sense. That would probably come in a day or two, a result of the inevitable congestion. Right now it seemed to be fully functioning. Ginger, lemon, rust. The ever-pervasive honeysuckle. The same general perfume, but more concentrated, more singularly identifiable than elsewhere in town. Twigs crunched under her feet as she reached for a tiny pinecone, perfectly intact. Above her a red crowned bird squeaked out a flute-like sound, and parallel to the path, a meandering creek gurgled predictably as it passed over moss-covered rocks. Closer to the water, Sarah could see a variety of species beneath the clear surface: crawdads, salamanders, snapping turtles, frogs. She observed them for a moment, their apparent harmonious existence, and thought of Darwin. Water, he said. We rose from the water. When Bryan asked Darrow whether he thought it insulting to say we "descended" from slime, Darrow responded that he thought it was insulting to the slime. He was joking, of course, but in principle not far from the truth. At least slime didn't deliberately kill its own.

She braced herself as they approached a roughly bordered area on the path, still delineated officially by rope and wooden poles. So this is where he died. She stepped to the side and gazed at the irregular space, tracing the entirety of its boundaries. Dirt and grass, a handful of brilliantly colored wild flowers. She kept looking, imagining the gun, point blank. Puncturing bone and muscle. Ripping tissue, splattering blood. Terrible, horrific. She waited for her gut to churn, but nothing happened. Her psyche evidently wasn't receiving. Perhaps because empathy takes a back seat to one's own pain. Or as her mother would say, the world might be coming to an end, but if you cut your finger it hurts. So does a sore throat.

Lena kept her eyes pointed straight ahead, and after a few minutes guided Sarah several yards down the path to a small clearing. They turned right, headed down another, narrower path, and walked about the length of a short city block. Lena then stopped before a massive oak tree with thick, gnarled roots.

"Here we are," she said. "This is what I brought you to see."

"The tree?"

"Not exactly." Lena pointed to what appeared to be a large, metal toolbox a few feet away. "Over there. Come on." Lena knelt down and motioned for Sarah to do the same. "Now," she said, opening the lid, "look at this."

Sarah held her breath. She didn't know if Lena had planned to be so mysterious, but Sarah felt as if she were about to gaze upon a long-lost, hidden treasure. What she actually saw was far more mundane. A feather pen, a couple of books, a miniature rebel flag. A few empty bottles, a corncob pipe and other such miscellaneous objects. She sat back on her knees. "So, what is this stuff?"

"A tribute to Nick."

"Another one?"

"The students had the idea, did it all on their own. Apparently, on the first day of class, Nick always told a story about that tree."

Sarah regarded the tree again. Beautiful in a macabre sort of way. The roots overlapping, twisting, turning back on themselves. "Well?"

"According to Jim, Nick said that it was right there his grandfather proposed to his grandmother, a beautiful Southern belle of sixteen. Although the girl had been promised to someone else, she unhesitatingly accepted his offer. Nick's father followed suit and so did Nick himself."

"Meaning what?"

"Meaning his mother and wife, neither of whom had any intention of marrying, both said yes in the very same spot. Nick concluded the story, Jim said, by telling the students that this was the place to come if they wished to make someone love them."

Sarah listened to this strange tale with knitted brows. Attributing mystical powers to a tree somehow didn't mesh with "survival of the fittest," particularly with Nicholas Manhoff's exceedingly ruthless version of the concept. Then again, nothing prevented a bigot from being romantic. No wonder young people liked him. Of course, he may have invented the whole thing precisely to win their favor. Sarah thought of his confession to Jacob and wondered. If it were true, was the black lineage on his grandmother or grandfather's side? Was the story of their love real or the way he wished it to be?

"Sweet, isn't it?" Lena said.

"A bit too for my taste. But what does it have to do with all this stuff?"

"In memory of Nick's connection to the tree, and the woods in general, the students started a collection of things they knew he valued. It's been growing daily. They hope to keep adding to it until everyone returns in the fall, and then bury the box right here. Something for Nick's spirit. That's how Jim described it anyway, invoking the Cherokee belief that anyone who was murdered would be forced to wander the earth, unable to go to the next world until the killer accepted responsibility and was put to death."

"That's interesting, I mean the Cherokee belief."

"Yeah, it has something to do with restoring balance."

"I'm a bit surprised that anything other than Christianity holds much sway here, though."

"Actually, Indian culture is used more superstitiously than anything. You know, everyone around here sees ghosts, and that's a colorful way to explain them."

"A little presumptuous too, I'd say, considering how the Indians have been treated." I wonder about the professor's spirit, Sarah thought. If there is such a thing, is it here or in a place less congenial? She knelt down and examined the items more closely. A tarnished silver crucifix. Light and delicate, but burdened with meaning. Ironic, considering Manhoff's views. There, a photograph of a uniformed soldier. Troubled eyes. Full, grey beard. Who else but Robert E. Lee? And then, the books. *Origin of Species*, of course. And the other, a collection of poetry by Alexander Pope. Sarah thumbed through the pages, stopping briefly at an underlined passage. Fortunately, her glasses were in her pocket:

> *All Nature is but art, unknown to thee; All*
> *chance, direction, which thou canst not see;*
> *All discord, harmony not understood; All*

*partial evil, universal good. And, spite of
pride, in erring reason's spite, One truth is
clear: Whatever IS is RIGHT.*

"Whatever is is right." If that were true, slavery would still be thriving.
And women never would have gotten the vote."

"Nick did adore Pope." Lena said.

"I can see why."

"Actually, Pope was a great humanist. You've taken that verse out of
context."

"Maybe your colleague did as well."

Lena frowned. "Perhaps. But I'll tell you something, Sarah. I wouldn't
mind students regarding me as highly as Nick's did him."

"Seems more like idol worship to me."

"I'll grant you, it does seem a bit excessive. Despite everything,
though, he did have some ineffable quality. I can't exactly explain it."

Sarah rolled her eyes. "So did Svengali."

"My dear cousin, you're comparing someone you didn't even know to
a character in a book."

"All right, Rasputin. You're the intellectual, Lena. History's full of real
men who use their charm for ill. Besides, since when don't you trust novelists
to portray characters realistically?"

"*Some* novelists."

"Okay, some. But all kidding aside, Lena, if you'd spoken to Jacob,
you'd understand. You're right. I didn't know your colleague. But I know he
was disturbed. Misguided if not sociopathic. I told you, he lied about his own
reproductive capacity. What kind of person would do that?"

"You only have Jacob's word on that."

"It seems too weird to invent. I'm serious, Lena. Professor Manhoff
must have been something of a mesmerist. I think he even got to you a little.
You must have had some idea about his views. Just now, for example. You knew
he admired Pope. And you were working with him on a paper, remember?"

Lena nodded. "I know, but I'm telling you he just didn't show that side." She looked away for a moment. "It's a funny thing about that paper, though."

"What's that?"

"We had a minor disagreement over who came up with the thesis." Lena raised her stylishly thin, artfully penciled brow. "If truth be told, it was mine. I'd worked on the thing for months. He suggested Edith Wharton, but I came up with the idea."

"You mean about literature for literature sake, or something like that?"

"Uh huh."

"Why didn't you tell me that before?"

"Why should I? Besides, Nick did make my idea better."

"Oh?"

"Yes. He improved upon it. Rounded it out, spiced it up." She sighed. "It doesn't really matter now, anyway. Although I guess I could still speak on the topic, with a posthumous acknowledgment."

Sarah marveled at her cousin's nonchalance. "Lena, when did you decide to work on the paper together?"

"A short time after I told him about it. He was highly complimentary. It was Nick, in fact, who suggested I submit something to the MLA."

"Why didn't you do it on your own, then?"

"Well, he said that because I was new to the organization, I'd have better luck if the paper had his name on it."

"I see."

"You do?"

"Yes, he wanted to take credit for a good idea, even if it wasn't his."

"Oh, come on. Well, sort of, maybe. But certainly not intentionally."

"Lena, I swear, you're still under his spell."

"And you're letting your obsession with that Colored get in the way of reason."

"Lena!"

Lena reddened, but didn't retract the statement. They stared at each other for a few moments unblinking.

"Look, Sarah," Lena finally said, "Nick's dead. I'd just as soon leave it be."

Sarah squeezed her hand. "All right," she said. In any case, it wasn't worth arguing about. Lena hoped this little visit would make Sarah more sympathetic to the professor, but it had not. That Lena, sharp as a tack, was still defending him, that she wanted Sarah to do the same, revealed the force—and the danger—of his personality. But murder? No, Sarah thought, checking herself again. He didn't deserve that.

Lena smiled. "Let's go. You look awful."

"Thanks."

"You're welcome."

"Let me just take another quick peek at these things." Sarah knelt down again and ran her eyes over the contents. Tokens offered to a favored god. She fingered the crucifix and picked up Origin of Species with her other hand. Darwin and Jesus held in the balance. She replaced them and examined the remaining items: a golf ball, a toy boat—did he like to sail or play in the bath?—and an empty bottle. An excellent sketch of an iris, the Tennessee state flower. Probably Eric's work. Then that rebel flag, the Southern Cross as they call it, a sight she was almost becoming used to. She glanced back at the bottle. Hmm. A bottle is a bottle, but that shape was somehow familiar. She reached for her glasses and raised it to the light. The label. Uh huh. She thought so. Authentic Chattahoochee River Water. Identical. How odd. But Jim didn't take it. No one did. She was sure, they left it there. "Lena, do you have any idea what this is?"

Lena read the label. Her eyes were still good. She shook her head. "Nope."

"Hmm. Then, I guess you don't know which of the students contributed it."

"No, I don't, but I'm sure we can find out. Why?"

Sarah sighed. "Don't you remember? I saw one just like it in the caves."

"Oh yeah, that's right. Paul said it was a cure for something. Probably from a hot springs. I think Nick frequented the baths."

"It says river water."

"What are you thinking?"

"Nothing. Actually, nothing at all." She was telling the truth. What was there to think? "Only if it's a cure, I could have used some."

Lena laughed. "Poor thing." She felt Sarah's head. "You're burning up."

Sarah returned the gesture. "You are too. It's hot out here!"

They laughed and turned to leave, putting Professor Manhoff, Jacob and all the rest on hold. Their bond was too strong, too important to let a disagreement over this or any other matter do it permanent harm. For most of the walk back, they in fact left the topic entirely, talking instead of things upon which they were in total accord: their regret over having never met their grandparents, their concern over Sarah's brother Harry's continued lack of employment, their disgust at Uncle Joe's lechery. "Eighteen Penny Joe," as Lena's mother called him, a mocking, inside reference to his private parts. The precise meaning of the term neither Sarah nor Lena ever wanted to know, but they were grateful that at least they'd only been victims of his wandering hands.

In the intimacy of the moment, Sarah also finally revealed the details of her night with Mitchell, to which Lena responded initially with annoyance for not having been told before but ultimately with joyous approval. Lena would definitely have to meet this man. Perhaps a foursome. With her and Paul. "Could you imagine," she said, "how much fun we'd have? Niagara Falls, New England, maybe even a trip to Europe."

"Not so fast," Sarah said.

"Okay, Atlantic City."

Had Sarah the energy, she would have reminded Lena of Paul's age and that Sarah's one night with Mitchell did not a relationship make—her own disappointment over not having spoken to him for twenty-four hours notwithstanding. But that would have to wait, because by the time they reached the house, she was ready to collapse. And it wasn't just the heat. The thermometer Nan reluctantly lent her read one hundred and three.

➻ 27

SARAH SPENT THE NEXT SEVENTY-TWO HOURS IN BED, her fever rising and falling to several more chapters of *Uncle Tom's Cabin*. On the first day, she read of the horrors of the slave trade, on the second, the compassion of the Quakers, and on the third of Tom's new home with the good-hearted St. Clares. She felt particular empathy for the sickly, young Eva St. Clare, whose condition worsened as Sarah's temperature spiked. Fortunately, however, life didn't imitate art. On day four, Sarah was back on her feet, but in the chapter where she left off, unambiguously titled "Death," sadly, the little girl passed away.

At times, a minor illness could be a relief. Once the acute stage passed, the subsequent dulling of the senses offered a welcome respite to the sharper edges of daily existence. For Sarah, this had been one of those times. No vague protracted malaise. No headache of unspecified origin. This was a garden-variety virus from which she would soon recover. Tangible, concrete, with a predetermined beginning and end. She gave in to the experience. To the muted tones and muffled sounds, the blurred, yellowish cast of the room, to each object melting into the other as she drifted in and out of sleep. She almost enjoyed the fact that everything, even Lena running in and out to check on her, appeared in slow motion.

In reality, however, a number of things occurred during that period that made Sarah wish she had been more actively in the world. First, Mitchell had called to say he was back in Toledo. Lena took the message, she said, because Sarah was sleeping. Thoughtful perhaps, but Sarah was disappointed. She should have been awakened. Lena claimed she was only looking out for her welfare, but Sarah suspected her mischievous little cousin actually had relished the opportunity of a one-on-one. God only knew the full extent of their conversation.

Nevertheless, Sarah should have been happy for Mitchell. The *Blade* had given him a new assignment about which, Lena said, he seemed very excited: a feature story on the continued appeals in the Sacco-Vanzetti case. Nicola Sacco and Bartolomeo Vanzetti, found guilty in 1920 of killing the paymaster and guard of a shoe factory in Massachusetts. Also of stealing a good deal of money. But the case became a real *cause célèbre*. Sarah, along with other Progressives hoping for a new trial, wondered. Were they guilty because of what they'd done or who they were: Italian immigrants and self-proclaimed anarchists who rubbed the Republican judge the wrong way, not to mention the Nativists who'd been calling for their death since before the verdict was announced. Progressive himself on most matters, Mitchell no doubt would try to get to the bottom of the appeals, which so far had been denied.

How times had changed. For a while, Mitchell had been *persona non grata* at the *Blade,* fired for refusing to tow the party line. Now, after covering an event for which any of his colleagues would have given their right arm, the paper had handed him another juicy plum. His work on Scopes must have been impressive. So, why wasn't she pleased? The trial was over; he had another assignment. Of course, he had to get back. She let out a little laugh. Why? She knew why. Deep down, not even that deep, she knew. She'd been hoping he'd come to Edenville. Change his schedule. Surprise her. She cringed, nearly gagged at the truth. Did she really desire that kind of romantic silliness? Yes, she actually thought she might.

Mitchell was gone, however, and she already felt herself coming down to earth. Phoning him now was out of the question. He would be busy, probably getting ready to leave town again. Sarah could read his remaining views of the trial in the back issues of the paper, and as for her lingering bit of laryngitis, well, Mitchell already asked Lena to apologize for spreading his germs. No, she would not call. Of course, nothing prevented them from seeing each other when she returned. But unique circumstances had brought them together. A confluence of forces creating a singular opportunity. No expectations. No obligations. Blessed anonymity. Here, in the cradle of slavery, they'd been free to explore. There, he had his life and she had hers.

And then, Jacob. Not that she could have done anything about it anyway, but it was nevertheless disconcerting to discover how swiftly things had progressed in her absence. Arrested with no bail, indicted on murder charges, jury selection underway, all over the past few days. Mencken may have known the Scopes verdict long before it was read, but he never could have anticipated the chain of events Sarah's meeting with him had set into motion. Naturally, as a small town with almost no serious crime, Edenville would seek to solve this case as soon as possible. But the speed with which the process had unfolded only increased her fear that the public's need for a suspect might very well trump any semblance of justice, especially since that suspect was black. Officer Perry had a job to do, and had done it. But to what end? With what consequences? Surely he hadn't exhausted all other possibilities. Faculty, staff, students. The summer holiday provided such a convenient escape. As he said, however, motive was another matter. Officer Perry may have been overly eager, but he wasn't stupid. Motive was why Jacob was in prison, that and the additional little factor of an eyewitness.

The *Edenville Times*, which Sarah read while letting her freshly washed hair dry enough to pin it up, listed the prosecutor, Henry Nelson, as "tough on crime." Tough on crime, a rallying cry for the conservatives. Not that she wasn't for it in theory. Who in their right mind wouldn't be? But in her experience, that term was often a euphemism for employing whatever means possible, legal or otherwise, to put defendants away; defendants, as in Sacco-Vanzetti, presumed guilty rather than innocent.

The accompanying picture showed the man to be about fifty, with a long narrow face, thick handlebar mustache and a tight-lipped smile. His look was one of self-assurance verging on cockiness, although, admittedly, her assessment may have been influenced by the paper's claim that he had not lost a case in ten years. On the opposite page, the court-appointed defense attorney, William Callahan, appeared more tentative. Younger, softer, with round searching eyes. A local man who had never defended a murder case. As for the judge, he was identified by name only, Cyrus "Whistler" Griffin. Sarah later learned that was because the town apparently knew everything about him they needed to know, including that he had a nervous habit of puckering his lips whistle fashion in-between trial witnesses. An Edenville institution, he'd presided over the criminal court for twenty-five years.

To top things off, the memorial service for Professor Manhoff had been moved up to this very afternoon. "Why?" Sarah asked Lena, by this point feeling a bit like Rip Van Winkle. Because of the arrest, Lena explained. Everyone was now riveted on that development and soon would be fixated on the trial. A few of the faculty, including Lena herself, might be called to testify. "Everyone agreed," Lena said, employing a metaphor befitting her profession, "it was time to close the book on Nick's death and allow the story of his murder to be told." Sarah couldn't agree more. The event, scheduled for two o'clock, would be simpler, more extemporaneous than originally planned as well. No formal eulogies. The men had relented, maybe even gratefully. Anyone who wished would be allowed to speak, including the students whom the faculty felt would benefit from this last, official farewell. Indeed, if not for the students, they might have canceled the event altogether. That, and the fact that Phyllis and Samantha had baked enough bread to feed an army.

Sarah felt her hair. Still damp, but it would have to do. Without even glancing in the mirror, she clipped it into place and grabbed her purse. It was now eleven a.m. She told Lena she would attend the memorial, but only after she paid Jacob a call, something that even back in her feverish state she knew was the right thing to do. Whatever his ultimate fate, she was in part responsible. Whatever the truth, at this moment he was suffering. If he turned out to be guilty, so be it. It wouldn't be the first time she'd consoled a murderer. If he were innocent, he deserved her support. Either way, she owed him a visit.

⇢ 28

MITCHELL BEGAN REPACKING THE CLOTHES that only yesterday he'd removed from his functional—the rope used to close it notwithstanding—leather suitcase. Christ, how he hated to pack. At least he'd had time to have his summer pants cleaned. Massachusetts might not be as hot as Tennessee, but the humidity at this time of year could be just as brutal. These should suffice, he thought. No one needed any more than two shirts and one pair of pants. Then again, didn't Mark Twain say something about the changeability of New England weather? Perhaps he'd throw in a sweater for good measure.

Ordinarily, Mitchell would be granted a few days off after an assignment of Scopes' magnitude. And in fact, his boss had given him an option: stay home for a week or leave for Boston in the morning. Whether this was a sign of the man's renewed appreciation of him or a test of Mitchell's commitment to the paper he wasn't sure. Either way, it wasn't a hard decision. The Sacco-Vanzetti case had interested him from the start, and the ruling in this latest appeal, scheduled for the day after tomorrow, was the most anticipated to date. Elizabeth Gurlye Flynn, founder of the Workers' Defense Union, raised twenty-five thousand dollars in only two days to pay the advance legal fee of Harvard Law School lecturer and Massachusetts insider William Thompson. Fred Moore, their initial flamboyant labor lawyer from California, had been ineffective.

Mitchell would have to do some further research for the story, but he already knew the basic fact: that the guilty verdict was based on circumstantial evidence. First, Sacco and Vanzetti owned guns similar in gauge to the one used in the crime. Second, eyewitnesses thought the murderers looked like Italians, and, of course, third, the men were anarchists, thus opposed to all forms of government, including the one that had found them guilty. As a reporter, Mitchell was obligated to keep his own views in check. But as with Scopes, that didn't mean they wouldn't occasionally surface in his writing. Especially when he felt as strongly as he did in this case. So much scapegoating of foreigners, communists and radicals had occurred over the past few years that he tended to look cynically on arrests of this sort. He wasn't alone. America was supposed to be the land of the free, but its Nativist bigotry and growing intolerance for dissent was making people wary, even those who normally held the country in high esteem.

On the other hand, these fellows might very well have committed the crime. Their alibis were weak, and anarchists were not opposed to violence. But though the judge insisted they be tried on the murder only—forbidding any reference in court to their radical politics—anyone who read the papers was well aware of their background. And that could tip the balance. Even the most well-meaning individual might have been persuaded to vote for conviction, succumbing to the "if it looks like a duck" mentality.

From what Mitchell learned from Lena yesterday, a similar situation might be brewing in Edenville. Jacob Lee, she announced, after refusing to let Mitchell speak to Sarah, had been arrested for the murder of Nicholas Manhoff. An amazing conclusion to what started out in Dayton as a wild— albeit highly pleasurable—monkey chase. Unlike Sacco-Vanzetti, however, the police had a reliable eyewitness. But Lena said that Sarah still had her doubts about whether the arrest was not, at least in part, racially motivated, which came as no surprise to Mitchell. And at that point, Sarah, whose illness Lena didn't hesitate to blame on him, didn't even yet know that the trial would begin almost immediately. When she found out, she would probably ask herself the same question he'd asked of Sacco-Vanzetti: would the jury judge Jacob on what he'd done or who he was? Yes, from what Lena said, that would be the first thing on Sarah's mind as soon as she was well enough to think.

Mitchell cinched the rope and lifted his suitcase to test its strength. Still okay. Then he checked himself in the mirror. Christ, whose face was that anyway? It seemed only yesterday he'd noticed a few wrinkles on his forehead.

Now they were everywhere, a map of intertwining lines and grooves. And what was that bit of extra skin under his chin? An inch at least. He wasn't a vain man, but he wasn't immune to the periodic, shocking realization of aging either. At least he had hair. Too much, even. His thick, overgrown salt and pepper locks had a mind of their own. But then, Sarah liked them. She told him so that night. That night. He smiled and started for the door. Perhaps he wasn't so old after all.

❧ ❧ ❧

"Reed's," Mitchell told the driver. "Reed's Chop House, across from Union Station." The restaurant was a popular haunt with newsmen, and prior to Volstead, Toledo's favorite watering hole. Mitchell himself had spent several long nights there before going on the wagon. At any rate, it was a convenient place to meet O'Brien, who had invited him to an early lunch. The judge was eager to hear his take on Scopes, and when he learned Mitchell was covering the Sacco-Vanzetti appeals, insisted that they get together before he left.

Strange. During the years Mitchell had reported on O'Brien, they'd never had a real conversation. But all that changed last summer, ironically when the reporting came to a screeching halt. Since then they'd talked often, were becoming friends. All because of Sarah. Like everything else lately where Mitchell was concerned. Had he spoken to her yesterday, he would have told her so, confessed that she was constantly in his thoughts. But Lena wouldn't hear of it. What a pert little thing her cousin was. Nosy too, although it gave Mitchell no small amount of satisfaction to know that Sarah had spoken of him to her.

Mitchell pushed open the restaurant's heavy glass doors. Before they closed behind him, he saw O'Brien's stocky frame flagging him down.

"Mitch, Mitch. Hello, my boy. Welcome home."

"Hello, Judge," Mitchell said, returning the man's strong grasp. "You look well. Very well." It was the truth. Ever since O'Brien had left the hospital, he seemed to be growing younger, as if the lifting of that burden he'd been carrying around was gradually taking him back to the day before it all started. Sixty years old, but so vital. His grey-blue eyes had always been striking, but now they shone, even in the dimly lit room. His thinning white hair seemed thicker. "Smoke?" he asked, opening a gold cigarette case.

"No thanks. I'm trying to quit."

"Ah, good man. I limit it to two a day myself, and a pipe, of course. So how much time do we have?"

"My train leaves at noon, so about an hour."

"Fine. I already ordered for us. A couple of those crab salads. You like that dish as I recall."

"Yes, I do. You've got quite a memory. It must have been six months ago when we last were here together."

"Seven, and I was still recuperating."

"I'll be careful then of what I say today. So, how are the Hens doing? I haven't had time to follow."

O'Brien frowned and threw a copy of the *Blade* on the table. "See for yourself. Your own paper tells the sad tale. But let's not talk about that right now, not on an empty stomach."

"Ha! All right."

"Actually, Mitch, I brought the paper just in case you hadn't seen some of the letters on Scopes. Your coverage really got people thinking. Look at this one," he said, pointing to the first on the page. Mitchell hadn't yet seen the Opinion section today, but there had been a steady stream of letters since the trial began. He moved the paper closer to the lamp and read:

> *If the eighteenth amendment cannot be isolated by the states, why should the first one be made null and void by the state of Tennessee? We must remember that all the opposition to evolution comes from religious sources. The question of its truth or falsity is no longer an open question among scientists. The constitution in article six provides for religious liberty, but our fathers thought it did not do so with sufficient definiteness, hence*

the first amendment to make it irrefragable.
After doing this, is it reasonable to suppose
they intended that the states should establish
religion? The Supreme Court, in my opinion,
would undoubtedly take this view of it. Then
the bigotry and malice of the Tennessee law.
It provides for fine and imprisonment for any
teacher who teaches evolution in any public
institution of learning, while it is no crime to
teach it elsewhere. Then, while a legislature
can make provisions for education and, in
a general way, decide what branches shall
be taught, no legislature can decide upon
the disputed points or a study. This must be
done by experts. The only way to handle false
teaching is through the fullest and freest liberty
of thought and discussion. If the teaching
of evolution is false, and that of Genesis is
true, are not religious people willing to leave
the matter to future investigations? If they
have any confidence in their cause, they are.
Scientists always have been.
—*Frank Steiner*

"I'm flattered if this is really a response to my work," he said. "But I have a feeling this Steiner fellow doesn't need me to make him think. He's right about the founders, isn't he?"

"Absolutely. You know, there isn't one reference to God in the Constitution. Not one. The founders knew what they were doing. They were believers, mind you, of a sort. But it was precisely to protect religion—religious liberty—that they created a secular state."

"Frank Steiner," Mitchell said. "Do you know him?"

"No, but that's what makes this all the more promising. There's an untapped resource out there. As you said, people are thinking. You know, Mitch, I'm a religious man too, but it's a sorry state of affairs when doctrine supplants the real value of faith. Love, tolerance and hope. That's what God means to me. That's what it's all about as far as I'm concerned. I'm not going to squabble over Adam and Eve in the face of geological evidence to the contrary. But I'll defend my faith in a loving God 'til my dying breath."

"We need more of your kind in the world, Judge."

"Can I bring you anything else?" the waiter asked, as he delivered the food.

"Mitch?"

"No, thanks."

"No, that will be all. Just charge it to my account."

"Now, Judge . . ."

"Never mind. I invited you." O'Brien flicked his ashes and stared at the ashtray. "So, what was your take on the trial? How'd it feel to be there?"

"Hot. Very hot."

O'Brien smiled.

"Seriously, it was a strange mixture. On one level, utterly absurd. A circus, you know, I wrote about that part of it, the balloons, the monkeys . . . animal and human. But that was surface stuff. Beneath, I felt something powerful at work. What started out as a gimmick, a way to bring money to a dying town, ended up provoking the entire world to think about themselves in the most basic way. Beneath all the mockery and cartoons, people were asking: who are we and where did we come from?"

O'Brien looked at Mitchell with a rapt expression. "It was a rare experience, then."

"Yes, I'd say it was." In more ways than one, he thought.

O'Brien picked up the Opinion page again and scanned the letters. "Ah, listen to this."

Mitchell dipped a piece of crab into the mayonnaise dressing and obeyed.

"Science is classified knowledge. It includes only those facts that have been proved to be true. It therefore follows that there can be no conflict between science and any intelligent religion. If any religion is not intelligent, it is not worth saving and cannot be saved. Truth is eternal and will prevail.

—O.A. Hammand."

"Interesting. Do you consider Christianity to be an intelligent religion, Judge?"

"Yes, when it uses its power intelligently, to help the poor, the sick, the disabled. When it encourages the God-given mind to grow. When it spreads love."

"Not like this, I take it." They leaned in toward the center of the table while Mitchell held the paper.

> *The unconverted church members who believe in the infidel theory of evolution must feel very proud over the kind of company they find themselves associated within the Dayton trial. The champion of the cause is Clarence Darrow, an avowed agnostic, who does not believe the Bible, who is a free thinker and a free lover, who says marriage is an unnecessary institution, and who for money secures Loeb and Leopold immunity from the death penalty they deserved. He objects to prayer in opening court and ridicules all who believe God's word and seek to obey it. The old adage "birds of a feather flock together" fits this motley crew of Unitarians, agnostics, and false prophets.*
> *—John M. Dunkerton*

O'Brien raised his eyes. "No, not like that."

Mitchell said: "Agnostics are false prophets. Science is an infidel. One would think we're back in the Dark Ages. And this reference to Loeb and Leopold. String 'em up, no matter what."

"Don't get me started on the death penalty. You know I'm against it."

"These are hard views to fight, though."

O'Brien nodded. "I know. But we've got to keep trying." He clasped his squat fingers together and smirked. "Clarence, a free lover. Well, well. I'll have to talk to him about that. Oh yeah. You said on the phone that he gave you an interview. How is the old boy?"

"Brilliant."

"Pretty impressive, eh? He and I agree on almost everything, you know, except he thinks because I'm Catholic I can't truly be a Progressive. What he doesn't realize, in fact what probably most of the folks who were in that courthouse don't realize either, is that Jesus was more progressive than Darrow himself."

Mitchell nodded. "You're right, or so I've heard. You know, I'm not a follower myself. But then again, that's what Bryan believes, too. In fact, that's where things get pretty muddy, isn't it? For all his fury against Darwin, Bryan's been loyal to the downtrodden. He fears for their welfare, views natural selection as their enemy."

"Yes, yes. Social Darwinism. Yes, we have to stay vigilant against it. But you don't throw the baby out with the bath water. Bryan lets doctrine interfere with his reason. But Mitch," O'Brien said conspiratorially, "now let's talk about what's really important. How is Sarah, anyway?"

Mitchell poked at another piece of crab and shifted in his chair. "Sarah. Yes, well I already told you about the murder and all. Unbelievable. The Mencken business, everything. It's been quite an experience for her, I'd say. I'm sure she'll tell you all about it when she returns."

"I hope she's not in over her head. You know better than anyone. I put her through hell last year. This holiday was a meager attempt to thank her for all she did. It doesn't sound as if she's having much fun."

"Oh, I don't know . . ."

O'Brien squinted at Mitchell, then raised and lowered his bushy, untamed eyebrows mischievously. "I see."

"Don't jump to conclusions."

O'Brien reached over and patted his arm. "I won't, but I can't think of anyone who'd be better for her."

Mitchell smiled. "Thanks. That means a lot to me, Judge. But you know Sarah, she's got a mind of her own."

"Do I ever. Too bad we can't get Darrow for her case. Her case. Listen to me. She'll make it her case all right. Sounds as if that young man could use a good lawyer."

Darrow, Mitchell thought. If he knew Sarah was involved he'd be in Edenville in a shot. Free lover. Huh. "Darrow would have been good for Sacco-Vanzetti too," he said. "It's unfortunate he wasn't their attorney."

"I wish I'd been the judge on that case, myself. Not that I'm certain they're innocent, but that so-called eyewitness—saying the suspects looked Italian. Come on. How many people fit that description. Oh, that reminds me of what I wanted to ask you. Take good notes on the judge, will you? Tell me if there's any funny business. I'm trying to keep tabs on what's going on in the courts, this growing conservatism. Pretty scary stuff. I'd like to write a piece on it for the *Judicial Review*."

"You should start with Judge Raulston."

"You're right. We'll have to talk more about him, too."

Mitchell checked his watch. "Shit, oh, pardon me Judge, but I've got to get going. You know, I haven't even asked how your family's doing."

"Oh, now there's a question. Wonderful," O'Brien beamed. "Absolutely wonderful. Margaret will be two, you know. Smart as a whip, and beautiful if I do say so myself."

"Time flies."

O'Brien winked. "Amen."

"Well, see you later, Judge. Thanks again for lunch."

"You're welcome. Next time it's on you."

"It's a deal," Mitchell said, as he raced out, wondering about the undoubtedly hidden costs of love that is offered for free.

⇝ 29

Officer Perry grimaced when Sarah appeared at the station unannounced. "I don't like it," he said. "The boy's lawyer should be notified."

"Then notify him," she commanded, darting him a look that indicated she would not be deterred.

"Ya watch how you talk there, ma'am. You're still in the presence of the law, ya know."

Sarah nodded.

"You wait here while I give the counselor a call."

When he returned, he looked defeated. "All right," he said begrudgingly. "Ten minutes. You've got ten minutes."

I should have as long as I damn well please, Sarah thought, but held her tongue.

The jail was like that in other small towns. Three cramped cells—two of which were unoccupied—each with a tiny barred window, washbasin, and pail. Suffocating in this heat, despite the sputtering overhead fan. Jacob lay on a sheetless cot, his elbows bent, fingers laced behind his head, staring at the ceiling. He didn't budge when Sarah approached. She watched him for a moment then moved in closer. "Jacob."

No reply.

"Jacob, I only have a short time. Please, may I speak to you?"

"Speak," he said, still motionless.

"I just wanted to say, that if there's anything I can do . . ."

He spun his head toward her. "You've done enough, haven't you?"

"I told you. I didn't know."

He rolled over and shot up. "And I told you. It doesn't matter. I'm here. It's over."

"Not if you didn't do it."

"Are you still singing that tune? I thought you had some brains."

"Truth is power," she said, only half believing it. "What is your attorney like?"

"White."

"That's not necessarily bad."

"What do you want, anyway?" he asked, pacing. "Why are you here? To relieve your conscience? There's nothing you can do, I tell you."

Sarah understood his anger, and at least he was talking. "Please," she said.

"What?"

"Do you know anything at all about the eyewitness?"

"No, nothing."

"How could he describe you so accurately, then?"

"Didn't you know, we all look alike?"

Sarah lowered her eyes. "But your height and weight, he got them right, even the set of your eyes," she said. "How would he know that? Are you sure you weren't in the woods that day, coincidentally?"

Jacob stared at her with knitted brows, then laughed cynically. "You're a breath away from believing I killed him, aren't you? Maybe less. Even so, I'll tell you straight. No, I was not in the woods."

Sarah stared back as he held her gaze. No side-glance. No blinking. No squirming.

"I did not kill Professor Manhoff," he repeated. "But you need not waste one more second trying to convince yourself otherwise. They've got their man, either way. It would be a lot easier if you'd just join them. A sprinkle of the Chattahoochee, that's what you need."

Sarah jolted. "What? What's that you said?"

"Chattahoochee River water, nectar of the bigots."

"Please, really, I don't know what you mean."

"The KKK. They use water from the Chattahoochee River to baptize new members. One drop and you'll forget all about me."

Sarah leaned against the cell bars. The KKK? Her thoughts raced. The cave, the box.

"Jacob, do they bottle the water? Transport it in little glass bottles?"

"Bottles? Maybe. Don't know exactly. "

"Why do they use that water?"

"What do you care?"

"Please!"

"From what I've heard, their leader, the Grand Dragon, Wizard, or whatever he's called, lived near the river. That makes it sacred, their version of Lourdes. Or maybe they have some other perverted reason. Why, have you already been invited to join?"

"I doubt whether I would. You might remember, I'm on their list of undesirables too."

He looked at her and nodded slowly. "So?"

Sarah just shook her head.

"See here, I know you mean well. But I'm tired, now," Jacob said. He walked back to his cot and resumed his former position.

"The offer stands," Sarah said. "If there is anything I can do."

He twisted his head toward her again. "There is one thing."

"Yes?"

"The trial starts next week. Find a way to explain my sentence to my mother. Down here, it'll be death by hanging," he said, and turned to the wall.

✈ ✈ ✈

The memorial was winding down by the time Sarah arrived. She didn't plan it that way, but she was not disappointed. As far as she was concerned, these farewell tributes had long since exceeded their time and purpose.

Chattahoochee River Water. On the way back from the jail, images of that mysterious potion dominated her thoughts. If only Mother Nature knew to what sinister purpose her life-giving force had been put. Chattahoochee River Water. Once, a curiosity. Twice a coincidence. Three times, an omen?

Of what? Sarah had no answer, and yet she wondered. The bottle she'd found in the cave; how it got there and who left it she didn't know. But what about the one in the chest, there among the things the professor had valued. Was it possible that Professor Manhoff himself belonged to the Invisible Empire? Considering what Sarah had learned of him, she wouldn't be surprised. Ironically, the Klan's brand of Christianity would perfectly complement his kind of Darwinism: perpendicular paths to the common goal of white supremacy. In Toledo, the group had been quite successful at recruiting seemingly respectable citizens precisely for this reason. But it was also a secret society. Members' identities were usually highly protected. Who would have known him well enough to possess such information? Another member? Surely, none of the students. Then again, children much younger than they had marched in that parade. But even if it were one of the students, what could that possibly have to do with the murder?

Probably nothing. Still, the improbable was all Sarah had to work with in her efforts to discover the truth, something she was now determined to do. Jacob had misjudged her. Despite the eyewitness, she was closer to believing in his innocence than ever. Close enough at least to do some further investigating on her own. Mitchell had a new assignment, and now so did she, even if it was self-appointed. For this, she would not request a badge.

Continuing toward the chapel, she had passed a vacant, hollow-cheeked beggar and immediately thought of Tillie. All things happen for a reason, she could hear her sister say. Sarah usually took objection to that claim, reminding her of all the senseless tragedies in the world. What did this poor soul, for instance, do to deserve his fate? Or the death of a child. If ever there were a case for the indifference of nature, the randomness of evolution, it was that unthinkable event. In this instance, however, she had to agree. Jacob's request to explain his sentence to his mother had forced Sarah to follow her destiny once and for all. Until now, she'd only been teasing herself, tinkering with a response. The easy part was going to Dayton. Now came the challenge: if it existed, finding the evidence that would reunite mother and son and return Jacob to the productive life for which he was certainly intended. Explain his hanging? Not if there wasn't one. Not if Sarah could help it.

Sarah caught Lena's glance as she entered the chapel and headed over to where she was seated among the other faculty. Despite the early planning, the event felt like an afterthought: hand-written programs, a few scattered flowers, a Victrola playing "Amazing Grace" to a group of about thirty.

Leaning on an easel in the front of the room was the painting of Nicholas Manhoff, staring back with that same inscrutable expression. At a nearby podium, Professor Lovell thanked his dead colleague for helping him get published, and then turned the floor over to Professor Byeerst who could think of nothing further to say. Jim and the twins followed, each emotionally lamenting his passing.

Then Penny rose to speak. Despite being almost too stylishly clad in a black, slinky chemise, the girl seemed genuinely distraught, choking up before she had even begun. Begging forgiveness, she reached in her purse for a handkerchief. "I'm Penelope Caldwell," she managed to get out again, but couldn't go on. Kathryn, vigilantly watching out for her friend, helped Penny back to her chair and then, planning to speak next anyway, returned to the podium with a notebook in her hand. Her wheat hair was softly pinned up, her light blue eyes glistening with tears. She wore a black dress as well, but in typical contrasting fashion, it was plainer than Penny's and hung loosely on her boyish build. Before beginning, she glanced up at Jim, who nodded back encouragingly.

"I know the faculty agreed to forego prepared speeches," she said, "but as a student, I'd like to be permitted to recite a short story in honor of Professor Manhoff." She smiled a little. "A very short, true story." No one objected, so she continued. "First, I'll read a passage which Professor Manhoff quoted the last day of spring term. It should not surprise any of you to learn that it is from Darwin's *The Origin of Species*: 'As many more individuals of each species are born than can possibly survive; and as, consequently, there is a frequently recurring struggle for existence, it follows that any being, if it vary however slightly in any manner profitable to itself, under the complex and sometimes varying conditions of life, will have a better chance of surviving, and thus be naturally selected.'

"You might ask, why this passage? Well, we all know Professor

Manhoff held Darwin's work in high esteem. But we also know he always tried to put the good of the whole ahead of his own desires."

Sarah observed several nodding heads, including Lena's.

"I'm sure many of you recall, for example, when the professor canceled a long-awaited trip to Germany to help the victims of the hurricane in Charleston."

Again, nodding.

"You might also remember the article in the *Charleston Daily* accusing him of studying rather than actually helping their town."

This time the nodding seemed somewhat reluctant.

"Remember? They claimed that he hadn't lifted a finger, that he was really only there to observe the struggle for existence, following a natural disaster. Now, on the surface, of course, this might seem selfish. But as we all know, as we students have been taught, studying with a purpose is just as important as fixing a fence. The results are just not as immediate."

Everyone in the room seemed to breathe a sigh of relief. Sarah herself was suspicious, but was impressed with Kathryn's articulate delivery.

"If it appeared Professor Manhoff was cruel, that his views were rigid, it was only that, unlike most people, he lived his philosophy." She closed her notebook. "Now, for my tale. Though true, it's a fable of sorts, one that relates back to the quote. When I was a young child, my parents, God rest their souls, had a full-bred show dog. A female, from fine stock, that they mated with an equally fine male. The result was a litter of adorable, perfectly formed puppies. All except one, that is, an undersized female with an abnormally large head. Water on the brain, the veterinarian said. The poor thing couldn't walk; its head was so heavy. The mother tried everything possible to restore her, but to no avail, and the puppy was constantly hungry. So one day, she simply laid on top it, softly, quietly, until it stopped breathing. Somehow she knew. This deformed creature was not, as Darwin said, 'profitable to itself.' So the mother took it out of its misery. She did it for the puppy and the good of the litter. If you knew Professor Manhoff, you knew that he was like the mother. Whatever he did, he did for the greater good." Now Kathryn choked up herself, left the podium and hurried over to Jim.

Lena turned to Sarah. "A little schmaltzy, but heartfelt."

"It's not the style that bothers me," Sarah said. "It's the message: kill the weak to protect the strong." There was a pattern here, she thought. Manhoff pressuring Jacob to withdraw his application, employing that example of the impaired cub. For God's sake, even removing himself from the genetic pool. These were the professor's ideas all right.

"I think you're extrapolating a bit. Have you read *A Modest Proposal?*"

"As a matter of fact I have. I'm not as illiterate as you think."

"Well, do you think Swift was really promoting eating children in that piece?"

"Of course not. But as I recall, that was satire. This is a true story Kathryn used to make a point about Professor Manhoff. And we know where she got her material."

"You're extrapolating again."

"Maybe, but that doesn't mean I'm wrong."

❧ ❧ ❧

When the tributes were done, Samantha and Phyllis announced that refreshments were ready in the conference room. Sarah always thought it strange that eating was so central to the mourning ritual. Even the most tragic of deaths seemed to spark everyone's appetite. And by the ravenous expressions, today was no exception. Sarah herself felt hungry for the first time in days.

The sandwiches were crustless and plain by Tillie's standards, but attractively displayed on a rectangular silver platter. Had her sister been here, she would have rolled her eyes at the limp cucumbers and wondered why they'd gone to all the trouble of baking the bread when they cut half of it off. Sarah would have preferred the crust too, for that matter, but that didn't stop her from gobbling a third ham and cheese. Afterward, she wiped her mouth, tossed out her napkin, and wandered over to the group of students huddled near the punch bowl.

Kathryn and Jim greeted her together. "Hello, Miss Kaufman."

"Hello. How are you two holding up?"

"As well as can be expected," Kathryn said.

"That was a sad story you told, Kathryn, about your dog. Well-expressed, though."

"Kathryn wants to be a writer," Jim said, wrapping his arm around her.

"It was sad when it happened," Kathryn said, leaning into him. "But I really do understand it differently now. I mean it would still be sad, but, well, you know what I mean."

Sarah in fact would have liked to ask her exactly what she meant, but decided it was neither the time nor place. Besides, perhaps in time the brainwashing would wear off. "Yes, I think I do," she said.

"Miss Kaufman, have you met the others? This is Timothy and Bill. They were Professor Manhoff's students, too."

Sarah extended her hand to the plain, shy-looking boys. "Hello, I'm Sarah Kaufman, Miss Greenberg's cousin."

"Nice to meet you," they mumbled.

"They were on vacation," Jim said. "Just got back."

"Oh," Sarah said. "Terrible thing to come back to."

They both nodded.

"Terrible for all of us," Kathryn said as Penny walked up.

Penny sniffed and looked toward Sarah. Her sculpted face was red and puffy from crying. Color also had fanned out in patches over her long, graceful neck. She pushed her hair behind her left ear, which was small and delicate. "Professor Manhoff was to be my advisor," she said.

"Did you take many classes with him?" Sarah asked.

"Only two. But they were better than all the rest combined." She sniffed again. "If you'll excuse me." She started to walk away, but Sarah gently took hold of her arm.

"Please, could you wait one moment?"

The girl seemed reticent, but turned back.

"I have a question, for all of you actually. Jim, remember when we went to the caves, and I found that bottle?"

"Uh huh. Yep, I do."

"Do you remember the name on the label?"

"A river, wasn't it? The Chattahoochee?"

"Precisely."

"Chattahoochee River water. Does that strike a chord with anyone?"

"A bottle of water?" Emily said frowning, with a name of a river?"

They shook their heads.

"Why Miss Kaufman?" Jim said. "Why do you ask?"

"Well, as strange as it may seem, I saw an identical bottle of the stuff in that chest you placed out in the woods for the professor. Do any of you know anything about that?"

They looked puzzled and shook their heads again.

"Huh. I wonder how it got there," Sarah said, sounding more accusatory than she intended.

"Probably a prankster," Eric said. "There've been a few things in there that seem to have been a joke. The golf ball, for instance."

They all chuckled. "Yeah," Emily said, "Professor Manhoff hated the sport. What did he used to say? Oh yeah. 'It is impossible to imagine Goethe or Beethoven being good at billiards or golf.'"

Kathryn twisted her fine features into a question mark. "What's this all about, Miss Kaufman? You seemed concerned."

"I discovered what that water is used for."

"Oh?" Jim said. "What?"

Sarah glanced at each of them before speaking, her pause intentionally pregnant. "To initiate new members into the Ku Klux Klan." She waited for a reaction. When only mild surprise ensued, she repeated the statement.

"Really?" Jim finally said.

"Yes."

"Why?" Eric asked blandly. "Why would they use that particular water?"

Sarah repeated what Jacob had told her about the location of the river and then said: "I wonder if there might be any connection, you know. If the professor was somehow involved with the group."

They seemed even less surprised by this remark.

"What if he was?" Penny said, now meeting her gaze directly.

"Do you know something?" Sarah asked.

"No. But I wouldn't see anything wrong in it." Penny glanced at Kathryn, as if for approval, but didn't wait for a response. "Professor Manhoff had a right to join whatever group he pleased. What business is it of yours, anyway?"

"Penny!" Jim said.

"Well, she's not a cop, is she? She didn't know the professor. She's not even from here!" Penny's face now appeared bright scarlet against her light hair. She glared at Sarah.

Eric touched her arm. "She's just trying to help, Pen."

"It's all right," Sarah said, more curious than hurt. "I understand."

Kathryn winked at them knowingly. "Penny's nerves are just raw. I'll take her back to the dorm."

"Probably a good idea," Jim said.

Sarah watched with the others as the two girls walked away. "I didn't mean to upset her."

Jim nodded. "I know. But Miss Kaufman, why are you asking all these questions? You aren't still working with the police, are you?"

"No, no. I'm just interested is all. You never know how things, even the most seemingly unrelated things, might fit together."

"You mean regarding the murder?"

"Yes. The murder."

"There's a pretty strong case against that Negro. Do you have another theory? I know how you Progressives are," he said with a half-smile.

"Ha! And you Republicans are a bit too quick to accept things at face value. But no, I have no theory whatsoever. Still, Jim, your friend's response was odd, though, don't you think?"

"As Kathryn said, she's just raw. Overwhelmed."

"I mean about the KKK," Sarah said.

"The Klan? Oh, I don't know. Not really. It's not such a big deal down here. A lot of people don't think they're so bad."

"What about you Jim?"

"Me? I don't care for their tactics. But I think they serve a purpose."

"Really. What's that?"

He thought for a moment. "Well, in a way, they're helping to preserve the American family. You've got to admit, Miss Kaufman, there's some pretty perverted behavior out there. Speakeasies, free love, who knows what else? Our country is in moral decline. The Klan may be prejudiced, a bit extreme, but they are strong family people, strong moralists," he said without a trace of irony.

"And you?" she said to the twins and the others.

They all just shrugged.

"I see. Well, may I ask one more question?"

"Sure."

"Was Penny particularly close to the professor? I mean more than any of the others?"

"Not that I know of," Jim said. She was an English major, of course, and, as she said, he was to be her advisor. But I think she just admired him like the rest of us. She's always been a bit high strung, especially since her father's death."

"Ah. Well, I do apologize for upsetting her."

"There you are," Lena said, still munching on a sandwich. "I hope you're not corrupting these young minds."

Sarah sighed. "No, I don't think so." Unfortunately that appears to have been accomplished already, she thought to herself.

⇝ 30

THE NEXT FEW DAYS PASSED QUIETLY. A bit too quietly. Lena was now down with the flu, and the others in the house were showing early symptoms, including Nan, whom Sarah tried at all costs to avoid. No telling what might happen if the woman was forced to cancel her trip to Atlanta. Moreover, with everyone sick, Sarah was afraid she might be called upon to prepare the meals. That would surely delay, if not prevent, their recovery altogether. Fortunately, however, Nan never developed the full-blown virus, something she jokingly attributed to survival of the fittest. It was the first time Sarah had heard the woman laugh, and Sarah laughed along with her, especially when she said she felt well enough to cook. "Y'all didn't think I understood what y'all was talking about the other day, did ya?" she said, still smiling as she pushed open the kitchen door.

Obviously, Nan understood the concept perfectly, and used it with surprising wit. But for Professor Manhoff, Darwin's idea had been deadly serious, a code to live and indeed to die by. For most of the weekend, Sarah rocked on the front porch swing, thinking about the professor, Jacob, and what to do next. She considered humbling herself before Officer Perry, asking him to check that bottle of river water for fingerprints. But then what? If they found any, other than her own, what would that prove? As she told Jim, she had no theory. Just a vague inkling, something that easily could be construed as a flight of fancy, or worse, women's intuition.

But the KKK. Here, now, again. How could she not wonder? Anything involving them had a sinister potential. What if Manhoff did belong to the Klan and had for some reason enraged another member? Maybe he suggested something impure about the person's lineage, or revealed something of his own, as he had with Jacob. Or, perhaps someone discovered he was a member of the group and hated him for it, some volatile individual who felt it his duty to make him pay. A Negro, other than Jacob. A Catholic. A Jew. The possibilities were endless. How to pursue them without the backing of the law was another matter entirely, seemingly impossible in such a short time.

The students' acceptance, if not benevolence, toward the Klan was disturbing as well. Sarah couldn't get Penny out of her mind, her venomous tone, how she defended the group and any possible link the professor might have had to it. Jim's comment bothered her too, that he respected the Klan's efforts to preserve the family; the traditional family. What was that exactly? Certainly Sarah's living arrangement with her adult siblings wouldn't qualify. A subservient wife? Children ruled with an iron fist? People who only love their neighbors if they're white and their god Christian? How could an intelligent, congenial fellow like Jim view the world so narrowly? Sarah sighed. How, indeed. The same inexplicable way countless others did.

By Sunday night, Sarah had come no closer to a course of action. So when Lena came downstairs in her robe and asked her to play a game of gin, she agreed. Perhaps it would clear her head. Lena blew her nose, shuffled and dealt. Sarah picked up her cards. Two queens, two consecutive clubs and six miscellaneous hearts and spades. Not great. As Tillie would say, she'd have to make a hand. She fanned them out, waited for Lena to move and stared at them unseeing. She might try and talk to Jim again. Or some of the others, probe them a bit about the eyewitness. Perhaps he had a connection to the Klan.

"Sarah, your turn."

"What?"

"Your turn," Lena repeated.

"Oh, sorry."

Sarah picked up a card. A queen! Then, Lena drew and threw down the last of the regal old ladies. That was more like it. Four of a kind. If only Sarah's "investigation" could go as well . . . and as quickly. By Tuesday, that is, the first day of the trial. She rearranged her cards, raised her eyes and tried to read Lena's mind. Lena drew again, glanced at her with a sly, half-smile, then laid down her cards. "Gin."

Sarah frowned. "Deal another," she said.

As Lena gathered the cards, Sarah decided this would have to be the last game. She had to speak with the students again tonight. That's all there was to it. She needed to know more about that witness. She'd go to their rooms, whether they liked it or not. A man's life was at stake.

A loud, insistent knock interrupted Lena in the middle of a masterful shuffle. Nan marched to the door as if preparing for battle. The man she eventually let in hardly looked her match, though. Bald, overweight and several inches shorter than she, he indeed seemed quite powerless in his dangerously tight seersucker suit. However, in his chubby hand was a paper that Sarah instantly recognized, one that granted him a unique, fearful authority. "Miss Greenberg?" His voice was smooth as silk.

"Yes, I'm Lena Greenberg."

"Here you are ma'am."

"You're being called to testify," Sarah said.

Lena blanched. "Shit."

"Don't worry. You knew this might happen," Sarah said. "Like I told you before, you'll probably just serve as a character witness. I'll help you pre . . ."

"Miss Kaufman? It is Miss Sarah Kaufman, isn't it," the man said with a glint in his eye.

"Yes?"

He bowed obsequiously and handed her a notice of her own. "You're both being called," he said, "as witnesses for the prosecution. See y'all in court."

Sarah looked at Lena dumbfounded.

"You were saying," Lena said.

"Shit. That's what I was saying."

❖ ❖ ❖

Why hadn't Sarah considered this as a possibility? Perhaps because despite everything, she was still a visitor, an outsider who happened to stumble upon a murder. But it should have been obvious. Without her, Officer

Perry never may have come across the name of Jacob Lee; Officer Perry, who no doubt was the driving force behind her testifying against the defendant. Witness for the prosecution!

Her revenge at gin would have to wait. So would her plan to badger the students. She needed advice, and she needed it now. The phone rang several times, then finally picked up. She nearly cried at the familiar, avuncular voice.

"Obee, Obee, thank God."

"Sarah! Hello, my dear."

"Obee, is this a bad time?"

"It's never a bad time for you, Sarah."

"Oh, it's so good to hear your voice. Are you well, is everything all right there?"

"Fine, fine. Not so with you, though, I take it."

"No. I've gotten myself into quite a mess. In fact, when I wrote you, that was only the beginning. Since then, well, I'll tell you, I don't even know where to start…"

"I already know, Sarah."

"You know? You know what?"

"The whole story. Mitchell told me."

"Mitchell!"

"We had lunch before he left for Boston."

"Oh?"

"Yes. We're becoming good pals, you know. Hell of a guy. But I don't need to tell *you* that."

"Obee!"

"Now, now, I just want you to know I approve. Anyway, Sarah, if you wanted to hobnob with celebrities, you should have told me. Henry Louis Mencken and my old pal, Clarence. My, my! And a murder! You were supposed to be resting. It's a terrible thing, of course, but I'm afraid you'll be quite bored when you return."

"Believe me, I'd like nothing better than to be bored to tears. But right now, I need your help."

"Of course, anything."

"There's one thing you don't know about this situation, Obee, because it just happened. I've been called as a witness . . . for the prosecution."

"Oh, my! Well, you do know how to make things interesting."

"Obee, is there any way I can decline? I'm almost certain this boy is innocent, but I know how a prosecutor could twist my words, especially one who hasn't lost a case in ten years!"

"Not if they've subpoenaed you. You know that, especially since, according to what Mitchell said, your testimony would be essential to the case. Isn't that true?"

"Unfortunately, yes."

"Of course, you'll be viewed as hostile."

"I *will* be hostile, there's no doubt about that."

"Sarah, you sure you're not letting your emotions cloud your judgment? And before you answer, you know you'd ask me the same question."

"Almost sure."

"Is the defense competent?"

"Probably just."

"Ah. Well, try to relax. Tell the truth. It'll come out the way it should."

"That's a bit Pollyanic, isn't it Judge?"

"If I sound that way it's your fault, Sarah."

"Mine?"

"For helping me get my life back. Even in my dire state, justice ultimately prevailed. How can I feel otherwise?"

"This is an entirely different matter, Obee, in an entirely different culture."

"Come now, Sarah, is it really that different?"

Sarah sighed into the phone. "Well, yes and no. Anyway, since there's nothing I can do, I may have to extend the trip again."

"Don't worry about that. I'm probably working against my own interests, but I want you to follow this thing through."

"What do you mean?"

"Sarah, my dear, I think you're destined for greater things. Maybe you'll get that law degree after all, or, ha, ha, open your own detective agency."

"I'm a little old for new beginnings, Obee. Besides, I want nothing more than to return to my job. By the way, how's Flora doing?"

"She's holding down the fort just fine."

"Good."

"Sarah, keep things in perspective."

"Right."

"Oh, and Sarah, I meant what I said about Mitchell."

"Judge . . ."

"He's a good man."

"All right, matchmaker, I heard you."

"Good luck."

"Thanks. I'll need it."

31

"ALL RISE." EASY TO OBEY AND PREDICTABLE. To Sarah, a phrase as familiar as hello. Today, however, the words sounded ominous, foreign. Not because of the bailiff's especially pronounced accent, but because now she was centrally involved, had become a key figure in a trial she had inadvertently precipitated. To her left, the Tennessee flag; to her right, the gloomy, handcuffed Jacob Lee. Behind her, her betrayer, Officer Perry; in front, the ruddy, triple-chinned judge whose proportionally undersized lips were already half-puckered. And in the jury box, twelve leathery men. Laborers and farmers, Sarah guessed, men who worked on machines and in fields, who barely scraped together a living, and who, she feared, were cut out of the same mold as that loudmouth brute at Cohen's.

Over the weekend, she actually had felt more optimistic. Everyone in the house was on the mend, the humidity had somewhat lifted and, despite her protests, she was secretly pleased Mitchell had mentioned her to Obee. Moreover, even though Obee had been unable to provide her with a legal out, he had helped her view the trial more reasonably. He was probably right, she thought. The truth—what she at least hoped was the truth—would win in the end.

Her trusted friend had calmed her down. And she remained calm, even when Lena continued to beat her mercilessly at gin. But now, in this stuffy courtroom, she was worried again. Worried about the slick, immaculately groomed prosecutor who appeared to know everyone in the room by name. Worried about the plain, earnest-looking public defender who appeared to know no one at all. And worried especially about those twelve jurors, each of whom, with very little trouble, she could envision in a white robe.

The irregularly shaped, brick and concrete space was packed too, with what were becoming familiar faces: teachers, students, others she'd seen in one place or another. Mr. Cohen himself was there, smiling warmly when Sarah caught his gaze. For a moment she relaxed, as if opening her front door after a long day. But only for a moment. As her eyes drifted around the room, they froze on a large group of Negroes standing in the back. Although segregation of this sort was not uncommon, symbolically it didn't bode well for a black defendant. Not even an exception was made for Jacob's visibly distraught mother, who turned away when Sarah offered her a sympathetic nod.

The tension was palpable as the prosecutor stood to speak. Edenville's version of Scopes, Sarah thought, including the press, the heat and furiously waving palm-leafed fans.

Henry Nelson's opening statement was brief. The case for the prosecution was open and shut, he said, snapping closed his notepad for emphasis. Indeed, he didn't need any notes, only twelve people prepared to right a terrible wrong. He twisted his long handlebar mustache and paced deliberately. Even from the fourth row, Sarah could smell his vile cologne. Vanilla was fragrant in the oven, but not on a man. "You will hear from a witness who is here begrudgingly," he said, staring at her directly. "But remember, even that person is obliged under the law and under God to tell the truth, the whole truth and nothing but the truth." He paced again, then stopped before the jury and leaned toward them confidentially. "You will hear how a young man unable to accept rejection, with a history of brutality, lashed out in violence, taking one of our town's own, our state's finest. And this was a boy who wanted to be a preacher. Who wanted to do God's work!"

"The devil's more like it!" someone in the crowd yelled out.

The judge, eyelids heavy, tapped his gavel. "Order."

"And you will hear from another young man," he continued, "by all accounts honest, kind and free of prejudice, who happened upon someone running from the woods. The very woods, at the very time, Professor Nicholas Manhoff, a pillar of our community, lay murdered. The person he saw is right there," Nelson said, pointing to Jacob accusingly." And that, gentlemen, is all you need to know."

Sarah sighed deeply. Simplicity. The approach could backfire with a thinking jury, but for one desiring an easy answer, perfect. The prosecutor winked at the men and sat down. Mr. Callahan then rose. Shorter, heavier and exceptionally pale. A marshmallow, with a few blond wisps of hair and sincere, brown eyes. He rolled up his white shirtsleeves, wiped his forehead and approached the jury.

Sarah held her breath, but then exhaled. He sounded more confident than he appeared. Although he admitted the State had an eyewitness, he argued there was no real hard evidence. The case was circumstantial. "You will hear," he said, in a light, pleasing drawl, "that the witness supposedly identified the defendant as he was running from the woods. Running. Now, I don't know about y'all, but I'd have trouble recognizing my wife doing that, let alone someone I supposedly never had seen before."

Sarah smiled, but the jury sat stone-faced.

He wiped his forehead again. "Mr. Nelson, here, made a point of telling you his witness is not prejudiced. I don't know if he is or not. But I do know that down here many claim not to be able to distinguish one Negro from another."

"I can't!" a voice loudly exclaimed.

Sarah turned. A small ruckus in the back of the room was put to rest by another, more forceful tap. "Order!"

"See there," the attorney said. "What'd I tell ya? And maybe, just maybe this witness, even unintentionally, got caught up in that same way of thinking. Because, I will argue that my client was not in the woods that day. No, instead he was at home, working on his wireless, one of many gadgets he ingeniously built with his own hands. Jacob Lee, my friends," he said, standing near the defendant, "is no more a criminal than any fellow in the height of youth. Over-anxious, hot-tempered, maybe. But not a cold-blooded killer. Does he own guns? Yes, but who in this room does not? Gentlemen and," he said turning, "citizens of Edenville. I want to warn you. In the course of my defense, you will hear some things about the professor that perhaps you didn't know, or don't want to know. Things that angered my defendant, yes. Things that would have angered anyone. But enough for him to kill? To leave the mother he loves? To abandon his religious ideals? No! Absolutely no."

Sarah stifled her applause as others whispered, like snakes hissing after their prey. She glanced at the jury. Still, inscrutable.

The audience settled in as Nelson called Professor Lovell, the first of several colleagues to offer Manhoff their unqualified praise. Nelson was as clever as his record indicated. With each of these witnesses, he raised the issue of the professor's radical views, effectively diffusing the defense before it even had begun. Yes, each of them admitted. The professor held strong beliefs where race was concerned, beliefs he, perhaps a bit overzealously, backed up with science.

"You mean, with Darwin's theory of evolution, don't you?" Nelson clarified, "the very theory I suspect my colleague here, Mr. Callahan, believes in himself."

"Yes."

And yes, they all agreed, Professor Manhoff was known to discuss these views with his students. But would he force them on anyone? Never! Those who agreed with him did so on their own accord.

"No one can be made to do anything he doesn't want," Professor Michelson said, echoing the others. "Even a mesmerist would admit to that."

"Now, a very important question," Nelson said. "Think carefully before answering. In your opinion, would Nicholas Manhoff ever let his views influence his official obligations? Would he use them to manipulate his students, or, more pointedly, the admission process?"

From each witness again came a resounding no. Whether they believed it or not, they unflinchingly rallied around the man, presenting a united front. Nor did they falter on cross-examination. Not that Mr. Callahan didn't try. Indeed, if Sarah were in his place, she would have taken the same approach, asking them how they—as men trained in critical thinking—would take such an uncritical stance where Manhoff was concerned.

"Y'all speak of the professor as if he were an angel," he said. "Now, I don't want to talk ill of the dead, but didn't anyone, especially educated, enlightened people such as yourselves, condemn his views? As we all know, Edenville was the first college in the South to admit blacks, and your Northern benefactors have required that this tradition continue. "Although," he said, "if my research isn't mistaken, the school received some sort of reprimand for not meeting its quota recently, did it not?" The question was posed to Professor Aurosa, the socialist with the stylish, gold cufflinks. He answered with a nearly inaudible "Yes."

Callahan then referred—sooner in the case than Sarah would have thought—to the comments Professor Manhoff had made on Lee's application. Deceptive, dangerous, godless. Why exactly was the boy dangerous, because he got into a few scrapes? Or because he was intelligent, too intelligent for a Negro? And how, the attorney asked, could a young man who had spent his life in the church, who planned to become a minister, be godless?

But even with this, they didn't budge. If Professor Manhoff was against Lee's admission, he had good reason. Besides, he was only one man. The board made the ultimate decision.

"Anyway," Professor Byreest said, "what does that have to do with the defendant's guilt? Professor Manhoff is not on trial. He didn't commit a murder."

Callahan rose. "Objection!"

"Just answer the question," the judge said obligatorily, knowing full well that as far as the defense was concerned, the damage was already done.

After lunch, the students—Jim, Kathryn, Eric, Emily and Penny— were called to the witness box. One by one they were sworn in and questioned, as Judge Griffin, living up to his moniker, fully puckered and released his lips. Their testimonies lived up to Sarah's expectations, too. Meaning they simply reiterated what they had said many times before: Professor Manhoff was the best teacher they'd ever had—with apologies to the others in the room, of course. There was something special about the man. His intelligence, wit, ability to inspire. But also his caring. He was protective of them, almost fatherly.

"All students felt that way, not just those of us testifying, not just those in this courtroom," Jim said, nodding to a group of about fifteen, including Timothy, Bill and a few others Sarah hadn't met.

"White students, you mean, don't you?" Callahan asked in cross-examination.

Jim started to respond, but the attorney dismissed him before he could finish his sentence. A powerful tactic, Sarah thought. Turning a good trait into a bad. Ending on a critical note. Then again, in this case the rhetorical flourish—focused as it was on the professor's racism—may very well have had the unintended effect of only improving upon his image.

❧·❧·❧

The trial resumed Wednesday morning with Lena's testimony. For the occasion, her cousin had selected the plainest, most respectable outfit she owned, a white button-down blouse and ankle-length navy blue skirt. For once, she admitted, she didn't want to draw attention to herself.

As Lena was rummaging through her clothes the night before, Sarah had tried to discuss her responses to the prosecutor's likely questions. But Lena would have none of it. She didn't want to sound rehearsed. She just wanted to tell the truth. "Did that include," Sarah gingerly asked, "Professor Manhoff's . . . borrowing of your work?"

"I don't see how that would come up, Sarah, do you?"

"No, no, I just wondered."

"To answer your question, no. There would be absolutely nothing gained in talking about something so inconsequential. And I might have something to lose."

Something to lose. Yes, of course. Lena was a newcomer, and an outsider at that. Tenure was years away. If she made such accusations, she might very well be out of a job. Sarah dropped the subject, and helped Lena pick out her shoes.

Lena placed her hand on the Bible, repeated the required phrase and sat down.

"I understand," said Nelson, "that you had a good relationship with Professor Manhoff. Is that true?"

"Brief, but yes, it was good."

"You were beginning to work on a paper together?"

"Yes."

"And in reviewing some of his writings, you, or rather your cousin,

Sarah Kaufman, discovered some notes about an appointment in Dayton, with Mr. Henry Louis Mencken."

"Yes."

"And am I correct that Miss Kaufman traveled to the town and kept that appointment?"

"Yes."

"And it was during that visit that the name Jacob Lee first came up. Is that right?"

"I believe so. Yes."

"And it was after your cousin's return that Lee's admission application was discovered, is that correct?"

"Yes."

"So, does that summarize the order of events, at least where you were concerned?"

"Yes."

"And now, Miss Greenberg. During the short time you knew Professor Manhoff, did he treat you with respect?"

"Yes."

"Did he ever indicate any hostility toward you because you were a woman?"

"No."

"Because you were Jewish?"

"No."

"So, all and all, you felt the professor was a good man."

Lena hesitated. "Well, after I discovered his views, I have to say . . ."

"I'm asking you, based on your experience with the man, whether he seemed like a good person."

"I suppose."

"Did he ever, in any way, act offensively toward you?"

Lena swallowed, glanced at Sarah and turned back to the attorney. "No."

"Thank you. I'm through with the witness."

"Any questions, Mr. Callahan?" the judge asked.

Callahan nodded and rose. "Miss Greenberg, ma'am, you said you were working on a paper with Professor Manhoff?"

Sarah braced herself.

"Yes."

"To deliver at some professional conference. The Modern Languages Association. Is that correct?"

"Yes, that's right."

"What was the nature of that paper?"

"Oh, some theoretical piece on the teaching of literature. I don't think it would interest you much. Rather dry stuff, really."

Sarah could hear a few of Lena's colleagues snicker, but Sarah sat motionless.

"You're probably right. But Miss Greenberg, regarding the subject matter. Now, I want you to think before you answer. Think very carefully. Did Professor Manhoff ever attempt to take any of your ideas, to pass them off as his own?"

"Objection!"

The room collectively gasped. Lena blushed, then turned white.

"Where are you going with this?" the judge asked.

"Your Honor, I'm just trying to clear up a rumor."

"All right. But be quick."

"Thank you," Callahan said, and then turned back to Lena. "Now, please, answer the question. I remind you, ma'am, you're under oath."

Lena stared at her hands for a moment, then looked up. "I . . ." Her eyes fell on the first row where her colleagues were seated. "No, of course not," she said. "We shared ideas, all academics do. But it was mutually agreed upon."

"You're absolutely sure?"

"Yes."

"Relevance, Your Honor," Nelson protested, half-standing.

"Never mind," Callahan said, "the witness is dismissed."

Lena left the bench shakily and shot Sarah a hard look. Sarah lowered her eyes. She knew she deserved it.

Yesterday, after court, Sarah had gone to see Jacob again. He wanted no part of her, of course, but Officer Perry, perhaps harboring some lingering regret over misleading her, let her into the jail anyway. Once she was standing before Jacob's cell, however, she fell mute. She wanted to appease him, offer sincere words of encouragement, but all she could muster were meaningless platitudes. "Callahan did a good job." "The jury seemed reasonable." And then, a careless remark. A slip of the tongue. Or perhaps subconsciously she intended to tell him all along, hoping it would somehow strengthen his case. In any event, she just blurted it out. Professor Manhoff had plagiarized, or at least had planned to plagiarize, her cousin's work.

"So?" Jacob barked.

"So?" Her question was genuine. "I'm not sure."

"Well, why tell me this drivel, then? To convince me the man was unethical? Thank you. I will die convinced. Now please, go."

Sarah thought. Why had she told him? So he might then convey the information to his lawyer? But to what end? Of what possible use could it be to the case? It certainly wouldn't solve the murder, wouldn't get Jacob off the hook. And at worst, it could put Lena's credibility into question at a time she was still being evaluated. It even could threaten her with perjury! What had possessed her? Some higher principle of right and wrong? A desire to gain justice for Lena, whether she wanted it or not? Sarah had been foolish, and after Lena's reaction last night to her question about how she'd respond if asked about the incident in court, she prayed that her lapse in judgment wouldn't come back to haunt her. But it had. Jacob had done precisely what she thought he might.

⇀ 32

"THAT'S TWICE, SARAH," LENA SAID BACK AT THE HOUSE. "Twice! First, keeping the contents of Nick's papers from me. And now, this." Lena was staring at her as if she were a stranger, first narrowing then opening her eyes wide. "Why, Sarah?"

Sarah shook her head. "I don't know. It was impulsive. I guess I thought it might help reveal something of Manhoff's true character."

"You don't know his true character, Sarah. Your entire notion of the man is based on hearsay."

"I tend to believe what you tell me, Lena."

"Not just me, and you know it. You've latched onto this thing and haven't let go. And really, you've only made matters worse. Academics stick up for their own."

Sarah hung her head. "Oh, Lena. I'm so sorry. I had good intentions, but it was wrong of me to go behind your back. I only hope I haven't done anything irreparable . . . to you I mean. I'd never forgive myself."

Lena was silent.

"You know," Sarah said, still gazing at the floor, "after I testify, I . . . I think I'll go back to Toledo." She waited for a protest, but it never came.

Instead, Lena said: "That might be a good idea."

⇀⇀⇀

The next morning Sarah somberly took the stand. The courtroom had thinned out a bit. Jim and Kathryn were sick. Probably others had caught the virus, too. Or maybe they weren't that interested in the testimony of an outsider. Just as well. She'd do what was necessary, answer the questions and be on the three o'clock train. Her bags were already packed. Not even her desire for truth could justify a rift with Lena.

Nelson got right to the point, asking her to recount her trip to Dayton; what spawned it, who she met there and what she learned. "You said that the famous Henry Louis Mencken provided you with Jacob's name. Is that correct?"

"Yes, well, indirectly. As I stated, a friend of mine, a reporter from the *Blade*, passed on the information."

"Yes. And Mr. Mencken also told you that Professor Manhoff was meeting him there to try and convince him to publish something that he had already rejected."

"Yes."

"What was the piece about, do you know?"

"Mr. Mencken said it was a story, something about a black president."

A few people snickered. "Over my dead body!" someone yelled out. Again the judge anemically called the court to order.

"And why wasn't he going to publish it?"

"Because of the subject matter, and because he said the writing quality was poor."

"Ah. But it wasn't primarily because of the subject matter."

"Not primarily, but . . ."

"In other words, he didn't think the content itself would be that offensive."

"I'm not sure, but then Mr. Mencken is rather tolerant of racial intolerance," Sarah said.

"Just answer the question."

"I'm not sure."

"Now, in your conversation with the defendant about his application, what did he say about Professor Manhoff?"

"He said that the professor discouraged him from applying to Edenville, that he told him he was too smart for a Negro, that he should help along the process of natural selection."

"Meaning? In the simplest terms, Miss Kaufman."

"Basically, that he should not permit his mind to grow, that he should remove his application."

Nelson chuckled condescendingly and smoothed his mustache. "Miss Kaufman. You've heard the previous witnesses. Their praise of the professor was unqualified. Would you really have us believe that he could treat someone so inhumanely?"

"Objection. Argumentative."

Nelson didn't wait for the judge's decision. "I must say this whole natural selection business sounds just a little convenient," he said, "with the Scopes trial going on nearby. You've already told us of the defendant's interest in the trial."

"Objection!"

"Please, Your Honor. Just a word more to the jury."

"Go ahead," the judge said, "but be brief."

"You see," he said, turning to the confused looking men, "natural selection is part of this whole theory of evolution that was on trial in Dayton—a theory that denies the Bible. I hardly think Professor Manhoff would bring this up to a God-fearing young man."

"Objection!"

"Sustained!"

"Professor Manhoff's papers indicated that he held such views," Sarah interjected. "And Mr. Mencken confirmed his beliefs."

"Only answer questions that are asked of you," the judge warned.

"Sorry," she said, although she was not.

"Did the defendant tell you anything else?" Nelson asked.

"Yes. He said that the professor told him that his claim that he was unable to bear children was false. That he himself had decided not to have any children . . . because, because one of his ancestors was black."

The courtroom erupted again, this time in anger. "Outrageous!" "Liar!" Mr. Nelson, however, just stood quietly with a satisfied look. So that was it. He had planned this. Get the crowd—and especially the jury—riled up. Over race, of course. Then they would transfer their indignation onto Jacob.

Sarah wondered how he had acquired the information. Probably from Officer Perry who likely badgered it out of his prisoner.

"Order! Order!"

"Well now, Miss Kaufman," Nelson said. "If the professor were physically able, how could he prevent a pregnancy?"

"There are methods. We all know that. If his wife were alive . . ."

"You know, ma'am, you make a lot of assumptions about the dead, don't you? Perhaps you can go to Preston Hall late one night and talk to the ghosts," he sarcastically joked. "Let the university know how they're doing."

Everyone now laughed. Lena tossed her a little sympathetic smile. Just a little, but enough.

"Don't you find it unusual that a distinguished professor would confide in a student, let alone one he'd just met?"

"I just know what the defendant told me."

"And you believed him?"

She looked at Jacob. "Yes, yes I did."

Jacob offered her a slight nod.

"Well, that says it all, doesn't it?" Nelson said. "I'm done," and he sat down, winking at the jury again.

Callahan was immediately at Nelson's heels. "Miss Kaufman, you're not a willing witness for the prosecution, are you?"

"No."

"Why is that?"

"Because I was manipulated into serving up the defendant," she said, staring unflinchingly at Officer Perry.

"Manipulated by the Chief of Police, is that right?"

"Objection. Leading, Your Honor."

"Sustained."

"Miss Kaufman. You work for the courts in Ohio, a probation officer in the women's and juvenile court, is that right?"

"Yes."

"For how long?"

"Twenty years."

"I imagine in that time you've become an excellent judge of character."

"I've been told I am."

"So, you must have had some pretty good reasons for believing the defendant."

"Objection."

"A professional opinion, Your Honor."

The judge glanced from one attorney to the other. "Overruled. You may respond, ma'am."

"Other than the obvious," she asked, "that he wanted to be a preacher?"

"Yes."

Sarah was prepared for the question. "Well, this may sound simplistic, but I've found it to be true. A man can usually be trusted if he treats animals with kindness and his mother with respect. Mr. Lee did both. The defendant's mind is curious, active, productive. He had and still does have noble goals. And his eyes. He didn't avert them when speaking to me, not even a little. A generalization perhaps, but people who are lying usually do."

"Thank you, ma'am. That's all."

"Miss Kaufman," Nelson questioned from his seat. "Have you ever heard of Al Capone?"

"Of course."

"Did you know he could stare down even the most seasoned interrogator? Nothing further, Your Honor."

❖ ❖ ❖

"The State calls Christopher Wilde to the stand."

Sarah had just returned to her seat near Lena when Nelson announced his star witness. Down the aisle walked the mild-looking young man, just as Officer Perry had described him. Medium build, neatly groomed, altogether average, with the exception of the purplish stain that nearly covered the left half of his face. Once sworn in, he took the witness box. Immediately, he leaned on his left elbow and cradled the birthmark with his hand, a gesture that by this point in his life was most probably unconscious.

After asking the boy to identify himself, Nelson proceeded to the day in question. "Now, Mr. Wilde, please recount in your own words, the events on the morning of June thirty-first."

"Well, I was waiting for my parents to pick me up. We were going to Atlanta to visit relatives. They were supposed to come to my dormitory, but since they were a little late, I decided to walk up to the school's entrance to meet them." His speech was soft and muffled due to his hand resting immovably on his face. The attorney requested that he speak up, which he did without changing positions.

"I'm housed with the engineering students, near the woods. As I approached the south trail, I stopped for a moment. I don't really know why. But just then, someone ran past me. Right in front of me."

"Describe that person, please."

Christopher shifted in his chair and looked directly at Jacob. "A Negro, tall, muscular with wide-set eyes that had a fearful, wild look about them. He was breathing heavily and sweating and turned his head around a few times as he ran, as if checking to see if anyone was following him."

"Did he look at you?"

"No. Honestly, I don't think he even saw me."

"You told the police that you forgot about him after your parents came."

"That's true. I was on vacation, sir."

"You didn't know Professor Manhoff, is that correct?"

"Yes," he said, glancing briefly at the students a few rows in front of Sarah.

"And you do not know the defendant either, do you?"

"No."

"And you harbor no ill will toward Negroes, do you?"

"Objection. Leading, Your Honor."

"Sustained."

"Do you harbor ill will toward Negroes?"

"No, absolutely not."

"In fact, your great-grandparents were Southern abolitionists, isn't that true?"

"Yes. I was schooled to be racially tolerant."

"Now, one further question. Is the man you saw that day in this courtroom?"

He hesitated for a moment and again glanced at the students. Sarah turned in their direction and observed what she thought was an exchange, a fleeting, almost imperceptible exchange between him and Penny.

"Yes."

"Could you please point to him?"

Christopher raised his right hand and pointed to Jacob.

"Thank you. Your witness."

Mr. Callahan slowly rose and approached the witness box deliberately. "Now, Mr. Wilde. You say it was definitely the defendant who ran past you."

"Yes."

"But you also say he didn't seem to see you."

"That's right. He was preoccupied."

"How can that be, if you were close enough to observe his features, so close that you can identify him?"

The boy again looked toward the students. This time Sarah was sure. Penny, the blond, bobbed beauty, nodded.

"Well, I only know what I saw. He ran past, like he was mesmerized or something."

"But you said he looked back. He wasn't completely in a trance."

"Objection, Your Honor. Badgering the witness."

"Your Honor," Callahan said, "this is critical to my client."

"I'll let it stand," the judge said, yawning.

"So you saw him, but he didn't see you. Is that what you're claiming?"

"Yes."

"Okay. Let's move on. You say that you have nothing against Negroes."

"That's right."

"In fact, do you feel sympathetic?"

"Sympathetic?" he asked, clutching his face tighter.

"Yes, I mean, having something physical that sets you apart."

Christopher lowered his eyes and said nothing.

"Objection, Your Honor." Nelson said. "Relevance. This is cruel!"

This *is* cruel, Sarah thought.

"Mr. Callahan. I assume you have a reason for this?"

"Yes, I do."

"Well, get to it."

"Mr. Wilde. I would imagine you've had a difficult time, with people staring at you, the way people do at anyone who is different."

No response.

"Has this made you have compassion for the Negro, understand his plight?"

The boy was still silent, but looked up. Sarah followed his eyes. Again. Again, they drifted to Penny. "My problem," he finally said in a trembling voice, "my problem has nothing to do with theirs. I am white. My blood is white. My father is white. My mother is white!"

"Hear, hear!" someone called out.

"Order."

"In fact, sir, you feel some hostility toward them, don't you? Despite your family upbringing. Perhaps you feel they are not your equal, although you are often treated similarly."

"Objection, Your Honor!"

"This involves motive, Judge."

"Motive for what?"

"For pinning the murder on my client."

From the audience now came a mix of sneers and groans. And from their chilled expressions, the jury wasn't buying the defense's theory either. But Sarah was beginning to, however vaguely.

The judge studied the attorney. "That is quite a leap, Counselor. But go ahead. Finish up."

Callahan paused dramatically and faced the witness. "Are you sure you're not trying to gain favor with people who have treated you badly? Are you sure you're not trying to prove you're just like everyone else? Mr. Wilde, are you sure that the man you saw, if you saw anyone at all, is the defendant?!"

Christopher pulled his hand down from his face, glanced once more at Penny, and then glared at Callahan contemptuously. "Yes. I am sure."

⇸ 33

LENA TOUCHED SARAH'S SHOULDER. "Lunch?" she asked. Sarah pressed her hand. "No, thanks. I'd like to stay here."

"Sarah . . ."

Sarah looked up. "I know," she said. "Go on, eat something before you waste away."

"I'll bring you a sandwich," Lena said, and she left not waiting for a response.

Sarah pulled out a handkerchief from her purse and dabbed her eyes. Lena apparently didn't possess the family tendency to hold a grudge. If it had been Tillie, Sarah would have had to think twice about biting into that sandwich. As she watched Lena push open the courtroom door, Sarah promised herself she never would keep anything from her cousin again. Starting now. As soon as Lena returned, she would tell her that she had decided to postpone her departure until tomorrow.

⇸ ⇸ ⇸

After lunch, the defense called its first witness, Mrs. Eldora Lee. Dressed severely in a mandarin collared navy blue crepe dress and head-hugging Joan Crawford style hat, Jacob's mother marched toward the front of the room defiantly, ignoring the stares and grunts. She took the stand and smiled lovingly at her son.

"Mrs. Lee, you know your son to be truthful, honest."

Mrs. Lee sat erect. "Always."

"What about his temper? My colleague here will no doubt ask you about the trouble he's been in."

"Sure, he's been in trouble. He's a boy, ain't he? But I'll tell you this. He would never hurt anyone intentionally. Never. I can't even get him to kill a spider."

"Jacob owns guns, though, doesn't he?"

"Course he does. You know anyone 'round here who don't? He's a fine shot, too. So was his daddy, taught him to protect himself."

"Jacob has been a good son, hasn't he, ma'am?"

"Objection. Leading."

"Has Jacob been a good son?"

"A mother couldn't ask for a better one. Ever since his father died, he's taken care of me."

"Tell me something about his father."

"His father? He was bricklayer. Faithful, wonderful man. Loved his son more than life itself. Died of a heart attack, a few years ago."

"I see. Well, now, Mrs. Lee, do you know where your son was on the morning of July eighteenth?"

"Yes, I do."

"Where?"

"With me, eating breakfast."

"Are you sure?"

"If he wasn't there, I'd have remembered. We always eat our first meal of the day together, have since he was little."

"Thank you, ma'am. Your witness."

Mr. Nelson stood up and rocked on his feet: "Mrs. Lee. I've heard you and your son go braggin' about some relationship to our great General Lee, is that right?"

"Oh, that's just a joke. Everyone knows that."

"Well, that's some joke, ma'am. I mean, really."

"Don't you think it's funny?"

"I suppose it is. But you know, there's a fine line between a joke and a lie. It might not be that hard to cross that line, where someone you love is concerned."

"There's a line all right, but I didn't cross it. And neither did my son.

He was home with me. You think you can fool a dumb nigger woman."

"You crossed that line at least once before though, didn't you? When you lied to the police about not knowing your son's whereabouts."

"I was just trying to protect him from . . ."

"Precisely. You were just trying to protect him. That's all."

"From injustice!" Mrs. Lee, said, forbidding him to cut her off. "From injustice!"

Judge Griffin tapped his gavel. "Mr. Callahan?"

"No more questions, Your Honor."

"Any other witnesses?"

"Not today, Your Honor."

"All right. Court dismissed until nine o'clock tomorrow morning."

❧ 34

THE EARLY RECESS AFFORDED SARAH THE OPPORTUNITY before dinner to act on her hunch, that those glances between Christopher and Penny had a deeper, perhaps ominous meaning. It may have been another case of wishful thinking, but she sensed that where Jacob was concerned, these two individuals had something to hide. First, however, she had to uphold her promise to Lena and tell her of her plan.

Her cousin was incredulous—after what they'd just been through, was she out of her mind? But eventually she realized it was a losing battle. As long as Sarah swore she would not involve her. "I'm a forgiving person," Lena said, "but I have my limits."

Sarah held up her right hand. "I swear."

"I don't need to remind you of the trouble you might get into with the police. I don't suppose you're going to inform them."

Sarah knew all about the possible legal ramifications, but she was willing to take the chance. No, she wasn't going to the authorities, not yet anyway.

"Well, you're on your own."

"I know."

And so now, by herself, she approached Simmons Hall, home to the students who would eventually build our bridges and light our homes. Here lived men who would find it easier to construct a soaring edifice than build a relationship. Sarah knew the type. She had several friends whose husbands were engineers.

In the fall, the Gothic structure would no doubt be bustling with the sounds of pencils, blackboards and erasers. At this moment, it was relatively quiet. Standing in the dim, empty lobby, Sarah could hear a few doors slam, a thread of laughter here and there. Summer students, she imagined, fell into two categories: either they had classes to make up or had little else in their lives. She assumed Christopher Wilde fell into the latter category.

"May I help you?"

Sarah jumped. She turned and saw why she hadn't heard any one approach. The wiry wisp of a boy standing before her was shoeless, his argyle socks rolled down on his child-size feet. He smiled politely.

"Yes, thank you. I'm wondering if you might tell me where Christopher Wilde's room is."

"I'm sorry. We aren't permitted to give out that information, ma'am. In fact, women aren't allowed in this dorm. May I ask who you are?"

"Oh dear. Now I'm sorry. I'm a relative of one of the teachers here."

"Which one?"

"Miss . . ." Lena's words echoed in her ears. You're on your own. "Look, could you just ask Christopher if he'd meet me outside. Tell him it has to do with the trial."

"Oh, the trial. All right. Where outside?"

"Didn't I see a bench, off to the right of the building?"

He nodded. "Okay. I'll tell him. If he's in. He's often off with that girlfriend . . . lucky dog. I'll let you know if he's not there."

Girlfriend? Sarah started to ask her name, but thought better of it. "Thanks," she said, and ambled toward the meeting spot, a wide, slatted wooden bench on which were carved numerous sets of initials. Were any of these lovers still together? she wondered. Were Christopher's among them? Then a voice called out, echoing through the tree-lined distance: "Ma'am?" Sarah turned. It was Christopher, standing near the dormitory entrance. "What d'ya want, ma'am?"

Sarah anchored her hand on her forehead to block the setting sun's glare and called back: "Christopher, may I speak to you a moment?"

"Why?"

"I have a few questions."

Their voices entwined and reverberated off one another.

"I don't think that's a good idea."

"Please. It's important." Her throat hurt from yelling.

He stood silently, digging his feet like a baseball player at bat. He glanced back at the dorm, to the side, and then slowly walked toward her. As he approached, his hand rose to his face. "All right," he said. "What can I do for you?"

"Please," Sarah said, "sit down." She exhaled and folded her hands, picturing herself back in her office, about to counsel a youth from the juvenile court. Her job? Extract the truth while preserving the boy's dignity. Show him compassion, but alert him to the seriousness of his actions. Give him hope but not pity. She felt the shift, and eased back into her own skin.

The look that passed between Christopher and Penny had been one Sarah had witnessed before. The specifics were of course different, but the dynamic at work was the same: power. Inequitable power. Penny's clenched jaw, hard, diamond eyes, slightly pouting mouth. Christopher's desperate, deferential nod. A bargain had been struck, and Sarah was betting her twenty years experience that she knew the nature of it.

"Christopher," she began. "I'd like to tell you something. When I was young, I was quite self-conscious about my appearance. I accept it now, but as a teenager I was miserable. I longed for blond hair and a straight nose, but instead . . . well, you can see."

"What do you want to ask me?" he said, standing.

"Please, hear me out."

He sat back down, staring at her icily.

"I had a particularly tough time with the opposite sex," Sarah said. "I wanted a boyfriend desperately, but none wanted me. Until a miracle occurred. Or so I thought. One of the most popular boys in my high school asked me for a date. I was beside myself with joy. But soon I learned that I had simply been the object of a contest. He and his friends drew straws, and he lost." Sarah winced. Even now, it wasn't easy to admit. "I felt horrible, humiliated," she said. "My need was so great, I did things with him I had never done before. I lied to my parents, to my friends, worst of all, to myself."

Christopher stood back up. "I don't know what you're getting at."

"I think you do," Sarah said, holding onto his arm. "How did Penny get you to lie?"

His hand dropped from his face, exposing his birthmark, an irregular, almost beautiful pool of color for which he must had suffered terribly. "You're crazy!" he said.

Sarah looked at him calmly. He was angry, but he hadn't moved. "Christopher," she said, "you're an intelligent young man with a bright future ahead of you. And you're a good person, aren't you? Ethical, moral. You've never done anything like this before, have you?"

He still didn't move.

"You know," she said, "after I discovered the truth about that boy in high school, I changed my attitude. I decided I never would allow anyone to degrade me like that again. And the funny thing is, after that, I never had trouble finding dates. Christopher," she said, touching his arm more gently, "there are many girls who would appreciate you for who you are. You don't have you sell your soul for love."

He shrugged her off and started to walk away.

"Sending an innocent man to his death will follow you," Sarah called out. "Do you think Penny will do the same?" She held her breath.

Gradually he slowed; slowed to a stop and finally turned.

⋇ ⋇ ⋇

Sarah weighed the options. Confront Penny directly, inform the prosecutor, tell Officer Perry. Each had their risks, not the least of which was the possibility of Sarah herself being arrested for witness tampering. Instead, she decided to take the revelation, along with Christopher, to the defense. There were disclosure rules, of course. But she'd let Mr. Callahan handle that part of it.

And what she presented to the stunned attorney was a revelation indeed, even though it was Mr. Callahan himself who had pointed the way. Christopher had not, after all, seen anyone running from the woods that day. And his decision to lie about it was, as Callahan suspected, related to his disfigurement. But sex, not race, was the motivating factor. He'd never been with a girl before, feared he never would. As Officer Perry had told Sarah, the boy had trouble with girls. And then, Penny came along. Offered herself. Penny! Edenville's Helen of Troy, the beauty all the fellas dreamt about. Sure, she asked for something in return. But everyone believed Jacob was guilty anyway, she said. All things considered, a little fib to rid the town of a killer in exchange for paradise seemed like a pretty fair deal.

But Christopher possessed a conscience, was an essentially good person temporarily led astray. And so Sarah had been able to reach him. The thing had been plaguing him so much, he said, he probably would have confessed eventually on his own.

Questions nevertheless remained. Penny had never met Jacob, or so she told Christopher. How then was she able to describe him so accurately? And of course, why did she attempt to pin the crime on him in the first place? By all accounts, Penny had adored Professor Manhoff, but enough to implicate a stranger? To invent evidence?

As Christopher repeated his story to Mr. Callahan, he pulled out a shiny pocket watch and laid it on the attorney's desk. "Penny gave me this," he said. "A souvenir, she said, something to remember her by. Never did tell time very well."

Callahan picked it up and examined the engraving: "P. C." Penelope Caldwell.

"Fool's gold," Christopher said.

"Maybe not. Hold on to it for now. It may come in handy," Callahan said. He moved closer to the boy. "Chris, I'm going to get you back on the stand. It may be rough. Can you handle it?"

"I have to, don't I? If I want to tell the truth."

Callahan smiled. "Good man."

35

"YOUR HONOR," CALLAHAN SAID AT THE OPENING OF COURT, "some new evidence has been presented to me that requires a change in the schedule."

The judge raised his heavily hooded eyes.

"I'd like to call Christopher Wilde back on the stand."

Nelson jumped up. "Objection, Your Honor! That's my witness, and I have not been informed of any new evidence."

"I just learned of it myself, Your Honor."

"From whom?"

"From the witness, from Christopher Wilde himself."

Lena nudged Sarah as Nelson turned questioningly to Christopher. Only his lips moved, but Sarah could read them: "What—in—the—hell?" She nudged her because she knew. The previous night, Sarah had relayed her discovery to Lena, who, though shocked about Penny and still recovering from what she referred to as Sarah's over-protectiveness where she was concerned, was glad her cousin had followed her instincts. She would think twice about challenging Sarah's judgment again, she said, unless of course it involved Lena's love life.

The judge swiveled on his chair, and then leaned forward. "Mr. Callahan, this is most irregular."

"This is a most irregular situation, Your Honor, and of utmost importance."

The judge puckered his lips, but then apparently changed his mind. "Gentlemen, approach the bench."

They whispered for a few moments before returning to their tables.

Nelson remained standing. "Your Honor, I request a recess to speak with the witness."

"Granted. Fifteen minutes. Be back at nine-thirty sharp."

"Don't let him bully you," Sarah murmured to Christopher, who was seated in front of her.

Christopher offered her a half-smile and followed Mr. Nelson out of the sanctum.

Excited chatter immediately ensued, everyone obviously wondering about the meaning of this development. Sarah eyed the students. Huddled together, mouths moving at high speed, they seemed as curious as the rest. Except for Penny, that is, who sat silently by herself. Only she looked concerned, on alert, like a deer hearing a distant gunshot.

It was a long fifteen minutes, but finally court resumed. Sarah watched Nelson lumber back to his table. He appeared simultaneously deflated and heavy. His tanned face had paled. Gone was the swagger.

Callahan wasted no time. "The defense calls Christopher Wilde."

Christopher took the stand and repeated the facts as he had told them earlier to the attorney. During his testimony, the room was eerily quiet. Heads periodically turned toward Penny, who seemed frozen into place.

"Do you know how Miss Caldwell knew so many details? How she was able to describe the defendant?"

"No, I do not."

"You didn't ask?"

"No, I should have, but I didn't."

Callahan was silent and paced, as if contemplating his next move. Sarah suspected he already knew what it would be. "Well, Your Honor," he said, looking directly at Penny, "there is one person who can help us answer these questions."

"No!" Penny was standing, shaking, yanking the knot on her sailor's blouse until it completely unraveled. "He's lying! He's lying!" she screamed.

"Order! Control yourself young lady."

"He's lying!"

"No, I am not," Christopher yelled. "And you know it!" He reached in his pocket and held up the watch, dangling the link chain in the air. A shaft of light caught the object's brassy sheen. Penny's perfectly shaped mouth opened. She hesitated for a moment, then fell back into her chair, sobbing.

The judge tapped his gavel. "Control yourself, or I will have you removed from this courtroom!"

The two guards monitoring the doors stiffened. Eric reached over and put his arm around her. From the other side, Kathryn did the same and calmly whispered something to her nearly hysterical friend. In a few moments, Penny quieted down.

Nelson, who had been silent up to this point, rose wobbily to his feet. "Judge, gentlemen of the jury. These are horrible accusations, and this poor girl has denied them. So let's not jump to conclusions. This . . . this young man, my witness, may be unstable." He wiped his forehead with the back of his hand. "The police obviously need to investigate."

"Your Honor!" Everyone turned again. The voice was heavy, reticent, but resigned. It came from a tall, dark-haired man in uniform, leaning against the courtroom doors. Sarah recognized him as one of Officer Perry's deputies. "Your Honor," he said again.

The judge motioned for him to approach.

He inched his way through the standing crowd, then walked slowly down the aisle and stood before the Bench. "If it pleases the Court, I wish to be sworn in."

"What's that?"

"I said I wish to give testimony, in support of this witness." He hung his head. "I think I can clear this matter up."

From the corner of her eye, Sarah could see Officer Perry frantically reaching for his tobacco.

The judge eyed the fellow up and down. "This better be good. Bailiff, do the honors."

Jacob exchanged glances with the deputy as he took the stand.

"Do you swear to tell the truth, the whole truth, and nothing but the truth, so help you God?"

"I do."

"State your name, age and occupation."

"Richard Blackstone, twenty-one, deputy for the Edenville police."

Sarah turned again to Penny. She was slumped over, hands covering her face.

Judge Griffin conducted the questioning. "What is it you wish to say?"

"Your Honor, I know how Penny, Penelope Caldwell, found out about Jacob."

"You do? How?"

The young man folded his hands, glanced sheepishly at Officer Perry and shook his head. "I told her."

"You?"

"Yes. I, I was seeing her and told her about the case."

"You revealed information about an ongoing investigation?"

"Yes, I'm afraid I did. It was not intentional. I had no idea . . ."

"You described the defendant to her?"

"Yes."

"Mr. Blackstone. Were you intimate with this girl?"

He nodded. "Yes."

Cursing and obscene gestures poured from the audience. Sights and sounds one never expected from such God-fearing people. The judge remained silent, his expression unreadable.

"Forgive me, Your Honor. Sir," Blackstone said to Officer Perry.

Sarah looked over at the prosecutor. He appeared to have perked up, taking pleasure in the chaos. When things quieted a bit, he smoothed his mustache and requested the floor. "Your Honor, gentlemen of the jury, members of the audience. I must tell you I am as shocked as everyone. Obviously, I cannot contest this confession. This girl, Penelope Caldwell, is obviously troubled, in need of help. Her grief over the loss of her teacher led her astray and my witness' need for her did the same to him. She must have been quite persuasive. Even this young officer fell under her spell."

People shifted in their seats as he continued. "There is no point denying that there has been a deception. But," he said, pausing dramatically, "not necessarily an injustice." He paced before the jury. "Gentlemen, think carefully about what I am about to say. This revelation does not preclude the defendant's guilt. Hear me, now. It does not mean Jacob Lee didn't kill Professor Manhoff. There is still the matter of his admission records. We know he had an axe to grind with the professor. And we know he has a history of violence. He is still the most likely suspect. The absence of an eyewitness does not make him less of a killer."

Nelson was grasping at straws. But the jury listened attentively, no doubt hoping for a way out of the confusion, for a reason to still find in the prosecutor's favor.

Callahan stood. "Is this my colleague's closing argument, Your Honor? Because if it is, I am entitled to my say, too."

"I don't know what anything is in this trial anymore. Mr. Nelson?"

"Suits me."

"All right. Deputy, you may step down. Go ahead, Mr. Callahan."

Callahan faced the jury. "Gentlemen, Mr. Nelson here is right. It is still possible that Jacob Lee killed Professor Manhoff. It is equally possible, however, that I did it. Or any of you. That's the kind of evidence there is against him. Reasonable doubt, my friends. This turn of events has cast not only reasonable, but probable doubt on the guilt of my client. Without the eyewitness, the case is flimsy at best. Reasonable doubt. It's what our legal system is built on. Here in the South, we often have let our prejudices get in the way of justice. Don't let that happen this time. It is your duty as Americans to find this defendant not guilty.

"Anything else?" the judge asked

"Yes, Judge," Nelson said. "I'd like to say one more thing to the jury. Mr. Callahan here is correct about reasonable doubt. But you must not abandon your reason for it. Y'all know who killed the professor."

The judge then charged the jury with the case. When he finished, he ordered Officer Perry to escort Penny, Christopher and Deputy Blackstone to his chambers. "Ladies and Gentlemen," he then said, "we will reconvene when the jury reaches a verdict. Court dismissed."

❧❧❧

"It doesn't look good," Sarah said to Lena over dinner. "Not good at all."

By rights, of course, it should have. An eyewitness discredits himself, a deputy lends him support. The case should have been open and shut. But Sarah knew juries. The smell and taste of them, and this one was hungry to convict.

She was still picking at her first biscuit when the doorbell rang. It was Kathryn and Jim. They had just come from the courthouse with news. First, Deputy Blackstone had been put on a month's suspension for talking about an ongoing investigation, punished but not fired. That was fair, Sarah felt. True, he had used poor judgment, but he publicly admitted his mistake. He was not penalized for being intimate with Penny. It would have been another story had Penny not been of age.

Secondly, Judge Griffin had dropped the perjury charge against Christopher, stating that the boy had suffered enough. This was heartening. Not just for Christopher, but for Jacob. Whistle or no whistle, the judge had exhibited compassion, and when it came to sentencing, that could mean the difference between life and death.

Mostly, the two talked about Penny, however. They simply couldn't believe their friend had resorted to such extreme measures. Degrading herself like that.

"And taking advantage of someone so vulnerable," Sarah reminded them.

"Yes, that too," Jim said.

"Why do you think she did it?"

Kathryn shrugged. "We don't know."

"So you had no idea?"

"How could we?"

Sarah wondered how they couldn't have, given their apparent closeness to the girl. "It is degrading for Christopher as well," she said. "And a nightmare for Jacob."

Kathryn nodded unconvincingly, and flipped back one of her long, braided pigtails. Free of make-up, she looked no more than thirteen. "If he's innocent. No offense, Miss Kaufman, but Mr. Nelson may be right."

"May means he didn't prove his case," Sarah said. "Reasonable doubt, remember?" But that's all she said. There was no point in arguing. If the prosecutor had convinced these bright, if somewhat misguided, young people of his position, the jury was a sure bet. The verdict was all but a headline.

Jim and Kathryn were clearly more concerned about Penny, who was now in custody and waiting to be officially charged, with what exactly they weren't sure. Kathryn had been allowed to visit her for a few minutes and said the girl was terrified. In fact, she feared Penny might have a breakdown. Ordinarily, Sarah would have had sympathy for someone like Penny, losing her father at such an important time in her life. Obviously, she had transferred some of her feelings onto Professor Manhoff. Penny needed counseling, the kind Sarah herself was accustomed to providing. But Sarah's concern was for Jacob. Whatever the cause, Penny's actions were deplorable, the extent of the damage yet to be determined. Besides, Kathryn said nothing about Penny feeling any remorse, the one thing that invariably caused Sarah to forgive.

All Sarah could do now was wait. For two agonizing days she listened to the clock chime, nearly lost her life savings playing cards and read her book:

> *What was once a smooth-shaven lawn before the house, dotted here and there with ornamental shrubs, was now covered with frowsy tangled grass, with horse-posts set up here and there, in it, where the turf was stamped away, and the ground littered with broken pails, cobs of corn, and other slovenly remains. The place looked desolate and uncomfortable; some windows stopped up with boards, some with shattered panes, and shutters hanging by a single hinge—all telling of coarse neglect and discomfort.*

Poor Uncle Tom, Sarah thought, marking her page once again. Taken from his benevolent, if nevertheless immoral, masters to the dilapidated plantation of the evil Simon Legree. Tom's family—not traditional, but more loving than any other in the story—left behind.

Then, at eleven a.m., Thursday morning, the announcement came.

Sarah watched the jury as they sullenly marched into the courtroom. Her eyes rested on one of the members who'd captured her attention because his mouth was in a perpetual frown. So he goes, so goes the verdict, she told herself. The slightest glance at Jacob and a shred of hope remained. But, no. He folded his arms tightly against his barrel chest and stared straight ahead. Though she expected it, her heart sank.

"Will the defendant please rise?"

Jacob stood up slowly.

"Have you reached a verdict?"

"We have, Your Honor," said the foreman, a stout, hirsute man of about forty.

The room contracted.

"We find the defendant, Jacob Lee, not guilty."

Sarah thought she misheard. So did everyone else, turning to each other silently with open mouths. Lena squeezed her hand.

"So say you all?"

"So say we all."

The group in the back cheered wildly. Sarah turned. "My God!"

"It wouldn't have happened without you, Sarah," Lena said.

Sarah rolled her eyes. "Yeah, I know."

"Oh come on, you know what I mean."

Gradually, the rest of the crowd chimed in. From what Sarah could tell, the overall sentiment was one of bitter disappointment. The judge pounded his gavel, called order, but eventually just sat back. Sarah had seen Obee do that on occasion too, when emotions were running high. Better to let them play out in the courtroom, he felt, than somewhere less controlled. Indeed, Sarah thought. Play them out and come to realize that it was their friends and neighbors, people just like themselves, who had reached this decision. She cast the still frowning juror another glance. Well, as Darwin proved, change is often imperceptible.

She wiped her eyes and turned to see Jacob's mother rushing to the front of the room to embrace her son. Jacob fell into her arms like a baby. Then, those in the back joined in the celebration.

Tomorrow Jim Crow would return, but for now, much to the dismay of the white onlookers, the boundaries had disappeared. Sarah wanted desperately to offer Jacob her congratulations too, but decided to let him be.

In a day or two, she promised herself. Before going home.

❧ 36

NOT GUILTY. Sarah could count on one hand the number of times she'd read a jury incorrectly, and even then, she'd had an inkling that it might go the other way. But she was usually able to maintain objectivity. In this case, she'd let herself be swayed by her own preconceived notions. These men were too ignorant to care about something as abstract as reasonable doubt, she had thought, too bigoted to separate their personal views from their public duty. Never was she happier to be wrong.

That night after dinner, Lena offered her own theory about the verdict. "I think it had to do with female sexuality," she said in a professorial tone. "From the jury's perspective, Penny is a disgrace, not because she harmed an innocent Negro, but because she was promiscuous. It wasn't what she did, but how she did it. In using her body, she dishonored the sacred tradition of the chaste Southern belle. "

Sarah nodded. "In freeing Jacob, they condemned Penny."

"Precisely."

The idea was certainly plausible, although Sarah would have liked to believe a more noble sentiment was involved. Either way, however, the system had worked. Of course, the murderer remained at large. No telling when—or if—they would ever discover his identity, although she thought re-questioning some of the professor's colleagues would be a good place to start.

Reveling in her previous wins, Lena challenged Sarah to another game of gin. Sarah declined. Why put herself through that agony? Besides, she wanted to take a bath and read a little. Lena sighed disappointedly, but licked her lips when Phyllis offered to play. She could already taste victory.

Sarah soaked until her fingers wrinkled, dried herself off, then stretched out on the bed and inhaled the exotic scent of Lena's jasmine bath beads lingering on her skin. She reached for her glasses and picked up her book. Only a few pages left.

Conditions at Simon Legree's plantation were further deteriorating. Legree's female slave, Cassie, had managed to escape, and now Legree was taking it out on Tom. Sarah sensed the worst, especially since the current chapter bore the foreboding title of "Martyr."

> *It was but a moment. There was one hesitating pause—one irresolute, relenting thrill—and the spirit of evil came back with seven-fold vehemence; and Legree, foaming with rage, smote his victim to the ground . . . Legree drew in a long breath; and, suppressing his rage, took Tom by the arm, and, approaching his face almost to his, said, in a terrible voice, "Hark'e, Tom! I'll count every drop of blood there is in you, and take 'em, one by one . . ."*

Sarah read on, as the doomed protagonist, like thousands of actual slaves, succumbed to his master's brutality. She heaved a deep sigh. "The savage words none of them reached that ear!—a higher voice there was saying, 'fear not them that kill the body, and after that, have no more that they can do.'" It was over. Tom was now with his God, reaping the rewards of his earthly sacrifice. Sarah sighed again. What about the here and now? Death, indeed, often had been the sad truth of slavery, but better for Tom that he fight Legree. Or try to escape. Better for his family that he had lived! Better for Sarah too, because now she felt slightly depressed. She closed the book, wrapped herself in Lena's robe and headed back downstairs. Maybe she'd take on her cousin again after all.

She listened for the slapping of cards, but heard nothing. She peaked into the dining room. Not there. Then into the kitchen. No one. Dirty dishes were still in the sink. The parlor was empty too. Where were they? She glanced onto the porch. Ah. "Okay, now I feel lucky," Sarah said, pushing open the front door.

"Sarah," Lena said. "Sarah."

"That's my name, all right."

"Oh God, Sarah."

Sarah smiled uneasily. "What's the matter?"

Lena averted her eyes. It was only then Sarah noticed Officer Perry, his bulky frame suddenly coming into sharp focus.

Sarah looked from one to the other. "What is it?" she said, feeling for her rings with one hand, grabbing hold of a chair with the other.

Officer Perry put his rough hands on her shoulders. His lined face glowed eerily in the full moonlight. "Jacob," he said.

She tightened her grip. "What about him?"

➔ 37

CAUSE OF DEATH: STRANGULATION. Method: lynching. A rope and a tree, turned into a deadly weapon. There were signs of a struggle; a bloody shoe a few yards away, skin under his nails. But, no matter. Jacob's neck hung slack in the noose when a neighbor found him, only a mile from his home. Jacob's mother had been planning a celebration and had sent her son out for ice cream. Friends now feared she might try to take her own life.

All signs pointed to the Klan, Officer Perry said. Clearly, it was their technique, their kind of target. And unfortunately, that made the chance of finding the specific perpetrators nearly impossible. They knew how to elude the law. Hell, some of them were the law. He would do what he could, but he was limited because the murder technically had occurred out of his jurisdiction. True, one Klavern served all the towns around here. But he only had so many resources. And now, once again, there was the Manhoff case to worry about.

Sarah heard all this as if through a leaden tunnel, one that blunted emotion as well as sound. She felt numb, hollow. If she had just stayed out, minded her own business. Officer Perry sensed her thoughts and tried to convince her otherwise. "Ya did what ya thought was right. I'm more to blame than anyone." But Sarah knew. She alone had put the ball into motion. Reading the professor's notes, as if she were a scholar. Deciphering them, as if she were Sherlock Holmes. Dayton, Mencken. If she just hadn't gone.

She drifted unresponsively past Officer Perry, Lena and the others. They tried, but there was nothing they could say. She went upstairs, unscrewed the lid of the still full flask, and downed half of its contents. Only Obee would understand. He knew about guilt, self-recrimination. She felt as if she were outside her body, saw herself go to the phone and start to call him, hang up, start and stop again. Yes, Obee would understand. He would console without patronizing. But suddenly Sarah realized that wouldn't be enough. She was aching, empty. The judge wasn't whom she needed, wasn't whom she wanted.

❖ ❖ ❖

Mitchell's gangly figure loping towards her, suitcase in hand, jolted her into reality. Be careful what you wish for, she heard Tillie say.

She had acted impulsively. Demanding his number from the *Blade,* repeatedly calling his hotel until finally he picked up. He had been working, of course. Sacco-Vanzetti. "Fascinating case," he said, "so good to hear your voice, Sarah." She stopped him mid-sentence, blurted out what happened, then lost all sense of propriety. "Mitchell, I need you."

He was silent.

"I know I sound crazy," she said. "Maybe I am."

"No," he said. "Just human."

Of course, he would be there. But two miserable, sleepless nights passed and still no word. She was heading for a third when he called to say he had gotten another reporter to finish up for him. He would be on today's noon train. "Thank you," she said, clutching the receiver. "Thank you."

Now that he was here, though, she wondered. Impulsiveness could be a sign of mental imbalance. She had been in shock, drunk even. She should have waited, gathered her wits. But it was too late. There he was. She tried to think her way out of it, but already she could see his desiring eyes, his insistent smile. What should she say? So good of you to come, Mr. Dobrinski? He dropped his suitcase, stretched out his arms. No words. No words at all. Her mind was one thing, her heart and body another. She sank into his chest; let his embrace enfold her completely. And then she wept, for the first time since she heard the terrible news.

❖ ❖ ❖

The introduction to Lena was brief. On these matters, her cousin was a pro, closing the bedroom door and assuring Sarah of privacy. Don't worry, she said. She would take care of Nan.

Mitchell stood by the nightstand thumbing through her book. She gazed at him hard, forcing him to look up. She closed the curtains, walked over and took the book from his hands. A clear message. No coyness. No pretense. Longing was all there was. The curtains filtered the sun only slightly. Unhampered by a cloudless sky, it streamed in, harsh and bright. Not a hint of breeze, nothing to soften the moment. Appropriate, Sarah thought. Romance was not what this was about. And she felt neither embarrassment nor disgust.

Holding his gaze, she slid off her dress and then, more clumsily, her undergarments. In seconds she was naked, every part of her tired figure exposed. No thinking, Sarah. No thinking. Mitchell followed her lead, lay on the bed and pulled her on top of him. Sensation. Pure sensation, the feeling of flesh against flesh. At first, they just held on to one another, kissing a little. But Sarah was impatient. A need to be met, freedom from grief, an absolution of sorts. The situation demanded a woman; a full-fledged adult who had experienced life's good and bad. And so, she surrendered, held nothing back. And Mitchell waited, let her build and release, build and release until the tension was gone, until her body and emotions were spent.

For a time afterward, they lay quietly, side by side. Then Mitchell turned, leaned on his elbow and studied her face. "Uh oh, I've seen that look before."

She traced the length of his aquiline nose with her finger. "What look?"

"Determination. You're supposed to be relaxed, dare I even say, tender?" He grabbed her other hand, stopping her rings mid-spin.

"I've got to find out who did this," she said.

"Sarah . . ."

"I know. But Jacob is different. I owe it to him, to his mother."

Mitchell rolled over on his side. He sucked in his slightly protruding belly and pushed back a strand of her hair. "You're setting yourself up for disappointment."

She didn't respond.

"And what would you do if you discovered the culprit? Burn a star of David on his lawn?"

She smirked. "I'd notify the authorities. That's all."

"I see you've made up your mind."

"Uh huh."

"So just how do you intend to go about it?"

She kissed him lightly. "With your help."

✺ 38

LIKE THE HEAD OF A SPY RING, Sarah had given Mitchell his assignment: infiltrate the local KKK—the Klavern, as they called it—and listen. Amongst themselves she'd bet members of the Klan were like hunters, bragging about their kill. She didn't think it would be difficult to find someone involved in the group.

"They were everywhere," she said. "And where they aren't, they leave a trail. Crosses, sheets, bottles. Bottles," she repeated. "Yes, what's a little pilfering, robbing the grave in the name of justice?"

"Talking to yourself now, are you?"

"Mitchell," she said, throwing on her clothes, stay here. I'll be back soon."

A half hour later, she returned with a small glass bottle inscribed with the words, Authentic Chattahoochee River Water. Sarah told him that the liquid these bottles contained was used to initiate new Klan members. He agreed that it might come in handy.

✺✺✺

Mitchell whisked his shaving cream into a rich lather and brushed it onto his stubbly face. His razor was dull, which usually translated into a few nasty nicks. But not today. The gods were with him, granting him a close and bloodless shave.

The last word Mitchell ever would have used to describe himself was lucky. Just now, however, standing before a cracked mirror in his dumpy hotel room, he felt as if he had struck gold. First, the Scopes trial, then Sacco-Vanzetti, a case which he'd already gathered enough information about to know the appeals would be denied. Right or wrong, the men would hang, he predicted, in an article that would soon go to press. But those were just the nuggets, enough to provide food and shelter. With Sarah he'd hit a vein, a rich, untapped resource that could make life worth living.

He closed his eyes. This time, she had been unequivocal. She wanted him and had not retreated. Throwing off convention, revealing her inner and outer self. She smiled and cried, made indecipherable sounds that somehow, vaguely, he understood. He had never known such intimacy, had shied away from it. But he had evolved. Darrow very well might have won the case with Mitchell as a witness.

So what was a little espionage? He would do anything for her. And actually, he knew more about the Klan than Sarah realized. After all, the Buckeye State had quite a following. With a membership of close to four hundred thousand, The Ohio Klan was one of if not the largest in the nation. The Toledo Klavern itself boasted close to a thousand members. There were even rumors that native son Warren Harding had been inducted.

As a reporter, Mitchell had been curious. And tenacious. So much so, he'd convinced the group to let him observe one of their meetings, with the stipulation that they review anything he planned to publish about them. As a result, nothing of any consequence saw print. But he carried with him a vivid memory of the event. The pomp, the commitment, the vitriol they spewed forth. And the costumes. Those had made it hard for him to keep a straight face, especially when he recognized the city attorney. There were only so many five foot, three- hundred-pound men in Toledo.

Mitchell picked up his notebook and sketched out a pyramid, the shape of their power hierarchy. The Imperial Wizard reigned supreme. Then came the Grand Dragon, the Grand Titan and the Exalted Cyclopes. Freud would have had a field day. Indeed, maybe that's what the group needed. A little time on the couch. Clearly, they were paranoid, going so far as to invent their own language to avoid detection. At first, Mitchell thought they were speaking in tongues, but eventually learned that a primitive, anagrammatic method underlay at least some of their madness. AYAK?: Are you a Klansman? AKIA: A Klansman I Am. And KIGY: Klansman, I Greet You!

The possession of knowledge was one thing, however. Applying it was something else. When he'd exited the Klan meeting in Toledo, he was home, in familiar surroundings. He hadn't worried that one of those dunces might come after him. This would be different. Foreign terrain, an alien culture, the very site of the Klan's origins. He would have to be very cautious, play it smart. That was the reason he wasn't with Sarah now, why he checked into this godforsaken place, he thought, looking around. He wasn't picky about décor, but he did care about cleanliness. The ripped curtains and worn carpet he could handle. But the crumbs on the supposedly fresh sheets turned his normally steely stomach.

Being a stranger could work for or against him, but being seen in Sarah's company, now that she had some notoriety, would eliminate any possibility of success. Everything depended on how he handled it. He lit a cigarette and thought, stared out the window, lit another and paced the room. Then, finally, he knew. If it worked, it would be the riskiest trick he'd ever pulled off. If not, well, he preferred not to think about it.

❧ ❧ ❧

Mitchell raised his thumb. The truck slowed. "Where ya headed?"

"Town."

"Hop in."

"Thanks, mind if I smoke?" Mitchell asked.

"Not at all. Got one for me?"

Mitchell lit him, and then sat back. Finally. This was the tenth vehicle that had passed. He'd started to worry that he'd gone a bit overboard with his down-and-out disguise. Torn overalls, muddy shirt, holey shoes. People would pick up a poor man, but not a lunatic.

"Not from around here, are ya?"

"Nope. New York."

"Long ways."

"Uh huh."

"What are ya doing here?"

"Lookin' for work."

"What type?"

"Anything."

Might as well test the waters, Mitchell thought. He took a deep drag and exhaled. "Niggers got all the jobs where I'm from."

The man was about fifty, flat-faced, with pale, flaky skin. He turned to Mitchell, eyed him, then said nothing else the rest of the trip. Mitchell stared straight ahead and smoked. That was obviously a mistake, he thought to himself.

When they got to town, the driver pulled to the side of the road and stopped in front of a dingy looking diner. "Can ya fry an egg?" he said.

"I do all right."

"Joe might have somethin.' Tell 'em Al sent ya."

"Thanks," Mitchell said, shutting the door.

He nodded, and Mitchell watched as he drove away. Then again, maybe not, he thought.

❧ ❧ ❧

At six the next morning, Mitchell was stirring pancake batter with one hand, thickening gravy with another. By eight, the place was packed. Not an empty seat, either at the dull, grey metal counter or at the old wooden tables, caked with grime. Not any women, either. Tough-looking characters mostly, even the few that wore suits.

In appearance, Joe was a carbon copy of his brother, Al. But he was cold and surly. He didn't want to hire anyone, he huffed. But he had no choice. His bursitis was "a bitch, fuckin' killin' him." Couldn't afford to pay much. But Mitchell could have the job if he wanted it.

At first, Mitchell just cooked and kept his ears perked. Fortunately, as a long-time bachelor, he knew his way around a kitchen. As of yet, nobody had complained about too much pepper or not enough salt. Not that the customers seemed terribly discriminating. Joe's was a typical greasy spoon, with double the grease. Per Joe's orders, Mitchell slathered bacon fat on everything from toast to grits. The place was certainly popular, though. Locals gathered here as much to talk as eat; about the price of gas, the effect of the heat on the crops, the upcoming church picnic. And as his string of good luck would have it, the recent lynching. A few people expressed lukewarm sympathy for the boy, but most felt he got what he deserved. One of the regulars was particularly vocal in this respect. Tall and handsome in a hard, military way, he complained that they'd "let the nigger off easy, should have tarred and feathered him first." Mitchell kept his eye on him. So did everyone else. He was a man who commanded respect. What's more, on his right forearm was a small tattoo of a cross, with the word CLASP written underneath. Clannish Loyalty A Sacred Principle. CLASP, Mitchell recalled, now that his memory had been triggered, was another of the Klan's anagrams.

The man came in every day for two weeks, during which time Mitchell kept his distance, but nodded approvingly whenever he spoke. When their eyes occasionally met, Mitchell made sure to offer him a deferential, knowing expression. A few times Mitchell thought he returned the gesture, but couldn't be sure. At the beginning of the third week, he decided there was only one way to find out.

As usual, the man sat down at the counter, ordered ham and eggs, and stuck his nose in the paper. Mitchell was hired to cook, but for his own purposes also had volunteered for counter duty. Joe had reluctantly agreed: "You ain't getting a dime more," he'd grunted, "but be my guest."

Mitchell prepared, and then served the man his meal. He stood close by, wiping off some sticky strawberry jam that had stubbornly clung to a plate. After a few minutes, the man tapped his cup. Now or never, Mitchell thought. He poured him a refill, then reached in his pocket. "Excuse me," Mitchell said, "but do you know a Mr. AYAK around here?" The man lowered the paper. Mitchell held up the bottle Sarah had given him, turning it in the room's grey light. The man gave no response, just glared at him icily. He gulped his coffee, threw down a buck and left.

The next couple of days he didn't show. Mitchell presumed he was the cause. The Klan was always looking for new members, but was extremely wary of strangers. Indeed, one of their other code words was SAN BOG. Strangers Are Near, Be On Guard. Mitchell began to wonder if he should try his routine on someone else. Fortunately, he didn't have to. On Tuesday, as he was about to leave, the man walked in. "We're closing," Mitchell said, trying to appear nonchalant.

The man nodded. His steely eyes gleamed. "Didn't come to eat," he grumbled. He glanced around, and then smiled at Mitchell, tight-lipped, knowingly. "Doleful," he said slowly. "Doleful. Twenty-nine Mills Road, seven p.m."

Mitchell returned to his room and excitedly scribbled the days of the week. It took him several tries, but eventually he knew he had it right, had managed to translate them into the Klan's alliterative rendition: From Monday: Desperate, Dreadful, Desolate, Doleful, Dismal, Deadly, Dark. "Doleful," he said out loud. Thursday. The meeting was Thursday night.

39

ORDINARILY, LENA WOULD HAVE BEEN PRESSING SARAH for details. But this time her cousin knew better. Sarah was relieved. Words could have only trivialized or granted the experience more importance than it was due. This had not been a casual romp in the hay, nor was it purely an expression of love. Raw, conflicting emotions had been involved. Still the feeling Sarah was left with was powerful. It didn't need a name for her to know that.

It was understandable, then, that she should now be concerned. Although she and Mitchell had agreed not to talk until he had something to report, it had been more than two weeks. Where was he? Had he, God forbid, been discovered? Her mind started to race, from one horrific possibility to the other. If anything happened to him because of her . . .

She took a deep breath. It wasn't very long really. Who did she think he was, Harry Houdini? This wasn't something that could be accomplished overnight. She was overly anxious. Give him another day or two, then panic, she thought.

At least she had spent the time wisely. To begin with, she had called Obee, whose support she was finally ready to receive. He did not let her down. Just the right amount of sympathy. And patience. "You stay there until you're done," he said. "If you leave now, my dear, you'll never forgive yourself." She was, however, a bit dismayed to learn that he already knew about Mitchell. Not everything, but enough. He had run into Mitchell's boss, who told him Mitchell was back in Tennessee, tracking down a hell of a story. Obee surmised it had something to do with Sarah.

More importantly, she had visited Jacob's mother. Sarah was not one to shrink from responsibility, but this tested her mettle. Why go, when it was almost certain the woman would refuse to see her? What good would it do, anyway? It would be self-indulgent, an attempt to salve her own conscience, she tried to convince herself. But that wasn't the whole truth. She also, more than anything, dreaded confronting the pain her actions had caused.

Mrs. Lee had been in seclusion since Jacob's death. Friends brought food that she didn't eat, uttered prayers that she didn't hear, sent condolences that she didn't read. So Sarah was doubly surprised when the grieving woman admitted her into her home. Hollowed out, empty of spirit, she opened the door and motioned for Sarah to sit in the chair on whose broad, soft arm her knitting lay undone. After a few moments of excruciating silence, she told Sarah that although she could never forget, she forgave her role in the tragedy. Not because the Bible commanded her to do so, she emphasized, but because she realized Sarah's intentions had been well-meaning. If she thought Sarah had really meant her boy any harm, she wouldn't have cared if God spoke to her himself. She'd curse Sarah to hell.

Hearing that, Sarah broke into tears, grateful, heartbroken and in awe. To rise above one's own suffering required a type of courage few people possessed. And the woman was suffering, terribly. Her son, her pride and joy, "my son" she kept repeating, "my son."

"Mrs. Lee . . . Eldora . . ." Sarah walked over to the couch, fell on her knees and took the woman's aching hands in her own. "Is there anything I can do for you?"

Mrs. Lee stifled her tears and looked up, then bore her dark eyes into Sarah's. "Just get these monsters. Don't let my boy die in vain."

❧ ❧ ❧

Sarah left with the promise that she would do everything in her power. To that end, as soon as she returned to Lena's, she called the *Baltimore Sun*. Amazingly, she was put right through.

"Well, Miss Kaufman, to what do I owe this pleasure?" The raspy voice was strangely comforting.

"No pleasure at all I'm afraid," Sarah said, then solemnly conveyed the facts.

Mencken fell silent. "Brutes, imbeciles!" he finally said. "Christ, this is one time I should have kept my mouth shut."

There was enough blame to go around, Sarah said. That wasn't why she was calling.

"Filthy lynchers! They need a dose of their own medicine."

Sarah told him she hoped he'd feel that way. Indeed, she hoped he'd be willing to administer his own special poison, his poisoned pen, to be exact. The law had their methods. Journalists had theirs. "You are a reporter, a celebrated critic," she said. "Write an article, Mr. Mencken. Strangle them with your words."

Sarah was now reading that piece:

> *If the Klan is against the foreign-born or the hyphenated citizen, so is the National Institute of Arts and Letters. If the Klan is against the Negro, so are all the States south of the Mason-Dixon line. If the Klan is against the Jews, so are half of the good hotels of the Republic and three-quarters of the good clubs. If the Klan is for damnation and persecution, so is the Methodist Church.*

And so on. Sarah thought it a brilliant indictment, denouncing the group by denouncing the culture that produced them. Brilliant, but she doubted whether it would have any immediate effect. More emotion, less intellect was what was needed. On this issue she would have preferred a direct attack.

The man was certainly capable of such an approach. On the opposite page was an excerpt from a piece he'd written about William Jennings Bryan—the late William Jennings Bryan, that is, found dead in Dayton! Like everyone else, Sarah was still in disbelief. The Commoner, dead, just after the trial; his diabetes, poor eating habits and, most felt, Darrow finally getting the better of him. Sarah first heard the news the day Mitchell arrived in Edenville. In an article he himself had already drafted, Mitchell said that Bryan, once Progressive, ironically had sought to hold back the modern era, to prevent the country from evolving. But Nature was against him. His lack of fitness hastened his own demise, a victim of the very theory he had fought against.

Mencken was not so philosophical. Driving a nail into the coffin was more like it:

> *It was hard to believe, watching Bryan at Dayton, that he had traveled, that he had been received in civilized societies, that he had been a high officer of state. He seemed only a poor clod like those around him, deluded by a childish theology, full of an almost pathological hatred of all learning, all human dignity, all beauty, all fine and noble things. What animated him from end to end of his grotesque career was simply ambition—the ambition of a common man to get his hand upon the collar of his superiors, or, failing that, to get his thumb into their eyes.*

This was more of what Sarah had in mind. If anyone deserved a "thumb in the eye," it was the KKK. Then again, as they say, there is more than one way to skin a cat, or in this case, unmask the villain. She should be grateful he wrote anything at all. Mencken was rough around the edges, but he had been generous to her. And like herself, he had meant well. That she wouldn't forget.

She turned the page. More eulogies. Since Bryan's death, they continued to flood the paper.

*No matter what Bryan did, he was always
sincere . . . The death of William Jennings
Bryan means a severe loss to the people of
our nation because of the taking away of his
religious and educational influence . . . He
died fighting for the word of God . . .*

"Sarah!"

Sarah raised her eyes.

"Mitchell. Mitchell is on the phone," Lena said.

"Mitch . . ." Sarah dropped the paper and ran to the phone, answering
out of breath. "Mitchell."

"I said I'd call when I learned something," he said.

"Yes?"

"Are you sitting down?"

❖ ❖ ❖

Sarah knew Mitchell was resourceful, but this exceeded her
expectations. In less than three weeks, he had gotten a job, passed himself off
as a venomous racist, and had been invited to and attended a Klan meeting.
Houdini wasn't so far off after all.

His account of the meeting, housed in the back of an old condemned
warehouse, sounded straight out of the Middle Ages. Secret passwords,
dragons, titans, "Klankraft," as they referred to it all. A few new inductees
knelt in prayer before a blazing cross in the center of a white-robed circle of
members, swearing obedience, fidelity and Klannishness. "Sworn in," Mitchell
recited, "on the Doleful day of the Woeful week of the Terrible month of the
Year of the Klan LVIII and the Year of the Reincarnation IX."

"I don't understand half of it. How did you get so smart?"

He chuckled, said she would have known, about that and many other
things, had she not tried to avoid him over the past year.

She sighed. "All right. Go on."

Which Mitchell did in unbelievable detail. The chairman, or the

Cyclops, as Mitchell said he was officially known, proceeded down the agenda. First, he encouraged those who had not purchased their robes to do so immediately, reminding them that they were essential to the full perfection of their order. Next he admonished members to stop buying their goods at Cohen's. "As the Klan, we can't sponsor this act, so kindly step to the next door and buy real honest-to-goodness American products, even if it does cost a trifle more." Then he lamented the poor recruitment numbers, and introduced Mitchell, or rather Robert Jones, a newcomer from New York. "Good material for knighthood," he said, slapping Mitchell on his back. Several more minor points of business were finally followed by refreshment: Ku Klux Klan cake, thick Klannish cream for their "Nigger Soup" and apples from the Garden of Eden.

"Oh, come on," Sarah said.

"No kidding," Mitchell said. "I only report what I hear."

After that, however, Mitchell said came the most interesting part of the evening.

"One Irishman, one Jew and one Negro," announced the chair. "Oh, wait a minute," he laughed. "Just one minute. I forgot." The group appeared to know what was coming, Mitchell explained. They snickered and clapped, waiting for the punch line. "Now, it is only one Irishman and one Jew we have to watch, isn't it?" The group went wild, hollering and flapping their robes in approval. Mitchell wished he'd had his camera.

"I wonder who the Irishman and Jew are? I mean, you can count the number of Jews in this town on one hand. Mr. Cohen, Lena, myself, temporarily, but go on."

"The Cyclops let them go at it for a while, and then hushed them with a raised finger. "As most of you are already aware," he bellowed, "we have the LOTIES to thank for this blessing." Again, there were cheers. "They informed us of his whereabouts. The darkie thought he'd gotten off. He was wrong. And now, because of the LOTIES' sacred loyalty to our noble cause, NM, our dear departed Grand Cyclops, can finally rest in peace." Loud applause ensued and then the singing of "America." The Cyclops, whose name by this time Mitchell learned was Gus Shelby, concluded the night with these words: "On

Deadly, we will all of us briefly mark the occasion together, the usual time at the Cavelern." He repeated the word very slowly. "C a v e l e r n."

"Gibberish," Sarah said.

"Not all of it. You know who the LOTIES are?"

"Obviously, no."

"You're going to love this, Sarah. Ladies. Ladies of the Invisible Empire."

"Ladies? Women?"

"Yeah, you know, Ohio has a small group."

"Uh huh, but . . . Mitchell, get to the point. What does this all mean?"

"In a nutshell? The Negro, who is no longer a problem, was Jacob. The women's group—or someone in the group—kept tabs on him, told the men where they could find him. Their Grand Cyclops, NM, was . . ." Sarah mouthed the words as he spoke . . . "Nicholas Manhoff."

"On Dark, which is Sunday," he continued, "both groups—men and women—will meet. The only thing I can't figure out is this reference to the Cavelern, some version of Klavern I guess."

Sarah nodded. It was all beginning to make a kind of crazy sense. Jacob, Professor Manhoff. And the women. "Mitchell" she said. "I think I might know what that word means."

➻ 40

SARAH HAD RECALLED FROM HER VISIT to the cave several hollows off the main cathedral. To ensure they found one adequate to their task, she and Mitchell had the driver drop them off at five p.m., two hours before what Mitchell assumed was the "usual" time. They glanced around, made certain they were alone, then crouched through the dark tunnel. After a bit of exploring, they located their spot, a tall, craggy alcove with a water-carved peephole; large enough for them to see out, but unnoticeable from the other side. They burrowed themselves in, turned out the flashlight and waited. It was cool and dark, Mitchell's warm breath on her neck. Under other circumstances, no telling what might have happened. Now they were just praying their instincts would not let them down.

Dim and muffled at first, then brighter, louder. Flashlights and footsteps. Sarah held her breath. They had started to arrive. How they didn't trip on their robes was a mystery. But soon the cave was full of them, Halloween caricatures of white, Gentile Americans.

Several lanterns were lit. A ceramic bowl was filled with water, a Bible laid open, the Stars and Stripes raised. Then the ceremony began. Men on one side of the cave, women on the other. The sinister, officiating voice Mitchell said belonged to Gus. As the men looked on, the women, ten in all, walked up, kissed the flag, dipped their hands into the water and saluted their supreme commander. "You are our only hope," Gus said, "the upholders of white womanhood." Each knelt before him as he touched their shoulder with a small sword. Then, one by one, they stood up and lifted their masks. Sarah's heart pounded. She felt around her face. Her glasses were on. She took them off, widened her eyes, put them back on, squinted, widened again.

No, dammit. She didn't recognize any of them.

"And now," Gus said, "for the induction."

Mitchell nudged her. From the crowd of men emerged a slender, hooded figure. Gus held up the familiar glass bottle and motioned for the person to approach. "As messenger, you have proven yourself worthy of membership," Gus began. "Without you, I could not have done what was necessary. And so, with this transparent, life-giving, powerful God-given fluid, more precious and far more significant than all the sacred oils of the ancients, I set you apart from the women of your daily association to the great and honorable task you have voluntarily allotted yourself as a citizen of the Invisible Empire, a woman of the Ku Klux Klan. As a Klanswoman, may your character be as transparent, your life purpose as powerful, your motive in all things as magnanimous and as pure and your Klannishness as real and as faithful as the manifold drops herein. You may remove your mask."

As he sprinkled their holy water on her wavy blond bob, Sarah exhaled. Her instincts had been right after all.

❖ ❖ ❖

Armed with names, places and dates, Sarah and Mitchell seated themselves in front of Officer Perry's cluttered desk. "We were witnesses," Sarah said. Penelope Caldwell and Gus Shelby. The whole lot of them obviously approved of the lynching, a few no doubt lent support. But Penny and Gus, they appeared to have been the organizers. For Penny, this was a rite of passage, a test of her worthiness to join the Klan. Penny formed the plan. Gus, quite literally, carried it out.

Officer Perry listened to their account with closed eyes. When he blinked them opened, they were filmier than usual and dark-rimmed. It was too familiar not to be true, he confessed. And heaven forgive him, he might have prevented it. After the trial, he had released Penny into the custody of her mother. She was a young girl, confused and vulnerable. She would change, he believed. Probation was a fair sentence. "I should've known," he said, shaking his head. "I should've known. Girl like that. Father dead. She was ripe for the Klan. Just the type they looked for. A girl in need of a cause."

Of course this was far from a done deal. A conspiracy to murder charge was hard to prove. As for Gus, he was a known scoundrel, a vicious but powerful fellow who was always one step ahead of the law. The good news was, he lived in Edenville. Officer Perry would send his boys out immediately. The man wouldn't surrender without a fight, but if they wanted to keep their jobs, they wouldn't return without him. It would be tough to get an indictment, of course, even tougher to get a conviction. Might take months. "Town's not as eager to try a white man," he said.

Sarah knew all that. She also knew that she and Mitchell would need to come back to testify should the case go to court. And that until then, as long as they remained in Edenville anyway, they would be in danger. Serious danger. Klan members didn't take well to any of their own being snitched on, let alone their first in command. When word got around who was responsible, they might add a Pole to that watch list of theirs. Best just to watch their backs and get out of town as soon as possible.

At least Sarah had done what she could, done her best to keep her promise to Mrs. Lee. In fact, as she thought about it, her need to fulfill that goal had jarred loose the grip of the past more than anything else since embarking on her strange trip to Edenville. Over the past year, the Klan had become more than just a criminal threat to her; it had become symbolic of fear itself. Of the unknown, of things dark, evil and hidden. Though still a formidable foe from which she would just as soon keep her distance, the robes had come off. Bigotry, hatred, even murder resided underneath, but they were embodied in a person as real as any who walked through the courtroom doors everyday.

Sarah shook Officer Perry's hand. "You've got your work cut out for you," she said. "Any new leads on Professor Manhoff's murderer?"

He sighed. "Not yet."

"Well, I wish you luck."

He sighed again, more deeply.

"Oh, by the way, sir," Sarah said, feeling a little sorry for him, "there's been an outbreak of guilt lately. Everyone I know seems to be suffering from it."

He looked up sheepishly. "That right?"

"Uh huh. I think there's a cure, though. And it's not in your waters."

"And what's that?"

"Justice, Officer Perry, justice."

❧ 41

THE NEXT DAY, SARAH AND MITCHELL WERE SUMMONED to identify the accused. Gus had been easier to capture than Officer Perry had thought. Apparently, he'd caught the virus and was in bed when the deputies arrived. That must have been quite a sight, Sarah thought, a Cyclops wiping his nose.

"Yeah, that's him," Mitchell said.

Gus sneered. "I'll be out of here by the end of the afternoon, and then, Mr. New Yorker, or wherever you're really from, you best be careful."

"You best be careful before then," Officer Perry warned Mitchell. "You too Miss Kaufman. An eye for an eye. They'll be seeking revenge."

"We know," Sarah said.

Officer Perry left the task of picking up Penny to himself. She was his responsibility, he said, his and his alone. Penny's mother begged him not to take her beautiful daughter back to that terrible place, but Penny offered no resistance. No explanations or apologies either. After arriving at the station, she asked for an attorney and told Sarah to "go fuck" herself.

Sarah, however, decided she would rather just go home, the day after tomorrow.

❧❧❧

Had it not been for Lena, she would have left the next day. But her cousin had made plans: one final day in the Smokies. Just the two of them . . . with Mitchell and Paul, who was due to arrive in Edenville any moment. Sarah shook her head, but didn't protest. Perhaps it was just what the doctor ordered.

The foursome would discuss the particulars of the hike over dinner, Lena said. Nan had agreed to make something special, provided the men left immediately afterwards. "I'm not stupid," she huffed. "I know what happened the other day, and it ain't gonna happen again. I don't care where they stay, but it ain't gonna be here."

Lena obliged by finding a room for them at one of the dormitories. Mitchell said he would have preferred to hide out under Sarah's sheets, but was grateful for the space nonetheless, a palace, he announced, compared to the joint he'd been staying in. He was already settled in, going over some of his notes. As for Lena and Paul, they were somewhere working up an appetite.

Meanwhile, at Lena's request, Sarah was on her way to Kathryn's. Combined with the professor's death and the fact that the murderer was still on the loose, she feared that Penny's arrest would be terribly upsetting to her. The girls were very close, she said, closer than any of the others. Lena knew Kathryn was strong, but if she had learned anything from Sarah at all, it was that even the strong had emotions.

"Why me?" Sarah had asked, not relishing the idea. She didn't think Kathryn was all that keen on her.

"Because," Lena explained, "you have experience in these matters, and," she said before Sarah could respond, "you owe me a favor."

"But you're her teacher."

"And you're a counselor. And you've gotten to know her a bit. But not too much. Now, who is better?"

Sarah continued to resist, but ultimately agreed and even came to think that maybe she could actually be of some help. Approaching Kathryn's dormitory, she ran into Jim and the rest of the gang tossing a football outside. Yes, they had heard the news. They didn't know what to feel, Jim said. But they shook Sarah's hand and wished her well. Sarah asked if Kathryn was in her room. Jim said yes, that she was writing.

Sarah knocked. No answer. She knocked again.

"Come in."

Kathryn was at her desk, her wheat hair loosely tied, strands popping out haphazardly. She turned around. "Miss Kaufman." She turned back and continued to write.

"Kathryn. I just wanted to say goodbye. I'm leaving tomorrow."

"Oh? Well, goodbye, then."

"Kathryn, actually, I also wanted to explain. I know you've heard about Penny. I worry about you and your friends."

"Worry about what?"

"Oh, that you might be upset, might find it difficult to reconcile your feelings. I know that you are particularly close with Penny. You've been through a lot."

"Thank you for your concern, but I'll be fine."

"Also, I have to say that I worry you might be persuaded by the Klan."

Kathryn put down her pencil and turned around. "By the Klan?"

"Well, yes, dear. You know, these people have ways of twisting the truth. And they play upon people's insecurities and fears. As they did with Penny. I know you are a strong young woman, but they can be quite seductive. It's easier to blame others for problems. And that's what they do. They scapegoat Negroes, foreigners, Catholics . . ."

"And Jews, Miss Kaufman?"

Sarah felt herself flush. "Yes, and Jews."

"What makes you think I'm not a member already?" She laughed. "Don't worry about me," she said. "I think for myself."

"I 'm sure you do. I know that. I didn't think you would fall for such ideas. And yet, that short story you recited, about your dog. I haven't been able to get it out of my mind."

"That story wasn't built on Klan thinking. That was Darwin."

"I know. And I'm all for Darwin. But taken to an extreme . . . Kathryn, do you think what Penny did was right?"

"Right? No. But Penny is a joiner. I've always known that. She does what she is told. Still, with all respect, ma'am, there's one thing you need to know. This is the South. We have our own ways of doing things."

"South, North. Bigotry exists everywhere, Kathryn. So does tolerance and compassion."

"Yes. I'm sure you're right." Kathryn turned back to her paper.

"Do you mind my asking what you're writing?"

"Another story. I have many of them." Kathryn handed her a thick folder.

Sarah opened the cover and started to peruse the neatly kept pages. *The Return of Light. Reversal of Time.* She flipped through a few more. *Darkness Before Dawn.* Sarah pulled that one out and started to read: "The year was 1975. The sun set earlier and rose later each day. All growth had withered. What was once white was black."

Kathryn leaned toward her. "That's one of my best pieces. I'm hoping to get it published."

"Interesting title. Sounds ominous. What's it about?"

"You wouldn't like it."

Sarah noticed the time on Kathryn's clock. "Oh, dear. I'm late," she said standing and handing her back the folder. "Kathryn, I hope you're not offended by my visit."

"Not at all."

"It was very nice to meet you. I hope when I see you again it will be under better circumstances."

"Yes, nice to meet you, too."

"Good luck on getting your work published."

"Thanks."

❧❧❧

Sarah had been rocking nervously on the porch when Mitchell arrived a half hour late, just as night overtook the last swath of orangey sky. Lena had shown Mitchell a shortcut through the woods, and he'd veered a bit off course before spotting the crooked path leading toward the house. Ordinarily, Sarah would have been irritated rather than worried. But with each minute that had passed, she became increasingly convinced that he was somewhere in a ghost-ridden thicket hanging from a tree. At the sight of his loping gait, she stopped rocking and breathed a heavy sigh of relief.

Nan's pot roast dinner didn't seem particularly special, and it certainly didn't do much to lighten their mood. Even the usually ebullient Paul was downcast. Slavery had ended a half century ago and yet the sentiment that inspired it was alive and well. In practice as well as theory. Would such madness ever stop? Was our species doomed to destroy itself? They tried to make the most of the evening, but they kept coming back to these depressing, unanswerable questions.

"If there is hope for the future, it will be in spite of the bigots, in spite of the Klan, in spite of people like Nicholas Manhoff," Sarah said.

Lena winced. "It's still jolting to hear that."

"And disillusioning," Paul added.

"Yet I know you're right," Lena said. "About Nick and Penny." She laced her short fingers together and nodded in resignation. "By the way, Sarah, I think I'm going to send that article off to a journal after all, with my own name on it."

Sarah smiled and gave her a little hug. "Good. I'm glad. As I've said before, I'm sorry about your colleague. Terribly sorry, she said, actually thinking of Jacob. But an English professor who can't write on his own, who steals another's ideas, well, it's criminal, that's all. You know, that's one of the things that must have made Mencken wary of your profession. How he detested Professor Manhoff's story. The one he actually did write. I mean, he really thought it was . . ."

"What?"

"Hmm?"

"Sarah?"

"He thought it was . . ."

"Sarah, what are you staring at?"

Mitchell touched her arm. "Sarah, what is it?"

I wonder, Sarah thought. "What was once white was black." She tried to recall. The beginning of the next paragraph. What did it say? "President Williams." Yes. "President Williams scratched his . . . his . . . wooly head." An eerie cold crept down her neck. She checked the clock. Not that late. She suddenly rose. "I'm going for a walk."

"She's lost her mind," Lena said.

Mitchell corrected her. "No, she's got something on her mind, don't you?"

"Something, yes, perhaps."

Lena sighed. "But didn't we just have a conversation about not venturing out alone? About the Klan seeking revenge and all that?"

"Yes," Mitchell said. "That's why I'm going with her."

"No, you stay . . ." A shadowy image of the woods flashed through her mind. "Yes, you're going with me."

"You're not going to tell me where you're going?" Lena asked, with a note of relief.

"No. It's probably nothing, anyway. If we're not back by ten, we'll see you in the morning."

"If you're not back by ten, I'm calling the police."

❖❖❖

Sarah had only an outline of suspicion, a vague inkling that she couldn't quite articulate when Mitchell pressed her for an explanation.

"Just keep guard," she said.

"Against what?"

"I'm not sure, but keep guard against it anyway."

"Right."

The lights were still on. She knocked.

"Who is it?"

"It's Sarah again, Miss Kaufman."

The door opened slightly. "Jim!"

"Shh. I'm not supposed to be here, you know."

"Yes. Well, don't worry. I won't tell."

Kathryn peered out around him. "I thought you were leaving."

"I know, I know, I'm being a pest, but, do you mind if I come in? I'll be quick."

Jim opened the door wider and motioned her in. "No problem," he said, "is it Kath?"

"No, no problem."

"I was just practicing my guitar while Emily Bronte here composes. I can't get her to do much of anything else these days. As you can see, I had to break the rules just to catch a glimpse of her. Maybe you can convince her that a boyfriend needs attention too."

"I don't know if I'm the right person for that."

Jim sat on her bed and strummed lightly.

"So," Kathryn said.

"Well, I was wondering if I could see that story of yours again. I haven't been able to get it out of my mind."

Kathryn looked at her quizzically. "Sure."

Sarah took the folder and reread to make certain. "President Williams scratched his wooly head. How would he answer the Senate's questions? He didn't even know what they meant."

"Kathryn, you say you wrote this?"

"Yes. Who else?"

"Oh . . . I, well, it's just funny, that's all, coincidental. When I was in Dayton, Mr. Mencken, you remember that I met with him, well he mentioned something Professor Manhoff wrote, something he wanted Mencken to publish . . . about a Negro president.

Kathryn reddened. "Oh?"

"Yes, I'm sure of it. Not a terribly sympathetic portrayal, as I recall. Remember, I mentioned it at Jacob's trial."

"You did?"

"Yes. Oh, that's right, you were sick that day, I think. Jim, you weren't there either, were you?"

Kathryn didn't wait for him to answer. "Well, it's a coincidence then. What of it?"

"Oh, I don't know. Did you ever discuss the premise with Professor Manhoff? I mean even a little?"

"What business is it of yours?"

The strumming stopped.

"None really. Like I said, I just thought it was strange, you know, because a black president is a novel idea for a story. Unique. Original. It seems nearly impossible that two people who worked together would individually come up with it."

Kathryn glared at her. Glared at her in a way that made Sarah begin to think that it wasn't just maturity she had once seen in the girl's eyes. "You've got it wrong," she said.

"I have what wrong, dear?"

"You think I stole Professor Manhoff's work."

Jim interjected. "Kathryn, Miss Kaufman didn't say that. Come on, you've been at this too long. He approached and put his arm around her, but she shrugged him off.

"It is what you were thinking, though, isn't it, ma'am?" Kathryn said, still glaring.

Sarah didn't know exactly what she had thought, but now . . .

Kathryn fingered the paper. "It was the other way around."

"What do you mean?"

Jim cocked his head confusedly. "Yes, what do you mean, Kath?"

"I mean Professor Manhoff put his name on *my* work." She looked out, somewhere beyond both of them. "This wasn't the first time either. He'd done it to me before."

"What?" Jim said, getting up.

"Sit down!" She shook her head. "You're so damn naïve."

Jim obeyed, looking as if he had been hit in the stomach. But Sarah believed the girl. The professor had done it before. To Kathryn . . . and to Lena, perhaps others. Sarah wondered. Plagiarism appeared to have been a habit with the professor. "Amateurish," Mencken had called the work. And now Sarah thought she knew why. All along, Kathryn had seemed intensely loyal to Professor Manhoff. But now, her expression. Bitter, vengeful. Sarah tried to control her breathing. One step at a time, she said to herself, one step at a time. "He had done it before?" she asked.

"Yes. But," she said, with softer eyes, "you have to understand. Professor Manhoff was a great man, and great men sometimes need to take liberties. They have a right to. Survival of the fittest, you know."

"But it still upset you."

"Not on the other occasions. They were minor. I understood, really, I did. But this time . . . well, this was my jewel, my child. I'd been working on it since I was a young teen. I told Professor Manhoff that, pleaded with him. But he'd not been productive lately, and the story was so good, he said, and well, he was more likely to get it published than I, and wasn't that the important thing, to have people read it?"

"I see."

"I don't," Jim said. "I don't at all. I thought you told me everything. What in the hell is this about, Kath?"

Kathryn didn't answer. She and Sarah just stared at each other, for what felt like an hour. Finally, Kathryn looked away. "I just couldn't let him do it this time," she said.

She couldn't let him do it? Couldn't let him? Sarah took some deep breaths. "No, of course not."

Kathryn's eyes started to fill. "He told me he wouldn't let me graduate if I made a fuss, that, that he would be forced to spread rumors. I was being selfish, he said, thinking of myself rather than the benefit to the whole."

"Tell me, Kathryn. Did you ever report this to anyone?"

"No. I didn't want to hurt him, you know. No one would believe me, anyway." She suddenly stiffened. "Miss Kaufman, you came to say goodbye." She grabbed the paper away from Sarah with a trembling hand. "Goodbye, then."

"Kathryn, please, one more thing. Professor Manhoff meant a great deal to you, didn't he?"

"The world. You know that. I loved him, like a father."

Sarah touched the girl's shoulder. "You must have felt . . . betrayed."

She started to nod, but then stiffened again. "Please, I've answered your questions. I'd like you to leave."

"Yes," Jim said, "yes," as if coming out of a daze. "Now I remember. You told me. You were angry that day. Very angry. You didn't want to see me. Don't you remember, Kath? Didn't he send you something? No, he delivered it. Or someone did. A note. A letter, right? I forgot. You'd gotten over it, and then he was . . . you never told me what it was about, though. Kathryn, what was it about? What is this about?"

Kathryn turned to them both. "You two just leave. Leave me alone!"

Sarah's work prepared her for this kind of situation. But she would have to play it very carefully. "I will. We will," she said calmly. But Kathryn, before I go, may I ask you something, about the story itself?"

Kathryn exhaled. "What?"

"How do you portray Negroes in the story?"

"Realistically," she said.

"Not with contempt?"

"Contempt? Not at all. I feel no contempt toward the race. As long as they stay in their place."

"And where is that?"

"I know what you're thinking. But like I said, you have to live here to understand. The Confederacy understood. Some day, the world will. All I show is that certain races are meant to lead, others to follow. In my story, I show the consequences of a black man fighting his nature."

"If you don't mind giving away the plot, what are those consequences?"

She was silent.

"Kathryn?"

"Assassination. Death."

Sarah drew a deep breath. "And then?"

"Things are put right. Balance is restored."

Delicately, Sarah. Very delicately. "Professor Manhoff taught you that, didn't he, Kathryn?"

"Yes. It was his ardent belief."

"So, let me get this straight. If someone isn't behaving according to their nature, some kind of intervention is needed. Is that what you believe?"

"Yes, I suppose I do."

"Would such intervention be required for a person who was, say, in a trusted position of authority. If they began acting immorally or unethically?"

"Yes," she said slowly, her cheeks blood red.

"You feel that certain people have a right to take matters into their own hands?"

"Not just a right, Miss Kaufman, an obligation."

"To eliminate the threat."

"Yes, the threat to the natural order."

"Like your dog, the one you wrote about? Smothering its baby."

"Yes, you do understand."

"That's similar to assassinating the Negro president."

"Yes."

"As you said in your story, it's a kind of natural selection, isn't it?"

"Yes, yes, yes."

"The black president."

"Yes," I said. "Yes!"

"The puppy?"

"Yes!"

"Like Professor Manhoff."

Jim groaned.

Kathryn stared at her wild-eyed.

"Professor Manhoff. He cheated you, took your work. He deserved punishment. More than that, he needed to be removed, selected out." Sarah held her breath.

For a moment, Kathryn's farm girl features hardened, like quickly drying plaster of Paris. But one by one, cracks appeared until the mask gave way and finally shattered. "Yes!" she screamed, her pale cupid lips now in wild motion. "Yes, yes, yes!"

➻ 42

THE NEXT MORNING THEY HIKED SINGLE-FILE up the same path she and Lena had taken several weeks before. It was still summer, the dog days. But the landscape had undergone a slight change. The greens were not quite as vivid, flowering had passed its peak. The overripe air was almost imperceptibly tinged with the smell of dry leaves.

Lena led, followed by Paul and Sarah. Huffing and puffing, Mitchell brought up the rear. "Need a push?" Sarah called out.

"Very funny." Mitchell leaned over to catch his breath.

"You'd do better if you stopped smoking."

"And you'd do well to throw out the rest of that hooch you told me about before we board the train."

"For my sake or yours?"

"Both."

"Uh huh." Sarah called out to Lena. "Go ahead. We're right behind you." Lena waved, and in a minute she and Paul were out of view.

"Well, you're not exactly breezing up either, you know," Mitchell said.

"I just didn't want to shame you. I know how fragile the male ego can be."

"Watch it or I'll have to prove my manhood to you right here."

Despite everything, Sarah had not resolved her ambivalence toward Mitchell, but she played along and pretended to flee from his clutches, scampering to a nearby ridge. There it was again, the vast Tennessee expanse. She'd barely scratched the surface of its hazy beauty. Yet, in a way, she'd seen much more than she'd wanted, lived its history, peeked into its divided soul.

To Sarah, Professor Manhoff was the symbol of the region's troubling complexity. Brilliant and bigoted, modern and backward, nurturing and abusive. And Sarah knew as well as anyone that even the most noble of spirits could be corrupted by his kind of abuse. But it was still hard to believe. Kathryn, so young and lovely. And female. Utterly defying the profile of a killer.

Sarah had worn her down enough to confess, to the murder as well as orchestrating the entire aftermath. Kathryn had been Professor Manhoff's favorite. Because of that, he had confided in her, about his mixed heritage—the real reason he remained childless—and about Jacob, a person Kathryn instantly knew would make the perfect suspect. Kathryn wasn't sure from whom the professor learned of the General Lee story, but she did know that he believed it. As Sarah suspected, he simply couldn't imagine a full-blooded Negro possessing Jacob's intelligence.

Kathryn's only mistake was Christopher Wilde. She had misjudged the depth of his loyalty. But she never doubted Penny's. Penny was a follower, she repeated, in her confession to Officer Perry. Although neither she nor the other students knew that Kathryn was the murderer, Penny had followed Kathryn all the way, had sacrificed her dignity and even her freedom for her. As for the Klan, no, Kathryn was not a member. But she was aware of Professor Manhoff's leadership role in the organization. She was friendly with many of its members and understood their mentality. As Professor Manhoff used her, Kathryn used them, and the other students, including Jim.

She and the professor were alike, Kathryn admitted. They both took what they wanted from people and ideas, twisted them to their will. Blame it on her parents' early death, on her grandparents' lack of involvement in her life. Kathryn herself didn't buy any of that. Like Professor Manhoff, Kathryn saw herself as one of the chosen, selected by nature to lead. She believed in her master's distorted teachings, so much so that she felt justified in using them against him.

Her confession was complete. But that was not quite the end. Sensing a problem when Sarah had taken so long, Mitchell had appeared just as Kathryn reached in her handbag for the pistol she had used to kill Professor

Manhoff. She hadn't even hidden the thing. Whether she was planning really to use it or not, Sarah didn't know since Mitchell grabbed it before any damage was done. After that, Kathryn refused to answer her questions. The only thing she said was that the authorities would have to drag her from her room, which they eventually did after Sarah called Officer Perry.

Mitchell came up behind Sarah, wrapped his arms around her waist. "Ready?"

"For what?"

"Whatever you want."

"What I want is for everyone to be safe. I'm worried about Lena. What if the Klan decides to take their revenge out on her."

"I wouldn't be concerned about that. They have too much to lose by going after another teacher. I think it's more likely they'll seek us out in Toledo."

"Oh, fine."

"The world is full of danger. You know that. This is just one more thing we have to worry about."

"I suppose you're right."

"So, I'll ask you the question again. What do you want?"

"Pancakes."

"And then?"

"Our hike."

"And then?"

"Home."

"And then?"

⇻ Acknowledgements

WRITERS OF HISTORICAL FICTION strive to make their stories contextually plausible and consistent with what is known about the characters they portray. Accomplishing this requires studying one's historical period in depth, both through primary and secondary sources. To represent the Scopes trial, its key figures, and 1920s Tennessee as accurately as possible, I am especially indebted to the following: *Inside the Klavern: The Secret History of a Ku Klux Klan of the 1920s*, ed. David A. Horowitz; *Hooded Americanism: The History of the Ku Klux Klan*, David M. Chalmers; *By Faith Endowed: The Story of Maryville College 1819-1944*, Carolyn L. Blair and Arda S. Walker; The *Jew Store: A Family Memoir*, Stella Suberman; *A Mencken Chrestomathy: His Own Selection of His Choicest Writings*, ed., Henry Louis Mencken, *You Be the Judge: A Day by Day Newspaper Account of the Scopes Trial*, ed. Timothy C. Cruver, *Summer for the Gods: The Scopes Trial and American's Continuing Debate over Science and Religion*, Edward J. Larson.

Many thanks to members of my book club who graciously agreed to read a first draft and then subsequently ripped it to shreds: Aubyn, George, Rob and especially Jackie. Your critique stung, but you made the manuscript better. Thanks also to my publisher and editor, Jim Smith, for believing in my work; to my daughter, Brooke Fruchtman, senior editor at the Los Angeles County Art Museum, who, in the early stages, wielded her red pen like a paintbrush; to Leigh Rathbone, for superb proofing; to my cousins, Lauren and Jeff Kahn for their humor-filled, incisive read, and to Lauren as well for again creating a book cover that imaginatively captures the essence of the story. Thanks to my son, Ben, for making me worry so much that I was forced to shift focus, to my parents, Rhoda and Marvin Kantor, just for being there, and to my husband, Dean, whose technical assistance, patience and love are far beyond what I deserve.

❥ About the Author

ONA RUSSELL HOLDS A PH.D. IN LITERATURE from the University of California, San Diego. She lectures nationally on the topic of literature and the law and is a regular contributor to Orange County Lawyer magazine. She also has been published in newspapers, scholarly journals and anthologies. She is the author of O'Brien's Desk, also from Sunstone Press, and is currently at work on her third Sarah Kaufman mystery, set against the backdrop of the 1920s Los Angeles oil boom. For more information visit: www.onarussell.com.

LaVergne, TN USA
07 April 2010
178380LV00006B/19/P